SHE CAN SCREAM
D0318734

# ALSO BY MELINDA LEIGH

*She Can Run*

*Midnight Exposure*

*She Can Tell*

*Midnight Sacrifice*

MELINDA LEIGH
SHE CAN SCREAM
Montlake
Romance

The characters and events portrayed in this book are fictitious. Any similarity to real persons, living or dead, is coincidental and not intended by the author.



Printed in the United States of America.



Published by Montlake Romance

PO Box 400818
Las Vegas, NV 89140

ISBN-13: 9781477807415
ISBN-10: 1477807411
Library of Congress Catalog Number: 2013908423

*To Annie, for making sure I came up for air now and then.*

# CHAPTER ONE

*Monday, October 21st, 6:10 p.m.*
*Coopersfield, Pennsylvania*

*Stalking used to be harder.*

He read the display on his phone: OFF 4 MY RUN!

Thank you, social media, for a generation of young women compelled to report their every movement to the world. Though it felt vaguely like cheating, a player who maintained a demanding career and hobby appreciated the amount of information willingly floated in cyberspace. There was only so much time in a day.

He set his phone on his thigh, picked up his binoculars, and adjusted the focus. A dead leaf drifted from the red maple branches above his car and landed on his windshield. At the other end of the street, Madison Thorpe exited her parents' bi-level house. She stepped out onto the stoop in between a pair of carved pumpkins.

Right on schedule.

Would she change her routine as winter approached and darkness fell earlier each day? He wouldn't take the chance. It had to be tonight. He was ready. For the last two months, he'd been watching and planning. Thanks to Maddie's online accounting of her every movement, he knew where she would be at any hour of the day. On Monday nights, Maddie ran in the woods. She lived with her parents, but they had theater tickets for this evening.

No one would miss Maddie until midnight.

A thrill heated his blood and throbbed in his temples. Their moment had arrived.

She turned and locked the door before trotting down the walk. Skintight pants and a formfitting pullover highlighted her firm eighteen-year-old body. All that exercise certainly paid off. Yellow neon running shoes would be easy to spot in the deepening twilight. The sun had dropped behind the trees. Maddie had thirty minutes of half-light left in the day. But no matter how fast she ran tonight, she would not be home before darkness fell.

This was almost too easy.

The faint buzz stirred in his blood. She was perfect. He'd made the right selection from his virtual catalog. He'd observed and researched a number of young women. Maddie had outshone all the others, and she was going to be his next star. The buzz grew louder, increasing from the faint drone of bees over a meadow to the deafening roar of a jet engine. He turned the key in the ignition halfway and cracked his window a few inches. Fresh air flooded the car. But the chill did little to cool his excitement.

His diligent observation and planning was coming to fruition. He wanted to freeze this moment in time, this revelation that in just twenty short minutes, her life would, literally, be in his hands.

His fingers clenched, imagining the slender column of her throat under his thumbs, each beat of her heart occurring only because he allowed it, every breath drawn into her lungs at his discretion, her life his for the taking. Her terror, her humiliation, her pain would fill him with power, and before he was finished, he would take everything from her body and soul. One hand drifted toward his zipper, but he stopped himself.

He wiped his sweaty palms and cleared his head. He was getting ahead of tonight's program. He needed to focus on the moment. Each step must be executed exactly as planned, every second of the night experienced to its full potential.

There wouldn't be another for some time. At least a year. His primary rule: one annual kill, like a deer hunter procures a seasonal doe permit. He was already breaking another important rule this evening by hunting so close to the northeastern Pennsylvania mountain town that he called home. But what fun it was going to be to watch the fallout around him instead of from a discrete distance.

Maddie stood on the uneven sidewalk for a few seconds, inserting her earbuds, selecting music on her iPod, and stretching her calves. Then she jogged off toward the footpath that led to her favorite trail. Her brown ponytail swished in rhythm with her toned thighs. Those bright sneakers arcing like beacons in the darkness.

His Maddie was routine oriented. He loved that about her.

There was no need to follow her. He knew exactly where she was going. The development of twenty-year-old homes backed up against township green acres that had been a working farm many years ago. For the next thirty minutes, she would jog on the rough trail that looped its perimeter. He glanced at his watch. Soon she would run through the wooded portion of her route, the location he'd chosen as their rendezvous point.

All he needed was the next quarter of an hour to proceed as usual.

He pulled away from the curb and drove out of the complex. A half mile down the road, he turned into an unmarked vehicle entrance. At the rear of the empty gravel parking lot, his tires crunched on the narrow dirt lane that continued past a retention pond. In the winter, the community used its frozen surface for ice-skating and hockey games, but the rest of the year, the area didn't get much use. He parked behind a clump of trees, where no one would see his car. The trail was just ahead. Maddie was slender, but dead weight was difficult to carry. He didn't want to work harder than necessary.

No point expending his energy when he had a whole night of fun planned.

He got out of the car. A chilly, wood smoke–tinged breeze crossed his face. Though the month had been unseasonably warm, the temperature was dropping with the light. He donned black nylon athletic pants and zipped a similar jacket over his clothes. The baggy outer garments disguised both his clothing and his shape. The trees thickened. Evergreens mixed with the red and gold of turned leaves, as many underfoot as overhead. He patted his pockets to check his supplies, though he knew he had everything he needed. Plastic ties, gloves, ski mask, check. He pulled the knit ski mask out and tugged it over his head. The gloves went on next. He rolled his neck until it cracked, then loosened up his shoulders. The hunt was on.

He glanced at his phone. Maddie would be passing in just a few minutes. This was true open space, just woods and trees and grass. No soccer fields, no baseball diamonds, no dog park.

And like tonight, typically, no other people. He only needed a few minutes to subdue her and secure her in his vehicle.

He heard the crunch of dead leaves and the soft thuds of her shoes on the trail before he saw her. As she approached, he tucked his head down and moved into the shadows at the edge of the path. Coming from the lighter open area into the darker woods, Maddie wouldn't see him. He knew because he'd checked during the dry run he executed the previous night at precisely the same time. He was invisible.

There was no hesitation in her stride as she ran past. Overconfident. That was Maddie.

Showtime.

The buzz in his veins heated and rushed into his head. It had been a long time since his last kill, but if Christmas happened every day, it would lose its holiday luster.

A burst of adrenaline fueled his steps as he charged her. She turned. Her eyes went wide. He launched his body at her, but she stumbled backward just before contact. He fell short, landing on his knees in front of her. Her mouth opened, and she turned to run again. Her shrill scream pierced the cool air and echoed in the woods. *Shit!* He caught her around the legs, tackling her to the ground. The impact with the earth cut off her scream. Her breath hissed from her lips.

He flipped her to her back, crawled on top of her, and pinned her body flat with his hips, then covered her mouth with a gloved hand. No more screaming. If people had heard, they would listen for another sound. When the noise wasn't repeated, they'd go back to their business, perhaps attributing the wail to a feral cat. Such was human nature. Given the option, most people would choose to believe they'd heard nothing.

Fresh terror widened her eyes as she registered his excitement, now pressed hard against her belly. He whispered in her ear, "That's right. Feel it, Maddie. There isn't anything I can't do to you."

Her trembling body was soft under his—weak, feminine, helpless. He inhaled. The pungent scent of her fear overwhelmed the musty leaf smell of the forest floor. Flailing, she struggled, the whites of her eyes shiny in the dim. He reveled in every useless slap of her hands. He'd waited a year for this moment. Every second was precious. But enough was enough. They needed to get moving in case someone had heard her cry.

But Maddie continued to fight with unexpected ferocity. She definitely wasn't going to be too easy.

He sat up and straddled her. "Fighting will only make it worse."

She bucked under him. His fingers found her throat and squeezed. Not too hard. He didn't want to kill her. Not yet. Not until he was finished. She would not be permitted to die until he commanded it. He applied just enough pressure to choke the fight out of her.

Practice makes perfect.

He leaned close to her ear.

"If you're quiet, I won't kill you," he lied. No matter what she did, he was going to kill her.

A few gurgles later, she quieted, eyes bulging, breaths rasping, limbs quivering. He removed his hands from her neck. A silver earring caught on his glove. He ripped it and its mate from her ears. Maddie whimpered as he shoved them into his pocket and dug for the plastic ties in his jacket.

Better. Much better. This was just the way he liked them.

Scared and submissive.

Her mouth opened. A shrill cry blasted out, loud as an air horn in the thin autumn night. He cocked a fist and punched her in the face. Her cheek split at impact. The sight of blood and her high-pitched cry of pain whipped his excitement higher. It blasted through his veins, eager to be unleashed.

Maddie was going to learn the hard way.

He raised his hand.

# CHAPTER TWO

*6:30 p.m., Coopersfield Community Center*

"This was my roommate, Karen." Brooke tapped the touchpad on her laptop and forwarded to the next slide in her PowerPoint presentation. She paused for a minute and stared at the picture. A young woman with clear blue eyes and long, shining brown hair laughed at the camera. Brooke had given this speech hundreds of times over the years, but the image never failed to squeeze her heart. She blinked a tear away.

*Tap.*

The next slide was a one-story brick elementary school in a northern suburb of Philadelphia, just a ninety-minute drive south on the Pennsylvania Turnpike. "Karen and I were both just out of school and had brand-new teaching jobs."

She changed slides. An apartment complex appeared on the screen. Exterior staircases on cement pads separated two-story buildings covered with gray aluminum siding. "We shared a two-bedroom apartment about a mile from the school. It was a nice neighborhood with lots of families and kids. Not far from the park. Karen minored in photography and always had a camera in her hand. She drove her red Trans Am with a heavy foot. Her favorite color was purple, and she had a weakness for macaroons."

*Tap.*

Brooke swallowed and studied the next slide. God, he'd been handsome. Short blond hair, blue eyes, and a killer smile beamed from the screen. "This was Karen's boyfriend, David Flanagan. They'd been dating for about six months when Karen decided to break it off with him. He was too clingy, too demanding with her time. She was only twenty-two and not ready to settle down yet."

*Tap.*

A dingy basement. On the left were locked storage units, one for each apartment. To the right, rusted washers and dryers sat on stained concrete.

"It was a warm October evening. A little after eleven, Karen went down to the basement to do some laundry. In our apartment building, there were only two washers and two dryers for a dozen units. Karen liked to do her laundry late at night when the machines would usually be empty."

Brooke paused and scanned the room. Nineteen college-age women sat on the waxed linoleum floor of the Coopersfield Community Center, their attention riveted to the screen. Cell phones were silent. No one texted. Even the first-timers sensed what was coming.

*Tap.*

A close-up of a dirty corner. Cobwebs spanned the angle from wall to wall. Dust and dryer lint coated the cinder blocks in bluish-gray. A dark stain blotched the cracked concrete like an ink blot test.

Brooke sipped water from a bottle. She swallowed the bitter clog of grief rising into her throat. "Her body was found here, behind the dryer, covered with the sheets she'd brought down to wash. She'd been raped, beaten, and strangled. There were no signs of a break-in. The police said he entered through an open basement window."

The picture on the screen switched back to the original photo and the flirty smile no one would ever see again.

"David and Karen had had an argument earlier that evening. He was angry that she'd dumped him. He said he was home alone when the murder occurred, but traces of Karen's blood were found in his car and condo. He was arrested and convicted of her murder."

Brooke told Karen's story to each group of girls she taught. It was the most effective means of punctuating her lecture on safe behavior. It was also her way of making sure Karen's death had meaning and that Brooke never forgot her friend.

Brooke stood. She motioned to a girl by the door. Fluorescent lights brightened the room. Everyone blinked.

"OK. We've been talking about staying safe and practicing basic self-defense for the last hour. When was the last time you heard about a group of girls being abducted?"

A tall brunette, Natalie, raised her hand. "Um, never?" On her left, her identical twin sister, Gabrielle, nodded.

"Exactly." Brooke let her safety-in-numbers point sink in for a few seconds. A wave of guilt doused her. If Karen hadn't gone into the basement alone that night, if Brooke had gone with her, Karen would still be alive today. But Brooke's secret was worse than that. Much worse. Luckily, the wound was old, the skin over it thick as scar tissue, and Brooke had years of practice containing her grief.

She glanced at her cell phone display. Her class had already run over nearly a half hour due to a mix-up with the room booking. Her kids hadn't been fed, and she had algebra quizzes that needed grading. A weary ache gathered at the base of her skull. She massaged the back of her neck. In twenty minutes she'd be home in Westbury, the neighboring town where she lived and taught high school math. "That's it for tonight. Thank you all for coming. Wednesday night is the last class in this unit. There'll be a padded attacker for you to practice the techniques on. You don't want to miss it. Stay together, and stay safe."

She closed her PowerPoint presentation, and Karen's picture vanished. There one second, gone the next. Just like Karen.

In two minutes, Brooke had packed her computer and projector into a cardboard box. Hefting it, she followed the girls toward the exit and thought of her dead roommate. She and Karen had been about the same age when it happened. Young, innocent, with endless years of life stretched out before them like an all-you-can-eat buffet.

Until it wasn't.

With a wave to the elderly night janitor, George, Brooke herded the girls outside. Streetlights cast yellow puddles of illumination in the parking lot. Natalie and Gabrielle folded their long legs into a red Mini Cooper parked next to Brooke's midsize SUV. They zoomed out of the lot with a short honk and a wave. The rest of the girls followed. Brooke loaded her equipment into her cargo area. She closed the rear hatch, opened the driver's side door, and tossed her purse onto the passenger seat.

A distant scream cut through her thoughts. Its raw tone and the way it cut off mid-wail disturbed the hair on Brooke's nape. She scanned the woods behind the center and listened, but all she heard was the muted sound of traffic on the main road and the wind chasing dead leaves across the parking lot. With less than a minute's hesitation, she grabbed a flashlight and cell phone from her car and popped her head back into the community center.

In the main room, George was clicking off the light switches. "Do you need something?"

"I think I heard someone scream in the woods. I'm going to check it out."

He pulled a huge ring of keys from his pocket, peered inside the supply closet, and then locked the door. "Lots of feral cats back there. Owls too."

"I know, but I'll feel better if I take a look." She hoped he was right, but to Brooke, the cry had sounded more female than feline.

More prey than predator.

"I'm sorry. I know I've already kept you later, but would you please call the police if I'm not back in ten minutes?"

Keys jangling, he crossed the room toward her. He shook his balding, white-rimmed head. "Nonsense. I heard you tell all those girls just a few minutes ago to avoid going places alone, especially at night." George opened a utility closet in the main hall and grabbed a heavy-duty metal flashlight from a wall hook. "I'm coming with you."

"Thank you." The Maglite wasn't exactly a sword, and George was an unlikely champion. But he was right, and she was grateful.

They rounded the building, waded through a strip of tall weedy grass, and headed into the trees. Despite a Santa belly and an arthritic hitch in his gait, George kept up. The forest was cooler, darker, and damper than open ground. They switched on their flashlights and played the beams on the pine needle carpet. A hundred feet into the forest, they stepped onto a path.

Brooke stopped and listened. George waited patiently beside her. A small animal scurried through the brushwood. Above, branches rustled in the breeze. They walked forward. Dead leaves crunched underfoot. A fresh scream came from the left, cut off abruptly by the *smack* of something striking flesh.

George silenced the keys on his belt with a fist.

"Shut. Up." A man's voice, terse and staccato, ordered. "And hold still."

A shriek, muffled. Another fleshy blow. Then crying.

Brooke dialed 911 and described the situation to the dispatcher in a low voice. Ignoring the operator's request to stay on the line, she ended the call and ran toward the sounds. George wheezed somewhere behind her.

She rounded a bend in the trail. Fifty feet ahead, shadows moved on the ground. Two figures, struggling. Brooke pointed her flashlight into the darkness. The bright beam spotlighted a masked man sitting on top of a young woman. His hands encircled her throat while the girl thrashed and gasped under him. His head jerked up and swiveled toward Brooke.

"Hey!" Brooke ran forward.

The assailant jumped to his feet and faced her. Hatred and hostility reached across the darkness. Brooke stopped. They stood frozen, staring at each other. Brooke's hearing blocked out everything but the sound of her own breathing and the throb of her pulse echoing in her ears.

# CHAPTER THREE

The assailant spun and took off down the path.

"Stay with her," Brooke shouted over her shoulder at George, still a hundred feet away. She sprinted after the black-clad man. The beam of her flashlight arced back and forth on the dark trail as she pumped her arms. With his head start, he pulled away. Though the five-minute mile from her college track days was no more, she kept in shape. She coached the high school track team and ran with the kids a few times a week. Brooke dug her toes into the sandy soil, pushing off with each stride, starting block–style. Her legs responded with a surge of speed. The distance between them closed. One toe caught on something on the dark trail. Her leg buckled, and she went down in a tumble of limbs. Pain, hot and sharp, burst through her knee. Her face struck the ground. Blood flooded her mouth.

She sat up and pointed her light down the path. He was gone. *Damn!* She shined her flashlight behind her. A gnarled tree root bulged out of the dirt.

Her clenched fist smacked the dirt next to her. She climbed to her feet. Her right knee wobbled, and when she tried to put weight on that leg, pain zinged from her toes to her hip. She couldn't inhale fast enough. Tiny pinpoints of light dotted her vision. She bent over and leaned her hands on her thighs. Her lungs bellowed, and her knee throbbed with each racing beat of her heart. Something gritty crunched between her teeth. She spat blood and dirt into the underbrush. Wiping her chin, she called 911 and gave them an update.

"He ran toward the Coopersfield reservoir." Lightheaded, she gasped between harsh intakes of cool air. "Average-size guy, wearing a ski mask, black pants, black windbreaker."

That's all she could say about him. Not much of a description. After being assured cars and an ambulance were en route, she ended the call.

The sound of someone crying summoned her. Brooke limped back toward the victim. The young woman was curled on the ground at the base of a tree. George stood a few feet away, shifting his weight from foot to foot. The woman cringed as Brooke's flashlight illuminated her. Brooke averted the beam, but not before she registered the young woman's battered condition. The left side of her face was bloody and beaten, her lips split, her eye blackened and swelling. She'd probably been pretty before he got his hands on her. Angry red marks encircled her neck. Pity blunted the ache in Brooke's leg. She halted and held her hands up. "It's OK. We're going to help you."

The woman held up shaking hands, bound at the wrists. She was trembling so hard Brooke could hear her teeth chattering.

"Here." Brooke stripped off her jacket and wrapped it around the woman's shoulders. "The police are on the way. What's your name?"

The voice was barely a rasp. "Maddie."

Maddie didn't look familiar. Since they were in Coopersfield, she'd probably gone to school here rather than at Westbury High where Brooke taught.

"I'm going to look at these ropes, Maddie." Brooke used her flashlight. Not ropes, but plastic ties encircled Maddie's wrists. Thin and unyielding, the binds had dug into her tender flesh.

Blood smeared her skin and stained her sleeves. "I'm sorry. These have to be cut, and I don't have a knife. Hold still so they don't hurt you anymore."

Maddie shook harder. Brooke wrapped her arms around the girl and held her tightly against her body. Hot tears soaked through her shirt.

A beam of light bobbed through the trees. George pointed toward the woods. The lights of the community center filtered through the half-bare branches. "Here are the police now."

An officer rushed in. Behind him, more lights approached. Two more uniforms burst into the clearing. Brooke pointed down the trail. "He ran that way."

Two cops jogged in the direction she indicated. One stayed behind. Tense and wary, he scanned the dark woods and spoke into a radio on his shoulder. A siren sounded. A few minutes later, two paramedics crashed through the underbrush.

Brooke eased the girl off her chest. "Maddie, I'm going to get out of the way so the paramedics can work."

Maddie didn't answer. Brooke leaned back. The girl's head lolled sideways. Brooke cradled it in one hand, easing it to the ground.

The paramedic knelt and opened his kit. "I've got her."

"Her name is Maddie." Brooke moved away to give them room.

The remaining cop pulled her aside. He looked to be about Brooke's age. It was hard to tell in the dark. "Your name, ma'am?"

"Brooke Davenport. I called 911." Hobbling, Brooke followed the policeman far enough away from Maddie so she wouldn't hear in case she regained consciousness.

"I'm Officer Kent." He shined his light on Brooke's face. "Are you all right, ma'am? Do you need medical attention?"

Brooke shielded her eyes, and the cop lowered the light. She ran her tongue over a swollen lump on her lower lip. "I'm OK." Brooke lowered her voice. "Did you catch him?"

"No, ma'am, but we're looking." He pulled out a notebook. "What else can you tell me about him?"

"Not much." She detailed the encounter from the scream to the present. "I didn't get that close. He ran. He wasn't excessively tall or short. Build appeared average. He ran like he was in decent shape, but he seemed . . . a little bulky."

"I'll walk you back to the parking lot." He started toward the trail.

Brooke turned to follow him, but as her adrenaline faded, the throb in her knee crescendoed.

"Are you sure you're all right?" The cop gave her leg a doubtful look.

"Just banged my knee. It'll be fine." But as they stopped next to her car, her knee gave out. Officer Kent caught her by the elbow.

He opened her car door and eased her to the seat. The overhead light gave her a clear view of the cop. He was blond and just shy of forty, with sharp eyes that dominated otherwise regular features. "You better have that looked at. Can I call somebody for you, ma'am?"

"No, thank you." Brooke perched sideways. Her jeans were torn and her knee skinned. Two years ago, before her divorce, she could've said yes. Scratch that. Even when they'd been married, her ex had rarely been around when she needed him. But now the only person she could call was her younger brother, Wade. Tonight, Wade was moving his stuff into her house to get ready for his deployment with the Army Reserve. And at the house with Brooke's fourteen-year-old son, Chris, was exactly where she wanted her brother to stay. Her fifteen-year-old daughter was at a high school field hockey team fundraiser. Haley was supposed to get a ride home from a friend, but the idea, which had been totally normal this morning, now made Brooke uneasy.

"Hang tight," Officer Kent said. "I'll get a paramedic over here."

Brooke opened her mouth to argue. But with her right knee in its current red-hot condition, she doubted she could drive. Without her jacket, a shiver swept through her. Chris had left a hoodie in the backseat, and Brooke gratefully tugged it over her head. She grabbed a bottle of water from the cup holder in the door, but her hands were trembling too hard to twist off the cap. She gave up and watched the scene unfold. An ambulance pulled into the drive, followed by two more marked police cars. A news van drove up. That was fast.

She did not want to be part of tonight's breaking news story. While she scanned the growing crowd for the officer who'd taken her statement, Brooke pulled out her phone and texted Chris to let him know she'd be late. The details would have to wait.

What happened tonight was not something she could tell him over the phone.

Where was the cop? Oh, no. A female reporter tottered across the asphalt toward Brooke's car. Using the car door, she pulled herself to her feet, grabbed her purse from the passenger seat, and hobbled toward the swarm of emergency personnel. Her vehicle chirped as she locked it with the fob. There was no way she wanted her photo on the news, not when the police hadn't found Maddie's assailant. Brooke had to face facts. Without an accurate description, catching him didn't seem likely. Once he'd left the area and changed clothes, he could be anyone.

And she was the one who'd stopped him.

With a sweep of headlights across grass, Luke turned at the metal mailbox and nosed his BMW onto the rutted drive. Ahead of his car, the dented black pickup driven by his friend, Wade Peterson, stalled. Luke braked. Wade's engine sputtered and then caught. The tires spun, spewing dirt onto Luke's silver sedan. A piece of gravel dinged off the hood.

Luke let the truck pull farther ahead. The drive curved around the big yellow farmhouse that Wade had grown up in. Luke parked next to the oversized detached garage that had once been a dairy barn. Wade didn't live here anymore, but he used the outbuilding as a base for his house-painting business. Luke got out and sucked in two lungfuls of damp meadow. Fresh air was one thing New York City was sadly lacking.

Wade backed the truck up to one of the two overhead doors and jumped down from the cab. He winced at the dirt showered on Luke's sedan. "Sorry about that. The truck needs a new transmission. Hope I didn't scratch your car."

"It's just a little dirt." Luke flicked a pea-size clump of soil from his windshield. "I'm not sure why I even bought it. I'm not home enough to drive it much." He stared at the old house. Memories stirred in his gut: girls, pizza, video games, first cars. Until high school, Luke had grown up in a posh suburb of Philadelphia, but he'd spent a few weeks every summer with his grandparents. After his parents had died, he'd come to live with his grandmother in Westbury. He and Wade had run the gauntlet of teen years together. "Just your sister lives here now?"

"And her kids. Brooke bought the place from my parents when they retired and decided to see the country by RV." Wade opened one of the overhead garage doors. "Speaking of leaving, when are you going back to work?"

"I report to the New York office next week." Luke followed his friend to the back of the truck. "Then I'm off to Argentina."

Wade climbed into the back, his boots clanking on the metal bed. Inside, furniture and boxes were packed like a 3-D puzzle. He squeezed between a cherry dresser and a headboard. He slid the dresser forward until the end protruded a few feet from the pickup bed. "Bet your grandmother is happy to see you."

"She is. I haven't been around much these last few years." Guilt nagged at Luke. He wanted to believe he was in Westbury to check up on his grandmother and see his best friend. But Luke's visit was just an excuse to get away from New York. There were way too many skyscrapers in the city for him to relax.

Luke steadied the heavy piece while Wade jumped to the ground. They lifted in unison. Luke's muscles strained, and the scarred skin on his back burned as it stretched.

"You OK?"

"Fine." Luke smoothed the grimace from his face.

They shuffled toward the open door.

"Are you sure you're ready to go back to work? You look like you could use some more R and R."

Three months ago in the Philippines, a terrorist bomb had blown a giant hole in a Manila high-rise one floor above Luke's meeting. He'd been pitching a comprehensive network security overhaul when the bomb had gone off. Six people had died and twenty more had been seriously injured, including Luke. "The doctor gave me the all clear." But his physical recovery wasn't the issue.

"Yeah, but are you really ready?" Wade tilted his head in the direction he wanted Luke to back up.

Luke glanced over his shoulder. The path was clear. "I need to get back to work." Face his demons and all that shit. Sleeping fourteen hours a day wasn't doing anything for his mental state. "I'm ready."

Wade raised an eyebrow in silent question.

"I'm here moving furniture for you, aren't I?"

"You are." Wade grinned. "Damn, I wish I didn't have to leave in the morning. But I'm glad you're going to hang for a while. A vacation in Westbury will be good for you."

"I'm sure it will." Just thinking about sitting in an office twenty stories up made Luke's skin itch and his stomach curl up like a scared kid. *Note to self: Most fire truck ladders don't reach above the seventh floor.* His boots scraped across a giant rust stain on the cement. The big white Peterson's Painting van was parked in the last bay. Supplies and equipment were stored on shelves next to it. "Where do you want this?"

"Let's squeeze it in with the rest of my junk in case Brooke needs space while I'm in Afghanistan."

Luke's gut soured at the thought of the danger his friend was heading into. "Do you need anything else taken care of before you go?"

"No. This is the last of my stuff to store." Wade shook his head. "The business is shut down. I let both my employees go."

"That sucks." Luke wiped clammy sweat from his forehead. They shuffled sideways and set the heavy piece down.

"One of the guys took it hard." Wade led the way back to the truck. He climbed into the bed, and they maneuvered the headboard into the clear. "He's been out of work before. In fact, can I give Brooke your number in case Joe bothers her this week?"

"Of course." Seeing Brooke again wouldn't be a hardship. He remembered the last time he'd seen her, ten years ago at the town's Fourth of July celebration. She'd been blowing bubbles to entertain her two young children, her smile wide as the kids raced in circles popping them. Watching them, emptiness had spread through his chest. She had married someone else, though her husband's absence had been as notable as Luke's heartache. Luke had cut his visit short and gone back to New York the next day.

"Luke?" Wade prompted.

Luke shook the vision from his head and rubbed his sternum. How could the memory be this sharp a decade later? "What's the guy's name?"

"Joe Verdi. Medium build. Extra-large temper."

"Great combo."

"Always." Wade said. "Just to round things out, he's a heavy drinker."

"Wonderful." Luke grabbed the end of the headboard. "Give her my cell number."

"Thanks."

"Hey, can I help, Uncle Wade?" A skinny teenage boy slouched behind the pickup. An unbuttoned plaid shirt hung over his T-shirt.

"Sure." Wade motioned between Luke and the kid. "Chris, do you remember my friend, Luke Holloway?"

Holy shit. *That* was Brooke's son? Luke still pictured him as a preschooler strung out on fireworks and cotton candy. The kid was adult-size. How the hell did that happen?

"Not really, but, hi." Like Wade, Chris was all dark brown hair and serious eyes. The teen wore his locks shaggy, while his uncle went with a buzz short enough to show scalp in the right light.

"Grab whatever you can lift, Chris." Wade hefted his end of the headboard, prompting Luke to do the same. Chris grabbed a box. With the kid's help, the unloading went faster than planned.

"You want these in the house?" Chris picked up a corrugated box marked CLOTHES.

"That'd be great. Thanks, Chris." Wade pulled his wallet from his back pocket and took out a couple of bills. "And you can order a couple of pizzas."

"Sweet. I'm starving, and Mom texted that she'd be late." The teen snagged the money and headed for the house.

Wade secured the back of the truck. "So, are you excited to get back to that jet-set life?"

"I guess." Luke dug a toe into the long grass. He looked out over the quiet yard. In the distance, foothills rolled purple into the darkness, the lights of civilization sparsely spaced. It was never dark or quiet in Manhattan.

"You guess? Most people would kill for your job. You lived in six different countries last year. Not bad for someone who almost got thrown out of school for hacking into the university's computer system."

"Not one of my finer moments. Now I use my powers for good." Luke faked a grin. He should be excited to get back to his job as a network security analyst, but just thinking of moving locations every four to six weeks made him tired. He imagined driving across the bridge, parking in a cement box, and riding an elevator high into a glass tower. He tried to stop there, but his brain conjured visions of the world exploding, of being stranded twenty stories up with no way of getting down except for running down a smoke-filled stairwell, of people screaming and bleeding and dying.

Of being on fire.

Pain burned a path across his back, and his heart sprinted into double-time.

"I understand why you're anxious to get back to the city. Westbury doesn't exactly have a roaring nightlife." Wade grinned. "But damn, it's been nice having you around this weekend. Come on. I stashed a six-pack in Brooke's fridge earlier today." Wade gestured toward the house. "I told you my sister's single again, right?"

"Twice." Luke stopped. "What's your point?"

"No point." The innocence in Wade's voice was overdone. "Just sayin' she's available, that's all."

"Are you trying to set me up with Brooke?"

"What if I was? What's so shocking about it?" Wade faced him. "You could do a lot worse than my sister."

"No, that's not what I meant. Brooke's terrific." Luke stammered, the argument rolling downhill faster than he could backpedal. "But I'm leaving town soon. She wouldn't be interested in me. I'm never around." Not to mention he was less stable than March ice on a pond, ready to crack at the slightest change in pressure.

"That's your choice."

"Yeah, it is." Luke *needed* to get back to work and get his life back on track. As soon as he got through a project or two, he'd be fine. This was no different than climbing back on a horse after a bad spill. All he needed was confidence.

"I just wish she wasn't alone. She takes care of two kids, teaches, coaches track, and devotes her few free hours to those self-defense classes."

When violence touched people, the damage didn't stop once the deed was done. It burrowed into the soul and made itself at home.

"How long has she been divorced?" Luke didn't know why he asked. He wasn't interested.

"About two years, but Ian traveled a lot. And even when Ian was around, he wasn't really around."

Luke kicked through a layer of dead leaves on the grass. The idea of Brooke being unhappy for years bugged him. The two-story farmhouse rose from the sloping rear lawn, blocking out the waning moon and a chunk of clear black sky. The yellow porch light highlighted weather-beaten trim. They climbed the steps to Brooke's back porch.

When would she be home? The quick stir of nerves in Luke's belly at the prospect of seeing her was as ridiculous as the teen crush he'd had on Wade's sister in high school. Other than being polite and sweet, Brooke, the hot college student, had barely noticed dorky Luke back then. Damn Wade for putting those thoughts back in Luke's head after he'd spent the last twenty years trying unsuccessfully to keep them out.

The back door stood open. Through the screen, Luke had a clear view into the kitchen. The space had been updated with bronze-toned granite and stainless-steel appliances since Luke had seen it last, but earth tones kept the room as inviting as it had been in his youth. The messy jumble of schoolbooks, folded laundry, and stacks of mail strewn across every flat surface spoiled the designer decor.

Luke thought of his absurdly expensive apartment with the minimalist furniture that came with the unit. What had looked sleek and modern when he'd moved in had felt cold and impersonal when he actually lived in the space for longer than a week. After three months of solid residency, the apartment still felt like a hotel. Its most attractive features were the third-floor location, way below panic height, and the sturdy fire escape outside his bedroom window.

Chris was standing in the kitchen, worried eyes riveted on a small countertop TV. An old collie snoozed on the tile next to his feet. A cool breeze swept across Luke's face, and clumps of dog hair blew across the kitchen floor like fur tumbleweeds.

Wade pushed through the screen door. "What's wrong?"

Chris pointed at the television, where a newswoman stood in a dark parking lot. Behind her, emergency lights flashed and swirled. "Somebody attacked a woman in the woods behind the Coopersfield Community Center. That's where Mom is."

# CHAPTER FOUR

Luke crossed the kitchen and turned up the volume, but the breaking news story segued into the weather report. Nails scratched on tile. The dog scrambled to its feet and stuck a narrow, whitening muzzle into his crotch. He gently averted the nose and stroked the bony head.

Wade pulled his cell phone out of his back pocket and punched a couple of keys. His mouth flattened out as he waited. "She's not answering."

"When she texted me that she'd be late, she didn't mention any of *that*." Chris gestured toward the TV.

"I'm going over there." Wade's phone buzzed. He yanked it out of his pocket. "It's Brooke." He slapped the cell to his ear. "Are you all right?" He listened for a minute. "I'll come and get you." He frowned. "Luke Holloway is here with me. He'll pick up Haley."

Luke could hear Brooke's disembodied voice. He couldn't make out the words, but the anxiety in her tone rang clear. He stood in the center of the kitchen, feeling useless, while Chris's bare feet paced the sand-colored floor.

"OK, I get it. You want me to pick Haley up," Wade huffed. "I'm sending Luke to pick you up. He'll be right there." Wade pushed END, cutting off the sound of Brooke yelling his name.

Chris stopped pacing. "What happened to Mom?"

"She's fine." Wade put a hand on his nephew's shoulder. "A woman was attacked. Your mom chased the guy off, but she tripped and hurt her knee." He turned to Luke. "Brooke is in the ER getting an X-ray. Do you mind going to get her? She wanted to call a friend of hers, but I'd feel better if she's with you. They haven't caught the bastard yet."

"Of course I don't mind," Luke lied. Hospitals were a close second on his list of places to avoid, right under high-rises, but he wasn't going to wimp out on his friend.

"Thanks. My niece is at the school. Brooke wants me to pick her up because Haley won't know you."

"Understandable. Your sister might not even recognize me." Luke pulled his keys from his pocket.

"Can I come?" Chris asked Luke.

Wade shook his head. "You're with me."

Chris opened his mouth.

Wade cut him off. "Your mom is worried enough right now. We're going to do whatever makes her feel better. This is about her, not us."

And that summed up Wade's motto. It was always about someone else.

"Whatever," the teen sulked.

"Don't worry. Luke will take care of your mom." Wade bumped a fist on his nephew's biceps. "And we'll pick up that pizza while we're out."

"I'll bring her back safe and sound." Luke headed out of the house. As he climbed behind the wheel, his phone vibrated. He glanced at the display, recognized the number, and ignored the call while nausea rolled through him.

*Can't think about* that *now. Focus on Brooke.*

He lowered the window. The air that flooded the car smelled of hayrides and bonfires. He backed out of the drive and pulled onto the country road that fronted the property. Like Gran's place just a few minutes away, there wasn't another house in sight. He glanced at his odometer when he passed the first neighbor—a full mile away. Who would Brooke call if she needed help in a hurry?

Fifteen minutes later, Luke parked in the ER parking lot. Double glass doors parted with a soft swish. He crossed the waiting room. A dozen people slouched in plastic chairs in a variety of miserable states telegraphed by ice packs and elevated limbs. A red-cheeked toddler slumped against his mother's chest while she stroked his sweaty head.

The nurse directed him to a long room with curtained-off triage bays. The glare of fluorescent lights brought back memories Luke tried his best to suppress on a daily basis. Sweat broke out between his shoulder blades, making his scars itch.

A uniformed policeman emerged from the middle unit. "Can I help you?"

"I'm looking for Brooke Davenport."

"I'm in here," a female voice called out.

"She's all yours." The cop gestured toward a gap in the curtains.

"Coming in." Luke ducked behind the curtain. At the sight of her, anger clamped his lips tight. One leg of her jeans had been cut off mid-thigh. Her leg was elevated on a pillow, her knee was covered with a square of white gauze, and an ice pack perched on top. Her chin was scraped, her lower lip swollen.

Shit like this shouldn't happen. Not here. This corner of the world was supposed to be insulated from violence.

"I appreciate you coming to get me." Brooke gave him a tight smile, then winced and touched her mouth. The sudden desire to press his lips to the injury shocked him.

Despite the decade since he'd seen her, his schoolboy crush hadn't faded one bit. Even with the passage of time, the mussed hair, and a puffy lip, she was still a gorgeous, capable woman. Her fair skin, shoulder-length dark hair, and athletic figure oozed small-town wholesomeness. Gran would say she had good bones, the kind of face that improved with age. As always, it was her determined brown eyes that drew him in, rich with the complexity of aged brandy. But meeting them tonight was a revelation. His soul recognized the damage behind her resolve and responded with a surge of need. Whether the demand was hers or his, he had no idea, but it didn't seem to matter. Something that was crushed inside of him stirred to life.

*OK. Overreact much?* Luke broke eye contact before he creeped her out.

A nurse came in with papers for Brooke to sign and a wheelchair. "Keep it elevated, iced, and wrapped."

"Thank you." Brooke tucked the pink copies into her purse.

From the open door, an alarm went off. A voice echoed "code blue" and a number. People ran in the hall.

"I'm sorry." The nurse hurried from the room.

Luke's gut twisted at the familiar sights and sounds of a medical crisis. "Are you ready to get out of here?" He sure as hell was.

"Definitely." She tossed the ice pack aside and slid off the table. Though average in height at about five-foot-five, standing next to his six-three, her head barely reached his shoulder. Their size difference and her injuries sparked a "me Tarzan" urge to swoop her up and carry her to the car. He restrained the impulse. She'd think he was nuts.

She hobbled toward the door. "Nothing's broken. Just a nasty scrape and a bruise."

"The nurse just said to stay off of it. You're going to make it swell even more." Annoyed, Luke grabbed the wheelchair. He released the brake and rolled it behind her. "Here. Sit down."

She *huffed* but dropped into the chair without a word. Luke pushed her down the hall, through the exit, and to the car waiting fifty feet away. He took her elbow and helped her into the passenger seat. "Lock the door." He left the wheelchair just inside the ER waiting room then returned to his car. He hadn't meant to be bossy, but damned if he'd let her make her injury worse under his watch, not after he'd promised Wade and Chris he'd look after her.

Escorting Brooke home was the biggest responsibility he'd accepted in months.

And it wasn't just any responsibility. It was Brooke.

He turned left on the country road that led toward her place. "What did the cop have to say?"

"He asked me some questions." Her head fell back onto the headrest. "They didn't catch him."

Luke clenched the wheel. To his right, the lights dotted the foothills. It was peaceful out here, but seclusion had its drawbacks. Wade was staying with Brooke tonight. But after that? She and her kids would be alone.

---

Brooke's knee was a hot, pulsing mess. She sank into the passenger seat as Luke steered through a bend. The recently repaved road stretched out ahead of them, the strip of tar shiny and black as an eel. They left the busy hospital and its brightly lit parking lot behind. A waning moon hovered, its outline crisp in a star-dusted sky. She'd lived in the country all her life. The dark had never bothered her. The small community of Westbury represented safety. But tonight, patches of impenetrable blackness crept among the foothills, and menacing shadows shifted in the moonlight. She pulled her gaze off the black landscape and studied Luke.

Wow. What a change. Of course, she couldn't remember the last time she'd seen him, but Wade had told her about the explosion. From her brother's comments, Brooke was glad to see Luke in one piece. She certainly hadn't expected him to look so . . . *Wow.*

Luke did not look like *that* in high school.

He'd been a sweet, geeky teenager with a lanky frame even the appetite of a starving wolverine couldn't fill out. But there was nothing gangly or geeky about him now. With his wavy brown hair tamed into a *GQ* cut and a car to match, Luke was sophisticated, successful, and much, much hotter than she remembered. His shoulders were broad and his chest muscular enough to make her look twice.

The dashboard light emphasized the sharp angles of his face and added to the intensity he'd projected even in his youth. Always a man on a mission. A few minutes ago, under the glare of the hospital lights, those piercing green eyes had focused 100 percent on her, cutting through her bullshit "I'm fine" act with the precision of a laser.

He stopped at an intersection. His gaze caught hers and held it for a second. There was a soul-deep sadness in his eyes that called to her. Like recognizing like? Her eyes filled at the unexpected reflection of pain. She blinked the connection—and the tears that threatened to spill out—away. Crashing adrenaline challenged her self-control, but she had plenty of practice keeping it together until she was alone.

"Are you all right?" Concern drew his brows together.

"Yes." She sucked in a deep breath and gathered her frayed emotions. "Thanks again for picking me up. I really needed Wade to be with my kids."

"No problem." Turning back to the road, he accelerated. Long, elegant fingers wrapped around the steering wheel. The tendons on the back of his hands corded as if his grip was excessive. "Do you want to talk about what happened?"

"I'd rather just do it once, if you don't mind. Wade's going to demand all the details. You know how he is." One retelling was going to be hard enough.

"I do."

Brooke wanted to think about something else for a few minutes. "How is your grandmother?"

"Pretty good." Luke made a left. "Busy with her charities."

"I haven't seen her in ages. Does she miss teaching?"

"I think so. She still teaches Sunday school. She was never one to sit around."

"Haley was in her fourth grade class the year she retired." Brooke lifted her head as Luke turned into the driveway.

He parked on her gravel drive and came around to help her out of the car, his hand strong under her elbow as she limped up the front walk. Luke wrapped an arm around her waist and lifted her up the three wooden steps to the porch with little effort. His body was rock solid against hers.

Wade opened the door. "I want to know everything." Irritation clipped his tone.

Heat emanated from the open door, welcoming Brooke home. "Can I go inside first?" After the violence of the evening, she needed to see her children, safe and sound. Wade moved back. Chris was behind him in the hall. Pulling away from Luke's supportive grasp, Brooke hobbled through the foyer. She hugged her son close. "Is Haley home?"

Chris patted her back. "Yeah, we got her."

Her muscles sighed in relief, nervous energy sliding out of her bones and exhaustion taking its place. Brooke called up the stairs, "Haley?"

"What happened?" Chris pulled back. His entrance to high school this year had shortened his tolerance for hugs. Since the divorce, Chris had matured beyond his years. Guilt tugged at Brooke's heart. Fourteen was too young to be the man of the house.

"If you get me a giant bag of ice, I'll answer all your questions." Brooke released her son, limped into the living room, and eased her butt onto her softest chair.

Luke faded back to lean against the wall, but Brooke could feel that intense green gaze still fixed on her. From across ten feet of hardwood, his attention heated her skin like the touch of his warm hand.

Chris slid the ottoman under her throbbing leg and fetched an ice pack. The cold barely made a dent in the heat radiating from her kneecap. Restless, Brooke shifted her position but couldn't get comfortable.

Sunshine clattered over and rested her head in Brooke's lap. She stroked the dog's head. "I'm all right, sweetie."

With an empathetic wag, the dog sank to the floor next to Brooke's chair.

Footsteps pounded on the steps, and Haley rushed into the room. Her face was flushed with a jumble of emotions.

"Mom!" She threw her arms around Brooke's neck. "Did you really save a girl from a rapist tonight?"

Brooke rested her temple against her daughter's head, taking another moment to be grateful that her children were safe. "How did you hear about it?"

Haley released her grip and perched on the edge of the ottoman. "Shannon's mother's sister works at the hospital."

"The police haven't caught him yet. Until they do, we're all going to be extra careful." Brooke looked from one child to the other, fear for them wrapping around her heart. "Neither of you goes anywhere alone. Promise me."

"OK," they said in unison.

"But you're all right?" Haley eyed Brooke's chin. "He didn't hurt you?"

Brooke adjusted her ice pack. "No. I tripped and face-planted on the ground. He was long gone."

Chris leaned down and gave her a one-armed hug. "I'm glad you're OK. Do you want anything before I go upstairs to finish my biology homework?"

"No, thanks." She squeezed his hand.

"I have to go take a shower." Haley followed her brother upstairs.

After the kids disappeared, Wade took a seat across from her. "Tell me everything."

Recounting the details of the night's events gave Brooke an icy ball in the pit of her stomach, as if she'd sucked down a giant Slurpee in one gulp.

"That guy could have killed you." Wade jumped to his feet and paced the room. "You should have let the police handle it instead of rushing into the woods."

"If I had hesitated, that girl wouldn't be alive right now." All the air whooshed out of Brooke's lungs and latent panic flooded in. She could still feel the malice and murderous intent emanating from Maddie's attacker. "I can't believe he got away. He'll do it again."

Wade shook his head. "You don't know that."

"Sexual predators reoffend. That's a fact." Brooke had been studying violent sex offenders and their crimes for years in order to arm her self-defense students with the best possible information. When these girls left the protection of their rural community, they'd be prepared in a way that Brooke and Karen hadn't been. "Do you really think I should have ignored her scream for help?"

"No, of course not." Wade dropped his chin. "But you can't save everyone. I know you're stuck on what happened to Karen, but it wasn't your fault."

*Wasn't it?*

Brooke wrapped her arms around her middle. All these years later, the scene was as real as if she stood there tonight. The sheet peeled down to reveal her friend's battered face and body. The milky glaze of Karen's eyes. The smell of blood and death overpowering the scent of dryer sheets and damp, vented air in the basement laundry. Pressure built behind her breastbone. She hugged herself tighter, holding it all inside, using the pain in her knee as an anchor to the present.

Wade walked up behind her and put a hand on her shoulder. "I worry about you."

"I worry about you too. I wish you weren't going back to Afghanistan."

Wade scratched his head. "I'm being deployed, Brooke. It's not a choice."

Brooke lowered her voice. “You re-upped with the reserve last year. You didn’t have to.” Worry, anger, and fear compounded in her chest until the force restricted her lungs.

“I’m sorry, Wade. I’m proud of you.” A hefty dose of guilt added to the mix. She shouldn’t make Wade feel bad about serving his country.

“Thanks.” Wade sighed. “Please be careful while I’m gone. Keep the heroics to a minimum.”

“I will if you will.” Seeking comfort, she reached down to rest a hand on Sunshine’s head. The dog’s tail thumped twice on the hardwood.

“Deal.”

The phone rang, startling them both.

“I’ll get it.” Wade turned away from her. “No. She isn’t available for a comment. I’ll give her the message.” He returned to the living room. Worry tightened his jaw to nutcracker. “That was a reporter for *Action-Packed News.* They want an interview.”

“That was fast.” Brooke rested her head back in the chair and stroked the old dog’s head.

“If the media got your name and number that fast, anyone could.” Wade paced. “I wish I wasn’t leaving in the morning.”

“Me too.” As independent as she wanted to be, she was grateful to have her brother in the house tonight.

“Luke and I will get your car.”

Brooke glanced at Luke, leaning on the wall, watching her. “The policeman said he’d have someone drop off my car.”

“Are you sure?” Wade’s forehead furrowed. “It might sit in the lot all night.”

“I can live without it,” Brooke protested. It felt stupid and weak, but she didn’t want to be alone right now. “I can’t drive with this knee anyway.”

"OK," Wade said.

"If you don't need anything else, I'm going to get going." Luke pushed off the wall.

"Thanks for helping." Wade moved toward the front door. "I'll walk you out." He glanced back at Brooke.

Luke followed him out onto the porch. Through the living room window, Brooke watched them confer.

Despite the fever in her knee, a shiver sprinted through her body. Putting aside the ice, she limped to the kitchen for a couple of ibuprofen. Pain or no pain, though, she was going to be up all night.

In fact, she might never close her eyes again.

# CHAPTER FIVE

He drove his car into his two-car garage and closed the overhead door, just as he would have done had his trip been a success. Luckily for him, his plan had included a quick getaway. Shedding his outer garments was all that was necessary to blend in. With the plastic bag containing his cover clothes tucked under his arm and a fast food sack in hand, he went inside. The basement door, the darkness, and the deeds he'd been anticipating beckoned.

His wrist stung. He set the bags down and pushed up his sleeve. Blood welled from three scratches just below where his glove had ended. Tree limb or Maddie's nails? There was a big difference between the consequences. He went to the sink and lathered up. As the soap burned the cuts, anger raged through his body. Never in all the years he'd indulged his *needs* had his plans been interrupted. Never had he left DNA behind. Never had he left a scene without the proper staging.

Tonight marked the end of his winning streak.

All because of *her.*

He applied antibacterial ointment and a flesh-toned Band-Aid, then rolled his sleeve back down over it. He grabbed his plastic bag and went into the basement. To the left was his carefully prepared workspace, empty and unused. Plastic sheeting crinkled underfoot as he crossed the space to the right. The cinder block wall was lined with storage containers. He knelt on the dirt floor in front of one and spun the numbers on the lock to the correct combination. Inside, he stashed his equipment bag, checking to make sure he hadn't dropped anything. Pants, jacket, ski mask. His lucky gloves were damp with blood, but they'd been stained with the blood of victims long before tonight. Guess they weren't quite so lucky anymore.

Not that it mattered. She hadn't seen his face. DNA was only a problem if he became a suspect.

He paused before closing the lid. Reaching into the bag, he rooted though the pockets for Maddie's earrings. He held one up by the post. A delicate silver music note dangled from his fingertips. His fist curled around it until the sharp points dug into his palm.

His gaze lingered on the other containers. If all had gone according to plan, he would have had new memories to catalog and store tonight. While he was at it, he would have taken some time to relive the evening—and to relish the hunts of past victims and sort through all the things that reminded him of their last, terror-drenched moments at his hands.

But his evening was spoiled. He'd failed.

He turned away from the bins. He couldn't look at his other keepsakes. How had this happened? He debated folding up the plastic sheets and returning them to their shelf. Hunger roiled in his belly. It was an appetite that would never be satisfied with food.

No. He wouldn't give up yet. He had needs he wouldn't be able to ignore for long. Unsatisfied, they might run unchecked. He was disciplined, but even his stringent self-control had limits. No matter how long a tiger is kept in a zoo, its predatory instincts cannot be contained. Given the opportunity, even a well-fed cat will kill. The need to hunt is ingrained in the beast's genetic code, imprinted into its brain stem.

Some creatures are programmed to kill.

Averting his eyes from his sturdy worktable, he returned to the main level and turned on the small TV in the kitchen. Tonight's event would be a big deal in the tiny, no-news town. Standing in front of the screen, he flipped to a major network. A female reporter stood in the parking lot of the Coopersfield Community Center. The words BREAKING NEWS scrolled across the screen.

The center was supposed to be closed before his hunt. He'd checked. The reporter summarized the incident. No accurate description. No clues. No leads.

Small favors, he supposed. He'd survived to try again, and try again he would. He was nothing if not determined.

Patience was one of the only virtues he possessed. Maddie would be his eventually. She bore some of the blame for his ruined night. If she hadn't struggled so hard, if she'd obeyed when he told her to shut up and be still, they would have been off the trail by the time the cavalry arrived.

The bag of greasy food called to him. He ripped it open on the counter. Next to it he opened his laptop. After it booted up, he signed in to the app that controlled all the social media pages under his secret identity, the profile of a nineteen-year-old man he'd established with careful attention to detail. Photos, hobbies, and a few expectedly inane updates provided his alter ego with a believable background. So far, very few young women had refused his virtual friendship.

He bit into the hamburger, his consolation prize. The tastes of meat and cheese, pickles and ketchup, exploded on his tongue. Tonight he'd indulge in some comfort food to make up for the evening's disappointment. But the meal was no more satisfying than a toaster to a game show contestant who pined for a Hawaiian vacation.

Tomorrow he'd return to his normal routine. He'd adhere to the diet and exercise plan that had helped keep him stalking fit. Considering the sprint speed he'd needed this evening, it was obviously an important part of his lifestyle, and yet more evidence that proper preparation would address any surprises. No plan was perfect. The actions of others could not be predicted in every circumstance.

Maddie wasn't the only one who was going to pay. Someone else owed him an exciting evening, a slightly older brunette who'd ruined his fun.

He thought back to another woman who'd stripped away his control. Even all these years later, those memories stained any reminiscence of his childhood. Never again would he be that powerless.

*"What are you doing?"*

*He paused. His older sister, Ellie, stood in the doorway.*

*"Put that down."*

*But he brought the hammer down one more time on the worn vinyl. The tiny bathroom in their rented trailer smelled funny. It wasn't as nice as the house he'd shared with his parents before they'd died. They'd had a whole house, with a yard and trees and a creek out back. He'd had to change kindergarten classes too. Not that he'd had many friends in his old school, but the classroom had been nicer.*

*Ellie snatched the hammer from his grip. She stared down at the damage. "Oh my God, you smashed it."*

*She grabbed him by the back of the collar and hauled him onto his feet. He dangled. The toes of his sneakers skimmed the floor.*

*"Look, I'm sorry that Mom and Dad died and that you're stuck with me. Trust me, waitressing and supporting you wasn't*

*my plan either. But I'd better not ever see you doing anything like this again." Ellie have him a quick shake, like a terrier shakes a rat, then dropped him. His teeth snapped together and rattled his head. She pinched the back of his neck. Anger tightened her grip. "Get out of here while I clean this up. Supper's in an hour."*

*She was a grown-up and he was just a kid. The shove sent him out the door into the cramped aisle that ran between the kitchen and the bedroom. He knocked into the wall. His elbow hit the paneling and a jolt of pain zinged through his arm.*

*He opened the squeaky screen door and went outside. It closed behind him with a* thwack. *A few dead leaves gathered on the steps. Rubbing his elbow, he sat down. The yard was a patch of dirt between their trailer and the next. No creek full of frogs here. Just weeds and rusted metal.*

*He wouldn't always be small. She wouldn't always be in charge. But until he got bigger than Ellie, he was gonna have to be more careful.*

# CHAPTER SIX

"I need to ask you for a favor."

"What is it?" Leaning on the porch railing, Luke clenched his fist around the car key until the teeth bit into his palm. He stared at the meadow that sprawled across the road from the house. He didn't have to look at Wade to know what was coming, and to know there wasn't a damned thing he could do about it.

"I'd really like you to keep an eye on Brooke."

The moisture evaporated from Luke's throat as if he'd swallowed a mouthful of sand. Responsibility for a woman's life was his personal nightmare. Literally.

"I'm really worried." Wade paced to the edge of the porch and back. His boots scraped the wide planks. "She interrupted some bad shit tonight. A reporter already called the house. It wouldn't take much for this guy to find her too."

"You're probably right." Violent people did violent things. Horrible acts that ordinary men couldn't comprehend. Innocents were murdered every day on this earth. No one knew that better than Luke.

"I know my sister. She's not going to let it go." Wade stopped. He swept both hands across his buzz cut.

"Because of what happened to her roommate?"

Wade leaned on the railing next to Luke and stared out over the field. "Brooke never got over it."

Tall grass rippled in the breeze. Silvery moonlight reduced the scene to shades of gray. There were some things a person carried to his grave.

"So, will you do it? At least for the next week."

The wind stirred dried leaves in the corner of the porch, and panic eddied in Luke's gut. He wanted to say no. The last thing he needed was responsibility. He'd come up here to hang out with his grandmother and relax, to clear his lungs and his head. But only a selfish bastard turned down a friend who was getting shipped out to Afghanistan, where distractions could get a man killed. And there was no way Luke could let anything happen to Brooke, with or without Wade's request. Luke's mouth was moving before he could stop it. "Of course I will."

Wade slapped him on the shoulder. "Thanks, man. I appreciate it. That gives me some peace of mind."

Ironic. The situation did the opposite for Luke. After all, the last woman who'd been his responsibility had ended up dead.

---

It was going to be a long night. Brooke lifted her head from the back of the chair as Wade came back inside. The deadbolt slid home.

Wade pulled up a chair. He spun it around, straddled it, and rested his forearms on the back. "I want you to make me a promise."

Suspicion cut through Brooke's exhaustion.

Wade interlocked his fingers, prayer style. "I asked Luke to look out for you for the next week. I want you to let him."

"You did what?" Brooke choked on her water.

"It's not a big deal." Wade shrugged. "He's around, visiting his grandmother."

"I hardly know him." Having him around 24-7 felt dangerous in a way that had nothing to do with tonight's attack. Luke roused emotions she had no desire to awaken. Emotions she'd worked hard to bury.

"I know him, and I trust him." Wade crossed his arms over his chest. "That should be enough for you."

"Oh, really?" A familiar mix of irritation and affection nudged some of her tension out of the way. "You're awfully bossy for a little brother."

Wade's face reddened. His eyes went sharp, already primed for what Brooke suspected was military mode. "I'm serious. Luke is a good man, and you could use one of those."

Mental warning bells clanged. "Are you trying to fix me up with your friend?"

"Maybe." Wade's shrug was too nonchalant. "You don't seem to be having much luck on your own."

Oh. Bull's-eye on her self-confidence.

Wade's eyes closed briefly, and his chest expanded in a deliberate heave. "I'm sorry. That was offsides." He reached out and gave her hand a squeeze.

Brooke accepted his apology by returning the clasp. "Luck has nothing to do with it. I'm too tired for the whole dating thing." Plus, she hadn't met anyone in years who made her body tingle. She was only thirty-eight. That wasn't too old for tingling, was it? She remembered the intensity of Luke's gaze. No. She could still tingle. Right down to her toes.

"In that case, I'm hand delivering you a man," her brother teased.

"Wade, that's not funny! You have to stop trying to fix me up with your friends." Since her divorce, she'd been disinterested in trying again. One failed marriage felt like enough. Why set herself up for more loss?

Her brother let out an exasperated give-me-strength breath. "Please, Brooke. For me. Just give me the peace of mind that Luke is here. You don't have to date him, just let him keep you safe. By the time he has to go back to New York, maybe the cops will have arrested this scumbag. I wouldn't want to be distracted over there. That might be dangerous."

"Now that's low." Brooke shook a finger at him. "I wouldn't do this for anyone else."

"I know." He grinned, then sobered. "You promise?"

Brooke held up three fingers. "On my honor." Her vision clouded with unshed tears. "What time do you leave tomorrow?"

"I'll be out of here before dawn. We'll get the good-byes out of the way tonight, OK?" Wade's eyes misted, and for the first time, Brooke realized how much leaving was costing him. "I'm sorry I didn't get around to painting this house."

"You'll do it when you get back."

The "if" hung in the silence between them.

Wade broke the sad tension. "You really should think about selling this place. It's way too much upkeep, and it's too isolated."

"I love this house. It's a lot of maintenance, but I have no mortgage. I can afford to keep it up. I've just been short on time lately."

"Still keeping up with those self-defense classes you teach, though?" Wade wanted the same thing as everyone else in her life, for her to move on.

"That's only two hours a week."

"Time isn't really what you sacrifice." Wade put a hand on her shoulder. "I appreciate that you want to give back, Brooke, but you should give yourself a break. What happened to Karen wasn't your fault."

Brooke wished he was right, but Wade didn't know the whole story. Other than Brooke, only two people knew everything that happened that night. One was in prison, and the other was dead.

# CHAPTER SEVEN

Boom.

*The force of the blast threw Luke to the floor face-first. Glass shattered. Smoke and falling dust filled the air. The echo of his heartbeat muffled sounds with an underwater effect, as if his head had sunken to the bottom of a muddy lake. Through the auditory haze, fire roared. People screamed.*

*An explosion. He needed to get out of here. Sherry. Where was Sherry?*

*He lifted his head a scant inch, but the pain that ricocheted through it blackened the edges of his vision. He inhaled, and the salty, coppery taste of blood ran down the back of his throat. He touched his nose, and his hand came away wet and red. He looked beyond his hand. There was blood everywhere. A lake of it spread toward him across the commercial carpet. Way too much to come from his nose. Just way too much.*

*Seeking the source, he lifted his head, slowly this time. His eyes drifted right. The horror made him want to squeeze them closed. But he couldn't.*

*His assistant, Sherry, was crumpled on her side. Blood splattered her skin and soaked her clothing. A gash in the side of her neck gaped. One arm stretched across the floor. Her fingers twitched. Luke grabbed hold. Her weak squeeze drenched him in terror.* Crack. *The world shifted. Debris rained down on him. Survival instinct kicked in, and his free hand covered his head. A heavy object landed on his back, the impact shooting the air from his lungs.*

*Yet his eyes were still locked on Sherry's face. Her body didn't move, but her eyes pleaded.*

*He was almost grateful for the pain that burned through the concussion and overshadowed everything. Agony seared a path across his back. He rolled, bumping up against something unforgiving.*

The impact jolted Luke awake.

Breathing hard, he took stock. Rag rug under him. Bed to his left. The dresser he'd just slammed into on his right. The steady tick of the grandfather clock in the hall. His grandmother's house. Not a burning high-rise in Manila.

Disappointment floored him nearly as much as the nightmare. After three months of intensive therapy, he thought he'd kicked the late-night creep show.

He glanced at the clock on the nightstand. Four o'clock was too early for breakfast. He sat up and waited for his heart rate to slow, his breathing to ease. Didn't happen. His body was convinced a full-flight response was warranted.

He had a choice. Crawl under the bed and hide or get moving. Option number one looked damned appealing, but he'd have to come out sooner or later.

Time to get his ass in gear then.

He dressed in sweats and a hoodie, laced up his running shoes, and headed out into the darkness. He gave his eyes a few minutes to adjust, then jogged down the brick walk, the chill stinging his face and his lungs like pinpricks, his breath puffing out in front of him. The best cure for the need for flight was to give his body exactly what it wanted, a hard run.

His feet hit the road. His stride lengthened. On either side of him, the warm ground and cold night combined into a floating mist that drifted like smoke. He passed a meadow and the neighboring farm, with its burned-out shell of a barn. Arson, Gran had said. Not even the idyllic community of Westbury could escape violence. The smell of charred wood drove him forward. Luke ran harder, adrenaline-charged muscles eager for action. In New York, he couldn't outrun the dream. The scents of diesel exhaust and burnt rubber followed him everywhere, reminding him of smoke and fire.

And death.

But here it was different. He put some distance between him and the rubble. Gradually, the sky lightened. The smell of damp grass and wet earth cleansed his nose. His pace and heart rate steadied. He pulled up suddenly. The old farmhouse rose in front of him, its solid bulk jutting into the predawn sky.

Not only had he run away from his past, he'd run all the way to Brooke's house.

His psychiatrist would have a party with this one.

But last night, the vulnerability in her eyes had shaken him and given him the disconcerting urge to camp out in front of her house with a weapon. The impulse was primal and disturbed him nearly as much as his promise to protect her.

The windows were dark. Nothing moved inside or out. Was she awake? How badly did she hurt this morning? Had nightmares ripped her from her sleep during the night?

Sweat dripped into his eye. He wiped it away and turned his feet around. Brooke's house was about four miles from his grandmother's place. He had a long run back. Gran was an early riser. She'd have breakfast on the table for him before six. No sleeping the day away in her house.

With the panic burned off, he eased his pace on the return run, enjoying the countryside. A stretch through the woods filled his nose with the scent of pine. He passed cows and sheep. A small herd of deer dotted an open meadow. Heads snapped up from the deep grass. With a flip of their white tails, the animals bounded away as he jogged by.

By the time he turned into his grandmother's driveway, he was covered in healthy sweat and more relaxed than he'd been in months, maybe even years. A light in the kitchen window told him Gran was up. He jogged up the porch steps and left his wet running shoes on the mat just inside the door. "Lucas?" His grandmother's call was punctuated by a cough.

He followed her voice back to the kitchen. Her head of precise gray curls barely came to his chest. He leaned over to kiss her on the cheek.

She held up a hand and blocked him. "You're going to catch my cold."

"Never. Living with eight million people is good for the immune system." Was it his imagination or was her papery skin paler than it had been yesterday? "You're up early."

"Couldn't sleep. No sense wasting the day." She cracked an egg into the same chipped porcelain bowl she'd been using for thirty years. Her nose wrinkled. "Go shower. Pancakes and bacon in twenty."

"Yes, ma'am."

The shower was stocked with a bottle of generic shampoo and a bar of Ivory soap. Letting the hot water sooth his tired muscles, Luke raised the white block to his nose. The familiar scent filled him with warmth. He'd had a New York address for years, but Gran's house was the place that always felt like home.

Though he'd only lived here for his high school years—after his parents had been killed in a car accident—they had been long years full of grief and turmoil and, ultimately, healing from his parents' shocking deaths.

Could this old house work its magic one more time? Probably not in a week.

Dressed in jeans and a T-shirt, he went back downstairs. The scent of frying bacon wafted down the hall. His stomach rumbled. He went back to the kitchen. As usual, the table was loaded with his favorites. He slid into a ladder-back chair.

Gran set a mug of coffee on the scarred table. "Eat. You have some weight to put back on."

"Yes, ma'am. This looks great." He filled his plate, the run establishing an appetite despite his rude awakening. Gran sat opposite him. One slice of bacon and a single pancake sat on her plate, but she didn't touch her food. "Are you all right?"

She cleared her throat and waved off his concern. "I'm fine. Takes more than a cold to keep me down."

She sipped her coffee, picked at her food, and let him eat in comfortable silence. After he pushed his plate back, Gran cleared the table. "Weren't you with Wade Peterson last night?"

"Yes, I was helping him get ready to ship out."

"Shame what happened to his sister."

"How did you hear about that?" Silly him. His grandmother knew everything and everyone in town. Since retiring from a long career as an elementary school teacher, she'd turned her attention to community service and raising money for local charities. Gossip was her fuel, guilt her weapon of choice, and figurative arm-twisting her superpower. At seventy, Gran could crack wallets like walnuts.

Gran set his dishes in the sink. “My friend Nancy called me. She’s the secretary to the police chief here in town. Did you see Brooke last night?”

“Yes.” He’d come in late. Gran had already been in bed. But he still suspected she already knew he’d picked Brooke up from the hospital.

“How was she?”

“Banged up her knee, but otherwise she seemed fine.”

“Good. I hear she’s quite the hero.”

“She is.” A picture of Brooke, with her stubborn and scraped chin lifted in determination, filled Luke’s head. Emotions shifted in his chest, like they were making room. Brooke had saved a young woman’s life. That was more than he’d been able to do.

The vision intruded. *Smooth olive skin streaked with blood. The mischievous eyes that had flirted with him not two minutes before the world exploded turned glassy with pain and fear.*

Now Brooke might be in danger.

“Lucas?” His grandmother was staring at him with sharp gray eyes that defied her age.

He cleared his throat and shook the image from his mind. “Is there more coffee?”

“Or course there is.” Gran refilled his cup. “Wade’s leaving soon, isn’t he?”

“Today. Soon, in fact.” Luke glanced at the digital clock on the microwave.

His grandmother sighed. “What terrible timing. I hate to see Brooke and her children alone with a violent criminal running around.” Was that a pointed statement?

Luke studied an errant ground swirling in his coffee. “I promised Wade I’d look after them until I have to leave.”

"Oh, that's a relief. I'll call Nancy and see what the Westbury police are doing about the situation. No doubt they're on the lookout, but Michael O'Connell—he's the Chief of Police—has been out on disability. I told you he'd been stabbed in the leg, didn't I?"

"No."

"Well, he was. But I'm sure he's keeping tabs on things." Gran opened the refrigerator and pulled out a covered rectangular dish. "I made a casserole for Brooke. Why don't you take it over to her?"

"How did you know I'd be going over there this morning?"

Gran put the heavy dish into Luke's hands. "Because I know what kind of man you are. You couldn't do anything else."

Luke left the house as the coming dawn warmed the horizon to dark gray. Gran's confidence in him felt empty, hollow, backed up only by her faith. Where had it come from? He'd never done anything to warrant her unwavering support. He'd gone to college, then devoted most of his time to his career, to himself, really. He had a fat bank account and plenty of expensive things to show for it. He couldn't think of one instance where he'd done significant good for others. In fact, the one time he'd been asked to help another person, he'd failed miserably.

He would keep his promise to Wade, but he didn't want to. He wanted to run back upstairs and crawl under the bed.

# CHAPTER EIGHT

"And now we go live to an update on last night's brutal assault in Coopersfield."

Riveted to the TV screen, he barely tasted his morning coffee. A blond reporter in a red suit stood in front of Westbury Community Hospital. "The young woman who was attacked last night while jogging is in stable condition at an area hospital this morning . . ."

*So close.* Maddie was barely a ten-minute drive from his house. He'd been denied, but that wouldn't last forever. He wanted so badly to see her. To watch her. To plan their next—their final—encounter.

An idea festered inside him. It might be fun to let Maddie know he was thinking of her. That he hadn't forgotten.

He let the newswoman's recap of his failure roll over him. It wasn't as much fun as listening to the news reports of his successful exploits.

Lady Luck had given him the metaphorical finger last night. Was fate telling him something? Perhaps that he'd been lazy. He hadn't challenged himself. He'd picked easy targets and relied on technology. And the worst offense? Last year's killing had been same old, same old rather that the fresh thrill it was supposed to be.

He started his laptop, opened his social media app, and checked on Maddie. Lots of well-wishes from her friends. No responses from his girl. Had he done more damage than he'd thought? A visit to the hospital was in order tonight. He had to know more than the official statement the hospital released on the news, and he was definitely going to plan a special surprise for Maddie.

"And a victim was saved by the intervention of one courageous woman." The reporter's sign-off caught his attention.

His head swiveled back to the TV. He stared at the photo of the attractive brunette on the big screen. Her age, her self-assured posture, and the determination in her gaze would normally cause him to cross her off his list of potential victims. It wasn't that he didn't find thirty-something females attractive, but younger women were often careless and therefore easier targets. But maybe picking off the easiest prey was killing his buzz. Pursuing a woman like that would change everything.

She'd be a challenge worthy of his talents.

# CHAPTER NINE

Brooke stared at her clock. The alarm wouldn't go off for another hour, but she'd slept off the worst of her exhaustion. Had the police caught the assailant during the night? There was no point trying to go back to sleep.

She swung her legs over the side of the bed and tested her knee. The joint was sore and stiff but not as painful as she'd expected. She hobbled into the bathroom and showered. The soapy water stung when it ran over the abrasion. She taped a fresh gauze pad over it and dressed in loose slacks.

"Time to get up!" She rapped on both kids' bedroom doors and waited for the morning moans and groans to seep through the wood before making her way downstairs. In the foyer, she stopped cold.

The hallway smelled like coffee. She heard the quiet slide of drawers opening and closing. Of someone looking for something. Already on edge, her nerves prickled.

Who was in her kitchen?

Wade should be long gone. The kids were still upstairs . . .

Get real. Criminals didn't make coffee. Wade must be running late.

Sunshine sprawled in the center of the kitchen floor. Instead of her brother, Luke was filling a coffee mug at the counter. As she limped into the room, he turned. Worn jeans sat low on lean hips, and a faded blue Penn State T-shirt highlighted his broad shoulders. Brooke ripped her stare off the giant letter *S* front and center on his muscular chest. “You made coffee.”

“I did. How’s the knee?” Deep green eyes gave her a critical once-over. Just like the night before, he saw through her brave face, as if he didn’t even have to ask about her emotional state. He knew.

“Not too bad.” She was instantly glad a few dabs of concealer had masked her scraped chin, which was ridiculous. Her appearance should be the least of her worries this morning. Unsettled, she hobbled around the sleeping dog and sat down. “How did you get in here?”

“Wade let me in before he left.” Luke poured her a cup of coffee and set it in front of her. “He gave me his key, too, in case of an emergency. I hope you don’t mind.”

Brooke didn’t answer. Wade trusted Luke enough to suggest she . . . No. She wasn’t going there before coffee. Luke having a key to her house shouldn’t make her nerves do a jig. But one thought dominated her brain. While she’d been naked in the shower, he’d been in her kitchen. Her skin warmed. She reached for her mug. It was too early to contemplate her brother’s attempt at matchmaking. Her own unfamiliar response to Luke was more than she could handle at the moment.

“Thanks.” She sipped, praying the caffeine would machete its way through the haze. Between her knee and the instant replays in her head, her night had been fitful. Was it just the residual anxiety from last night’s attack that unsettled her? Or did Luke’s masculine presence in her kitchen add to the jumble? Her last smooth nerve threatened to wiggle free, and she fought to restrain the irritation in her tone. “Why are you here?”

“Wade asked me to keep an eye on you.”

"I know. He told me, but I didn't expect to see you this early." Sadness fractured her heart. Her little brother, soon on his way to a hostile country, was still looking out for her. But he should have asked her before giving his friend a key to her house. "You didn't by any chance catch the news this morning, did you?"

His mouth tightened. "They haven't caught him."

With that one sentence, Luke's presence shifted from unsettling to reassuring. "The more time that passes, the less likely it is that he'll be caught."

For a brief second, fear flashed in Luke's eyes. Or was that a reflection of the panic brewing inside her? Out the back window, a gray predawn mist rolled across the foothills. A secluded location and expansive windows were two of the house's best features, but this morning the lovely view represented sheer vulnerability.

"Let's hope they find him this week." He blinked the raw emotion clear and turned away. At the sound of pans rattling, the dog lifted her head. "How about some eggs?"

Sunshine scrambled to her feet, arthritic limbs sliding on the tile with the shaky grace of a newborn fawn.

He gave the dog a pat. "I wasn't talking to you."

Sunshine's tail arced in a slow, hopeful wag.

"She wants her breakfast." Brooke put a palm on the table and started to push to her feet.

Luke raised a hand in a stop gesture. "Sit. I'll do it."

"OK." Brooke eased back down. "There's a bag of kibble in the pantry. Thank you."

"I like dogs. I wish I was home enough to have one." Luke fed the dog and filled her bowl with fresh water. He returned to the stove. "How many eggs can you eat?"

"Just one. I'm not a morning person." As if the traumatic connection between them wasn't hard enough to resist, he was good-looking, had a sense of humor, was kind to pets, *and* he cooked. She was in trouble. Brooke gulped her coffee. Another gallon and she might wake up and come to her senses.

Karen's death and a failed marriage had ruined Brooke. She stared at Luke's broad back. The explosion had damaged him. She could sense the broken pieces under his polished veneer. Putting all their baggage together would be insane, right?

"How about the kids?" Luke cracked eggs into the pan.

"We don't usually eat breakfast." Brooke had given up years ago. Haley was too crabby and Chris too sleepy in the morning to get any food into them.

While the pan sizzled, Luke grabbed the ice pack from the freezer and handed it to her. "How's the swelling?"

"Went down some overnight."

"If you stay off of it, it might be even better tomorrow." He gave her another one of those appraising looks.

More heat flushed across her skin. *Ugh.* "Look, I appreciate you coming over here at the crack of almost dawn, but we're fine. Really."

"I promised Wade." The jut of his jaw told her that was that. "He's worried about you."

"I'm worried about him too." A small piece of her heart sheared off the way a hunk of glacier slides into the sea. Her temper dropped off with it. Please, God, let nothing happen to her brother.

Luke slid a fried egg and a slice of toast onto a plate and set it in front of her. Brooke tested the egg. Perfect. She forked some on top of her toast and bit in. "This is good."

Luke rinsed his mug and stowed it in the dishwasher. "How are your parents?"

"When I talked to them last week, they were headed to Arizona for the winter."

"Too bad. No chance they'd come home for a visit?"

"My mother's emphysema is irritated by the damp and cold of winter. The last two years they've wintered in the Southwest. It's the healthiest she's been in a long time."

He tossed a hunk of toast to Sunshine. The dog missed the throw and snuffled along the tiles for the food. Brooke scratched the dog's back as she passed by. A pungent odor wafted across the kitchen.

"Sunshine, you smell awful." Still scratching, Brooke wrinkled her nose. "What did you roll in? As soon as my knee is better, a bath is going to the top of my to-do list."

Unconcerned, Sunshine turned so Brooke could reach her head.

Luke took his plate to the sink. "I'm more worried about her lack of watchdog skills. When I came in, she was sound asleep in the hall and didn't wake up until I tripped over her."

Sunshine's back paw twitched as Brooke's nails found an itchy spot beneath her ear. "Give her a break. She's eleven years old. Her hearing isn't what it used to be. Besides, she's the friendliest dog on the planet. When she was younger, she was more babysitter than watchdog."

With a final pat, Brooke turned her attention back to her breakfast. Appetite dulled, she offered a toast corner to the dog. "I wish they'd have caught him."

His expression went grim. "I'm in town for the next week—"

"It's all right, Luke. I appreciate your help, but ultimately I'm not your responsibility. I doubt we're in much danger. I don't know who he is. I can't identify him. He has no reason to bother us." But her statement rang empty. The media had her name.

Had they broadcast it yet? Regardless, it was only a matter of time until her involvement was public information. She didn't exactly keep a low profile. For the first time, she regretted her public devotion to her cause.

If this criminal found her, he found her children as well.

"I'd like to check your windows and doors while you're at school. Is that all right with you?"

Brooke shrugged. "Sure. Go ahead, but I check them regularly. The locks should all be in working order."

"Can't be too careful."

The kids pounded down the stairs. They stopped at the sight of Luke in the kitchen. He slid two plates of eggs and toast onto the table. With confused, half-asleep expressions, Haley and Chris sat. Luke poured orange juice.

Chris bumped Brooke's arm with an elbow. "What's he doing here?"

"Uncle Wade asked him to look out for us."

"Oh." Chris shrugged and started forking eggs into his mouth.

Haley frowned at her plate. She tasted an egg with the suspicion of the king's poison taster. Her brows lifted, she ate a few bites, and then moved on to the toast.

They never ate breakfast when Brooke prepared it for them. Were they being polite to Luke? Probably. Good kids.

Chris scraped his plate clean. "If we don't get moving, we're all going to be late."

After a quick scramble for briefcase, backpacks, and shoes, everyone followed Luke to the door.

"Uh-oh." Looking through the prism glass of the sidelight, Luke stopped them with an outstretched arm.

Brooke peered out. A news van was parked on the street. "I really wish I had an attached garage."

"Do you want to wait?" he asked.

Brooke reached past him and unlocked the door. "For what? I doubt they're going anywhere." She opened the door and pushed Haley and Chris behind her. Luke stepped in front of them all, shielding her and the kids as much as he could with his body.

The skinny blond newswoman jumped out of the van and sprinted on her toes across the frost-covered lawn. Juggling his equipment, a cameraman jogged in her wake. "Ms. Davenport!"

They scrambled into the car. Luke locked the doors and pulled away, leaving a frustrated reporter behind.

Would they follow her to work?

"Maybe I should just give them an interview." She lowered the window an inch. The scents of wood smoke and wet earth rushed in. She'd lived in this house, on this property, for most of her life. Even her parents had moved on, while she was mired in the past. But Karen's murder had left an indelible mark on Brooke's life, a permanent stamp she would never allow to fade.

Luke steered through a bend in the road. "This is not a good time for your face to be on TV."

Unfortunately, the cameraman would have to be the worst in the industry to have missed a shot of Brooke. She pressed a hand to her belly, where paranoia had disturbed her breakfast. She'd always felt safe in her hometown. Always. But last night's attack pointed out that evil was everywhere—even here.

---

Carrying her briefcase and lunch, Brooke limped through the door Chris held open. Inside, the high school was a chaotic moving mass of bodies. The metallic slam of lockers echoed in the cinder block and linoleum hallway. "We'll meet right here after school. Please wait inside."

"OK." Haley split off to the right, her bobbing ponytail disappearing as she was swallowed up by the throng.

Brooke ducked into the main office to pick up her mail. When she exited, Chris was waiting in the hall. A bright flash burst in Brooke's face. She held up a hand, colored dots swirling in her vision. Her briefcase fell off her shoulder and dropped to the ground. While Chris stooped to pick it up, Brooke blinked and focused on the man with the camera. He was average size, fortyish, with a head he shaved as a concession to a rapidly receding hairline. "Owen, what's the deal?"

"Sorry, you're big news today." Owen Zimmerman, local photographer, lifted an unconcerned hand. "The *Coopersfield Daily* wants your picture." In addition to shooting school portraits, Owen freelanced.

"What if I don't want them to have it?"

"The public has a right to know." Owen shrugged. "I'm not giving it back."

"I'll have your contract with the school cancelled," Brooke threatened. The school was in the middle of picture week. Guaranteed income every year.

He blanched. "You wouldn't."

"Oh, yes I would." Brooke used her school teacher voice.

Owen turned his camera around. The LCD screen showed Brooke's picture. It wasn't flattering, with her swollen lip, tired eyes, and surprised expression. She should have worn more makeup. Owen pushed the trash can button. "Happy?" But a nasty glint in his eyes said he wasn't.

Brooke stepped back. "Yes, thank you." Juggling her lunch and mail, she turned to take her briefcase from her son.

Chris held on to it. "I'll carry it to your classroom."

"You'll be late for class."

"So write me a pass." Her son shot Owen a squinty glare. Chris had noticed Owen's hostility and wasn't leaving her alone. Her son's protectiveness warmed Brooke's heart, but she wasn't ready to switch roles with him just yet.

Tony Grassi emerged from the office. "I can help your mom, Chris." Tall and thin, Tony's salt-and-pepper hair stood a head over the young crowd. Matching salt-and-pepper brows dipped into a concerned *V*. "I'm headed that way."

Tony looked precisely as a history teacher should in a tweed blazer over outdated trousers, an oxford shirt, and a dark red bow tie. His classroom wasn't anywhere near Brooke's, but she didn't point that out.

Chris gave her a questioning look. Brooke nodded. "Thanks, Chris. You go on."

"OK. See ya later." Chris handed Tony the briefcase and threaded his way through the crowd.

Tony moved slightly ahead of Brooke to clear the way. An endless surge of teens swept around them in the homeroom-bell rush. A fast-moving backpack jostled Brooke. Her balance didn't suffer, but Tony grabbed her arm anyway. Hmmm. His touch didn't make her skin heat the way Luke's had. In fact, she found Tony's grip irritating enough to twist her arm out of his grasp.

Her classroom was near the back of the school. A line of students had formed near the door. She put her key in the lock. "Sorry I'm late, everyone."

The kids filed in. Tony placed Brooke's briefcase on her desk. Behind wire-rimmed glasses, sincere gray eyes settled on her. "Are you truly all right?"

"I'm fine."

He glanced around. The kids were murmuring to each other, not paying them any attention. Tony lowered his voice. "I'm sorry I didn't call last night. I didn't hear about what happened until this morning. I was reading a new account of the Siege of Bastogne. I got caught up and missed the news."

"I said I'm fine, Tony." Brooke plastered a faux smile across her face. Her sore lip protested, but she ignored it.

"Let me bring you lunch. It'll save you the walk to the cafeteria."

"I already have my lunch, but thanks." Brooke held up the brown bag.

"We could still eat together." A hopeful lilt colored his voice.

Brooke searched her brain for an excuse. She couldn't handle an entire lunch hour discussing the key battles of World War II.

"We're still on for lunch, right?" Fellow math teacher Abby Foster poked her blond head though the door. Abby's classroom was across the hall. God bless best friends.

"Right." Brooke smiled at Tony again. "Sorry. I promised Abby."

"I'll put that in the fridge for you." Abby walked in and took Brooke's bag.

"Thanks," Brooke said.

Abby flashed a conspiratorial smile.

Tony sniffed and straightened his tie. "Well, call me if you need anything."

Brooke nodded sincerely. "Of course. Thank you."

But as he turned to leave, an angry scowl passed across his face. Brooke sank into her chair. Enough with the paranoia. Tony was harmless. He hadn't been at the school as long as

Brooke, but they'd worked together for several years. He wore a bow tie, for heaven's sake.

The homeroom bell peeled, and Tony withdrew. Brooke turned her attention to taking roll and reading the morning announcements. The morning passed quickly. At the beginning of sixth period, she limped to the end of the hall, where the math teachers shared a combination lounge and office. Supplies occupied the metal shelves lining one wall. Cabinets were topped with a coffee maker and a copy machine. Brooke slid into a chair at the tiny table in the middle of the cramped space. Abby zoomed in a minute later, her slim figure dwarfed by a loose-fitting sweater and shapeless slacks, her clothes too frumpy for a pretty, single thirty-year-old. She grabbed their lunches from the fridge and sat down.

Abby's brown eyes were doe-wide. "You're so brave. I wouldn't have been able to react."

"You should take one of my courses," Brooke suggested. "Last night's attack proves that there's no escaping violence against women, not even in the boonies."

The color in Abby's fair skin faded. "I know I should. I've been really busy."

Brooke lifted an eyebrow. Other than helping Brooke coach the track team, Abby didn't exactly have a thriving social life. Brooke touched her friend's arm.

"Honey, you've been saying that for two years," Brooke said gently.

Abby's gaze darted away like the prey animal she so often resembled.

Brooke packed up her frustration and emptied her bag. Her friend never talked about her past. With a smile, Brooke changed the topic. Someday Abby might be ready to talk to her, and Brooke would be there when her friend was ready. "Thanks for saving me this morning."

Composed again, Abby opened her lunch. "You're welcome. It's weird the way he fixates on someone. Margery Collins said it took her months to shake him off after they went for a cup of coffee. There wasn't even food involved."

Why *had* Brooke said yes to Tony's invitation to grab a sandwich after last month's PTA meeting, when all the other teachers had bolted for the nearest exit? The meal had been as stimulating as proctoring the SATs. She pictured his face as he left her classroom. "I always thought he was harmless and lonely. But I have to admit, his behavior does feel a little obsessive. But I might just be paranoid after last night."

"You can't be too careful." Abby examined her sandwich as though she'd never seen it before. Brooke knew why she was suspicious of everyone today, but what was Abby's reason? Oh, well. Brooke should understand more than anyone how hard it is to open up to other people. She'd never told anyone the whole story of Karen's murder.

"True." Brooke's leg throbbed from her ankle to her tailbone. She hoisted her foot up on the chair next to her. "Can you run track practice solo today?"

"Sure. You should go home and put that up."

"That's the plan." Brooke dug in her purse for ibuprofen and swallowed two tablets.

Fellow math teacher Greg Fines strode into the room. "Hey, Brooke. Abby." His gaze lingered on Abby a fraction of a second too long. She flushed. Attraction or discomfort? She leaned a few centimeters closer to Brooke. Anxiety, definitely.

Greg blinked back to Brooke. "Hey, I heard about last night. Are you OK?"

"Fine, thanks for asking." Brooke twisted the cap off of her water bottle and drank. She stopped swallowing at Greg's glare. Uh-oh. An avid environmentalist, Greg ran the Green Club and the school's annual Earth Day celebration.

"Bottled water is a drain on our environment," Greg lectured as he dumped his insulated lunch bag on the table and withdrew his stainless-steel water bottle. He set it on the laminate table with an angry *thunk*. "Transporting bottled water uses forty-seven million gallons of oil a year—"

"I know." Brooke cut him off before he really got rolling.

Greg sneered down at her paper bag.

Brooke played her pity card. "My brother packed my lunch last night while I was at the hospital. I guess he couldn't find my lunch bag. It won't happen again. He's been sent to Afghanistan."

"Oh." Greg smoothed out his expression. "You *are* usually good about keeping Green. I'm sorry I got excited."

"That's all right." Brooke smiled. "Your intentions are good."

Abby covered a short laugh with a cough.

Mollified, Greg dropped into a plastic chair. "So, Brooke. What the hell happened last night?"

Brooke didn't take his abruptness personally. That was just Greg. She shrugged off his less-than-tactful question. "Not much to tell that the media hasn't already covered."

Which was true. The attack had been a breaking news story all night long. So far, her name hadn't been put out there, but it was only a matter of time. They'd stated that she was teaching at the community center before the attack. Her identity was only a few mouse clicks away. Brooke didn't hide her background. For the first time in sixteen years, she wondered if she'd made a mistake keeping Karen's story alive. She could have used a story without a personal connection to illustrate her points, one that didn't chisel away at her heart every time she told it.

A story that wouldn't come back to haunt her.

# CHAPTER TEN

Luke carried the last bag of hats, coats, and gloves from his grandmother's trunk to an empty room in the Methodist church. "Here you go, Gran."

"Thank you, Lucas." Gran took the bag and dumped it on a long folding table. The three older women helping sort winter clothes smiled at him. Gran beamed in an I'm-proud-of-my-grandson way.

"Can I help with anything else?" he asked.

"No, you've been a huge help already," Gran said.

"OK, then. I'm headed back to fix your fence. I have to pick Brooke and her kids up at school later too." Luke kissed her on the cheek. "Do you have your cell?"

Gran pulled the smartphone he'd given her for Christmas last year out of her sweater pocket. "Of course. I'm going to take some pictures today for the church's Facebook page. See if we can drum up some more volunteers." She coughed into her sleeve.

"Call me if you need anything." Luke grinned. His gran wasn't the type to let technology skip ahead of her. "And don't tire yourself out."

"Bah. I'm fine."

He drove back to Gran's house and let himself in. In the detached garage, he grabbed an old wooden toolbox, and went back outside. He reattached a few sagging pickets and then moved around to the porch to fix the loose steps. Both the porch and the fence would need painting in the spring. Would Gran be able to manage that on her own? He pulled out his phone to set a reminder in his calendar app for April. He stopped. Should he need an electronic memo to take care of his grandmother?

No. From now on, he'd visit her every single time he was back in the States, and he'd call her every couple of days no matter where he was or what he was doing. It wasn't likely he'd be back for Thanksgiving, but Christmas was a possibility. What was he thinking? He should be here for Christmas with Gran no matter what.

He felt like his world was shifting. Everything that had been a priority three months ago now seemed trivial.

A glance at his phone display told him he had several hours until he needed to pick Brooke up from the school. He drove to her house and used his key to unlock her door. He stepped through the doorway. His foot caught, and he tripped.

The dog yelped. Luke caught his balance with a hand on the doorjamb. "Sorry." Sunshine got up and wagged her tail. He scratched her behind the ears. "I didn't hurt you, did I?"

She stretched and yawned.

"You look OK, but this isn't the best spot for a nap." The rank odor drifted up to his nose. He straightened. "You really do need a bath." Maybe he'd do it tomorrow. Brooke loved that dog. Wait. Was he thinking about bathing the dog to impress her? And what was with this sudden urge to do things for her? Whatever. He was overanalyzing, as usual. Sunshine was too heavy for Brooke to lift, even after her knee healed. How hard could it be to wash a dog?

He started checking the windows in the basement, one big open space with a cracked concrete floor. The washer and dryer were on the near wall. Boxes, some labeled, some not, lined metal shelves on the opposite side. The middle of the space was clear, and a large padded exercise mat occupied the center. Next to it, a heavy bag, the kind that professional fighters used, hung from the rafters. The skinny windows were locked.

The first floor was as secure as possible, considering the big expanses of windows. Luke went upstairs. The kids' bedroom windows were secure and anyone who broke in would likely break his neck tripping over mounds of dirty laundry. Luke paused at the doorway to the next room. Brooke wasn't much neater than her kids. The hamper overflowed. Books and papers cluttered her nightstand. A few pairs of shoes had been kicked into the corner. Luke lingered by the unmade bed, a sudden vision of Brooke rising sleepily from the twisted sheets, her hair tousled, eyes heavy with desire.

Whoa! Hold the phone.

Not cool. Not cool at all. Damn Wade for putting the idea of Luke and Brooke as a couple in his head. He got back to business. Opening the blinds, he checked the lock on the window. A movement outside caught his eye. A black pickup cruised past much too slowly to be normal traffic. The vehicle stopped next to the mailbox. The driver seemed to be leaning across the passenger seat. The afternoon sun glared off the windshield, and all Luke could see was a shadow. He needed a better angle to read the license plate. He went downstairs and tried the living room window. Damn, he still couldn't read it. The driver must have seen his movement. The truck roared down the street.

Luke rubbed the quivering hair on the back of his neck. Should he call the police? And tell them what? A black pickup truck, probably an American make, drove by Brooke's house too slowly? Right. Ridiculous.

He imagined Brooke in bed again, but this time the shadow of an intruder fell across her tousled head. She bolted to a sitting position and screamed. The scene shifted to Sherry bleeding out in front of him. He closed his eyes, willing it away. *Shit. Shit. Shit.* He needed to banish his flashbacks, not give them a life of their own.

Luke wasn't in Manila, and Brooke wasn't Sherry.

Tentatively, he looked back down at the floor. The image was gone. Brooke's hardwood needed a good cleaning, but no blood puddled on its planks.

Sweat broke out on Luke's forehead. He pulled at the neck of his T-shirt. It wasn't tight, but he was too aware of the fabric encircling the base of his neck. His pulse shifted up a gear. No. He couldn't be having a panic attack. He wasn't anywhere near a skyscraper. Was he getting worse? Had his mental health improvement not been a real recovery, but a remission? A cancer that could return at any future time. Obsessing about a future he couldn't control wasn't healthy. He'd paid a therapist a lot of money to hammer that into his brain.

Breathing through his nose, he rushed from the room. He shut the door behind him and leaned on it.

He shouldn't have promised Wade he'd watch over his sister. Obviously, three months wasn't enough time to truly put the trauma behind him. Not only was the weight of his new responsibility taking its toll, but how the hell was he going to protect Brooke if he freaked out at the thought of her in danger?

He knew only one thing for certain. He couldn't let his involvement with Brooke grow any deeper.

The final bell pealed through Brooke's classroom, eliciting groans from the six students who hadn't finished their tests. The rest of the kids were ready as runners at the starting block. Chairs scraped as they hustled for the door. The harried stragglers slapped their tests on the corner of her desk as they rushed for the exit. She shoved tests that needed grading into her briefcase, slung the strap over her shoulder, and limped toward the door. Now to make her escape before Tony could show up and offer his assistance.

"Brooke, let me carry that for you."

Shoot. Too late. He must have let his class go early to have gotten here so quickly. Not a good sign.

"Ah, thanks." Not.

He reached for the strap. His finger lingered on her shoulder. She rocked back to move out from under his touch. Impatience narrowed his eyes, but he smiled over it.

Brooke started for the door. The sooner she could get out of here the better.

Tony fell into step beside her. "I'm worried about you all alone in that big house."

"I don't live alone. I have two kids."

"But there's no man in the house."

"We're fine. Thanks for your concern."

"I'm serious, Brooke. Why don't I stay at your house for a few days? You could use someone to take care of you."

Yeah. That was not happening. Tony's industrial-strength Velcro attachment to her already gave her the willies. Yesterday, he'd been merely irritating. Last night's attack had intensified his behavior. Was he worried or just weird?

"That's very sweet of you, Tony. But I can take care of myself. I have sturdy locks, and remember, I teach girls to defend themselves all the time."

Tony gave her a doubtful glance. “You’re still a woman.”

“Well, I can’t dispute that.” Brooke paused at an intersection then threaded her way through the sea of moving bodies.

Another wave of irritation passed over his face. “I’m sorry. I didn’t mean that as a sexist statement, only that women are more vulnerable than men.”

A fact that was making her increasingly uncomfortable with Tony’s dogged pursuit. Brooke was probably being overly sensitive, but in case he was unstable, Brooke trod lightly. It did not seem wise to provoke a possible nut today. “You’re right, Tony. I’m sorry for snapping. My knee hurts, and I’m cranky.”

They passed the cafeteria and turned down the hall that led to the main office. The cinder block walls shifted from blue to yellow. Dozens of sneakers squeaked on the scuffed linoleum.

“Exactly why I should come home with you. I could take care of you.”

Beams of sun shone through the glass exit doors. Freedom! “Thanks for the offer, but I have to say no. It wouldn’t be professional. We’re colleagues. We wouldn’t want to damage our reputations.”

“You have a point. But I’d take that risk to protect you.”

*Sheesh.* She couldn’t win here. Thankfully, her son was waiting by the office.

“I’ll take that.” Chris relieved Tony of her briefcase.

No sign of her daughter. “Where’s Haley?”

Chris held the main door open. “Out in the car with Luke.”

Tony stiffened.

“Thanks for the help.” Brooke smiled at Tony, then turned and hobbled outside. *Please don’t follow.* Ack. He was right behind her. Lord, he was harder to get rid of than lice in a kindergarten class.

"You're welcome." Tony's voice sounded strained, as if he were forcing the words through his teeth.

Luke's silver sedan idled at the curb. He got out of the car and came around to open the passenger door. His scrutiny sliced through Tony's arrogance with the subtlety of an axe, and the possessiveness in his demeanor filled Brooke with guilty pleasure. What was wrong with her? She should not be enjoying any of this.

Luke held out a hand, but his green eyes flickered with irritation as they locked on Tony. "Luke Holloway."

"Tony Grassi. I teach history. How do you know Brooke?" Tony stared down his nose at Luke's hand, but he shook it. What, no knuckle-crushing contest? Not that it would be much of a contest. Luke's body was rock hard and just thinking about it made Brooke's hands itch to touch him, while Tony looked like he confined his heavy lifting to General MacArthur's autobiography. It'd be like watching a panther eat a house cat.

"I'm an old friend." Luke gave Brooke a heated glance, hot enough to disperse a delicious flush across her skin. "Let's get you home. You should get off that leg." He claimed her elbow with a firm grip. She eased onto the seat and swung her leg under the dash. Luke closed the car door.

As the car pulled away from the curb, Brooke looked out the window. Tony was standing in front of the office, his posture rigid. Was he angry or hurt? Probably both. Guilt and worry badgered Brooke. She tried to brush it away. She hadn't done anything to lead him on. If anything, she'd done everything to discourage him over the past couple of weeks. Why was he so hung up on her? Was Tony lonely or obsessive?

She turned forward as the car pulled out into the exit lane, but she still could feel Tony watching them. "Why did you do that?"

"Do what?" Luke asked with mock innocence.

"Act like we're involved."

"I have no idea what you mean." Luke's face split in a feral grin. The masculine glint in his eyes made Brooke's toes curl inside her practical pumps. What the hell was that all about? She squirmed.

Luke turned onto the main road. "Come on, your body language couldn't have been more obvious. If you could have run away from that guy, you would have."

"Tony's harmless." Probably. Brooke sank lower into the plush leather. Low-grade pressure built in her forehead. "He's just—"

"Jealous? Possessive?" Luke suggested.

*Ugh.* Brooke closed her eyes without responding.

"He's a creeper," Haley chimed in. "What were you thinking when you went out with him?"

"I did not go out with him!" Brooke massaged her temples. "We grabbed a bite after a PTA meeting. Once!"

Once was more than enough.

# CHAPTER ELEVEN

Luke gripped the wheel tighter. Brooke had dated that oddball? Luke had done business on four continents. He'd learned to read body language like written text. The history teacher had been jealous as hell.

What happened to Luke's determination to protect Brooke without any further involvement?

It's not like she was *his.*

Luke rubbed the center of his chest, where a completely irrational turmoil churned like a tropical depression forming in the Caribbean. Brooke set off more than his protective instincts. His desires went beyond keeping her safe. Seeing another man's interest in her hollowed him out just as seeing the evidence of her marriage to another man had all those years ago. He'd been blatantly rude to the history teacher, and worse, he didn't feel a single ounce of regret. Given the chance, he'd do it again.

*Get a grip.* In six days, he'd be back in New York. But what if she was still in danger? What then? He squashed the thought. There was no point worrying about something that was out of his control.

A few minutes later, Luke turned at Brooke's mailbox and parked in front of the house. Everyone piled out. The kids left the front door yawning. Sunshine trotted out to the car. Luke leaned down to scratch her head. The dog arched her back. Nails dug into the ground as she stretched, then she ambled out onto the front lawn to sniff the grass.

Luke turned to look for Brooke. She was limping down the driveway toward the mailbox. "I'll get the mail."

"I'm not helpless." She pulled it open and stumbled backward. One hand shot to cover her mouth, and the color bled from her fair skin.

Luke sprinted to her side and pushed her behind him. The rotten scent of decay floated toward him. Flies buzzed around the opening. Luke peered inside. A flat bloody mass of fur had been stuffed into the metal tube. Squirrel? "Looks like roadkill."

Brooke was leaning on her thighs. She kept her gaze firmly on the clover under her feet. "Lovely."

"I should have thought to check the mailbox." He explained about the truck he'd seen that afternoon. "Let's go inside. I'll call the police."

He took her elbow and steered her to the house. At the door, he whistled for the dog, and she followed them into the foyer. Music blared from upstairs.

Brooke beelined to the living room and dropped into her chair. Exhausted lines fanned her eyes and mouth. Luke angled the ottoman so she could put her leg up. While he was in the kitchen calling the cops, he grabbed an ice pack from the freezer.

"Thanks." Brooke clenched her shaking hands.

A deep-seated, primal urge roared inside Luke. He wanted to find the truck's owner and beat him to a pulp as bloody as the animal he'd stuffed into Brooke's mailbox. Then he'd hold Brooke until she stopped trembling.

"You haven't seen a pickup following you?" He paced the living room in front of her chair.

"I haven't gone anywhere without you since last night."

"Does anyone at school drive a black pickup?" Luke stopped. "What does that history teacher drive?"

"I don't know." Brooke leaned forward and rested her elbows on her knees. She dropped her forehead into her hands. "But Tony would have been at school all day."

"He gets a lunch break, doesn't he?"

"I suppose, but I can't see Tony shoveling a road-killed squirrel into my mailbox." Brooke straightened. Her brown eyes went wide. "Today he kept insisting he come and stay here to protect us."

"So maybe he thinks if he scares you enough, you'll let him."

Brooke leaned back in the chair and closed her eyes, as if the thought exhausted her.

The doorbell rang. Sunshine's head shot up. She let out a loud *woof* and trotted toward the front door.

"You're supposed to bark *before* they get to the door," Luke joked, following the dog. He checked the peephole. "It's the police."

Brooke sighed and hauled herself out of the chair.

A young, black-haired officer came to the door. "Hey, Brooke."

Brooke stepped out onto the porch. "Luke, this is Officer Ethan Hale. Ethan, Luke Holloway."

"Call me Ethan." The cop shook Luke's hand. They walked to the mailbox.

"That's nasty." Ethan grimaced. "I'll write up a report, but honestly, unless you know who did it, there isn't much we can do about a prank like this."

Luke told him about the black truck.

Ethan made a note. "Did you get the license plate number?"

"No." Luke clamped his teeth together until his jaw ached.

Ethan went to his vehicle for a camera. He snapped a picture and jotted down some information. "Call us right away if you see that truck again or if anything else unusual happens."

Brooke climbed the porch steps. A sedan pulled into Brooke's driveway, and the officer who'd interviewed Brooke in the ER the night before got out. The cops exchanged a quick greeting in the driveway.

The cop looked rough. Stubble and dark circles said he'd been up all night.

"Luke, this is Officer Kent." Brooke waved a hand between them. "Please, come inside. Is something wrong?"

"No, ma'am." Officer Kent followed them into the living room. "I live out here. I stopped by on my way home to give you an update."

"I appreciate that," Brooke said.

Luke told him about the roadkill and the truck.

"I don't like the sound of that." Kent grabbed a straight-back chair from the corner and set it next to Brooke's chair. He pulled out a small notebook and turned to Brooke. "First of all, let me say that we're grateful you stepped in last night and stopped a terrible crime. Most people don't want to get involved."

"Brooke isn't most people." Unexpected pride laced Luke's voice. Where the hell did that come from? He perched on the arm of the sofa.

"How is Maddie?" Brooke leaned forward. Her eyes misted.

"Good enough to give us a statement thanks to you," the cop said.

"Thank goodness." Brooke clasped her hands together in her lap. Had they stopped shaking? "I didn't see her last night. She was getting a CAT scan, but her parents were there. They told me she had a concussion from repeated blows to the head. I'm glad to hear she was coherent enough to talk to you."

"We haven't found her assailant yet." The cop rested his forearms on his thighs. "But the good news is that Maddie had some skin under her nails. We're going to run the DNA through CODIS. It'll take time, but if the same guy ever left DNA at another crime scene or if he's registered in the convicted offender database, we'll be able to match it."

"What's CODIS?" Luke asked.

"CODIS is the Combined DNA Index System. It cross-references the DNA of convicted criminals with DNA found at crime scenes," Kent explained. "We're also going through our lists of sexual offenders in the area. That might narrow it down. This guy didn't come out of the blue. Sexual crimes tend to be habitual. There's a good chance he's done something like this before. Maddie got lucky."

"She fought hard," Brooke said.

"She did." The cop sounded impressed. "Is there anything else you can tell me about last night?"

Brooke's eyes unfocused as she searched her memories. She blinked and shook her head. "No. If I remember anything, I'll call you."

"How much danger do you think Brooke is in?" Luke asked.

"Hard to say." The cop tucked his notebook back in his pocket. "She didn't see his face, so she isn't an eyewitness or anything like that. But you never know with these violent types."

"Chances are he knows Maddie from somewhere." Brooke tapped a forefinger on her lip.

"Maddie didn't recognize him." The cop yawned.

"He was wearing a mask. This doesn't seem like a random attack." Brooke leveled the cop with a hard stare. "I've lived in this area most of my life. Hardly anyone uses that trail. A rapist lying in wait for a hapless female jogger might have had to wait for days. It's much more likely he knew Maddie would be coming along."

"Maybe," Kent admitted. "We'll consider all the evidence and *then* come up with some theories. Don't worry. We'll be looking at every scenario."

But Brooke's eyes were plenty worried.

The cop handed Brooke a business card. "Call me if you think of anything else." Kent stood and stretched his back. "Maddie asked if you would visit her. She wants to thank you in person."

"I'll go over there today." Brooke struggled to her feet.

"Please, don't get up. I can see myself out."

"I don't want to get too comfortable if I have to go out again." She followed Luke and the cop to the foyer. Kent went out.

Luke hesitated at the open door. "I'll be outside for a few minutes."

"OK. If we're going to see Maddie tonight, I need coffee." She headed for the kitchen. "Do you want some?"

"Yes, please. I'll be right back." Luke went out front, cleaned out the mailbox, and buried the flat squirrel behind the garage before joining her in the kitchen. Brooke, already halfway through a mug of coffee, poured him a cup.

"Thank you." Relief softened her voice. "I don't think I could've handled that."

"You're welcome." Their fingers brushed as he took the cup from her hand. The slight contact made Luke want to perform more manly chores for her if it led to additional touching.

The doorbell rang again, and irritation buzzed through Luke as he went to answer it. The buzz went ballistic when he saw Tony the teacher on the porch, a bouquet of flowers in his hand. Instead of letting the teacher in, Luke went out onto the porch and barged into the guy's personal space. Wide-eyed, Tony backed up. He dropped the flowers. The glass vase hit the porch with a *thunk*. Water spilled out and spread across the boards.

Ignoring the mess, Luke pressed closer. "Did you pay Brooke a visit this afternoon?"

"N-no." Tony's butt hit the railing. His Adam's apple quivered.

Luke glanced at the driveway. Tony drove a navy-blue Volvo. Anger batted reason aside. Tony could've borrowed a truck. "Can you prove you didn't leave the school today?"

The front door opened. "What's going on?" Brooke limped out.

But Luke didn't move. Tony sidled out from behind him. He stooped, picked up the vase, and thrust it at Brooke. "These will need fresh water."

Brooke didn't accept the flowers. She hugged her arms in a defensive gesture that tempted Luke to pick Tony up by his scrawny, pompous neck and toss him onto the lawn.

"Why are you here?" Luke loomed. He had a few inches of height on the teacher.

"I just wanted to make sure you knew my offer was sincere." Tony jerked the flowers back to his body.

"I said no this afternoon, and I meant it. As you can see, I'm not alone." Brooke gestured to Luke, and her tone iced over. "Tony, we had dinner as friends and colleagues. There will never be anything more between us than that."

"Well then. I'm sorry to have bothered you." Tony's head bowed, but under his apologetic façade, Luke sensed the undercurrent of anger still ran strong. With a final glare at Luke, the teacher backed off the porch and walked back to his sedan.

Shivering, Brooke limped back into the house. Luke closed the door behind them. In the foyer, she spun to face him. The circles under her eyes deepened in the overhead light, highlighting her vulnerability and exhaustion. "You shouldn't have done that."

"Done what?" Luke shot back. "Let that creep know I won't stand for him stalking you?"

"You're leaving next week." Brooke pointed at his chest. "I need to handle men like Tony on my own. Besides, he's a coworker. I have to see him almost every day."

"I can't let anything happen to you."

Brooke softened. "I know you promised Wade to look out for me, but you can't just take over. After you go, I still have to live my life. Otherwise, once you're in another country, what's to stop Tony from harassing me again? Facts are facts. This time next week I will be on my own. It's far better if Tony respects *me* rather than *you*."

She was right, but facts had no effect on the storm brewing inside Luke.

"You don't understand." Luke paced the foyer, nerves seething from the mailbox find and the encounter with Tony. He hit the wall with both palms. Pausing for a deep breath, he pulled his shit together by sheer force of will. His promise to Wade was stretching his tenuous thread of recovery to the breaking point. Shame flooded him. Brooke was in danger because she'd risked her life to save another. Her courage humbled him. How could Luke resent his best friend's request to protect her? Oh, who was he kidding? Luke wasn't here because of Wade. He was here because of Brooke.

More worry spun in Luke's gut. Wade wouldn't be here tonight. Someone had played a nasty prank on Brooke today, she had a creepy coworker to worry about, and Maddie's assailant was still on the loose.

What had Brooke said to her brother the night before? Sexual predators reoffended. It was the way they were wired. So, whether the attacker went after Maddie or another woman, this guy wouldn't stop until someone made him.

He crossed the hardwood and crowded her against the closed door. Her brown eyes darkened. Surprise or desire? His body hardened as he hoped for the latter. He leaned close to her ear. Her hair smelled soft and fresh, like the meadow that fronted her house. "I *won't* let anything happen to you this week. You're just going to have to deal with it."

---

Brooke froze. Her nerves, already tested by the week's events, locked in indecision. Her brain was screaming that she wasn't a let-the-man-take-charge kind of girl, but her body was shamelessly reveling in the whole alpha-male display. Primed from confrontation, Luke's body was hard as stone and just inches away from hers. Tension radiated from his skin like an electrical field, and she wanted to absorb his energy.

Too cultured for jealousy or possessiveness, intellectual Ian wasn't prone to emotional outbursts. He hadn't even lost his cool when he'd left her.

She'd never had a man act this primitive and protective over her. My God, what would it be like to have Luke exercise that dominance over her naked body? A warm shiver slid through her belly. Cripes. Why the hell was she even thinking about sex?

Must be some physiological response to stress. Whatever the cause, it was powerful and primal, calling every female molecule in her body to sit up and take notice.

His gaze dropped to her mouth. Was he going to kiss her? Did she want him to? The scent of warm male and soap flooded her nose and drew her closer. Oh, yes. She did.

"Mom?" Haley called from upstairs.

Luke backed away, regret thinning his mouth.

"Yes?" Brooke answered, thankful for her daughter's interruption. Luke might fan her hormones into a frenzy, but her heart couldn't take being left behind one more time. Her ex-husband had left Westbury for the excitement of the city. She and the kids hadn't been enough for Ian. He'd had zero interest in soccer or Scouts or any of the small activities that were part of raising kids, a sad fact that left jagged holes in all of them.

Haley jogged down the stairs. Chris was right behind her. "We're hungry."

Thanks to the wonders of blaring pop music, the kids had missed all the drama.

"How about a snack?" Brooke walked into the kitchen, opened the pantry, and pulled out a bag of pretzels. The kids took it to the table, and the dog took up a hopeful position on the floor.

Seeking the strength to finish the day, Brooke gulped tepid coffee.

Haley's phone buzzed, and when she looked at it, her mouth curved into a small smile that suggested she was communicating with the new boy on her radar.

*Ugh.* At fifteen, Haley hadn't gone boy-crazy yet, but her sixteenth birthday was approaching fast, and her hyper-focus on this particular boy gave Brooke an instant headache. She was not ready for the older-boy-with-car situation.

She addressed the kids. "I need to go to the hospital and visit the woman from last night."

"OK," said Chris.

Engrossed with her messaging, Haley gave her an absent nod.

"I am not leaving you two here alone." The caffeine wasn't giving Brooke the boost she needed.

"You promised we'd work on my costume tonight for the Halloween dance this Friday." Haley bit into a pretzel. Crumbs dropped to her lap. "And I have tons of history homework."

"Pack your stuff up and do it in the hospital waiting room," Brooke said in her do-not-challenge-me voice. "We'll work on your costume when we get back."

Haley crinkled her nose. "Hospitals are gross."

Brooke didn't dispute the statement. "Do you have homework, Chris?"

"Done." He shoved a whole cookie into his mouth.

"Why don't we drop the kids with my grandmother?" Luke said. "She'd love the company."

Brooke turned to Haley. "Luke's grandmother is Mrs. Holloway."

"Mrs. Holloway?" Haley brightened. "She was one of my favorite teachers."

Brooke considered. "Are you sure she wouldn't mind?"

"Positive," Luke said. "But I'll call her and make sure if it makes you feel better."

One quick call and fifteen minutes later they were in Luke's car parked in front of a trim two-story. Luke's cell buzzed on the console. An incoming call notification popped onto the screen. He picked it up and looked at the screen. His mouth tightened. The phone vibrated again, but Luke just stared at it.

"Not going to get that?" she asked, leaning forward to peer at the display.

"No." He turned the phone off and reached for the door handle.

*Oookaaay.* Disappointment prodded her. But Luke had every right to keep a phone call private. As they got out, the front door opened. Mrs. Holloway stood at the threshold. The petite gray-haired woman wiped her hands on the front of her apron. "You're in luck. I just took a batch of cookies out of the oven. Go on back to the kitchen if you'd like some."

Chris led the charge. Haley trailed behind him.

"We won't be long." Brooke sniffed. The scent of melted chocolate lingered. Her stomach rumbled. "And thank you so much for the casserole. It'll be appreciated tonight."

"You're welcome. It was nothing." Mrs. Holloway waved her off with a blue-veined hand. "Take your time. The kids will be fine."

"I know, and thanks again." Satisfied the kids were safe, Brooke followed Luke outside. The sun was falling toward the treetops and taking its warmth with it. Chilled air rushed across Brooke's skin. She zipped her jacket to her chin.

Westbury Community Hospital sat on the outskirts of town. Fifteen minutes later, Luke dropped her off at the concrete apron in front and went to park the car. In the shade of the covered entrance, Brooke shivered. Discomfort crept along her nape, an instinctive tingle that signaled danger. A nurse pushed a wheelchair out of the revolving door and waited with her bundled patient. A large sedan pulled up to the curb in front of them.

Brooke pivoted and surveyed the parking lot, three-quarters full. A few people walked to and from their vehicles. Nothing seemed abnormal there either. She rubbed the back of her neck and went inside, very glad to see Luke parking in the fourth row. At the sight of him getting out of the car, a rush of security swept through her. She turned away from it and went into the hospital lobby. As much as she appreciated his presence this week, there was no point in getting attached. Luke wasn't sticking around. The needs he stirred up inside of her would have to go unmet. She couldn't deal with one more failure.

# CHAPTER TWELVE

The smart move would be to start his car, turn around, and drive home.

But he couldn't.

Maddie was inside, waiting. The need inside him was swirling, growing, strengthening like a tropical storm over warm ocean waters. If he didn't discharge the force constructively, it could overwhelm him. He'd learned that early in life. His darkest desires couldn't be stopped, but they could be channeled.

If he proceeded, he would need to use caution.

Leaning over, he opened the glove box. Keeping his head down and pretending to look for something, he peered over the dashboard and watched Brooke Davenport enter the hospital doors. A fresh burst of excitement rushed through his veins. What would she say to Maddie? Would they talk about him?

He should wait until Brooke left, but curiosity gnawed at his discipline. The need to see them together grew to a feverish intensity.

He recognized the risk, the departure from the rules and self-control that had kept him safe from discovery so far. But it didn't matter. Desire paced his bloodstream like a caged panther.

He stared at the brick façade of the hospital. They were inside. Together. And he had a present for Maddie.

What to do?

There was a time in his life when he'd had no control, when someone else had been in charge, when his smaller size had rendered him powerless.

*"Stop it!"*

*He looked up from his play. The hand caught him on the cheek, the sting resounding through his skull.*

*His older sister, Ellie, stooped down in front of him, her face contorted in fury. "What the hell is wrong with you?"*

*He put a hand to his face.*

*"I asked you a question." Ellie raised her hand. He tried to back away, but there wasn't much room for evasion in a trailer. He waited for the blow. Her fist clenched over his head for a long second. She dropped her hand and grabbed him by the back of the collar. "What am I going to do with you? Why can't you just behave?"*

*She opened the closet and shoved him inside. "Maybe a time-out will teach you a lesson."*

*In a single-wide trailer, the coat closet wasn't much wider than a skinny five-year-old. He barely fit. The door closed. He pushed a couple of pairs of shoes aside, squatted down, and huddled on the floor. The shoes smelled like sour feet. The hems of jackets brushed the top of his head. Might as well get as comfortable as possible. Who knew how long his "time-out" would be? It might be morning before she let him out.*

*Good thing he wasn't afraid of the dark. In fact, he liked it. Shadows were great places for a little boy to hide.*

*He closed his eyes and tried to picture the house he'd lived in until just a few months ago. He imagined the quiet creek that meandered through the patch of woods behind the tiny property. They hadn't been rich, but he'd had a lot more freedom there. With busy working parents, he'd been mostly left alone to roam in the hours between school and dinner. He'd gotten good at catching frogs. How long had it been since Mom and Dad had died and his sister had brought him here to live?*

*Probably longer than it seemed.*

*Someday, he'd be big. He would be the one in control. No one would tell him what he could and couldn't do. No one would hit him or lock him in closets either.*

*He hunkered down in the dark and waited.*

# CHAPTER THIRTEEN

Brooke went into the building and approached the front desk. The elderly guard on duty could've stunt-doubled for Don Knotts. Brooke gave him Maddie's name. He typed it into his keyboard, squinted at the monitor, and wrote out a guest pass for Brooke.

"I'll need two passes," Brooke said. Luke walked into the lobby and joined her.

The guard shook his head. "I'm sorry. Only three visitors per guest. There are already two out for that patient."

Luke shrugged. "I'll wait here."

Brooke headed for the elevator. Inside, she glanced at the handwritten number on the pass. Maddie was in room 310. Brooke pushed the number three on the panel. The elevator groaned its way up to the third floor. She followed the wall signs to the right hallway.

Brooke tapped on the doorframe. "Maddie?" she called in a soft voice in case the girl was sleeping. "It's Brooke."

"Come in." The voice was stronger than Brooke expected. Still, she braced herself for Maddie's appearance and strode into the room. In the bed closest to the door, Maddie reclined on two pillows, the white sheet folded neatly over a thermal blanket at her waist. The bed in front of the window was empty, the center curtain pulled open to expose the black glass. The lights were dimmed, but Brooke could see more than enough.

The battered right side of Maddie's face looked worse than the night before. The bruises had purpled, her eye was nearly swollen shut, and a row of tiny black stitches closed a cut on her cheekbone. A few more sutures closed the slices in her earlobes where her assailant had torn her earrings free. An obscene necklace of bruises circled her throat like fat black pearls. Though her body lay quiet, Maddie's hands fingered the edge of the sheet in an unconscious, repetitive motion.

In a vinyl recliner angled between the beds, Maddie's father sat with a folded newspaper on his lap. He stood and ran a hand through his thinning hair. Mr. Thorpe clearly hadn't slept since Brooke saw him in the ER the night before. His eyes were watery, his clothing rumpled. Could a man age overnight?

"Thanks for coming." His blue eyes misted over as he grasped Brooke's hand, holding on for several seconds. He glanced at his daughter, then back at Brooke. "I'll just go get a fresh cup of coffee. Are you going to be here for a few minutes?"

"I won't leave until you come back," Brooke promised. If it were her daughter in that bed, Brooke wouldn't leave her alone for a moment either. Nausea rose in her throat at the thought. She swallowed, grateful that Haley and Chris were stashed with Mrs. Holloway.

Mr. Thorpe blinked hard, took off his rimless glasses, and rubbed one eye with a knuckle. "I'll go catch up with my wife in the cafeteria. Thank you." He nodded and, with a tight glance backward, walked out the door.

Brooke went to the bedside. Maddie lifted a hand to grab Brooke's. The IV line got caught on the bedrail. Brooke untangled it and squeezed Maddie's palm.

"Thank you." A tear slipped down Maddie's unmarred cheek. "I thought I was going to die."

"I'm just glad I was there." Still holding Maddie's hand, Brooke eased into the chair Mr. Thorpe had vacated. "How do you feel?"

"My head hurts."

"I'll bet it does. You tell me if it hurts too much to talk, OK? I'll still stay here with you until your dad comes back."

"No. I want to talk to you." Maddie shuddered. "You were there. You're the only one who understands."

Brooke gave her a gentle, close-lipped smile. "Do you mind if I ask you a few questions?"

Maddie lifted her chin a millimeter, enough to exhibit the spunk that had likely saved her life. "You can ask me anything at all. They already sent a psychiatrist to see me. She said I should talk about it."

"How much of a description were you able to give the police?"

"Not much." Maddie's voice dropped to a whisper.

"Was there anything about him that seemed familiar?"

"No." Maddie reached for a cup of water on her wheeled tray and sipped through the straw. "Nothing at all."

Brooke switched tack. "Do you have a boyfriend?"

Maddie frowned and shook her head. She closed her eyes for a few seconds, as if the movement caused her pain. "We broke up."

"Was he upset about the breakup?"

"A little." Looking down, Maddie picked at the edge of the sheet, rolling it between her finger and thumb, over and over. "I met someone else I thought I liked. I didn't think it was right to keep him on a string."

"Could it have been him last night?"

"No way."

"How do you know?"

"Because my ex, Tyler, is Asian. This guy was not."

Brooke froze. "How could you tell?"

"I saw his skin!" Maddie brightened. "His sleeve was pushed up. Even though it was dark, I could see that his skin was very white. Also, Tyler is thin. The man was bulkier, older maybe?"

"Did you tell the police this?"

Excitement glittered in Maddie's good eye. "No. I just remembered it."

"Let's call them." Brooke pulled out the Coopersfield officer's card and dialed his number. The call went to voice mail, so she left a brief message.

Maddie looked pleased to have contributed some information. While they waited for the cop to call back, Brooke fished for more information. "Do you have any hobbies?"

"I like Zumba."

"That does look like fun."

"It is. The classes at Forever Fitness are great."

More meat market than fitness center, Forever Fitness was in a strip mall a few miles away. A greater percentage of floor space was devoted to the juice bar than the exercise equipment. Brooke had toured it when it first opened, but found she much preferred the heavy bag in her basement. Beating on her punching bag relieved stress the way no treadmill ever could.

"Head hurt?"

"A little."

"We don't have to talk." Brooke patted her forearm. "Why don't you close your eyes?"

"I don't want to." Maddie studied her fingers. The nails were ragged, torn below the quick. "Did you sleep last night?"

Brooke thought of her own restless slumber, full of wooden creaks and shifting shadows. "No."

"I know I'm safe here in the hospital, but every time I hear a noise, every time I close my eyes, he's there." Maddie's voice trembled. “He’s going to come after me. I know it. What if the police don’t find him? What will I do?”

Brooke wanted to make everything right, but she was powerless and almost as frightened as Maddie. “I don’t know.”

“Are you afraid he’ll come after you?”

Brooke was tempted to lie. She’d been denying her fears for a long time, but Maddie deserved better. She needed to know she wasn’t alone. Brooke looked her straight in the eye. “Yes, Maddie. I’m scared. I’m going to be extra careful, but I’m not going to feel safe again until this man is caught. Until then, all I can do is face one day at a time.”

Maddie sniffed. “The policeman said you teach self-defense classes. When I’m better, I’d like to take some.”

“That’s a great idea.”

Maddie crumpled the sheet in a tight fist. “He kept telling me to be quiet and stop fighting, but I couldn’t. It was like I didn’t have any control over that. The screaming, the struggling, I couldn’t stop.” She paused, sniffed, and braced herself. “Do you think he wouldn’t have hurt me as much if I’d been quiet, if I’d cooperated like he said?”

Good God. She thought she’d caused her own injuries.

Brooke held the girl’s hand in both of hers. “No, Maddie. You did exactly the right thing. If you hadn’t screamed, I wouldn’t have heard you. All that fighting bought you time. Time for me and the janitor to find you.”

A relieved Maddie dozed off a few minutes later. While she waited for Mr. Thorpe to return, Brooke slid down in the chair and rested her head. Her phone buzzed. Officer Kent’s number showed on the screen. She answered it with a whispered, “Hello,” fumbling with the button and hobbling to the doorway so she didn’t wake Maddie. She explained what Maddie had remembered to Kent, who promised to come to the hospital immediately. Brooke returned to the chair.

Ten minutes or so passed. Then rolling carts full of dinner trays clanked down the hall. A green uniformed woman brought Maddie's dinner and set it on the wheeled tray by her bed. Maddie stirred and opened her eyes.

"Your dinner's here."

Footsteps in the doorway caught Brooke's attention. Mr. and Mrs. Thorpe walked in.

"I'm going to leave." Brooke gave Maddie's hand a last squeeze. "When Officer Kent gets here, tell him exactly what you told me."

Mrs. Thorpe hugged Brooke hard. Moisture glistened in her eyes. "I can't thank you enough."

"I'm just glad I was there." With a last glance at the battered young woman, Brooke left the room. Brooke shuddered as she walked toward the elevator. Without that snafu in event scheduling, the class would have ended on time last night, and Maddie would be dead.

---

Maddie watched Brooke leave with a fleeting surge of panic. She sipped some water and swallowed the salty clog in her throat. Brooke could hardly stay with Maddie 24-7.

She closed her eyes and repeated her new mantra. *I am safe. I am safe. I am safe.*

How many times would she have to say it to feel secure?

When Brooke had been here, Maddie had stopped staring at the door, waiting for a dark shadow. Waiting for *him*. Brooke had saved her once. Maddie had no doubt she would do it again.

Would he really give up so easily?

Her dad eased back down into the chair next to the bed, while her mom fussed with the rolling tray, adjusting the height so she could push it across Maddie's lap. She wanted to tell her mom not to bother. The scents coming from the covered dishes weren't all that appetizing. But Mom needed to stay busy.

Her father hadn't left her bedside for more than five minutes since the attack. He would protect her with his life. But Maddie still didn't feel safe.

Brooke was smaller than Dad, but there was something in her eyes: ferocity.

Maddie eased forward and let her mom stack the bed pillows behind her. The back of her neck prickled, and she glanced at the doorway. Of course no one was there, but a quiver of panic slid through her. Gooseflesh rippled along the bare skin of her arms.

"Do you want another blanket?" Mom shook out the napkin and draped it across Maddie's lap.

"No. I'm OK." A blanket couldn't cure her paranoia, not as long as he was still out there.

Mom lifted the insulated cover from the dinner plate.

Maddie stared down at her mashed potatoes.

*No.*

It couldn't be. Not here.

A scream ripped through Maddie's swollen throat, along with the certainty that she would never be safe again.

---

A scream, high-pitched and frantic with terror, echoed in the hallway.

Brooke stuck a hand between the elevator doors. They

bounced back and separated. Ignoring her knee, she rushed back toward Maddie's hall. Medical personnel gathered outside the doorway. Through the open door, Mr. and Mrs. Thorpe clutched their daughter. A security guard talked on his radio just inside the door.

Maddie was sobbing, a hysterical hitch in her voice that cracked Brooke's heart.

Mr. Thorpe met Brooke's gaze. He kissed the top of Maddie's head and left her in her mother's arms. He pulled Brooke outside the hospital room.

He exhaled and pressed his lips together, as if composing himself enough to speak. "*He* was here."

Brooke tracked Mr. Thorpe's gaze to the dinner tray. The rolling cart had been pushed away from the bed. A lump of mashed potatoes sat on the plate. Standing in the well of gravy like a conquering flag was one of Maddie's missing earrings.

---

Luke tossed the newspaper back onto the chair next to him. He sat forward and rested his forearms on his thighs to take the pressure off his back. Leaning on it for too long irritated the sensitive scar tissue.

A security guard ran across the lobby. Agitated people were moving and making calls at the front desk. Alarm buzzed in Luke's gut. Something was up. He got up and strode across the lobby. He pushed the elevator call button. He fished his buzzing phone out of his pocket and opened a text from Brooke.

COME TO 3RD FLOOR.

He waited. One elevator was on three, the other on four.

Luke bolted into the stairwell. No one stopped him. He took the steps two at a time. On the third floor, he followed the sounds of commotion. Two security guards talked into radios. Nurses and other staff milled in the hall.

Someone was crying softly.

He spotted Brooke in a doorway. She saw him and hobbled over. Her face was pale as skim milk, her eyes a composite of fear and fury.

"What happened?"

"*He* was here."

"You don't mean . . . ?"

"Yes. Last night, he ripped her earrings off and took them. Maddie said they got in his way as he was choking her." Brooke glanced over her shoulder at Maddie. "One of them was on her dinner tray."

"Jesus." Luke's exclamation took the air from his lungs. He followed her gaze to the room's occupants. A parent sat on each side of the hospital bed. A young woman was sandwiched between them, the left side of her face battered, bruised, and bloody. Her quiet sobs were wretched and beyond distraught. They were the sounds of a soul breaking, of someone suffering beyond comprehension.

Her despair radiated to Luke, like a palpable current in the air. Pity and anger welled up in his throat.

Luke turned back to Brooke. She was watching Maddie break down.

Brooke's chin lifted and her jaw tightened as fury beat back fear with a stick.

Luke whipped out his phone. "I'll call my grandmother and make sure everything is all right there."

"I already checked with the kids. They're fine."

"Did you tell them what happened?"

Brooke shook her head. "Not over the phone. It might upset them too much."

Footsteps clomped in the hall. Two uniformed police officers conferred with the security guards. Luke recognized Ethan, the young black-haired cop who'd responded to the vandalism call that afternoon. The middle-aged cop with him was clearly senior. "I'm Lieutenant Winters. I'd like everyone except Mr. and Mrs. Thorpe to clear out of the room, but please don't leave. Officer Hale will be taking a statement from each and every one of you."

Twenty minutes later, Brooke was ushered into a small waiting area at the end of the hall. "Hi, Ethan." Grimacing, she lowered herself into a chair.

"What can you tell me, Brooke?" Ethan's pen hovered over a notebook.

"I didn't see anything." Brooke summed up her visit with Maddie.

The cop took notes. "We have your personal information. Give us a call if you think of anything else."

"I will." Brooke pushed to her feet. Pain lined the corners of her eyes and mouth. "In the meantime, are you going to make sure Maddie is protected? He's obviously fixated on her."

"That'll be the chief's decision, but you know how he is. He'll look after her." The cop's assurance seemed to satisfy Brooke, but all Luke could think was, what about Brooke?

Luke escorted her to the elevator. The doors slid open and Officer Kent from Coopersfield walked off. Brooke filled him in.

The cop swept a frustrated hand across his short blond hair. "There was a girl raped three weeks ago in Hillside. She was also attacked while jogging. DNA was collected in that case, so we're hoping for a match. The victim survived and got a good look at her attacker. The Hillside PD has some leads on the composite sketch." Kent took a step toward Maddie's hall. "I'll let you know when I have more news."

Luke and Brooke rode the elevator down in silence. Brooke's jaw was shifting back and forth. He watched her sift through the information the cop had given them.

Outside, dark had fallen. The parking lot was well-lit, but rows of cars provided too many places to hide.

Luke debated getting the car so Brooke wouldn't have to walk through the parking lot, but he didn't want to leave her alone. Not for a second. The hospital had already proved to be a vulnerable location.

"You OK with walking to the car?"

"Yes." She answered quickly, stepping off the cement curb and onto the asphalt.

He kept her close, scanning the lot for any sign of movement or shadows that didn't belong. As they approached each row of cars, Luke bent over and glanced under the vehicles. A car drove up the row, slowed, and pulled into an empty spot. Luke circled Brooke so he was between her and the man climbing out of the sedan. He kept one eye on the guy's progress through the lot and into the entrance of the hospital.

In the fourth row, he let out a tight breath as he helped Brooke into the car. He slid into the driver's seat. But he didn't breath easily until the car was locked, the engine started, and they were pulling out of the lot onto the rural highway. He drove toward his grandmother's house.

"Do you know all the local cops?"

"Just the Westbury Police Department. They help me with my self-defense classes. In the last class of each unit, I bring in a padded attacker and let the girls practice the techniques they've learned. The Westbury cops take turns. Ethan's helped out quite a few times."

Brooke leaned her head on the passenger window. "He still wants her." The statement was issued without emotion, as if she were rambling off a fact sheet. "He won't stop. And if he's willing to take the kind of risk he took tonight just to see her, to give her that message . . ." A shudder rolled through her.

Luke turned up the heat.

The desperate edge in her voice worried him.

"The police officer said Maddie would have a guard all night."

"Sure, tonight, and maybe for a couple of days. But what about after that? What's she going to do in two weeks if the police haven't caught this bastard? They're not going to give her a permanent police escort."

"There are security cameras all over the hospital. One of them had to have gotten this guy's picture." Luke stopped at a traffic light. "It sounded like the Hillside cops were close to making an arrest."

"Let's hope." But her tone implied she wasn't counting on it.

Brooke was right. Maddie's assailant had waltzed right into a crowded hospital to leave her his message, a move too bold for Luke's comfort. This guy was either crazy or confident. Both of those options gave Luke a huge dose of paranoia.

# CHAPTER FOURTEEN

Physical exhaustion oozed over Brooke, saturating her muscles. Limping up her porch steps depleted her last ounce of *oomph*. The wind kicked up. A sudden gust streaked across the yard, chasing dead leaves on the lawn into swirling piles. Cold air slipped into the neck of her jacked, and she hunched her shoulders against the chill. All she wanted to do was flop into bed and pull the covers over her head. Unfortunately, her nerves were still humming like transformers.

The kids were already at the door. Haley slung her heavy backpack over one shoulder. Chris held a container of chocolate chip cookies. Luke stepped in front of them. He unlocked the door and crossed over the threshold.

Brooke remembered the dog. "Watch—"

"Ah." He stumbled, throwing a hand out to steady himself against the wall.

"Out," Brooke finished.

Under his feet, Sunshine scrambled upright, tail wagging. Luke reached down to scratch her head. "Sorry, girl."

Flipping light switches as he passed them, Luke walked through the living room and dining room on either side of the main hall. He went into the kitchen, opened the pantry, and looked inside.

"Wait here." He grabbed a flashlight from a wall peg and disappeared into the basement.

Brooke sank into a chair.

"I'll take care of Sunshine." Chris tossed Brooke an ice pack and scooped kibble into the dog's bowl. Sunshine crushed through her dinner and *woofed* at the back door. Chris let her out.

Brooke settled the ice on the only part of her body that wasn't freezing, her flaming knee. The cold sent a shiver rattling through her skeleton.

Haley dropped her backpack on the floor. "I'll pack lunches."

"Thanks." Her kids' unsolicited help warmed Brooke's cold bones. Haley tossed yogurt and fruit into two insulated pouches. Chris preferred cafeteria food.

Haley stashed the lunch bags in the fridge and sat down next to Brooke. "Is Maddie going to be OK?"

Brooke wrapped an arm around her daughter's shoulders. The kids were still processing the news. Heck, *Brooke* was still processing what happened at the hospital. The attacker had waltzed into a busy hospital, and no one had noticed. It seemed unreal. Impossible. "The police are going to watch her 24-7. They won't let anything happen to her."

Haley twisted a lock of hair. "She must be scared."

"I'm sure she is."

Chris was filling a glass with water, but his head was tilted as if he was listening.

"Are you scared?" Brooke asked.

Haley looked away. She shrugged.

Brooke's chest ached. She wanted to tell them there was no danger, that they were completely safe, but they weren't babies anymore. A stuffed bear standing guard at the foot of the bed wasn't enough. They deserved the truth. "We're going to lock the house up tight, and we're not going anywhere alone until this man is caught. OK?"

"OK." Haley nodded. "I'm going to bed."

"Wake me if you can't sleep." Brooke hugged her. "That goes for you too, Chris."

"I'll be fine." He set the empty glass in the sink.

Luke clumped up the wooden basement steps, passed through the kitchen, and headed upstairs. Five minutes later, he reappeared. "Coast is clear."

Exhausted, the kids went upstairs.

"Can I make you something to eat? Casserole?" Luke asked.

"I'm not hungry. Maybe some tea."

"Tired?" He filled the kettle and lit the burner under it. Branches scraped the kitchen window as wind rattled the oak out back. At the dog's bark, Luke let her in. Sunshine ambled to Brooke for a head scratch, then stretched out on the floor next to her chair.

"Yes, but I'm in no rush to close my eyes." She was going to relive Maddie's despair all night. The frantic hopelessness in her voice and the raw terror in her eyes would haunt Brooke for a long time.

"Maybe the cops will catch this guy fast. It sounded like the Hillside PD is making progress and that the towns are coordinating their efforts in the investigation."

"Even if they catch a rapist, the DNA tests will take weeks, at best." Fresh horror swept through her. "What if the Hillside police make an arrest and feel strongly that it's the same man? They'll likely pull Maddie's guard. And it'll still be possible that they have the wrong man. She'll be terrified and vulnerable."

As would Brooke and her kids.

"How are the kids coping?" Luke asked.

Brooke adjusted her ice pack. "I'm sure they're more frightened than they'll admit. Since the divorce, they both seem to think they have to act like adults."

"Was the split hard on them?"

"Ian traveled a lot. They were already used to him not being here. He liked the idea of having a wife and kids more than the reality." Sadness filled her throat. Her kids were too old to be shielded from the truth. "I can tell them the divorce was a mutual decision until I'm blue, but Ian moved two hours away. He only sees them twice a month. They're smart kids. Their father chose his lifestyle over them. They know it."

"It must be hard not to be able to shield them."

Fear welled fresh in Brooke's chest. "God, Luke. What am I going to do if they don't catch this guy?"

The tea kettle hissed. Luke froze for a few seconds. Then, with a harsh breath, he poured steaming water over tea bags in two mugs. "Maybe it's too early to think of the worst-case scenario."

Where else would she start? One thing was certain. She couldn't just sit around and hope the police solved the case. "I'd like to check my notes on this other rape case. Let's go into my office."

Luke, carrying the mugs of tea, followed her to her office down the hall. Brooke cringed. There were piles of books and folders and papers on every available surface. She shifted some piles from the desk to the floor. Luke set the mugs down and cleared a chair while Brooke booted up her laptop. She sipped tea while the machine chugged to life. The hot liquid did little to dispel her chill.

The home screen appeared. Brooke typed HILLSIDE JOGGER RAPE into the search engine. While the computer chugged away, she pulled a file out of her desk and removed a local newspaper article. She skimmed the details.

Luke pulled out a chair and dropped into it. “You knew about the Hillside case?”

“I keep up with sexual assaults and homicides in the surrounding area. The Hillside victim was grabbed while jogging at twilight. The guy dragged her off the main path, hit her a couple of times, and raped her. The attack was interrupted by a couple of mountain bikers.” Brooke scrolled down the page. “But he didn’t wear a mask, just a hood and a bandana over his nose and mouth.”

Luke pointed to her laptop. “Your search is up.”

She went back to the computer, selected a link, and clicked. “The bandana fell down during the struggle, giving the victim and witnesses a look at his face. The police put up a composite sketch.”

She turned the computer to give Luke a better view.

“With the facial hair and hoodie, he looks like the Unabomber.”

Brooke studied the drawing. “Maddie’s assailant wore a ski mask.”

“Maybe be learned his lesson.”

“Maybe.” Brooke pulled up a second article. “But this guy didn’t wear gloves either. Or a condom. He left DNA behind.”

“Except for the gloves and mask, it sounds a lot like Maddie’s attacker,” Luke pointed out. “You don’t know if he was going to use a condom or not. Thanks to you, he didn’t get that far.”

But something about the idea wasn’t right. “It wasn’t cold enough for gloves last night. He wore them because he didn’t want to leave fingerprints. I doubt very much that Maddie's attacker wouldn't have used a condom."

Luke considered her argument. "Yeah, that doesn't make any sense."

"The Hillside attacker was careless. That attack doesn't have the same planned feel as Maddie's. Also, the Hillside rapist didn't choke his victim."

"So?"

"So, Maddie's assailant wanted to kill her." Brooke tapped her fingers on the table. "No, I don't have any proof of this, just the way he was choking her . . ." The sheer level of violence sent a fresh chill sliding through Brooke's belly. She sipped more tea. "At the time, I had no doubt killing her was his ultimate intention."

Luke didn't respond.

"Statistically most women are attacked by men they know, though not necessarily know well. She might not have noticed him, but she caught his interest somewhere. School. Work. Maybe he sees her in a coffee shop every morning or goes to her gym. He could have done work on her parents' house or fixed her car, but there's usually some connection."

Luke tested the tea, then set it down and pushed it aside.

He reached across the table and squeezed her hand. Heat seeped from his skin to hers. Much better than the tea. "The police will figure all that out. They have DNA to compare. No guessing there. It's frustrating the results take so long, but when they're in, everyone will be sure, one way or the other."

But for now, a violent man was free. No one was safe—not Maddie or Brooke or her kids.

"They'll do everything they can." She grabbed a small tablet and flipped to a fresh page. She wrote down the name of Maddie's ex and the boy she liked. Next she listed all the places Maddie had mentioned: Forever Fitness, Lark County Community College, her place of employment.

Luke cocked his head to read. "What are you doing?"

"Just making a list of the places Maddie goes regularly. Her attacker knows her from somewhere. He picked her. He stalked her. He fixated on her."

Brooke would bet on it. Real predators didn't wait for a victim to wander into striking distance. They hunted.

She listed the similarities and differences in the two cases. With her thoughts jotted down, she felt more settled. Weariness sagged over her. She started a file for Maddie and put her notes inside it.

Luke glanced around her office. "Why didn't you chuck teaching and become a cop?"

"After Karen died, I moved back home. Ian and I got married right away and the kids came along pretty fast. I wanted *normal* so badly, I did everything I could to get it." Brooke paused, the memory raw as a wound. "Anyway, doing what I do," she swept a hand in the air over her files, "lets me help hundreds of young women. I can give them an edge Karen and I didn't have when we went out into the world. We were so naïve." She swallowed her bitterness.

Luke moved his hand as if he was going to touch hers, but he pulled away before making contact. Disappointment added to Brooke's exhaustion. What did she expect? That he was going to swoop in and carry her off on a white horse? Even fairy tales were usually pretty grim.

"I need to go to bed." She powered down her computer.

Luke got up. He took both mugs to the sink, rinsed them, and put them in the dishwasher. Brooke placed her palms on the table and pushed to her feet.

"You don't have to get up," Luke said. "I can let myself out and lock up. Unless you want your key back?"

"No. You hold on to it." She wasn't sure why this gave her some comfort, but it did.

Brooke followed Luke to the front door. One glance at the painted white steel door brought the memory of their almost-kiss flooding back. Her exhausted muscles loosened. If her kids weren't there, and if he weren't so obviously trying to keep his distance, she'd have taken him by the hand and led him to her bedroom.

But that wasn't going to happen.

God, she was tired of maintaining control.

"Thank you for everything today. I don't know what I would've done—"

"Sh." He pressed a finger to her lips. The green of his eyes darkened to emerald. Was he thinking about their earlier moment? "I'll be back early. Call my cell if you need me. I'm only a few minutes away."

He stepped back and stared up the stairs, tight-lipped, for a few seconds. Then, as if he'd made a decision, he jerked open the door. Cold air blasted into the foyer.

"Goodnight, Brooke," he said without looking back at her.

She watched his sedan back out of the driveway. Red tail-lights faded into the night. She closed the door and secured the deadbolt. She limped upstairs to her room. Tossing her clothes on top of her overflowing hamper, she tugged on loose pajamas. Face washed and teeth brushed, she slipped between the sheets and stared at the ceiling. After spending an entire day in Luke's company, his absence was glaring. She swept a hand over the empty bed next to her. Tugging the extra pillow closer, she hugged it against her body, but a pillow was no replacement for a warm body. Her mind refused to shut off. She lay still, concentrating on every noise and categorizing its probable source.

She got out of bed and went to her closet. In the back was the gun safe her father had installed when Haley was born. She entered the combination and opened the heavy door. Inside, one lone weapon, her dad's old shotgun, leaned in the corner. She slid the gun under her bed and tucked a few shells into her pocket, but she didn't feel any safer.

If someone broke into the house, would she hear? Would she wake in time to use the gun? She lay still, listening to the trees move outside her window. The house settled with a low groan. Brooke burrowed under her comforter, but the fear lodged in her bones chilled her from the inside out. A gust of wind pushed against the glass, seeking weakness, looking for a way in.

---

Luke zipped his jacket against a current of air that slid into his collar and encircled his neck. He walked to his car and stood beside it. Behind him, the glare of Brooke's porch light and lamppost were the only visible sources of light. No streetlights out here. None of the neon signs or headlights of New York City.

His eyes adjusted to the dark, and he scanned the fallow fields that surrounded Brooke's house. Across the road, the slope climbed to a distant stand of trees, black and shapeless in the dark. Behind the house, grass rolled down into the shadowed foothills.

He looked at the old house, standing alone on the hillside. The front of the house was dark, but Brooke's bedroom was around back. Was she getting ready for bed? How soundly did she sleep? Would she wake up if someone broke in? And what would she do if she encountered an intruder?

*Blood spreading toward him. Sherry's glassy stare.*

Sweat dripped down Luke's back.

He stomped to his car, yanked the door open, and climbed behind the wheel. Shifting into reverse, he gave the car more gas than he'd intended. His tires spit gravel. He eased off the pedal and backed out of the driveway.

The drive to his grandmother's house took less than ten minutes. The house still smelled of cookies. Luke walked back to the kitchen. Gran sat at the table, a mug of tea at her elbow, a crossword in front of her. A dark blue robe covered flannel pajamas. She always seemed to be cold lately. She looked at him over the top of her reading glasses. "Is everything all right with Brooke and the children?"

"Yes, ma'am." Luke dropped into a chair. He turned her puzzle toward him and read one of the clues. ORANGE _____ TEA.

Gran watched him. "What's wrong, Lucas?" When Luke was young, he could hide things from his busy parents, but he'd never been able to pull anything over on Gran. He might not have told her about Sherry, but she knew something was up.

"I don't like leaving them alone." Luke picked up her pencil and filled in nine across, PEKOE.

Gran sipped her tea.

Luke dropped the pencil. "I'm going back over there. I'm sorry, Gran." Luke stood and bent down to kiss his grandmother's cheek. "I'm not comfortable leaving them alone all night."

"I would hope not." His grandmother clutched the lapels of her robe at the base of her throat. "Why would you be sorry about that?"

"I came here to spend some time with you."

Gran squeezed his hand, her seemingly frail fingers surprisingly strong. "I love that you've come to visit me, but what's important right now is protecting Brooke and her children."

It was bad enough he'd failed Sherry. Luke couldn't let anything happen to Brooke or her kids. "Thanks for understanding."

She released his hand. "Go on. Get out of here."

Luke ran up to his room. He yanked his overnight bag from the closet. A change of clothes and his shaving kit went inside. He jogged back down the stairs. His grandmother was in the hall.

"Lock the door behind me."

Gran touched his forearm. "Be careful, Lucas. I love you."

"Me too." Luke drove back to Brooke's house. In the driveway, he paused. He didn't want to scare her by just walking in. He could knock. No, waking the kids wasn't necessary. He sent her a text.

OUTSIDE. COMING IN.

Hoping she would agree to let him stay, he waited a couple of minutes. Then he unlocked the door and went inside, careful to step over the sleeping dog. He heard the slap of her tail on the hardwood. Sunshine scrambled to her feet as Luke secured the deadbolt.

"Brooke?" Scratching the dog behind her ears, he called softly up the stairs.

Floorboards squeaked at the back of the house. The hall light snapped on. Luke blinked.

"Luke?" Brooke stepped into view. "What are you doing here? Did you forget something?"

"No. After what happened with Maddie today, um . . ." Warmth flooded the back of Luke's neck. What was that behind her? "I thought I'd crash on your couch. Is that a gun?"

"Yes." She hefted it higher. "I hate that I got it out."

"Not me. I'm damned glad to see it." Luke walked down the hall toward her. The overhead light glared down on her face. Exhaustion bruised the thin skin under her eyes. He wasn't much of a hero, but she didn't know that. With no warning, there hadn't been anything he could do for Sherry. But he knew about the danger to Brooke, and he had to do everything in his power to protect her.

"Thank you." Brooke's voice was weary. "I'd say it wasn't necessary, but I feel better now that you're here."

Her affirmation unleashed a few gallons of testosterone. The heat from his neck flushed right through his face, then lower. "I thought you went to bed?"

"I couldn't sleep. I went down to my office to grade some tests." She ducked into her office and turned off the light. "You don't have to sleep on the couch. You can have Wade's room upstairs. He's not using it."

And be that close to her all night? Probably not a good idea. Not only would he lie awake thinking about her, sleeping in the next room, but what if his nighttime horror flick decided to run a midnight showing? There was no way he could handle anyone seeing him thrash around on the floor like he'd been Tased. "I'd rather be down here where I can hear someone outside."

"All right. You can sleep in the den. The sofa is longer, and you'll have more privacy than in the living room."

Luke followed her through the kitchen, past her office, and into a comfortable room with a medium-size flat screen.

Under the TV was the requisite plethora of teenage-boy electronic toys.

Brooke leaned the gun in the corner and opened a closet. She pulled out a pillow and sheets. "There's a blanket on the back of the couch. The sofa opens into a bed, but honestly, it's more comfortable as it is." As usual, she put everyone else's well-being before her own needs. Like now, when he should be waiting on her.

Luke dropped his overnight bag on the floor and walked over to take the linens. "I can get everything. You should get off that leg."

"Thank you for doing this." She looked up into his eyes. The rich brown was brimming with an emotion he couldn't quite identify. Gratitude? He leaned closer. His gaze dropped to her mouth. For the second time, the desire to press his lips to her injured lip shocked him. And the scrape on her chin? He wanted to kiss that too, then maybe work his way down the delicate column of her throat, where her pulse throbbed.

He jerked his gaze back to her eyes. They widened as gratitude shifted to surprise, then darkened with the first stirrings of desire.

He'd always thought Brooke was beautiful, but had he ever looked closer, to see the complexity of the woman beneath her exterior? She was a cocktail of strength and vulnerability, intelligence and beauty, compassion and resolve.

Teenage crush aside, her sensuality was something he'd never truly appreciated.

Luke lifted the sheets and pillow from her arms. He backed away before he was tempted to ease her down on the sofa and explore every inch of her courage. "Thanks."

He couldn't get any closer to Brooke. Sherry had been his assistant. There hadn't been any relationship between them beyond a little harmless flirting. But her death had left him devastated. If he fell for Brooke and couldn't protect her, he'd never recover.

She blinked, breaking the connection. "Thank you."

He cleared his throat. "Can I use your computer?"

"Help yourself." She gave her head a slight shake and moved toward the doorway. "It's in my office. Do you want this?" She raised the shotgun.

"No. I'd feel better if you keep that with you. Goodnight, Brooke."

She fled as fast as the bad knee would allow. Sunshine followed her, nails tapping on the floor as the dog went back to her spot by the front door.

Luke should have asked if he could take a cold shower, but he hadn't anticipated what had just passed between them. Still keyed up, he went into Brooke's office and booted up the computer. Her machine could use a tune-up.

While he waited, he opened the file drawer. Folders were labeled with names and dates. Luke slid one out. He opened it. Inside were printouts of Internet articles. PHILADELPHIA WOMAN MURDERED IN FAIRMONT PARK. Luke returned the file and selected another. YOUNG PITTSBURGH MOTHER RAPED AND STRANGLED. He flipped through the pages. A few more articles. Some notes made by Brooke on key facts of the case. He returned the file and thumbed through the rest. Dozens of files detailing the stories of women murdered in Pennsylvania. In the very front of the drawer was a fat folder full of statistics and reports from the Bureau of Justice. The files she'd started on Maddie and the woman raped in Hillside were right behind the stats file.

No wonder Brooke knew so much about rapists and killers. She was doing more than teaching self-defense. There was an undercurrent of obsession in Brooke's preoccupation with violence.

He turned back to the computer, accessed the system files, and started cleaning up the hard drive. The laptop chugged. With all the extraneous files on Brooke's computer, his task was going to take a while. But he wasn't ready for sleep anyway.

Luke thought back to Brooke's friend's death. He vaguely remembered Brooke moving back home afterward and getting married, but he'd been in college and hadn't been around much. Clearly, that violent act had reshaped her world and changed her.

Would Sherry's death haunt him forever?

# CHAPTER FIFTEEN

The alarm blared. With part of her brain locked in the dark recesses of sleep, she slapped the OFF button. Her eyes snapped open, the erotic images of her dream imprinted in her mind.

Luke. Her. Naked. Doing sweaty things she hadn't even thought about in years.

She rolled onto her back. A twinge shot through her knee. The pain helped suppress her reawakened libido like shock therapy. Part of her was glad; the other part wanted those visions back.

They were pretty hot.

She moved her leg experimentally on the bed. Still stiff and painful, but she could bend and straighten it a few inches, a definite improvement in range of motion from yesterday.

Her grogginess persisted as she pushed back the covers, almost embarrassed at how well she'd slept with Luke downstairs. She barely remembered climbing into bed.

*Do not get used to having him here.*

Swinging her legs over the side, she tested a bit more weight on her leg. Better. She locked up her shotgun, then went into the bathroom, showered, and dressed in another pair of loose slacks and a light sweater.

"Time to get up." She rapped on the kids' doors on her way down the hall.

The kitchen was empty but smelled of coffee. Brooke poured a cup, downing half while standing over the sink in an effort to clear her head of the fuzziness left by hard sleep. She left her mug on the counter and moved stiffly toward the den.

Where was Luke? A small flurry of nerves swirled in her belly. Had she imagined the moment between them last night?

"Luke?" Conscious of his privacy, she knocked on the doorjamb.

"In here." His voice came from the direction of her office.

"Morning." She poked her head inside. Luke sat at her desk. Her laptop chugged in front of him.

He shifted his attention from the computer to her. "Good morning."

Something warmed in his eyes, just for a second before he cooled it off, but it had been there. Desire. For her.

Oh. Her face heated. She hadn't imagined it. How did she feel about that?

Confused, she decided, and pushed it away. The whole interaction needed some time to settle in her mind.

"What are you doing?" she asked.

"Your hard drive was bogged down. I cleaned it up some last night. Your antivirus software is updating now." He stood and stretched. His clothes were wrinkled from sleeping in them. His dark hair, rumpled out of its precision *GQ* cut, fell over his forehead. The shadow on his jaw made her wish he'd woken up in bed with her. *Sheesh*, what was wrong with her? "Coffee's ready. Are you hungry?"

Erotic images reeled through her mind. A lovely warmth bloomed over the rest of her skin.

"Um. I'm good with coffee, thanks. Plus, I'm running a little late this morning." She shifted back, lifting the hem of her sweater to cool her skin. Maybe she should change into something lighter.

Luke followed her into the kitchen. “Well, I’m hungry. Do you have cereal?”

“In the pantry.”

He selected a box.

“Bowls are over the range.” She sat at the table, glad to have a solid piece of furniture between them. “While I’m thinking of it . . .” She gave him the location and combination for the gun safe. “In case of emergency. It’s of no use if you can’t access it.”

“Got it.” Cereal tinged into ceramic. He poured milk, then turned and leaned against the counter while he ate. Brooke grabbed her coffee with both hands and chugged it. Her wild response to Luke had to be a remnant from her sleepiness. Surely the caffeine would wash it all away. She could go back to normal.

Luke turned and rinsed his bowl in the sink. Brooke watched the muscles of his broad shoulders and back shift under his shirt.

*Ack!*

“Could I use your shower? I’ll be two minutes.”

“Of course.” Getting those erotic visions out of her head was not getting any easier. “Use the one in my bedroom. Towels are in the linen closet in the hall.”

“Thanks.” He stopped in the den for his bag and disappeared down the main hall. Brooke heard his footsteps ascend the stairs.

He was going to be naked in her shower. She couldn’t handle the mental image. Needing a distraction, she switched on the countertop TV and poured herself a bowl of cereal.

She ate her way through the weather report and a traffic update. “Now for a special update on the vicious assault of a young woman in Coopersfield.”

The camera panned to another news desk. The same relentless blond reporter that had chased her through the community center parking lot Monday night. Dressed in a striking suit of cobalt blue, the blond sat in a modern newsroom. "The victim of Monday night's brutal assault has been released from the hospital and is recovering at home."

The reporter rehashed the attack. Then Brooke's picture appeared in the corner of the screen. Fear turned her stomach.

The blond continued, "Tuesday night's hero, Brooke Davenport, is no stranger to violence. At age twenty-two, her friend and roommate, Karen Edwards, was murdered by an estranged boyfriend in the basement of their apartment building."

Karen's photo appeared next, then a picture of the apartment building where they'd lived. The pictures that flashed onto the screen looked nearly identical to the ones she used for her own presentations. And she suddenly had no desire to ever see them again.

"Ms. Davenport teaches math at the Westbury High School, and she devotes much of her spare time to helping others as well. Once or twice a week for the past decade, Ms. Davenport has taught a women's self-defense class in the surrounding communities . . ." The newswoman droned on.

Brooke tuned out the rest of the story.

"Well, that's a problem, isn't it?"

Brooke's head swiveled. Luke stood in the entrance to the kitchen, freshly shaven, his hair damp. She stared at him, but his eyes never left the screen. He didn't move, except for the twitching of a muscle in his jaw.

When the piece was over, the program switched to a soldier homecoming piece that didn't lighten the dead weight in Brooke's chest.

Luke turned to her. "That reporter broadcast everything except your address and phone number." He paced, raising a hand to his temple. "If that creep didn't know who you were ten minutes ago, he does now."

The phone rang. The hour of the call sent alarm buzzing through Brooke. The phone was on the counter next to Luke. He looked at the caller ID: IAN DAVENPORT.

"My ex." Brooke reached for the phone. "Hello."

Ian's voice came over the line. "I just saw the news report. Are you all right?"

She sighed. "I'm fine, thanks."

"I doubt you really are," Ian said. "Have you seen the therapist?"

"Not yet." Irritation rubbed at Brooke's frazzled temper. "It just happened, Ian. Give me some time."

They both knew she probably wouldn't go. The last one wanted her to take a break from teaching self-defense, to stop beating herself up about Karen's death, to let go of her guilt.

Something Brooke wasn't able to do.

"Brooke . . ." Disappointment carried on the connection from Philadelphia to Westbury.

"Ian, I have to go to work. Thanks for calling."

Anger and bitterness crept into his voice. "I don't understand why you just can't let the past be in the past."

"I know you don't." She shot back. "That was part of the problem."

She ticked off the seconds of silence. One, two, three.

"Let's not argue. That's all water under the bridge at this point." Ian's voice was cool as usual. "I'll see you next Friday when I pick up the kids."

"Right." Brooke jammed the phone back in the charging cradle. In her opinion, a few good arguments would have been better than Ian's chilly reserve.

He'd married her assuming a few trips to an expensive psychiatrist would restore the carefree woman he'd dated in college. He'd been very disappointed to learn Karen's death had changed Brooke forever. He'd been disappointed in everything about their marriage. He'd grown up in a country club, au pair, dress-for-dinner kind of family. But their kids weren't the perfectly mannered violin prodigies he'd envisioned. They were loud and boisterous, often covered in mud and grass stains. Rather than embrace the chaos, Ian had kept his distance.

He'd said it best the day he'd moved out: They just weren't compatible.

Luke had withdrawn into the den to give her privacy. He came back out. "Everything OK?"

"Fine." It was too early in the morning, and she was still reeling from the news report. There was no way she could have a discussion about Karen now. She needed to compose herself and get to work. "Ian was just checking in."

Luke raised a disbelieving brow. Feet thudded down the stairs. Chris skidded into the kitchen, feet sliding on the tile. He gave the stove a hopeful glance.

"Did you want me to make you breakfast?" Brooke asked, surprised.

"No!" Chris opened the pantry and pulled out a box of granola bars. "I mean, I'm not hungry yet. And it's a little late. I'll take these with me."

Haley swooped in, grabbing two bars and shoving them into her backpack. "Ready."

Brooke set her coffee aside.

Luke was quiet with the kids in the room, but his expression told her their discussion wasn't over. Like everyone else, he was going to ask her questions she couldn't answer.

# CHAPTER SIXTEEN

Time to catch up on the news. Specifically, his news. What did the media have to say about him this morning? Was he still a star? With a jittery stomach, he placed his mug and a plate of scrambled eggs on the coffee table and settled on the couch. He picked up the remote. The TV was already set to the local news station. It was all he'd watched since Monday night.

Five minutes into the hour, the same female reporter sat in the newsroom and began her spiel. Maddie was home! Now *that* was good news. Appetite whet, he dug into his breakfast. The police had no leads. *No kidding.* Except for the scratches, he hadn't left them any.

The reporter started in on Brooke Davenport's history. He hit the record button on the remote. No interview. Interesting. Was she uncooperative? Did she eschew the spotlight?

He went granite hard in one beat of his heart, the response he *used* to have at the thought of any of his kills. Was that what was missing lately? A good fight? That spark of hope that had to be beaten out of a victim? The rush of adrenaline when she realized all her efforts were pointless. He was going to hurt her, and then she was going to die.

The strongest woman was powerless against him.

"This isn't Brooke Davenport's first encounter with violence."

He shut down his imagination as the reporter detailed Brooke's involvement in an old murder. The cold eggs in his mouth became tasteless. His fork bounced off the carpet.

It was Karma, fate, divine influence for those who believed in that sort of thing. Brooke Davenport's maiden name was Peterson, and she'd once found the body of her murdered friend.

His stalking options burst wide open. A beam of light and chorus of . . . The heavenly metaphor didn't ring true. Did demons sing? Probably not.

He'd followed dozens of women over the years, tracked their every move, predicted their every response. Watched. Waited. Then leapt with precision and timing to rival the best natural predator. But he'd never let one of his subjects know he was on the prowl. To have them anticipate their encounter with the same intensity as him. It was a rush to know that as he was planning their fate, they were fearing his intentions.

He pictured Brooke's lovely face. She would know.

Every time she closed her eyes, she'd think of him.

Her life was going to come full circle, from her friend's death to her own, and he was going to make sure she knew her end was coming the exact same way.

If he killed her, he might have to move. She was too well-known in the community. People would insist her case be solved. Even if he managed to brush the crime off on someone else, staying here for next year's kill wasn't an option. He'd lived here a long time, too long maybe. Change wasn't necessarily a bad thing. Avoiding patterns was important. And the winters here sucked. Cold, damp, and nasty weather from December through April.

Maybe he'd head south. No Texas or Florida, though. Those states were way too quick to flip the switch for his comfort. Death row was practically an express lane. New Mexico maybe. They'd abolished the death penalty a few years ago. Not that he was going to get caught, but it paid to be careful.

He would kill Brooke Davenport, then he'd move to New Mexico.

On the TV, the reporter had moved on from Brooke's background to a bit of information about the young woman she'd saved. The victim's name wasn't given, but he knew it was Maddie. He bristled at the praise for her actions, her will to live, her fighting spirit.

Maddie hadn't cooperated the way he'd predicted. Why? What personal trait had he missed in his evaluation of her that allowed her so much spirit?

He went down to the basement. Maddie's file was in the first storage container. He spun the combination lock and lifted the lid. The manila envelope filled with pictures, schedules, and notes rested on top of an empty scrapbook. Acid-free to preserve his memories for as long as possible. Rocking back on his heels, he opened the file and paged through his notes. Nothing. He returned to the main floor and fired up his laptop. He reviewed his virtual catalog of potential victims. Maddie shone here as well. Every aspect of her behavior indicated she was perfect for him. Nothing predicted her refusal to give up, nothing rebellious in her background. Perhaps Maddie was an anomaly.

No worries. Maddie would learn her lesson in time.

He moved two fingers on the touchpad, absently scrolling through his early notes on all the candidates. A new thought flashed into his head with the Billy Mays enthusiasm of an As Seen on TV commercial.

*But wait! There's more. This week only, kill two women for the price of one, the ultimate BOGO.*

After all, what did Brooke care about more than herself? What act would break her the way that stopping his annual hunt was torturing him? He would make her watch him rape and kill another before he extracted his pleasure from her. Her dread would make the act so much sweeter.

He took his notes upstairs. He was going to start a new book on Brooke. Catching two women at the same time would take some planning, but he was up to the task.

The thrill rejuvenated his enthusiasm.

It'd been a long time since he'd taken on a new adventure, demanded something extra from his skills. Had he gotten lazy? Maybe. But that was no more. His new scheme broke the rules that had kept him from detection over the years. There would be consequences. But the payoff would make the cost worthwhile.

His next hunt would be double the challenge and twice the pleasure.

# CHAPTER SEVENTEEN

"*X* equals fifty-two," Brooke said as she wrote the answer to the problem on the dry-erase board in black marker. She turned to face her Algebra I class. "Does anyone have any questions about today's lesson?"

She scanned the classroom. Twenty-eight faces blinked back at her with varying degrees of comprehension. In the front row, Sara, a pretty blond with perfectly straight hair and teeth, copied the problem with her usual diligence. Derek dozed in the back row, head tilted back, long jean-clad legs stretched out under the seat in front of him. Brooke sighed. Derek would snooze his way to an effortless A on the next test, while poor Sara would scratch and claw for a C.

The bell clanged.

Lunchtime.

Brooke raised her voice over the sounds of bodies moving, backpacks zipping, and chair legs scraping on linoleum. "Don't forget, page seventy, problems sixteen through thirty for tomorrow." She pointed to the other end of the dry-erase board, where she'd written the homework assignment.

Students bottlenecked at the exit. Brooke wiped the eraser across the board, clearing the lesson for the next class. The door opened and the change-of-class cacophony of voices, footsteps, and slamming lockers filled Brooke's classroom. She dropped into her chair.

Sara stopped in front of Brooke's desk, twirled the blunt end of a few blond locks. "Ms. Davenport, I'm really confused. Are you going to be here in the morning?"

Poor Sara worked her tail off.

"I'll be here about twenty minutes before homeroom tomorrow. I'm available eighth period and for a little while after school today."

Sara shook her head. "I have field hockey practice after school. I'll come in the morning."

"OK." Brooke set her marker on its ledge. She watched the perfect fall of Sara's hair swish out the door.

After the room emptied, Brooke locked the door and started toward the math teachers' lounge. Her stomach rumbled, and she wished she'd brought more than yogurt and a banana for lunch. Was she hungry enough to trek to the cafeteria?

Abby emerged from her classroom and fell into step beside her. "How's the knee?"

"Better today." But probably not better enough to zip down to the cafeteria and back in her short lunch period. Yogurt and fruit would have to suffice, which was probably a good thing since she hadn't exercised since Monday.

They reached the lounge, and Abby led the way into the tiny room. "Don't forget we have track team yearbook pictures first thing in the morning."

"I won't." The smell reached Brooke before she got through the door. Fresh cookies. The aroma should have made her drool, but instead the familiar scent staunched her appetite on the first whiff.

"Oh, look." Excitement raised the pitch of Abby's voice.

Brooke stepped around her friend. She stared. Homemade macaroons were piled on a round platter. A Post-it note bearing her name was stuck onto the plastic wrap. In her peripheral vision she could see Abby at the refrigerator, opening the door, sticking her head inside, and pulling out their lunches. But her voice had faded to a vocal blur.

The aroma filled the room. Memories swamped Brooke.

"They smell fabulous. I'm starving. I want to skip lunch and just eat those." Abby tossed their lunch bags on the table. "Aren't you going to open the card?"

"Of course." She was being ridiculous. She could not freak out every time she encountered coconut cookies. This weekend, she was going to eat macaroons all day long to desensitize herself to the sight and smell and taste. Determined, Brooke checked the outer wrapping, then lifted the tray and checked underneath. "No card."

"Maybe it fell off." Abby pulled out a chair and sat down. A quizzical furrow formed between her eyebrows. "Is something wrong?"

"No. Not at all. This is a thoughtful gesture." It was. Someone baked her cookies, and she was being weird. She shook it off. "I wish I knew who sent them so I could thank them."

No student at Westbury High could possibly know that macaroons were Karen's favorite cookie, or that Brooke hadn't been able to eat one without crying since her friend's death.

"You should take them home."

"No. I'll leave them here for everyone to enjoy."

"Cool." Greg walked in, sniffing the air. He took the chair opposite Brooke and snatched a cookie from the tray. "These are good. Did you make them?" He mumbled the question at Abby around a mouthful of cookie.

Abby shook her head. "Wasn't me."

Greg opened his lunch box and took out a sandwich. He glanced at Brooke. "We all know it wasn't *you*."

"What do you mean by that?" Brooke snapped the end of her banana and peeled the top half, but the scent clashed with the lingering smell of coconut. Her yogurt didn't go down any easier.

Greg rolled his eyes. "Oh, come on. Remember those peanut butter things you made at Christmas last year?" He shuddered.

"He's being melodramatic," Abby said. "They weren't *that* bad."

Brooke shrugged. "I won't make you any cookies this year."

Greg lifted his sandwich. "I can live with that."

Brooke should have acted appropriately insulted, but the usual banter didn't appeal. The scent of coconut had lodged in her nose. It was going to remind her of Karen for the rest of the day.

---

"Gran?" Luke carried his bag into the foyer. The sound of coughing led him down the hall to the kitchen. His grandmother stood at the counter. She was filling a mug with coffee.

"Lucas." She set the pot back on its burner and smiled at him. "I haven't heard anything from Nancy at the police station, so I assume all is well with Brooke."

"Yes, ma'am. So far, so good." Luke dropped his bag on the floor. "How are you feeling?"

"I'm fine." Gran coughed into her fist. She waved him toward a chair. "Sit. I made an apple strudel. Coffee?"

While Gran scrubbed her hands at the sink, Luke dropped into a chair. She poured him coffee and sliced a chunk off the end of the fresh pastry. "You can take the rest back to Brooke's with you."

"Don't you want any?"

"I'm not terribly hungry." She took the seat across from him.

He picked up the fork. "They why did you make it?"

"I was bored, and I like to bake." She wrapped her hands around her mug. "I thought someone was sure to drop by and eat it. And here you are."

He slipped a forkful into his mouth, chewed, and swallowed. "Perfect, as always."

Gran blushed, the pink rising into her pale cheeks like a fever.

Luke lowered his fork. "Are you sure you're all right? You look tired."

"I appreciate that you're worried about me, Lucas." She smiled at him. "I have a cold. It's cruddy, but I'll get over it."

Luke ate more strudel. Probably if he'd been around more in the last few years, he'd have seen his grandmother with a cold before, and he wouldn't be so paranoid.

"Now tell me how Brooke and the children are doing."

Luke told her about the special report the news had played that morning.

"I saw that." Gran's eyes narrowed and her face sharpened to the look that meant someone was going to get a stern lecture. "I'd like to call that news station and give them a piece of my mind."

Luke grinned. He wouldn't want to be on the receiving end of Gran's wrath. "Freedom of the press and all that."

Gran pursed her lips at his statement. "Rubbish. The press has the same responsibility as anyone else not to put people in danger. They just want to milk the crime as long as possible."

"Probably."

Luke finished his dessert, retrieved more clean clothes from his room, and said goodbye to his grandmother.

He stopped at the pet store for bathing supplies on his way back to Brooke's house. Sunshine greeted him at the door. He let the dog out onto the lawn for a few minutes. She did her business and followed him back into the house. He scratched her head. He'd never had a dog, but washing one seemed simple enough. He wanted to do something nice for Brooke. The last few days had been rough.

In the upstairs bathroom, he lined up the new items next to the tub: hydrating shampoo for sensitive skin, a conditioner for thick coats, and a brush recommended by the sales clerk. He grabbed a plastic cup and fetched a stack of towels from the linen closet.

At the top of the stairs, he slapped his thigh. "Come on, girl."

Sunshine wasn't in sight. He went downstairs. Where was she? A quick tour of the house revealed the dog cowering under the kitchen table.

Luke leaned over. "Oh, come on. You can't possibly know."

She backed up. Luke pulled out a chair and crawled under the table. He wrapped his arms around her the dog and gently pulled her into the open. With a firm grip on her collar, he stood. "Let's go."

Sunshine sunk onto the tile.

"Passive resistance?" He picked her up. She didn't fight but went limp in his arms. Luke carried her upstairs and into the bathroom. He closed the door with his foot before setting the dog down. "This is ridiculous. It's just a bath. You smell awful."

He ran the water. Watching, the dog shivered. Her brown eyes accused him of committing all sorts of atrocities.

"You're not even wet yet." When a few inches had accumulated, Luke stirred the water with his hand to check the temperature. Perfect. Warm, not hot. He spread a towel on the floor and lifted the dog. She flailed as he set her down in the tub. Water splashed over the edge and onto Luke's jeans. He grabbed for more towels.

"Relax," he soothed. "Sit down. You're going to feel much better afterward."

Using the cup, he thoroughly soaked her fur and lathered her up with shampoo and rinsed her about a thousand times. Collies had a lot of fur. Luke let the water out of the tub twice before he was satisfied her coat was completely suds free. He pulled the plug for the last time. "Don't you feel better?"

He turned and reached for a towel. The dog leaped from the tub. Water splashed. Scrambling on the slippery floor, Luke grabbed for her collar. She ducked him and shook hard. Water sprayed in every direction.

Luke reached for another towel, but they were all soaked.

"Stay." He pointed at the dog as he cracked the door and backed out the narrow opening. She lunged, streaking between his legs and out into the hall. "Stop!" He chased her, sliding across the water-splattered hardwood. She scrambled faster than an old dog should be able to move. Breathing hard, Luke cornered her in the kitchen. He tried to lead her by the collar, but she planted her butt firmly on the tile. "Come on. We're almost done."

He hadn't brought a towel with him. He picked up the sopping dog and carried her back upstairs. He pushed her into the bathroom and grabbed more towels from the closet. Twenty minutes of rubbing later, Sunshine's coat was still damp. Luke found a hair dryer under the cabinet. With the air on low, he brushed the tangles out of the thick coat. Satisfied she was dry enough not to get sick, he turned off the dryer and sniffed her fur. "Much better."

He opened the door. The dog bolted from the room. Luke looked down at his clothes. His jeans and shirt were wet and coated with dog fur, and so was the bathroom, the hall, the stairwell, and the kitchen. With a sigh, he carried the wet towels to the basement and started the washer. He found the cleaning supplies and attacked the explosion of wet fur. An hour later, the bathroom sparkled, and the floors were mopped. He stowed the mop and bucket in the basement, transferred the wet towels to the dryer, and started a second load. Back upstairs, he checked the clock.

Time to pick up Brooke and the kids at school. No time to shower. Wonderful.

He sniffed his shirt. He smelled like the dog—before the bath.

# CHAPTER EIGHTEEN

Brooke climbed into the passenger seat of Luke's sedan. She sniffed. A familiar foul odor filled Luke's car. Had he taken her dog somewhere? Already in the backseat, the kids grinned.

"Luke gave Sunshine a bath." Chris snickered.

"Oh." Brooke raised a hand to her nose. "That was really nice of you."

He muttered something under his breath and turned the car toward home. "The dog looks great."

At home, a fluffy and clean Sunshine greeted them at the door. Brooke ran a hand through the silky fur.

"She looks beautiful and smells even better." Brooke touched Luke's arm. "Thank you."

He flushed. "That's because she gave me all her stink. I'm going to take a shower."

Brooke went back to the kitchen. Her floors were noticeably free of fur and dust. She heard the faint buzz of the dryer. He did wash? "Chris, would you go down and get the laundry?"

"Sure, Mom." A few minutes later Chris brought an armload of towels upstairs. "There's another load in the dryer. Looks like all the towels we own." Chris grinned.

She held back a snort of laughter. Barely. She folded towels and stacked them on the table. "It was really nice of him to bathe the dog. You could have done it."

"I know better." Chris laughed. He dropped into a kitchen chair and started pulling books out of his backpack.

Brooke eyed the pile of towels on the table. Were there any left? She grabbed the stack and went to the second floor. The upstairs hall was just as oddly clean. She glanced in the bathroom and saw nothing but gleaming surfaces. Her bedroom door was open, the shower running.

She'd just leave the towels by the bathroom door. Except it wasn't closed. Luke stood in the doorway, wearing what must have been the last clean towel draped around his hips. Oh. She got an eyeful of long, lean man. His muscular chest and shoulders tapered to abs flat enough for a fitness magazine cover. Her libido did a cartwheel, while her imagination was busy editing the previous night's erotic dreams. Her gaze tracked the sprinkling of hair across his chest down to . . . "I'm sorry. I thought you might need a towel."

Red-faced, Luke backed into the bathroom. "I found one, thanks." He firmly shut the door, leaving Brooke to close her mouth. And possibly wipe some drool from her chin.

Mentally fanning herself, Brooke returned to the kitchen. There was no way she could pretend she hadn't seen that. Wow. No worries on the tingling thing. She was tingling to her core. Muscles and sexy green eyes aside, how did a woman resist a man who bathed her dog and mopped her floors? He hadn't done that for Wade. He'd done it for her. He might brush off his protection as a promise to her brother, but this afternoon he'd shown he cared about *her.*

"Mom, can you check my costume now?" Haley called from the stairwell.

"Yes." Thankful for the distraction, Brooke grabbed the rarely used sewing kit from the closet.

Haley swept in. A long white robe cinched at the waist by a length of gold braiding, sandals, and a gold-leaf head wreath transformed her daughter into Aphrodite. Haley's phone went off with the opening chords of a pop tune.

"Hold still." Brooke lowered her aching body to the floor and eyed the hem of the costume. "You can text him back after I make sure this is straight. Sewing isn't one of my talents."

Her daughter lowered the cell phone and grinned. "Sorry."

"I think it looks good." Or at least as good as it was going to get.

"I love it." Haley fluffed the flowing skirt. The dog ambled over and sniffed at the costume. "I'm going to change before Sunshine gets dog hair all over it." She bounced down the hall, already texting again.

In fresh jeans, Luke entered the room, his damp clothes and towel balled up in his hands. "Did you make her costume?"

"I didn't have much choice." Brooke climbed to her feet. *Do not picture him naked. Too late.* This might get awkward. "The children's costumes were too small, and the adult costumes were too *adult*. The packaged costumes should have been labeled GREEK GODDESS PROSTITUTE."

"I can see where that might be a problem." Luke's laugh eased the tension.

"You can just toss those things down the basement steps. I'll throw them in with my next load. Thank you again for bathing the dog and cleaning the bathroom and mopping the floors."

With a fresh surge of color to his face, he did as she suggested. "It wasn't really an option. She got away from me mid-bath."

"Happens every time." Brooke covered her grin with a fist. "Coffee?"

"Sure. When is the big Halloween event?" Luke took the mug she handed him and sat across from Chris.

"The Halloween dance is Friday night." Brooke's stomach rumbled. She opened the freezer and considered the contents. "Let's order a pizza."

"With sausage and pepperoni?" Chris brightened.

She phoned in the order, then filled a mug with fresh-enough coffee, and carried it to the table. Sipping, Brooke slid into the chair next to her son. She fished a Hershey's Kiss from a small bowl. The chocolate melted in her mouth. Despite her determination to desensitize herself to coconut, she'd chickened out and left the platter of cookies at school. The memories were too painful to bring home, which was ironic because she willingly lived with the horror of Karen's death every day. Why could she face her friend's murder but not the happy life she'd lived before violence had ended it? What was wrong with her?

Haley returned, dressed in the skinny jeans and sweater she'd worn to school. She opened her laptop on the table and tapped the touchpad. "Look. Cindy posted pictures of her new puppy." Haley turned the computer around so Brooke could see the screen. In the photo, a beagle puppy sat on a patch of grass.

"Cute," Brooke said.

Haley signed out of her profile. "I'm going upstairs to study." She left the laptop on the table and disappeared down the hall.

Brooke stared at the computer, her mind still fixated on Haley's Internet profile.

"What are you thinking?" Luke asked.

"I'll bet Maddie has accounts and profiles too. If she's anything like most of my students, it's full of personal information." Brooke logged in under her own name.

"You have an account?" Luke sounded surprised.

"I do. I use it to keep track of what my kids are doing online. I have rules for social media use, and I'm not afraid to police them." Brooke smiled.

"There's nothing like a nosy mother to keep kids honest."

"Exactly." Brooke found Maddie in less than a minute. The young woman was very active. "Wow. He didn't have to physically follow her much. She practically posts her minute-to-minute daily agenda online, and she doesn't have her data fully protected."

Brooke scrolled through pictures of Maddie and her friends. There were long lists of places she'd been and organizations she belonged to. "There's no way she knows all those people."

Forever Fitness was on her list, as was the law firm that employed her. The community college she attended and her former high school were both listed. Brooke scrolled through pages and pages of pictures. She stopped on a photo of a group of skirt-clad girls holding sticks. Shock rippled through her.

"Hey, that's Haley's field hockey team. Why is it posted on Maddie's page? She didn't go to Westbury High." She swept the mouse over the picture. Players' names popped up every time she hovered over a face. She paused on her daughter's image. "It's the local newspaper shot from their first big win last year."

Luke leaned over to get a better view of the screen. "On sites like this one, anyone can post pictures and tag them with names. Maddie didn't post this picture. She just shared it. From the number of links attached, it's made the Internet rounds. She's shared dozens of pictures and articles about all the local high school field hockey teams."

Unease lodged in Brooke's chest. Labeled pictures of young girls all over the Internet were a predator's dream. Brooke clicked on another link. "Maddie played for Coopersfield High. Here's a picture of her team. They won the state championship last year. It was a big deal. Lots of news coverage. I didn't realize she just graduated last June."

"It's hard to estimate her age with her face all swollen and bruised." Luke's voice was grim.

She flipped back to the picture of Haley's team. Her daughter's smiling face stared back from the first row. Brooke went back to Maddie's profile. "Everything about Maddie's life is right here."

"If he used the Internet to find her, then there should be a link to him somewhere."

"To use this site, he has to have an account, right?"

"Yes, but it can be a fake account with fake personal data. All you need to provide is a working e-mail address."

Brooke paged through Maddie's profile. Every page went to another page, which was connected to its own set of people, and so on. "I wonder if he interacted with her on one of these pages."

"It's possible."

"We need to narrow it down." Brooke continued to scroll.

"Narrow what down?" Suspicion tinted Luke's voice.

"Where Maddie's attacker found her."

"Brooke, this is a police investigation. You can't interfere."

Panic rose behind Brooke's breastbone, the pressure building with no outlet, constricting her lungs. Her next breath was tight. Westbury police could hardly keep a guard on Maddie forever, and there was no police cruiser parked in Brooke's driveway. Luke was leaving in five days. Then what? "There are two different towns working this case: Coopersfield, where Maddie was attacked, and Westbury, where her assailant left the earring for her. Three police departments are involved if you count the Hillside rape. What if they don't coordinate? What if the

Hillside rape and Maddie's attack in Coopersfield aren't even related?"

Luke put his hand over hers. "You aren't with the police. You need to let them do their job."

"So I should do nothing?" That wasn't an option for Brooke.

"You should stay informed about the case." Luke squeezed her hand. "And you should be very careful."

"This guy is focused on Maddie." Brooke needed to move. She pulled her hand out from under his and stood. She went to the cabinet, pulled down a glass, and filled it with water at the tap. "He went into a crowded hospital to let her know that."

"And the police have an officer with her right now."

"But for how long?"

Eventually Maddie would be alone and vulnerable—and so were Brooke and her kids.

---

"Brooke, you have to let the police handle this." Luke pushed to his feet. He rounded the table and crossed the room to face her.

Her hands were trembling, her skin had paled, and her movements lost their grace. She looked like he felt when he had a nightmare. Shaky, full of energy that had no outlet. She lifted her cup to her mouth and drank. Nerves radiated from her jerky motions.

The phone rang. Brooke jumped. Choking, she sputtered coffee and reached for a pile of napkins on the counter. A second digital ring reverberated through the kitchen. She coughed and pressed a hand to her chest, but she didn't move toward the charging cradle on the counter.

Luke picked up the phone. "Hello."

"This is Officer Ethan Hale. May I speak to Brooke?"

Brooke's coughing slowed. She took a deep breath, and Luke gave her the handset.

"Hello." She rubbed her temple. "Of course I understand. It's not a problem. Thanks for calling." She hung up the phone. "Ethan was supposed to help with my class tonight but he's tied up. He didn't say, but it's probably because they have a man at Maddie's house. Westbury is a small police force. They only have a handful of officers. No doubt watching Maddie is straining their resources."

Luke held a hand up to stop her speech. "Wait a minute. You're teaching class tonight?"

Brooke's forehead crinkled. She tilted her head. "Yes. Why wouldn't I?"

"Because you're hurt." And upset and obsessed.

"It's the last class of the unit. I can't miss it." She waved away his concern.

He gave her knee a pointed stare. "Can't you reschedule?"

"No." Her tone sharpened. "My knee is much better, and the community center books the room out months in advance."

"Brooke, I'm sure your students would understand if you couldn't make it tonight."

"No." Brooke's voice rose. "This is an important lesson."

"I'm sure it is, but—"

"I won't let them down. What happened to Maddie could happen to any one of those girls. *He* is still out there. You don't understand. I *have* to teach tonight." She set the empty mug in the sink with a shaky hand. "Do you remember my roommate, Karen?"

"The girl that was murdered by her boyfriend?" Wade had said Brooke felt guilty about her roommate's death. "Brooke, she was killed by an angry ex. That's not your fault."

"It doesn't matter." Brooke interlaced her fingers and brought her knuckles to her chin, as if she was praying. "If I can prevent just one woman from being killed . . ."

"You've already done that."

She paused, opening her mouth as if she was going to say something else. Then she clamped her lips together and shook her head. "It's not enough."

"OK." Luke raised his hands, palms out. Brooke's agitation and sense of responsibility were out of proportion. But maybe teaching her class was the best thing for her, a constructive outlet for nervous energy. "I do understand. How much did Wade tell you about the explosion I was in?"

Brooke blinked. "Just that terrorists bombed the building, and you were burned."

He would give almost anything to make his story that simple. "My assistant was killed in the blast." Luke closed his eyes. He could see Sherry bleeding out in front of him. But Brooke didn't need all the gory details. "It was her first international project. It was my job to take care of her, but I failed. She died." His throat tightened as if clogged with smoke, and he struggled for his voice. "Her name was Sherry. She was twenty-eight, beautiful and vibrant, with a wicked sense of humor. I'm as obsessed with keeping you safe as you are with your girls."

Horror filled her eyes. "Wade shouldn't have asked you to protect me. It wasn't fair."

"Wade doesn't know. No one knows except my shrink." Luke met her eyes to see his pain reflected back at him. "And you." He reached out to touch her, but his hand fell short. Who would want a man as messed up as him? Brooke had enough baggage of her own. She didn't need to lug his around too.

"I'm sorry to be so much trouble."

Why had he told her? He'd intended to let her know she wasn't alone, but he hadn't succeeded. Now she felt like she was a burden. "None of this is your fault."

"I guess." She didn't sound convinced.

"I've had some other issues too. Going into a high-rise is still really hard. That's why I've been out of work so long." *Huh*. Sharing that humiliating fact was easier than he'd expected.

Her palm settled on his forearm, and instead of the pity he'd dreaded, understanding passed between them. "Fine pair we are."

"Seriously." He covered her hand with his for a few seconds. Unexpected emotion swelled in his chest. *Whoa*. Overload. He drew back a few inches. "Now, what was the cop going to do for you tonight?"

Brooke smiled. "He was my attacker."

"Excuse me?"

Brooke's expression lightened and the corners of her mouth turned up. "He was going to wear the padded suit and let my girls beat on him." She turned thoughtful. "I suppose I can wear the suit."

*Like hell.*

"No, you can't." Luke scowled. "You're already injured. Can I do it?"

She considered him with a quick head-to-toe appraisal. "We'd have to practice."

What? He knew he'd lost weight, but dammit, he wasn't weak.

"Seriously?" Luke lifted his hands, palms up. "I've taken Krav Maga on and off for years. I don't need practice to let someone hit me." Krav Maga was the fighting style of the Israeli military, known for its blunt and brutally effective techniques. A typical class involved plenty of contact.

Brooke stopped. New interest sharpened her expression. "You took Krav?"

"Whenever I'm in the States, I go to a class or two." Luke shrugged. "I travel all over. Sometimes, the locations can be dicey." If only the worst thing he'd faced was a mugger. All that training hadn't done a damned thing against a briefcase full of explosives. "What about you? Where did you learn all this stuff?"

"I've done some mixed martial arts along with plenty of basic women's self-defense," Brooke said. "Nothing fancy. I prefer simple, effective, and easy-to-remember techniques. Come on. I'll show you." Brooke headed for the basement. Luke followed her down the wooden stairs. She pulled down a large, black hockey-equipment bag from the wall shelves. She set it on the floor and unzipped it. "Do you want to try the suit on?"

Luke pulled a padded vest out. Underneath was a heavy-duty groin protector. He didn't want to think about why he'd need that. But the prospect of practicing with him had shifted Brooke's demeanor from paranoid to productive. So he'd do whatever she wanted.

He was hardly one to judge. What would he do if he woke up from a nightmare and couldn't go for a run? Sitting on the floor shaking like a cold kitten sucked enough when he was alone. The only thing worse was having someone watch him disintegrate.

"There's a helmet too."

"I think for now we can just pretend." He zipped the bag. "Are you sure you're up for this? You're still hurting."

"We'll just go over the mechanics. We don't have to get physical." Brooke limped to the middle of her mat. She waggled her fingers at him, and he went to her like a puppy.

Sad. Pathetic even.

But he'd do anything to keep that helpless, panicked look off her face.

"For the purposes of this class, I stick to a few basic grabs and strikes. Most of the girls have no martial arts experience. Grab my wrist." She held one arm out. "I want you to use enough pressure to provide some resistance, but not enough to leave a mark. The girls have practiced these moves with each other, but there's an entirely different feel between the grip of a man than that of another girl."

He wrapped his fingers around her slender wrist. Her pulse throbbed under his thumb, the beats rapid considering they weren't doing anything physical.

"Perfect." She broke his hold with a twist of her arm. "That's the first escape we practice."

They went over the mechanics of a few other techniques for hair grabs and chokes. Brooke's hold breaks were simple and effective. Strikes were focused on soft targets: the eyes, nose, throat, and groin.

"Last one. Give me a bear hug."

Luke stepped behind her and wrapped his arms around her. The softness of her body nestled against him. Her hair smelled like flowers. She shifted sideways and mimicked dropping a hammer fist into his groin. Luke flinched, though she didn't make contact. That blow could be a total mood killer.

"That's it. I keep it pretty basic. This isn't a martial arts class. The class is designed to get them used to practicing safe behavior and learn that they can fight back." She pulled against his arms.

But Luke didn't release her. Her body snuggled up against his felt right. He turned her around and did what he'd been thinking about for two days—no, his whole life. He pressed a gentle kiss to her injured lip. She froze. Luke didn't, couldn't stop. He shifted his lips to take her whole mouth. She responded suddenly, as if there was a two-second delay between her brain and body. Her hands splayed against his chest, then clenched in his shirt, pulling him closer. Her mouth opened under his. She tasted of chocolate and coffee.

Instinctively, he leaned in. The full body contact set off a buzz in his blood, a need to be even closer. His mind drifted to the hungry look in her eyes when she'd seen him outside the shower earlier. He'd backed away before she could get a look at his back. How would she react to his scars?

Maybe he could just keep on kissing her all night. His tongue slid passed her lips. She responded with enthusiasm.

The muffled ring of the doorbell echoed above their heads. They froze. She released his shirt and pulled her head back. Her eyes reflected the bewilderment he felt to his bones. The connection between them went further than mouth-to-mouth. It had speared him through his damaged soul.

How did he let this happen? Luke wanted to run, but he was trapped by his promise and by the bone-deep yearning to maintain his connection with Brooke.

"I can't." She splayed a hand in the center of his chest. "I don't do casual flings. I'm sorry."

He had no response. He had no right to start a relationship he couldn't maintain—definitely not with Brooke. She deserved more. But her eyes were darkened with desire, her lips swollen from his kiss. Selfishly, he wanted to keep going. Disappointment rumbled through him.

"The pizza's here." She pivoted and headed for the stairs at too brisk a pace. Running away from the kiss? He didn't blame her. One thing was certain. No more of that mouth-to-mouth or full-on body contact for them. He could no more taste her than an alcoholic could have just a sip of wine.

With a vow to keep his physical distance, and an adjustment of his jeans, he gathered up the equipment and hauled it upstairs.

The pizza was consumed in rapid-fire, mostly by Chris. Brooke didn't make eye contact throughout the meal. Not a good sign. But every time he looked at her she flushed, which gave him a big boost to his masculine pride, even thought he'd sworn it would never happen again.

Brooke stashed the sole surviving slice in the refrigerator. "We have to leave in a few minutes."

Neither Chris nor Haley argued. Both likely sensed it was pointless. Twenty minutes later, Luke's breath locked up as he parked in the lot in Coopersfield. The woods stretched out behind the community center, dark and threatening. A vicious assault had occurred just a few hundred feet away.

He scanned the area before escorting Brooke and her kids into the building. She was favoring her leg more than she had earlier.

A group of young women gathered in the main room. They surrounded Brooke with a chorus of, "*Omigod*, Ms. Davenport. Are you *OK*?"

"I'm fine." But Brooke sank into the chair one of the girls brought her. "This is my friend, Mr. Holloway. He's graciously agreed to let you all practice on him tonight."

The glances turned on him varied from the shy interest from a set of tall dark-haired twins, to *holy shit*, blatant flirting from a tiny blond. Luke was tempted to hide in the car. It wasn't the girls' fists that scared him.

Haley joined the class. Chris burrowed into a corner with a book.

Brooke paired up the girls and ran them through a quick review of the same techniques she'd shown Luke in her basement. Luke zipped and Velcroed his way into the thick foam pads. He took particular care with adjusting the groin protector.

The girls bunched up, high-pitched giggles projecting nerves. No one took point.

"Natalie, why don't you go first?" Brooke suggested.

One of the twins stepped forward. Her identical sister fell in behind her, and the rest of the girls queued up.

Luke tentatively took her slim wrist in a gentle grasp.

"No!" She broke the hold just as Brooke had taught her.

Once they warmed up, the girls' voices grew louder, their responses stronger as their confidence was bolstered. Thirty minutes later, they were yelling in his face and hitting him like they meant it. Haley must practice with her mother because she drilled him in the chest with a palm strike he felt through the padding straight to his solar plexus.

"OK, everybody. You all did great tonight. How about a round of applause for Mr. Holloway?"

They clapped, and Luke smiled as he stripped off the sweaty protective gear. A sense of belonging, of contributing, put new energy into his step. He carried the equipment to his car and loaded it into the trunk. Chris and Haley jumped into the back.

"Thanks, Luke." Brooke stood next to his car, her attention on making sure all her girls were safely in their cars before she slid into the passenger seat. "I really appreciate you pinch-hitting for me."

"They were great." Luke got behind the wheel. He reached across the console and touched her hand. "I'm glad I did it. You make a difference. I didn't realize how much until I saw the class."

Brooke blushed. Heat flooded Luke's face and bloomed in his chest.

He wasn't bullshitting. She gave each of those girls a chunk of her strength, and they gave her something back. He could feel it inside of him too, a charge to batteries long dead.

But Brooke had panicked at the thought of cancelling class. Could she go on without it? The class and her obsession with crimes against women seemed to be more of a lifeline than a sideline, and her devotion cost her. There was no way she could hope to protect all these young women from harm. Assuming responsibility for their welfare was an enormous load for Brooke to carry.

She'd suffer if anything happened to any of them.

# CHAPTER NINETEEN

Twilight settled over the trees.

He slumped down in the driver's seat and raised his binoculars to peer over the dashboard. At the other end of the street, Maddie's house called to him. But a Westbury Police Department cruiser was parked at the curb, and three other vehicles occupied the driveway. He recognized both her parents' cars. The third must belong to another visitor.

How long would they stay?

He shifted his view to examine the house. Maddie's room was at the back on what was technically the second floor. But in a bi-level home, the first floor was partially underground. Maddie's bedroom window was only ten feet above the backyard. He knew from earlier reconnaissance that a large deck spanned the rear of the house. If he stood on the wooden railing, he'd be able to see her. Another possibility was to circle around the back of the property and use his field glasses to get a glimpse inside.

Was he that bold, and would darkness and some trees be enough cover?

And could he snatch her from her home?

Maddie was so close. He could practically feel her squirming body bucking under his again. He glanced at the ketamine on the seat beside him. Imagine how terrified she'd be if she woke up in his trunk? Or on his worktable?

His attention turned back to the house. He'd need to watch closely. To plan her abduction with greater detail than he'd ever constructed before.

Was he up to the challenge?

# CHAPTER TWENTY

A creak sounded outside. Maddie startled. She lifted her aching head from the pillow and stared at the window, eyes open wide enough to burn. A branch scraped against the glass.

Just the wind.

She eased her head back down and closed her eyes. Too quiet. Her hand sought the TV remote. She flipped through stations. News. *No.* Melodrama. *Double no.* God knew she'd had enough drama. She needed something distracting and relatively mindless. Ah, a rerun of *Project Runway.* Perfect.

Someone knocked softly on the door.

"Come in," Maddie said.

The door opened and her mom came in, a glass of water in one hand, a small white bottle in the other,

"Everything all right, honey?" Mom sat on the edge of the bed. The mattress dipped, and the pain in Maddie's head amplified.

"Yeah." Maddie struggled to a sitting position.

"How's your head?"

"Hurts."

"You can take more ibuprofen now. Maybe that will help."

Oh, yeah. It had definitely worn off. Maddie took a few pills and swallowed them with water. Mom fluffed up the pillows so she could sit up.

"Can I get you anything?"

"No." Maddie lay back. "Soon as these kick in, I'll be fine."

"Eat the crackers. It's not good to take medicine on an empty stomach." Her mom glanced at the window. The view of the wooded backyard had turned black and reflected their images. With a puzzled frown, Mom crossed the room, checked the window locks—again—and yanked the curtains closed with a determined snap.

Maddie's phone buzzed next to her head. She looked at the screen. Tyler. He'd been messaging her nonstop since Monday night. The smile hurt her bruised face, but she couldn't hold it back. She put a finger to a scab on her lip. Mom had offered to cover the mirrors, but Maddie was all right with seeing the damage to her face.

This was the first time in her life that she simply appreciated being alive.

Besides, it looked bad now, all swollen and angry red, but the doctors assured her the bruises should heal completely. They'd called in a plastic surgeon to stitch the cut on her cheek to minimize the chances of scarring. It was unlikely to leave more than a small mark.

Physically, Maddie would be all right.

But how would she heal on the inside? Two days after her attack, she knew the terror wasn't going to fade like her bruises.

*He* was still out there.

"Are you sure you don't want to come downstairs with me and your dad? We could rent a movie." Mom's smile was too bright, her voice too sunny, to be real. She was as terrified as Maddie.

"I was down there all day, Mom. I really need to be alone for a little while."

"Of course. I understand. Call me if you need anything." Her mom backed out of the room, hesitant to leave Maddie's side.

Maddie picked up her phone and texted Tyler back. He wanted to visit her tomorrow. A tiny fragment of hope bubbled up in her belly. They'd had their disagreements, but his concern for her was the single bright spot in her day.

Maddie blinked at the TV. Contestants discussed colors and fabrics. Not paying attention, she let the conversation flow around her.

The branch scraped on her window again. She jumped.

*Chill.*

She was in her own room. The house was locked up tightly. In the morning, a man was coming to give her parents an estimate on a security system, and Dad's freshly cleaned and oiled hunting rifle was at his side.

She was safe here. Maddie picked up the remote and turned up the volume. But when would she stop feeling as if someone was outside, watching?

---

Brooke settled at her desk. Teaching her self-defense class, and the glass of merlot at her elbow, had done wonders for her earlier panic. She opened her briefcase and took out a pile of tests and her answer key. Lifting her red pen, she started on the first paper. Through the ceiling, the muted sound of running water drowned out her thoughts.

Luke was upstairs. Naked. In her shower. Again. Her imagination conjured up the image of him wearing only a towel and then shifted to the smoking-hot kiss they shared in the basement.

She lifted the front of her shirt away from her skin. Was it hot in here?

*X* equals sixty-eight. Check. Next problem.

The rush of water stopped. He was done. He was rubbing one of her towels across his skin. This was ridiculous. She had a serious case of hormones gone wild. But after seeing him work so carefully with her class, paying attention to each girl and adjusting his level of aggression accordingly, his hotness rating had skyrocketed.

And she wasn't even going to think about the kiss. Drat. There it was, front and center in her mind, the taste of his mouth, the explorations of his tongue, other places she could imagine it . . .

If only the attraction was limited to her physical reaction. That she could resist. Probably. But Wade was right. Luke was a good man. Kind, intelligent, funny. He only had one major fault: he wasn't sticking around Westbury. He was off to Buenos Aires next week. Who in his right mind would stay in this little town when his life could be one exotic adventure after the next?

Besides her.

There was nothing she could do to change matters. The situation was no more Luke's fault than it had been Ian's. But her heart couldn't take not being enough for a man again. *Y* equals twenty-seven. At this rate, she was going to be up until midnight. She cleared her head and applied red pen to paper. In the next half hour, she plowed through half the pile.

A knock on her doorframe interrupted her concentration. Luke walked into her office. The man could sure fill out a T-shirt and jeans. His hair was damp, his feet were bare, and he smelled like soap. Why did it seem like he was always showering? "Chris just scooped a monster bowl of ice cream. Do you want anything?"

He had no idea. What she needed was a handful of ice in her shirt.

"Um, no." She smiled. *Act casual.* "I'm full. Thanks."

"Do you have a lot of work?" He asked. "I was going to watch a movie." His eyes glinted as if he was thinking of doing more than *watching a movie*. Rats, now so was she.

She glanced down at the pile of tests, then back at Luke. The thought of sitting on the sofa snuggled up with him was tempting. Too tempting. "I wish I could, but I really should finish grading these tests."

Disappointment dimmed his eyes. "No problem. I'll be in the den if you need me."

She hunched over the stack of papers. She heard Luke and Chris talking in the kitchen. The dog barked. Brooke tracked Chris's voice as he let Sunshine out then went upstairs. Brooke focused on her work. She set aside a poor test from a usually good student. She'd have to talk to him in the morning and find out what went wrong.

Glass smashed. Something thudded. *What was that?* Brooke ran through the kitchen and joined Luke in the main corridor. Outside, a horn blared, and Brooke flinched.

"Hey, Peterson!" The voice came from the front of the house.

"Call the police and wait here," Luke whispered. He crept down the hall.

Brooke picked up the cordless phone and followed him. Chris and Haley were upstairs. If there was danger at the front of the house, she was putting herself between it and the stairwell that led to the second story—and her kids. She stopped at the entrance to the living room. A rock lay near the baseboard. Dents and scratches in the oak planks tracked its path across the floor. Wind blew through a jagged hole the size of a softball. The living room curtains were open, and yellow porch light filtered in and glittered on shards of broken glass.

Luke shoved his feet into his sneakers. "You were calling the police?"

"Peterson, I'm calling you!" A man's voice, loud and slurred, brought her attention back to the front of the house. She made the call to 911.

Skirting the debris, Luke walked to the side of the window. He peered around the edge. "There's a man and a black truck on your front lawn."

Brooke checked the deadbolt on the front door and squinted through the decorative glass sidelight. The view was distorted by the leafy pattern and metal framework, but she could see the blurry shape of a man swaying in the center of the front lawn. He held a bottle in one hand. Behind him, a pickup was parked askew on the grass. The cab door hung open, and the interior light spilled out onto his work boots. The man reached into the car. The horn blared again. The sound sent a fresh shot of adrenaline through her veins.

"What happened?" Chris asked from the stairwell. A wide-eyed Haley was at the top of the steps, clutching the banister.

"Go back upstairs, Chris," Brooke said over her shoulder. "You too, Haley. Stay out of sight, and there's broken glass all over the living room."

Chris bent and squinted through the transom. "It's Mr. Verdi."

"He gives me the creeps." Haley's voice trembled. Hugging her arms, she sat on the top step. Chris backed up the stairs and eased down next to her. "His daughter's in my English class. She never says a word."

Brooke grabbed a pair of boots from the hall closet and stomped in them. Anger and fear churned in her belly. Damn Joe for scaring her kids. She moved to the window beside Luke and looked out the clear glass. "That's Joe all right. He worked for Wade."

Luke nudged her behind him. The protective gesture eased the slamming of her heart in her throat. Chris and Haley were safer because Luke was here.

"Joe was really upset when Wade let him go. Wade tried to find him another job, but the market is tight around here," Brooke said.

"Throwing a brick through your window seems extreme."

"I heard his wife left him too." Brooke leaned around him and frowned. "He looks drunk. Joe's not the most personable guy sober. Maybe I should go get my shotgun."

Luke turned back to the window. Joe honked his horn again. How long would it take the police to get out here? "I don't see a gun on him, and the police will be here any minute. Any idea why he's here?"

"Technically, my house is the official address of Peterson's Painting. Wade stored his stuff in the garage. The crew met Wade here and left their cars out back every day."

"Wade Peterson, I'm talking to you." The man on the lawn called out. He swigged from his beer.

Brooke leaned on Luke's shoulder. Whether she needed physical or moral support, the way she fit against his body buoyed her spirits.

Joe weaved across the lawn a few steps.

*Woof.* Joe's head swiveled. His gaze shifted to the side of the house.

Dread strangled Brooke's next breath. "Oh, no."

Sunshine was still outside.

"Oh, hell." Luke was unlocking and opening the door before Brooke could protest. "Lock this again behind me."

"Luke," Brooke called out, but he'd already slipped outside. She loved Sunshine but didn't want Luke to get hurt. With a glance at the kids still sitting at the top of the steps, she locked the door and hurried back to the window. Sunshine was rounding the corner of the house. Brooke scanned the road for the bright lights of a police car but saw nothing. How long would it take her to grab her shotgun? If she shot Joe to protect her dog, would she go to prison?

Joe's face swung back. His attention sharpened as he spotted Luke.

"You're Joe, right?" Luke went down the porch steps and stopped on the walk. He whistled. The dog changed course and headed for Luke with a wag.

"Yeah. Who're you?" Joe drained his bottle. Fifteen feet of lawn separated the two men.

"I'm Luke. I'm a friend of the family."

Joe lurched forward a few steps. "Where's Peterson?"

"Wade's not here."

"I don't believe you." Joe flipped the bottle to grip it by the neck. "You're all a bunch of liars."

Luke held his hands up in front of his face, palms forward. "Whoa. It sounds like you're upset with Wade, but he's not here. Let's calm down before anyone gets hurt."

"Too late. I've already been hurt because *Wade* had to go play fucking hero." Joe's face twisted in an angry sneer. He raised the beer bottle over his head and lunged at Luke. The bottle swung down toward Luke's head, but Luke side-stepped out of its path. Joe's hand arced downward through empty air. Luke grabbed Joe's wrist with his left hand and plowed his right elbow into Joe's face.

Brooke heard the crunch of bone through the broken window.

Joe's head rocked back. Blood streamed from his nose. His eyes rolled back in his head, and he crumpled onto the grass.

Relief washed through Brooke. She leaned on the wall for a few seconds and sucked in a few deep breaths.

Luke hadn't exaggerated when he said he could fight.

Swirling lights of red, white, and blue signaled the approach of a police car. The cop pulled up behind the truck and got out of the car. It was Ethan, the young black-haired cop that had taken her complaint about the mailbox. Joe moaned. He put a hand to the ground to push himself up. The cop was on Joe in a second, flipping him over and cuffing his hands behind his back. Ethan went to his cruiser, leaned in, and spoke into the radio.

Brooke turned and limped to the front door. She crossed the porch and walked toward Luke. He met her halfway and wrapped an arm around her shoulders.

"Thank you," she said.

He smiled, but a shudder passed through his lanky frame. Sunshine sat down next to Luke's legs. His free hand dropped onto her head.

Joe mumbled curses into the lawn.

"Do you know this guy?" Ethan nodded toward the cuffed man.

"Yes," Brooke said. "His name is Joe Verdi."

Ethan took their statements. She filled him in about Joe's relationship to Wade.

Ethan nodded at the black pickup. "I'll bet he was the one who left the roadkill in your mailbox." The cop hauled Joe to his feet and stuffed him in the back of his cruiser. "Brooke, you seriously need to catch a break."

"Isn't that the truth?" Brooke rubbed her arms. Luke pulled her closer, and she leaned into him, grateful for his masculine presence.

"Please stop by the station tomorrow and sign your statements." Ethan got into the car.

"All right." Taking the dog by the collar, Brooke turned and hobbled back inside as the police car drove off. Luke closed and locked the door. The kids were in the foyer. Neither were wearing shoes. "Stay out of the living room until I get that glass cleaned up. Chris, put Sunshine in the den. I don't want her to cut her feet."

"Is he going to come back?" Haley twisted a lock of hair over her shoulder. A tear rolled down her cheek. Chris's eyes were wide. Her kids had seen too much over the last few days. They hadn't needed one more display of violence. How dare Joe come to her home and frighten her children.

"Not tonight." Brooke hugged her kids hard.

Joe had looked like he was going to pass out before Luke likely broke his nose. Even if someone bailed him out, there was no way the police would give him his vehicle in his inebriated state. But tomorrow, who knew? Brooke was putting on a calm façade for her kids, but inside fear and fading adrenaline churned into nausea.

"Why would Mr. Verdi do that?" Haley sniffed.

Brooke brushed the tear off Haley's cheek. "He's angry, and he's been drinking. That's a bad combination."

Brooke leaned back to assess her son. Haley's emotions were transparent. But just because Chris contained his emotions better didn't mean he wasn't upset. "Are you OK?"

Chris nodded. "Yeah. Good thing Luke was here, though. Mr. Verdi might have hurt Sunshine."

"I'm glad Luke was here too." And Brooke meant it. "How about some hot chocolate?" The mess in the living room could wait.

They went back to the kitchen and spent a quiet half hour settling before the kids trooped back upstairs.

As soon as they were out of sight, she dropped onto a chair, her legs going rubbery with equal parts relief and shock. She knew the world was full of violence and did her best to prepare both her kids and the young women she taught. But she'd thought the danger would be waiting when they left this rural community. Never had she thought she'd have to fear for her children's safety in her hometown.

"Normally, I hate when the kids go with their dad for the weekend." Brooke's hair fell in front of her face. She shoved it behind her ear. "Not that he's not a good father, because he is. Just because he didn't want me anymore doesn't mean he doesn't love them. It's just that I miss them when they're gone. The house is too empty and quiet. But I almost wish they were going to Ian's this Friday instead of next."

Luke squatted in front of her. "Are you all right?"

"Not really." The kids had calmed down quickly, but Brooke's heart still rattled behind her breastbone.

He took her hand in his, but he made no promises, which reminded her that his protection was temporary. "I think you should consider a security system."

"I'll make some calls tomorrow." The idea of taking action to protect her family steadied her. She stood. "Time to clean up."

Luke led the way back to the living room. "I'm going out to the garage to see if there's anything to board up this window."

"I think there's a sheet of plywood behind Wade's van." Brooke fetched the dustpan from the pantry. She picked up the larger pieces of glass and swept up the small shards. Dragging the vacuum from the closet, she gave the floor a thorough cleaning before she let the dog out of the den.

Luke nailed plywood over the broken window while Brooke watched, restless. She was too unfocused to return to grading tests, but heading to bed wasn't an option either.

"Hey, you're bleeding."

She looked down. Blood welled from a cut on her thumb. "I must have cut it on a piece of glass."

"Come on." Luke steered her toward the kitchen. "Do you have a first-aid kit?"

"In the pantry."

Luke grabbed the small white box and opened it. He wrapped his fingers around her wrist. Brooke's pulse kicked up its heels, and she was powerless to stop it. The incident with Joe had left her nerves raw. Her self-control held on by a fingernail. Not even the burn of antiseptic as he poured it over the wound dampened her response to his touch. What was a woman to do? Luke had stood between her family and danger. The man had taken down a bottle-wielding drunk to protect her dog.

He leaned over her hand and examined the cut. "I don't see any glass."

"I'm sure it's fine."

He applied a Band-Aid.

She tugged at her hand. "I should finish my work." She should do anything but stay this close to him. There was only so long she could keep biology at bay.

Luke shook his head. "Come with me." He led her into the den and guided her to the sofa. Brooke sat upright, too keyed up to relax. The cushion dipped as he dropped down next to her and picked up the remote. He clicked through some channels, settling on an old black-and-white comedy. He took her shoulders gently with both hands and drew her back against him. She let him. Joe's act of violence had shattered her confidence. Luke's body was solid and reassuring behind hers. His arms surrounded her. She knew she should resist, but she couldn't.

Sunshine followed them into the den. She jumped onto the sofa on Luke's other side, curled up, and settled her big head in his lap.

"She's drooling on your leg."

"I know." Luke stroked Sunshine's head. The dog gave him the big-brown-eye treatment while her tail slapped against the leather couch.

Brooke gave up and rested her head on his shoulder. How long had it been since she'd connected with a man?

Too damned long.

As long as she kept it in her mind that he wasn't going to be around long, could she indulge? Nothing serious, though. He wasn't staying. But even as her body relaxed against his, she knew it was a mistake. Leaning on him would make it harder to stand alone after he left.

# CHAPTER TWENTY-ONE

Excitement roared through his veins as he pulled into his garage. He shut the car off and pushed the button clamped to the visor. The windowless overhead door cranked down with a *whirr* and shuddered as it hit the concrete.

He jumped out and rushed to the rear of his vehicle. His hands clenched with anticipation as he popped the trunk with the keychain fob. The lid sprang open with matching enthusiasm.

She was still asleep, her body still on the plastic sheeting. Perfect. He'd be able to get her settled in with less fuss than usual. Like social media, using ketamine could be considered cheating, but he rationalized that he'd pulled this snatch off with barely a day of preparation. Allowances must be made.

He reached down and stroked her dark hair. *Mm. Mm. Mm.*

Gorgeous.

Brunettes were his favorites, though he tried his best not to establish a type or pattern with his victims. Working in the occasional redhead was also a nice change. He might love steak, but that didn't mean a pasta dinner didn't appeal now and then. Never blonds, though. Like sushi, they held zero appeal.

But tonight it was a juicy prime rib all the way.

He dragged her bound arms, limp as string, over his head and heaved her onto his shoulders. He swayed under her weight for a few seconds before widening his stance to create balance.

All those trips to the gym were never a waste. People had no idea how physically demanding it was to move unconscious and dead bodies. Lifting weights regularly was a necessity.

He carried her through the house and down into the basement. More plastic crunched underfoot as he eased her onto the worktable with reverence. Her long hair trailed across the clear tarp. He brushed it aside to secure her hands to the steel frame at the head of the table. He selected a utility knife from his toolbox. A quick slice severed the plastic ties securing her ankles. He separated her feet, then stood back and considered her position.

What was he in the mood for this evening?

The overhead pulley he'd installed over the summer caught his attention. Yes. He had a new toy to play with tonight. It had worked nicely with his practice mannequin. He moved it experimentally, grimacing at an annoying squeak. A few quirts of WD-40 resulted in the smooth silence he expected.

He unsnapped the D-hook connecting the chain from her wrists to the table, let out some slack, and transferred it to the pulley. Her arms extended straight up, lifting her shoulders just a millimeter from the table. Now he could put her anywhere he wanted. To prevent her from sitting up until she was properly subdued, he wrapped a length of chain around her neck and tied it to the steel frame of the table above her head. She'd have to arch her back to take the pressure off her throat.

Grabbing two cinder blocks from the corner of the room, he put one on the floor on each side of the table. He wrapped a plastic tie around each ankle and secured each to its own block.

He stepped back to survey his work. She was immobile, but her position would be easy for him to adjust. By releasing her neck and sliding the pulley forward, he could pull her off the table without setting her hands free. The cinder blocks attached to her feet would prevent her from kicking him, yet enable him to move her on and off the table at will.

A fresh thrill coursed through him at his ingenuity.

This would be no quick kill. He had big plans for tonight. He had two days' worth of frustration to purge from his system.

Satisfied that she was adequately restrained, he checked his supplies and then went upstairs. He dialed the temperature of the thermostat up a few degrees. Cold flesh was not as appealing as a warm body.

In the kitchen, he prepared a protein shake for sustained energy that wouldn't weigh him down.

Then he went back downstairs to wait for her to stir.

He watched her sleep, trussed like a Christmas turkey, completely under his control. He was the one in charge. No question. Old memories stirred.

*"What the hell?" The screen door opened. A mosquito buzzed inside the trailer.*

Uh-oh. *Leaning over his bowl at the kitchen table, he froze. His spoon hovered over his noodles.*

*"You're early." He'd thought he would have another hour to clean up.*

*Ellie stared at him. Stains and wrinkles marred her black-and-white uniform. She looked a lot older than she had when their parents died three years before. Her blond hair was frizzy instead of smooth and pretty, a by-product of running in and out of a hot kitchen with trays of food, she said. Ellie worked a lot, which was good for him. He was home alone most days after school. He liked that. No Ellie screaming at him. He could relax and be himself.*

*"Not again. What do I have to do to get you to straighten out?" Ellie cuffed him. The strike hit his ear and jarred him. He tried to*

*scramble out from behind the table, but she was still bigger, still stronger, still faster. She jerked him back by the arm. Pain zipped in his shoulder and she dragged him off the chair.*

*Her hand reared back and slapped him hard across the face. He felt the blow to his toes. Eyes tearing, he put a hand to his stinging face.*

*"What am I supposed to do with you?"*

*He stared at the curtains billowing in the hot evening breeze. Answering would just make her madder. He didn't know what to say anyway.*

*"I do not have the energy for this." She twisted his arm behind his back and marched him down the narrow hall toward the closet.*

*He pushed his sneakers into the vinyl but they didn't hold, just squeaked as Ellie dragged him across the floor.*

Not the closet. *"I'll clean up the mess, Ellie."*

*"I can't even look at you right now." She opened a door. One hard push sent him into the cramped space. He barely fit these days. With no room to squat on the floor, he was forced to stand. He leaned against the back wall and listened to his sister rant. At least she wouldn't hit him while he was in here. A scrape against the knob told him she'd barred the door with a broomstick.*

No! *He slumped against the wall.*

*It was going to be a long night.*

# CHAPTER TWENTY-TWO

Luke circled around the sprawling dog. He pulled a box of pancake mix from the pantry and measured into a mixing bowl. He needed a real breakfast after a night of tossing and turning. Between worrying about the incident with Joe and the yearning of his body to slip upstairs to Brooke's bed, sleep had remained elusive.

Yeah. Holding her in his arms for a two-hour movie had been a not-so-brilliant maneuver for a man who wanted to keep his distance. But damn, it had been nice. In fact, even without sleep, he was in a stupidly good mood.

"I'm an idiot," he said to the dog.

Sunshine kept her eyes on the food.

Soft footsteps in the hall signaled Brooke's entry. "Good morning."

With a mass scramble of long limbs, the dog got up and shuffled over to her mistress. Brooke gave Sunshine a scratch.

"Morning." Luke poured her a cup of coffee. He almost leaned in to kiss her good morning but stopped himself just in time.

She took her mug. "Thanks."

"Did you sleep?"

"Some." She turned away from him. "You?"

"Some." Luke watched her walk away. She was barely favoring her injured knee this morning, and her dress slacks weren't as loose. This pair, a soft fabric in dark gray, clung nicely to her fit frame. She took a seat at the table, on the opposite side from him. Her hair tumbled over her shoulders, and Luke itched to sink his fingers into the silky, dark mass. Sunshine followed, sticking her head in Brooke's lap.

"Thanks again for helping us. I don't know what I would've done if you weren't here last night."

"You're welcome." He put his eyes firmly back on the stove. "Pancakes?"

"That would be great." She sipped, then scanned her kitchen. "Did you clean up?"

"Maybe a little." All he'd done was organize her clutter and wipe down the counters. Oh, and he'd polished the stainless. And scrubbed the range. "I was up early."

"You didn't need to do that."

Actually, he had. First of all, the clutter was giving him hives. Secondly, he'd been up at four and had time to spare.

"And you don't have to cook us breakfast every day."

"I know." But he wanted to do it almost as much as he wanted to kiss her again. Since he couldn't explain why, he changed the subject. "What's the plan for the day?' He added milk and cracked eggs into the bowl. With a handful of eggshells, he crossed to the trash can. Luke tripped. Shells splattered on the tile. He looked down at the big dog under his feet. "Where did you come from?"

Sunshine wagged and lunged for the eggshells faster than Luke had thought an old dog could move. He grabbed her collar. "Oh, no, you don't."

Her tail sagged. A string of saliva dripped from her mouth to the floor.

Brooke was on her feet moving toward the paper towels. One hand was pressed against her mouth. Her eyes were laughing.

"She used to be so well-behaved. The older she gets, the more of her obedience training she conveniently forgets."

Luke let her mop up the mess while he returned to making breakfast. A few minutes later, pancakes sizzled in butter. Outside the windows, the yard was frosty and dark, but the kitchen was warm, as were the emotions filling Luke's chest. Not even slimy raw eggs or equally slimy dog slobber could spoil his mood. "Back to the plan for the day."

Brooke went back to her chair. Her face tightened. "I have to go to the police station and sign papers. I'd like to drop the kids at school first. I called and got someone to cover my first two classes."

The feel-good homey moment Luke had been enjoying came to a crashing halt. Back to reality. "That makes sense." The kids had been traumatized enough by Joe's freak-out.

Brooke blew out a long, worried breath.

Thuds sounded on the wooden steps. The kids filed into the kitchen. A bleary-eyed Chris sniffed the air and brightened. Brooke shook off her mood and smiled at them. "Good morning."

"Hungry?" Luke slid plates of pancakes onto the table.

"You bet." Chris dropped his backpack next to a chair. He detoured to the fridge for the butter dish.

Haley slumped into a chair and frowned at the plate Luke set in front of her. "Thanks," she mumbled. Obviously, the kids hadn't slept well either.

Luke joined them at the table. Brooke paused, her fork over her plate. "Why is it that you two don't eat when I make you breakfast?"

Chris's plate was empty. He pushed his chair back. "Oh, look at the time. I have to go brush my teeth." He bolted for the hall.

"Me too." Haley set both dishes on the kitchen floor. A few crumbs remained on her plate.

"What are you doing?" Luke stared.

Sunshine ambled over, held the first plate down with a paw, and licked it clean. She moved on to the second.

"What?" Haley picked up the dishes and put them in the dishwasher.

"Nothing." Luke dropped his head into his hand. After Haley left the room, he turned to Brooke. "That's disgusting."

Laughing, she raised both hands, palms up. "Why? The dishwasher sterilizes everything. Sunshine's tongue is more thorough than any dish sponge."

"Still . . ." Dog slobber on the floor was one thing. Luke looked down at his empty plate and wondered if the dog had ever licked it. *Ugh.*

"Besides, germs are good for you. It isn't healthy to be a clean freak."

"I'm not a clean freak."

Brooke pointedly glanced around her formerly messy, now tidy kitchen.

"I've traveled all over the world. Internationally, most cultures do not share Americans' fixation with bathing. I've eaten things that would make your skin crawl. But the dog licking plates is still gross."

Brooke was still laughing in the car, and since he liked the sound of it, he didn't even mind that she was laughing at him. They dropped the kids at school and drove to the one-story brick building that housed Westbury's limited police force. Inside, a white-haired woman met them at the reception desk. A pumpkin on the counter was the sole concession to the upcoming holiday. She was the only person in sight. The office in the back, labeled Chief of Police, was dark. Luke introduced them. "Brooke is here to sign a statement."

"I'm Nancy Wheelen." Ah. His grandmother's source of information. "Officer Hale is off duty, but he left the papers for you to sign."

She handed Brooke a manila file. Brooke dug a pair of glasses out of her purse and read through the pages. Nancy handed her a pen.

Brooke signed a box next to a Post-it flag and handed the forms back. "Thank you."

Nancy took the folder with an approving nod. "Please give my best to your grandmother, Luke."

Ha. Like Nancy wasn't going to call Gran right now. "Yes, ma'am."

Outside, the early morning sun shone weakly on his back, and the crisp air smelled faintly of smoke. He'd forgotten how much he'd missed autumn in the mountains. Cities had their own scents, but most of them weren't pleasant.

They crossed a square of asphalt to the car. He opened the passenger door, and Brooke climbed in. She picked at a fingernail. He knew that look. She was thinking about something he wasn't going to like. He got behind the wheel and waited.

She dropped her hand and checked her phone. "Do you mind making a stop?"

Bingo. "Where do you want to go?"

"I have an hour before I'm due at school. I know Joe's wife. Their oldest is on Haley's field hockey team. I want to stop over and see her. Maybe she'll talk to me. I need to know if I have something to worry about. Was he just drunk and confused about where Wade is? Or does he include me in his crazy conspiracy?"

"All good questions we should probably leave to the police to answer. It isn't safe for you to poke your nose into Joe's business."

"But the police don't know Lisa. How much is she going to tell them?" Brooke shook her head. "I think I can safely talk to another mom. Besides, for her own safety she should know what happened last night."

Unfortunately, Luke couldn't think of a refuting argument. The heavy ball of unease in his gut was too vague to verbalize, but that didn't make it any less valid.

"If you have somewhere you have to be, I can always pick up my car and go by myself," Brooke said.

*Not happening.* Luke put the key in the ignition. Brooke wasn't going anywhere alone.

---

*But will she talk to me?* Brooke and Lisa were friendly, but they weren't exactly BFFs. Most of their conversations had revolved around coordinating fund-raisers and snacks for the field hockey team. Brooke had learned about the separation from Haley.

"Where does she live?" Luke asked.

The edge in his voice sent a small wave of guilt through Brooke. Her blatant manipulation was inexcusable, but she meant every word. If Luke didn't take her to see Lisa, she'd go by herself. Her reasons for wanting to talk to Lisa were twofold. She wanted info on Joe, sure, but she also want to make sure Lisa knew the full scoop. Estranged wives were common outlets for spousal fury. Brooke knew too well that female homicide victims were often murdered by their current or ex-partners. If anyone was at risk of injury from an enraged Joe, it was Lisa.

"She's staying with her mom. It's just a few blocks from here. Take a left at the stop sign." She directed Luke to a quiet street of modest homes on narrow lots. "Slow down. I've only been here once when it was my turn to carpool." Which house was it? "There it is. White house, black shutters."

Luke pulled up to the curb in front of a neat saltbox. Like most of the houses on the block, it wasn't anything fancy but was meticulously maintained. No weeds, fresh mulch, recently painted shutters. The flowerboxes under the windows were empty. Ornamental cabbages unfurled purple leaves in the flower beds that flanked the front door. Lisa's minivan was parked in the drive.

Brooke got out and walked up to the front stoop. She rang the bell. Lisa opened the door, her blue eyes cloudy with exhaustion and mild confusion. The morning light wasn't kind to her paler-than-pale Irish complexion or the bottle dye job that tinted her hair a dark shade of red nature hadn't considered. She squinted. Lines fanned out from her eyes. "Brooke?"

"I'm sorry for bothering you." Brooke had forgotten Lisa was a nurse and worked nights. "Did I wake you?"

"No. I haven't gone to bed yet." Lisa stepped back. "Come on in."

Brooke stepped over the threshold. The front door opened into a living room decorated in 1980s country style, heavy on the country blue and oak.

Lisa closed the door. "I get home just in time to send the kids off to school. Then I try to unwind a while before going to bed."

"Where's your mom?"

"Work. She gets home at five. We all have dinner together before I leave." Lisa's forefinger traced a square on the tablecloth. "It's actually working out better than I expected."

A square of hardwood the size of a parking space separated the foyer from the creamy carpet of the living room. Lisa led the way back to the kitchen. The country blue and oak motif carried over. A steaming mug sat on a pedestal table. "Want coffee? Sorry, it's decaf."

"No, thanks. I won't stay long." Brooke took a seat facing a window that overlooked a chain-linked yard barely twenty feet deep. The rear neighbor wasn't as tidy. Hedges planted to screen the view weren't tall enough to block the sight of a rusted metal shed.

Lisa set a mug on the vinyl tablecloth and sat opposite Brooke. "I heard what Joe did last night."

"News travels fast in this town."

"Always." Lisa wrapped her hands around her cup and sighed with as much defeat as exhaustion. "Why are you here, Brooke?"

Brooke hadn't really thought about how she'd broach such a delicate topic. Probably best to be vague and see what Lisa wanted to tell her. "I wanted to make sure you knew what happened last night. Did Joe talk to you about what happened with Wade?"

"No." Lisa gave her head a hard shake. "Joe and I haven't spoken since the day I left him."

Oh. Guilt tapped on Brooke's shoulder. Lisa didn't need more stress. "Wade didn't want to lay him off. He even tried to find him a job, but I know Joe was upset, and it was hard on your marriage."

Lisa froze. “Why would you think the layoff caused our split?”

“That’s what Joe said.”

“Of course he did.” Lisa set her mug down hard. Coffee sloshed over the rim. “I did not leave him because he lost his job.” She pulled up her sleeve. Fading bruises encircled her forearm. “I left him because he hurt me.”

Words eluded Brooke. She stared at the mottled yellows and greens on Lisa’s skin. “I’m sorry.”

“We’d been fighting a lot the last couple of years. The last three contractors he worked for went out of business. He’s been out of work three times. He’s been drinking more and more. But this is the first time he ever laid a hand on me. I can’t believe anyone would believe that I left him because he got laid off. What kind of person would leave their spouse because of the economy or a job?” Lisa yanked her sleeve down. “That’s what I get for trying to keep our personal problems private.”

“I had no idea,” Brooke stammered. She should have considered the possibility of domestic abuse.

“He’s probably telling everyone I’m a moneygrubbing bitch that took off when the gravy train pulled out.” Lisa’s eyes filled. A tear rolled down her face. “And obviously everyone believes him”

“Lisa—”

“Well, here’s some news for everyone. I’ve made more money than Joe for the last five years, and he’s the one who can’t deal with it. Joe and his damned macho male ego.” Lisa swiped a hand across her cheek. “I’m sorry. I need to sleep. I’m working again tonight.”

“I’m so sorry.” Brooke paused, debating whether or not to invade Lisa’s privacy any more. Fear for her own kids made her plow ahead. “Did you file charges against him?”

Lisa stared out the window. "No."

"You should think about it." Brooke pointed at Lisa's arm. "Before those fade any more. Has he come here?"

Lisa shivered and picked up her coffee. Her knuckles whitened. "He sat in the driveway one night and watched the house."

A chill crept into Brooke's belly. Two women and three kids didn't stand a chance against a guy as strong and aggressive as Joe. "Have you seen him today?"

"No."

"He's out on bail."

"Thanks for the warning." Deflated, Lisa slumped over her mug. "Joe has parents in town and two sisters who are pretty close."

"You should think about a restraining order too. For your kids' sake."

Lisa sniffed and straightened her shoulders. "Maybe I will."

"I'll let you get some rest," Brooke said. Though she doubted Lisa would be getting the sleep she needed, not after Brooke had rehashed all her marital problems.

Lisa walked Brooke to the foyer. Light streamed in through glass panes in the front door. It would take seconds for a burglar, or Joe, to break in through this door.

She turned to Lisa. "You should have a steel door with no glass. All he has to do is break a pane and stick his hand through to unlock the deadbolt."

Lisa's mouth tightened. "The way Joe's acted lately, if he wants to get in, he's coming in. No steel door or piece of paper will keep Joe out if he's mad."

Luke's car was cold when Brooke slid into the passenger seat. He started the engine, and she burrowed into the heated leather.

"She hasn't seen him." She summed up her conversation with Lisa.

"That's not encouraging news." Luke pulled away from the curb.

"No, it isn't. Joe is out there, and he's angry."

# CHAPTER TWENTY-THREE

Luke parked in front of Brooke's house and the family trooped inside. Tired from school, the kids and Brooke shed backpacks and purses as they walked. Luke itched to put everything away, except he suspected the closets were as disorganized as the rest of the house. "I fixed your windows while you were at school."

"Oh, thank you. I appreciate everything you've done for us." Brooke flashed him a grateful smile that made it all worthwhile. She headed for the stairs. "I'm going to change."

The slight limp didn't affect the sway of her hips or the way his blood heated as he watched her go up. He wanted to follow her up to her bedroom and watch her undress. Better yet, help her. The more his protective instincts kicked in, the more he ached to be with her.

Instead he went back to the kitchen, filled a glass with ice water, and drank half of it. It did little to cool his blood.

Brooke walked into the kitchen in a pair of slim jeans and a sweater. Yikes. The faded denim hugged her curves even more. Luke gulped more cold water. "Have you heard from Wade?"

She shook her head. "Not yet. He'll e-mail as soon as he gets settled. Last time he was deployed, it took a few days."

Her cell buzzed. She glanced at the display. "Excuse me." She answered the call, "Hello." A man's voice responded.

A thin wisp of jealousy swirled in Luke's belly. Which was ridiculous. Brooke could see anyone she wanted. One kiss was hardly a commitment, and he was purposefully not getting involved with her. But why did the thought of another man calling her fan that wisp into a spark of jealousy?

"Who called you?" Brooke's voice rose. "Well, I think it's relevant."

She ducked into the den and closed the door. Guess she wanted privacy. Luke strained to hear her voice through the doorway. He couldn't understand the words, but her tone was plenty pissed off.

She walked back into the kitchen. "That was my ex-husband, Ian."

She paced across the room, turned, and strode back. Shoving a straggling piece of hair out of her face, she dropped into a chair. Her head fell into her hands.

"What's wrong?" Wanting to touch her, Luke put a hand on her shoulder. Her muscles were tight and knotted under his fingers.

"Someone called Ian and told him about Joe coming here last night."

Luke circled his thumb at the base of her neck.

"The kids are supposed to be here this weekend. But he's insisting they go to his place. They have a teacher in-service day off on Monday. Maybe by Monday night, the business with Joe will be sorted out."

"But you don't want them to go."

She rubbed her forehead. "He has a point. If Joe comes back, they'll be safer with Ian." Brooke rolled her neck.

Luke put both hands to work kneading the tense muscles of her shoulders. "What's the problem?"

"Haley's going to be heartbroken." Brooke's hand dropped to the table. "She's been looking forward to the Halloween dance for ages."

"There'll be other dances."

"That's what Ian said." Her tone disagreed with both of them. Luke wasn't thrilled with the comparison with her ex-husband.

"The dance is her first date with this new boy. We've been working on her costume for weeks." Brooke closed her eyes. "Trust me. As far as Haley's concerned, this is the most important night of her life."

"Can't you just say no to Ian?"

"It's complicated. Our custody agreement actually gives him much more time with the kids than he takes. If I say no, he threatened to take me back to court. His bank account is bigger than mine. He can do that over and over and he knows it."

"That's not right."

"Anyone who says the court system is fair hasn't spent any time in it."

"Wouldn't a judge let Chris and Haley choose where they want to live? They're hardly little kids."

"Maybe." Brooke rubbed her forehead. "Unless Ian convinced the judge that their safety was at stake."

"Good point."

"It doesn't really matter." Brooke straightened her spine. "I won't put my kids in the position of having to choose between me and Ian if it's avoidable. It wouldn't be fair to them. Besides, I know he isn't really being a bastard. He's not perfect, but he's worried about the kids and trying to do what's best for them. He's never yanked any of the custody agreement strings before. And what if Joe *does* come back? What if he does something more violent than toss a brick through my window? Ian's right. I have to put their safety first no matter how much it's going to break my daughter's heart."

Luke gave her shoulders a gentle squeeze. "There *will* be other dances."

"I'm not the one who has to be convinced." Brooke stood. Dread weighted her steps as she turned around. "I might as well tell her now. On the bright side, it gives me four days to figure out what's going on with Maddie."

Wait a minute.

"Don't you mean four days for the police to figure things out?" Luke took a step back to give her room to pass.

"Right. Isn't that what I said?"

"Not exactly."

She walked down the hall to the foyer and called up the stairs, "Haley? Chris? Would you come downstairs, please?" The kids appeared a few seconds later and she filled them in on the decision.

"I can't go to Dad's tonight," Haley protested. Shock shifted to comprehension. Panic edged in, and her voice rose. "I'll miss school tomorrow, and the dance is tomorrow night."

"I'm so sorry, honey." Brooke's voice was heavy with sympathy. "You can miss one day of school, and you're going to have to miss the dance. There are too many things going on around here. Your dad and I have decided you'll be safer at his apartment."

Brooke could've tossed the blame on her ex, but she didn't.

Haley's face reddened. "But that's not fair—"

"I know." Brooke sighed, her eyes misting. Luke had no doubt she felt every ounce of her daughter's pain.

Tear welled in Haley's eyes. "I'm not going."

"This is not up for discussion." Brooke's voice was level and firm. "Go get your things together."

"What about you?" Haley argued. "If it isn't safe here for us, it isn't safe for you."

"It'll be much easier for Luke to look after just me rather than all three of us."

"This was Dad's idea, wasn't it?"

"Your father and I made the decision together."

"This is all him. I know it. He barely wants to see us, but he still has to be in control." Haley's face reddened. "Why do you always stand up for him? He left you too."

Brooke pulled back. "I don't want your relationship with your father to suffer because of the divorce."

"What relationship?" Haley said. "He put more than a hundred miles between us. He sees us on his terms. Twice a month. No more. Only at his apartment. He never comes here. He has no interest in any of my friends. He's never even seen me play field hockey."

Brooke had no defense for Ian's behavior. She'd always thought she was doing the right thing by sticking up for him. Now she wasn't sure. Ian loved his kids. He'd just never been able to show it.

Every tear that welled from Haley's eyes cracked Brooke's heart. Haley ran upstairs.

Brooke put a hand to the ache in her chest, where her daughter's pain was amplified. *Haley will be safer with Ian.* For all his faults, he wouldn't let anything happen to his kids.

She turned to her suspiciously quiet son. "No argument from you?"

"Nope." Chris grinned. "I'll have a long weekend to finish my English paper."

Brooke's face sharpened. "When's it due?"

He waved a casual hand. "Tomorrow."

"When were you going to finish it?" Brooke crossed her arms.

"Tonight." Chris patted her on the shoulder. "It's all good, Mom. If I get to miss school tomorrow, I gain a couple of extra days."

She stabbed the air with a finger in his direction. "You cannot leave long-term assignments until the last minute!"

"It all worked out. It always does." Chris turned to Luke. "You swear you won't leave her alone?"

Luke held a hand in front of him Boy Scout–style. "Swear."

"I'm holding you to that." Chris sauntered off. "I'll go grab my stuff."

Brooke pinched the bridge of her nose. "How can they both be made from the same genetic material?"

Luke assumed the question was rhetorical. "There's no chance he'd bring her back for the dance tomorrow night?"

"I already tried that. Ian refused to drive her back, and when I offered to come and get her just for the dance, he said he doesn't want the kids anywhere near Westbury for the next few days."

"Where does he live?"

"Philadelphia. Usually I'm annoyed that he moved so far away. It makes things difficult. But tonight I'm relieved. I'll feel a lot better when they're away from Westbury—and me."

Luke hugged her shoulders.

She leaned on his arm. "My knee is better. You don't have to drive us if you don't want to. It's a long trip."

"I don't mind." There was no way Brooke was getting hurt on his watch. All he could do was hope the police caught the assailant before he left for New York on Monday morning.

Two hours later Luke exited the Schuylkill Expressway onto Broad Street in Philadelphia. The kids sat silently in the backseat,

Chris upbeat, Haley sullen. She stared out the car window, occasionally wiping a stray tear from her cheek.

Brooke's head was back, her eyes closed. What was she thinking?

Luke followed his GPS, threading through the city streets until he pulled into the parking garage underneath Ian's building. He walked around the front of the car, but Brooke was already climbing out.

She glanced up at the ceiling. "Are you going to be all right going up? Ian's apartment is on the twentieth floor. I can take the kids up by myself."

"I can do it." Luke wasn't as sure as he tried to sound, but he wasn't letting her out of his sight for a second. Obviously Brooke felt the same about her kids or she would have sent them up on their own.

They walked toward the lobby. In the middle of the marble floor, a guard sat behind a desk.

Brooke approached the guard. "Brooke Davenport to see Ian Davenport. Apartment 2015."

The guard made a quick call. "Go on up."

The elevator opened. With a deep breath, Luke herded the family on board. Brooke pushed a button. They were halfway to Ian's twentieth floor apartment when Luke realized he wasn't sweating. He froze. His pulse was normal. The slight churning in his gut was worry for Brooke and her kids, not himself. Not the blind panic he'd experienced every other time he'd been in a skyscraper since the explosion.

Where was the nausea? Where were the clammy palms? Sure, he was on edge trying to watch everyone who came within ten feet of Brooke. Every male who so much as glanced at her was suspect. But the uncontrollable panic was absent.

What. The. Hell?

Was he too preoccupied with protecting Brooke to worry about his own safety? That must be it. How else could he explain the fact that he was twenty stories up in a glass rectangle and not freaking out?

The car stopped, and he ushered the group into a plush hall. A fortyish man was waiting, gray temples, fairly fit, nice suit. Chris gave his mom a hug and a goodbye. Haley put her head down and stomped off. The kids headed for an open door. Brooke hung back.

"Nice to see you, Brooke." Her ex stuffed his hands in the pockets of a pair of dress trousers. "You look tired."

"I'm fine." Brooke's face was devoid of emotion. Her voice sounded deliberately polite. She gestured to Luke. "Luke Holloway, Ian Davenport."

Ian held out a hand. "So, you're a friend of Wade's."

Luke shook it. "I am."

"Thanks for driving them down here." Ian crossed his arms over his chest. His lips pursed. Was he unhappy seeing Brooke with Luke? Too bad. Ian had tossed her away. His loss.

"You're welcome." There didn't seem to be much more to say.

Ian focused on Brooke. "Are you sure you don't want to stay too?"

"Yes, I'm sure." Brooke's tone went subzero.

Ian rocked back on his heels. "Offer stands. Just because we're divorced doesn't mean I don't still care about you."

"Thank you, Ian." Her voice warmed from freezer to fridge.

Her ex nodded. "Nice to meet you, Luke." Ian headed for the open door. "Please be careful, Brooke."

She didn't respond, but her lips flattened out as she turned away from her ex.

The elevator doors closed. Brooke turned to him. "How are you?"

"Fine." Did he sound as shocked as he felt?

"Ian seems OK." Which almost annoyed Luke.

"That's Ian. Always calm. Always composed. Nothing can rattle him." Her eyes were wet. She swiped a finger under her lower lashes and sniffed. "I can't thank you enough for bringing us here. I can't imagine how hard it was for you."

"No really. I'm fine. I can't believe it, but I'm having no issues at all." The elevator opened and they made their way through the lobby to the garage. He steered her toward his car. He watched between the rows and under the vehicles for movement. "Before the explosion, I wouldn't have wanted to celebrate a successful elevator ride. But now, I want to pop the cork on a bottle of champagne, which is actually kind of sad." He reached for her door, then paused and stepped in close.

"No, it's great." Her were misty. "I'm happy for you."

It wasn't the best time for a romantic moment, but there wasn't anyone else who would understand the importance of his milestone. "I'm glad you were here with me."

He stared at her mouth. So tempting.

"Me too." She smiled. "I guess this mean you're cured. You can get back to work."

"Maybe not cured, but it's a definite improvement." Why did the thought of going back to work ruin his mood? He should be thrilled.

Brooke went quiet. Was she thinking about the danger that waited for them back in Westbury or the fact that her children weren't safe in their own home? She was vulnerable physically and emotionally. As Luke well knew, psychological trauma could be the more debilitating of the two. Her vulnerability was one more reason Luke should keep his hands to himself and concentrate on her safety.

Luke scanned the rows of cars. Lots of places for someone to hide. He opened her door, the concrete seeping cold through his shoes. Between Monday night's assailant and Joe, danger could lurk in any shadow.

---

Brooke slid into the plush, black leather, glad to be out of the subterranean damp. She shivered, and Luke switched on the seat heater. Her butt warmed in a few seconds. "I could get used to this."

"I'm not in the country much. I've had the car for over a year, and I've barely driven it. I'm enjoying tooling around in it this week."

Soon he'd be back to traveling the globe. She tried to summon up some enthusiasm. He'd been stunned and relieved in the elevator. He deserved his happiness, but she was going to miss him. She still couldn't believe he walked right into that elevator knowing how uncomfortable it could have been for him. He'd done it with no hesitation because he cared more about her and her family than himself.

No wonder her brother trusted Luke.

He pulled into traffic and headed back up Route 676. On the Schuylkill Expressway, bumper-to-bumper traffic slowed their trip home, but once they hit the Northeast Extension of the Pennsylvania Turnpike, the traffic thinned.

Brooke's stomach rumbled as the car exited the interstate toward Westbury. A shopping center appeared in the distance, and an idea popped into Brooke's head. "How about some food?"

Luke rolled his head on his shoulders. "Good idea. I'm starving."

"Do you like Chinese?"

"Chinese is fine."

Brooke pointed ahead. "Then pull into that strip mall. The Jade Dragon has terrific pot stickers." She didn't mention that Maddie's gym anchored the center.

Luke slowed the car and turned into the entrance. He drove past Forever Fitness. Ads in the front window obscured the view inside. He parked the car in front of the restaurant. Brooke got out of the car and stretched. Her limbs were stiff from the four-hour drive to Philly and back. Luke followed her into the restaurant. Soft, instrumental flute music played in the background. The smell of food sent Brooke's stomach into another rumble.

They stepped up to the hostess podium. A tiny woman greeted them with a wide smile and slightly accented English. "Welcome to the Jade Dragon. Would you like to eat in or take out?"

Brooke glanced at Luke. The restaurant was quiet, but she had no desire to sit here and eat. What she really wanted to do was snuggle on her couch and watch another movie with him. "Do you mind takeout? I'm bushed."

"Fine with me."

The hostess handed Luke a paper menu. Brooke leaned close to read it. How did soap smell so good on him? "The pot stickers and an order of ginger chicken."

"One egg roll and beef lo mein." Luke handed the menu back to the hostess.

She gave him a short bow. "Ten minutes."

"Let's walk. My knee needs to loosen up." Brooke checked the time on her cell phone, then led Luke back outside. They ambled along, looking into storefronts, until they came to the end, Forever Fitness. "I'm going to stop in the gym and ask around."

Luke's face fell in a suspicious frown. "Why?"

Brooke lifted a casual shoulder. "I'm just going to ask for membership information and take a quick tour. Nothing wrong with that."

"Brooke, the police might not like your interference." Luke's tone dropped to low and serious.

She raised her chin. "I've been thinking about joining a gym for quite a while now. This is the closest one to my house. I heard they give discounts to teachers."

"I'm not buying it, and I don't like it." He said, but he followed her inside.

Brooke stopped at the reception desk. Behind it, a juice bar offered smoothies and protein drinks. A large matted area divided the workout area into thirds. Cardio machines were lined up in three rows on the left. A decent selection of weight machines occupied the middle of the space. Free weights spanned the right third of the room. A dozen members were spread out over the equipment.

"Can I help you?" The man at the desk said over the clink of weights and the steady thump of sneakers on treadmills. He was muscular, but not in the bulky, deformed way she'd seen at the other gym in town, a hard-core facility that trained bodybuilders. His lean physique suggested an active sport like track and field or rock climbing. Brooke read the name tag pinned to his navy blue logo T-shirt. ZACK.

"Hi. I'm a teacher at Westbury High. A friend of mine suggested your gym. Maddie Thorpe. Do you know her?"

Zack paused. He blinked away for a second. "No. I can't picture her, but we have a lot of members. I can't remember everyone."

*Liar.* "Could I look around?" Brooke smiled.

"Of course. We give discounts to teachers and students," Zack said.

Brooke raised a "told you" brow at Luke. He didn't look impressed.

Zack motioned to a teen in a Forever Fitness T-shirt. "Watch the desk, please."

He stepped out from behind the counter and led them into the main space, pointing out the obvious as they walked. "We have state-of-the-art cardio equipment, free weights, and machines. Have you ever belonged to a gym?"

"No." Running and cross-training on her heavy bag had always been enough. She eyed the defined muscles of a young girl on an elliptical trainer. Maybe she *should* add weight training to her regime.

"Every membership comes with three free personal-training sessions to get you started. Our trainers will show you how to set up and operate the machines, plus they'll develop a beginner program for you." Zack opened the door to a large room with a wood floor. Brooke stuck her head in and looked around. The front wall was mirrored; equipment lined the other three. Music blared. Two dozen men and women hoisted kettle bells. "This is our fitness class studio. We have everything from boot camp to Zumba. That's a Latin dance–based class. It burns a ton of calories." Zack's attention strayed to a well-built redhead in ultra-skimpy spandex shorts in the back row. She sensed his stare and shot him a get-real-creep eye roll.

Zack closed the door and circled back to the front desk.

"Why don't I set you both up with free two-week memberships? You can try a few classes and see what you like."

"That sounds great." Brooke filled out a short form and passed the pen to Luke.

Zack handed them two paper IDs. He slid a paper across the counter to Brooke. "Here's a class schedule." He circled five blocks on the grid. "These are the Zumba classes."

"Thank you." Brooke folded the paper and stuffed it into her purse. She turned away from the desk.

"Hope to see you soon." Zack smiled.

"Hey, Brooke."

She spun.

Greg Fines was exiting the locker room, gym bag in hand. "What are you doing here?"

She shrugged. "I've been thinking about joining."

"Don't you run all the time with the track team?" Greg asked.

*Snagged. Think fast.* "I need to start cross-training," Brooke said.

"That is important." Greg looked to Luke.

"Oh, I'm sorry." Brooke introduced them. "Have you been working out here long?"

Greg's eyes wandered to a twenty-something in spandex that was leaving the gym.

"Greg?" Brooke prompted.

"Oh, sorry." He gave her a sheepish grin. "Yoga pants are the greatest invention of the twentieth century." Greg gave Luke a nudge-nudge look.

Luke gave Brooke a what's-with-this-guy shrug.

Brooke resisted the urge to snap her fingers in Greg's face. "I asked you if you'd been working out here long."

"Years." Greg nodded like a bobblehead. "It's not like I'm going to get a workout coaching the robotics team."

"Good point." Brooke laughed.

"Well, I have to run." He was watching yoga-pants girl get into a baby-blue Prius. "See you tomorrow." He bolted through the door, stopped cold in the lot, and gave the girl a dorky half wave. She backed out and zoomed off. She did not flip him off, but it was close.

Greg pivoted and jogged across the lot. A huge grin split his skinny face.

Yup. Greg was clueless.

"I bet our food is ready." Luke held the door open.

"Probably." Brooke exited. She hugged her biceps against the dropping temperature. "Maybe I'll come to a Zumba class."

Luke sighed. "You can barely walk without limping. I think Zumba is a stretch."

Damn. He was right. "What I need is a member roster."

"I doubt Zack will give you one."

"I know. Speaking of Zack, did you catch the way he was staring at that redhead? It was creepy. She wasn't happy about it."

"I agree he was kind of a jerk about it, but those were some small shorts."

*Hm.* A pang of jealousy shot through her. "You noticed her?"

"Just vaguely." He leaned back and looked at her. "You'd look better in those shorts."

"Nice cover." Brooke snorted. Her underwear covered more.

Luke laughed, and they walked back toward the Jade Dragon. Inside, a brown bag waited for them on the counter. The aroma of fried dumplings carried to the doorway.

Brooke unzipped her purse and fished inside, but Luke already had his out. “I’ll get it.”

“Thank you.” It felt almost like a normal date.

Except they were trying to find a killer.

# CHAPTER TWENTY-FOUR

He tilted her head. The angle had to be just right. There. Perfect. He rubbed an aching muscle in his neck. Who would have thought she would've been so hard to maneuver through the narrow window? Her limbs were immobile, and her joints were stiff from being in his cellar for such a long time.

Despite the damp chill of Brooke's basement, sweat dripped down his face.

Wiping his brow on a sleeve, he straightened and assessed the scene. He moved back to stand in front of the washing machine. With the top open, Brooke wouldn't see her at first. No. She'd add clothes and detergent and then close the lid and start the unit.

That's when her eyes would pick up the anomaly. The thing that didn't belong.

Excitement hummed as he pictured Brooke freezing at the sight, then walking toward it hesitantly. Would the terror strike right away or would it take a while to sink in? Would she need to peel down the sheet before panic sprinted through her veins?

He visualized Brooke kneeling on the concrete, lifting the corner of the sheet, gasping in horror. Would she faint?

No. Not Brooke. She'd fight the terror like a champ.

His hand dropped to his groin, and he rubbed the hard bulge in his pants.

Tonight hadn't been enough. His appetite was whetted rather than sated by the evening's activities. His victim hadn't fought hard enough and had died far too quickly. He was to blame. He lost control. Choking the fight out of her had escalated to strangulation before he'd even gotten to try out the pulley system. Damn. He'd been counting on a dress rehearsal before the main show.

He adjusted the sheet over the bloody face and pulled some dark locks down over her shoulder. Better.

Now for part two of tonight's plan. He crept up the stairs and carefully opened the door to a dark kitchen. His hand swept along the wall for a light switch. He found it but hesitated. Brooke didn't have neighbors to see the light, but a car driving by wasn't out of the realm of possibility. Shuffling across the floor, he fished in his pocket for his flashlight. He palmed it and pushed the switch with his thumb. Where was the big man sleeping? Brooke had two children. She wouldn't sleep with a man while her kids were in the house. So, the big man would be sleeping on the couch. He shone the light around the kitchen and walked toward a dark hallway. He passed an office and found a cozy den. He swept his light in a wide arc. A black duffel bag was in the corner.

*Woof.*

He froze.

A car door slammed outside.

His pulse jolted.

She was home. He glanced at his watch. The basement setup had taken much longer than he'd anticipated. He turned back toward the basement door.

His feet tangled, and he fell forward. What the fuck? Brooke's damned dog cowered under his legs. Blinding anger surged through him. He kicked at the stupid creature and rooted through his pockets for a knife.

# CHAPTER TWENTY-FIVE

Brooke carried the take-out boxes into the den while Luke took the dog out back. She spread the food out on the coffee table and went back to the kitchen for forks and napkins. Luke and Sunshine walked into the room.

"She's favoring her right foreleg." Luke put a worried hand on the dog's head.

Brooke ran her hands down each of the dog's legs. "I don't feel anything. Maybe her arthritis is acting up. If it doesn't clear up in the next day or two I'll have the vet check it out."

The dog beelined for the food, the limp not slowing her down much.

"Oh, no you don't." Brooke grabbed Sunshine and gently guided her out of the den. "You had your dinner."

She closed the door.

"Poor old dog." Luke sank onto the couch.

Brooke eased down next to him. "You wouldn't say that if she crawled into your lap and stuck her nose in your carton."

She flipped on the TV and picked an old black-and-white movie. She opened the box of ginger chicken and sniffed. Her stomach growled.

Luke handed her a pair of chopsticks. "Sounds like you're hungry."

"I'm not very good with these." She reached for her fork. "They always seem like so much work."

"It's simple once you get the hang of it." He pulled another set out of the bag and ripped off the white paper wrapper. "I'll give you a quick lesson."

"All right." She opened hers.

Moving closer, he took her hand in his, the heat from his body crossing the few inches of space between them. Brooke inhaled the musky scent of his aftershave. This was definitely worth the effort of eating with giant toothpicks. Luke rested the first stick between the base of her thumb and her ring finger.

"This one stays still." His fingertips stroked her hand as he released it to reach for the second chopstick. Brooke's toes curled. Only their hands were touching. How could it feel so erotic? She became acutely aware that they were alone in the house. They could . . . She stopped that train of thought before it gathered any steam. Luke was a traveling man.

He placed the second stick between the tips of the forefinger and thumb. His fingers glided along her skin as his hand encircled hers. "Only the top stick moves." He opened and closed her fingers, pinching the sticks together.

"Give it a try." He released her hand.

Whew. Was it hot in here? She picked up a fried dumpling and dropped it on the table. "Maybe I shouldn't have locked the dog out."

Luke laughed. "Try again." He grabbed a hunk of lo mein and stuffed it into his mouth. "Slurping the noodles is perfectly acceptable."

Brooke picked up the carton with her free hand and selected another dumpling. This time she kept the container underneath as she brought the food to her mouth.

"Just bite it in half." Luke demonstrated, plucking a dumpling out of her carton and eating it in two bites. "It'll work on the rice too. You'll see."

She gathered a clump of rice and only lost a few grains on the way to her mouth. "We'll let the dog in when we're done."

The chunks of chicken were easier. It took a bit of extra time, but she got through her meal without resorting to a fork. She set the white carton down. Luke's stare was hot on her face. She turned. "What?"

"You have some sauce . . ." He leaned in and licked the corner of her mouth. "Got it."

He certainly did.

He kissed her, nudging her lips open and sliding his tongue inside her mouth. He tasted of the sweet-and-sour blend of Asian spices. Brooke's muscles went lax, her blood hummed, and the nerve endings in her lips took on a whole new life as Luke explored her mouth. Her body thought of other things that could be slipping and sliding.

Was there a reason she shouldn't get naked with him? Right here, right now, nothing seemed important enough to deny the empty ache building deep inside her.

A groan rumbled through his chest. His lips trailed to the side of her neck. His body shifted, turning toward her, seeking more contact. A big rough palm slid up her arm to her biceps and stopped inches from her breast. Her skin heated at his touch. Desire was a drug chugging through her veins. Wanting his hands on more of her, Brooke's arm moved to give him better access.

She dropped the chopsticks. A water chestnut bounced down the front of her sweater, leaving a trail of ginger sauce behind.

Luke moved back. "I'm sorry." Breathing hard, he straightened and adjusted the fit of his jeans.

Whoa. *Do not stare.* But, um, yeah. Impressive.

Brooke studied the stain on her sweater.

"I'm sorry. I shouldn't have done that." Luke retreated to the other side of the couch. "I'm not going to be here long. I have no right to start something between us."

Her heart pinged. Too late. Emotions welled into her throat, the empty ache spreading through her chest. Her desire for Luke already went beyond the physical. She needed more space than the span of a sofa between them. "I'm going to change."

She bolted for the hall. Upstairs, she rooted through a basket of clean laundry and pulled out the least sexy thing she could find, a sweatshirt at least three sizes too large. Her eyes filled as she tugged the soft fabric over her head. Damn it. How could she like him this much already? Luke was the first man who'd stirred her blood in years, and she couldn't have him. She'd thought the sexual part of her soul had died. Now she knew it was just a contrary bitch with a sick sense of humor.

She snatched her stained sweater from the dresser and went downstairs. In the kitchen, she did a one-eighty and descended the basement steps. She flipped the wall switch. Bare bulbs attached to ceiling joists cast the dusty space in harsh light. The unfinished wood steps creaked under her socks. At the bottom, she automatically scooped up Luke's dirty clothes on her way across the cracked concrete to the washer. She sprayed spot remover on the stain and tossed everything into the wash. A cap full of detergent went into the dispenser. She closed the lip and pressed start. The machine clicked, and water rushed into the tub.

A faint smell teased her nostrils. Cloying. Raw. Familiar. Brooke froze. The hair on her nape lifted, and the pit of her belly went icy. The ginger chicken and dumplings did a slow, uneasy roll.

Something was wrong. Air passed over her skin. A wave of goose bumps followed. Looking for its source, she scanned the room. Her gaze zeroed in on the small, rectangular window at the top of one cinder block wall. Open.

Panic washed through her, pushing cold sweat through her pores.

Someone had broken in. Had he left or was he still here? She wanted to shout for Luke, but fear closed around her throat like a garrote.

Heart pounding, she scanned the shadows of the basement. The punching bag cast a long shadow from the bare bulb behind it. Lots of junk down here to hide behind. Why couldn't she be organized like her brother?

She should run back upstairs and get Luke. But the smell . . . It pulled at her, the same as it had one night a long time ago. She shuffled forward. Her toe caught on the edge of the mat. Her knee twisted. The pain that zinged up her leg felt far away, as if it were emanating from someone else's body. Numbness blanketed her. She welcomed it. She moved past the washer and dryer. Her eyes riveted on a sheet-draped lump in the corner. Her lungs locked up.

*No.*

*It couldn't be.*

One of the kids had to have left something there.

Lightheaded, she shuffled forward, heart pounding in her chest, pulse echoing in her ears. Her hand reached for the edge of the sheet. Nausea rippled through her belly as she peeled it down.

She sprang backward and fell on her ass on the cement. Pain zinged up her spine from her tailbone to the base of her skull. The world spun. Her lungs constricted with shock as if she was drowning in memories.

Under a fall of dark brown hair, a bloody face stared back at her.

---

Appetite squashed, Luke gathered up the leftover Chinese and stacked the containers in the fridge. He returned to the den. Sunshine was licking rice off the carpet. Whatever. Luke ignored her and paced the room. The ceiling creaked as Brooke moved around in her bedroom.

Damn it.

*You really fucked that one up.*

Floorboards groaned in the hall. A door squeaked in the kitchen.

When Wade suggested Luke might be interested in his sister, mauling her was probably not what he had in mind. Luke took another turn around the small room. He watched in disbelief as Sunshine moved to the couch and shoved her nose between the cushions to look for stray crumbs.

He turned away. How could he criticize Brooke for living in a disorganized house and letting her dog be the vacuum cleaner? Luke's apartment might be spotless, but that was because no one lived in it. He had a service that took care of just about everything. And seriously, his emotional state was a fucking mess. What were cluttered closets in comparison?

Luke rubbed his temples. The dog snuffed and licked her way back into the kitchen.

A scream ripped through the house.

Panic grabbed Luke by the heart. He ran for the kitchen. The basement door was open. He tore down the stairs, his boots sliding on the cement as he hit the bottom. Brooke sat on the floor.

Hugging her knees and rocking, she stared straight ahead, her eyes glassy. Luke tracked her line of sight to the dim corner behind the washing machine. A woman, partially concealed under a sheet, was crumpled against the cinder blocks. He jolted, his mind briefly superimposing Sherry's face on the huddled figure. He shook the false image from his head.

*Sherry wasn't here.*

And something about the body's position didn't look right.

He walked closer. It took his brain a minute to register the disjointed limbs, the shiny plastic instead of skin, the featureless face beneath the red smears and long brown hair.

A mannequin.

*What the fuck?*

He scanned the room, felt the shift of air, and spotted the open window.

Guilt almost knocked him off his feet. He didn't go through the house tonight when they got home. They'd been gone more than five hours. He did a quick sweep of the basement. It was empty.

Brooke's erratic breathing spun him around. He went to her and squatted down. He took her hands. They were cold as the slab under his feet.

He moved his head until she couldn't look around him. "Brooke, it isn't real."

She didn't respond. Her eyes were bleak and lost.

"It's a mannequin."

She blinked.

"In a brown wig."

Her chest expanded in a huge breath. Her eyes met his, and confusion wrinkled her forehead. "It's not Maddie?"

"No."

Her muscles gave out. She collapsed forward into his arms. He picked up her shaking body and carried her upstairs. In the den, he set her on the couch. Her teeth chattered. The blanket was folded on a chair. He wrapped it around her. "I'll be right back. I'm going to call the police and check the rest of the house. Stay here."

He went into the kitchen and picked up the cordless phone. As he dialed, anger bled through his guilt. Someone had broken into Brooke's house. The dispatcher promised a quick response.

Luke hung up and checked the rest of the house. Except for the prank in the basement, nothing else looked out of place. Back in the kitchen, he grabbed a tumbler from the cabinet. Where had he seen that bottle of liquor? He opened a lower cabinet next to the refrigerator. Ah, there it was. A bottle of brandy was visible through the glass jar of a blender. He poured a long shot into the glass and returned to the den.

Brooke hadn't changed position, but Sunshine had crawled up onto the sofa and rested her head in her mistress's lap. Empathy poured from the canine eyes as she gave Luke a quick glance. Brooke's hand stroked the dog's head in an automatic motion.

Luke sat on Brooke's opposite side. He pushed the glass of liquor into her hand. "Take a sip."

She raised the glass, sniffed the contents, and wrinkled her nose before setting it on the table. "The wig was meant to look like Maddie." Brooke's voice broke.

Luke wrapped an arm around her shaking shoulders. "I know."

"But he set her up just like Karen."

Luke picked up the brandy and tossed it back. The intruder knew Brooke well enough to exploit her biggest weaknesses.

# CHAPTER TWENTY-SIX

Luke looked through the sidelight. Through the distorted glass, he saw a powerfully built man of about forty leaning heavily on a pair of crutches. Luke opened the door.

The visitor was dressed in khaki trousers and a light blue oxford shirt. A police badge was affixed to his belt. His skin was ruddy-Irish, his red hair was gray at the temples, and his nose had been broken at least once. In the driveway was the police cruiser driven by the officer who had arrived a half hour ago. Behind it sat an SUV with a circular emblem on the door.

"Police Chief Mike O'Connell." He held out a beefy hand. "Call me Mike."

"Luke Holloway." Luke shook it, then stepped back to admit him to the foyer.

The chief limped in with a grimace. "How's your grandmother?"

"OK, except for a cold. Thanks for asking."

O'Connell frowned. "I need to ask Brooke some questions."

"Of course. She's in the kitchen." Luke turned. "Gran didn't know if you were back on duty."

The chief followed. "Officially, I'm not, but I wanted to see this personally."

Luke led him back to the kitchen. Brooke sat at the table, a cup of steaming tea clutched between both hands. Sunshine had followed her from the den. The dog sat next to Brooke's chair. The big head pressed against her mistress's hip.

Brooke's eyes were locked on the basement door. Ethan was downstairs taking pictures and collecting evidence.

"Hey, Brooke. I'm going to take a look downstairs. We'll talk in a few minutes." The chief walked to the doorway and began a slow and obviously painful descent, crutches in his left hand, the handrail gripped firmly with the right.

Luke followed him down. His boots hit the concrete. The chief went to the center of the room. His blue eyes scrutinized every inch of the space.

"What do you think?" Luke hung back, out of the way.

"I think whoever did this is ballsy, and that makes me uncomfortable." Mike moved toward the window, where the black-haired officer was taking close-ups of the neatly cut glass pane. "Find anything, Ethan?"

"Some fibers caught in the window frame." The flash went off as Ethan snapped a photo. "He cut the glass, then reached through to unlock and open the window."

Simple and efficient. Discomfort stirred in Luke's chest. "Can't be fat or unfit if he came in through that window."

"Or big. I sure as hell wouldn't fit." The chief looked back at Luke. "But you could squeeze through it."

"He had to be strong enough to get that mannequin in here too," Luke said.

"Get big-picture shots too, Ethan, from every angle." O'Connell walked over to the corner and stared at the mannequin. "How much do you think it weighs?"

Luke considered. "Forty pounds, maybe, but the arms and legs only bend at the shoulders and hips. It wouldn't be easy to maneuver."

The chief leaned closer. "Looks like real blood."

"Smells real too." Unfortunately, Luke's nose recognized its raw stench.

"We'll find out for sure. And see if we can figure out where the mannequin came from. That's not something most people would have lying around." Mike gave Ethan additional instructions, then headed back to the stairs. Luke hung back, not rushing him.

The chief made a slow ascent back to the kitchen. He sank into a kitchen chair and let out a hard breath. "When was the last time someone was in the basement?"

"I went through the whole house when I brought Brooke and the kids home this afternoon. *That* wasn't down there." Luke bit back his guilt. "I didn't check it when we returned home about ninety minutes ago."

"So it was put there this evening." Mike studied Brooke. "Does it look like what I think it looks like?"

Brooke stared into her cup. A wispy swirl of steam rose from her mug. "Yes. The setup is just like how Karen was left."

"You found her, right?" Mike asked in a quiet voice.

Still studying her drink, Brooke nodded. A tremor surged through her frame, and Luke's heart cracked. He'd known Karen was killed but not that Brooke had been the one to find the body. No wonder she'd never gotten over it.

"How many people know about Karen?" the chief asked.

"Everyone. You know I tell her story ever time I teach a women's self-defense class." Brooke's voice was flat, disturbingly unemotional. "And the media rehashed the story on the news Wednesday morning."

The chief pulled a small notebook from the chest pocket of his button-down shirt. "Karen's case was closed, right?"

"Yes, her ex-boyfriend was convicted of her murder. He's still in prison." Brooke fingered her mug.

"Does he have any special reason to hold a grudge against you?" Mike asked.

"I testified about the argument he had with Karen the night she was killed." Brooke heaved a defeated sigh. "And I appeared with Karen's parents at his parole hearing two years ago."

The chief made a note. "OK. I'll verify Karen's killer is still in prison and see if he's had any interesting visitors or letters lately. It wouldn't be the first time a convict arranged criminal activity from inside prison."

"I doubt it's him." Brooke set her mug down and leveled a gaze at the police chief. "He's up for parole again next year. Why would he do anything to jeopardize that?"

The man had already committed murder. A bold threat didn't seem like much of a stretch to Luke. "Maybe he doesn't want people to protest at his next parole hearing."

"That's what I was thinking." Mike nodded. "And if it isn't him, then we're looking at someone who is doing this to torment Brooke."

Luke leaned back on the kitchen counter and crossed his arms over his chest. "Do you think it was Maddie's attacker?"

"That's another possibility." The chief rubbed his temple.

"What happened with the security cameras at the hospital?" Luke's cell phone vibrated in his back pocket. He pulled it out, glanced at the display, and shoved it back into his pocket. He had enough on his plate without past trauma adding to the mix.

"Not a damned thing," the chief said. "We couldn't find a single frame of anyone messing with the dinner trays."

"What about Joe Verdi?" Luke's phone buzzed once, indicating a voice message that Luke knew he would delete without listening to.

"Do you really think Joe would do something this calculated?" Brooke asked.

"Who knows what he's capable of when he's sober," Luke said.

"We're going to find out where Joe was tonight." The chief nodded. "Is there anyone else who might have a grudge against you? You have an ex-husband, right?"

"We split up two years ago. Nothing has changed since then. Our divorce was as amicable as any." She stopped, let out a breath. "It was Ian who left me. He has a whole new life and seems content. Plus, he was in Philadelphia when this happened." She gestured toward the basement door.

"Was he around when your roommate was killed?"

"Yes." Brooke stared at her clenched hands. "We'd been dating since junior year in college."

"Then I'd still like to talk to him. He might remember something you don't."

"I remember *everything* from that time. Every single thing." Brooke gave the chief Ian's contact information.

Mike wrote it down. "No one else? You haven't gotten into any arguments lately?"

Brooke shook her head. "No."

Mike made a notation. "Do you live here alone with your kids?"

Brooke nodded. "Luke and I dropped them off at their father's house for the weekend. After Joe's visit last night, I felt better if they were away from here for a few days."

The chief closed his notebook. "Is there anyone *you* can stay with for a few days? Give us some time to figure this out."

Brooke shook her head. "All my friends live here in town, and I won't put any of them in danger."

"How about a hotel?" Mike said. "I don't like the idea of you here alone."

Luke leaned on the back of a chair. "She won't be alone. I'll be here until Monday."

"I'm thinking about a security system. Can you recommend anyone?" Brooke asked.

Mike nodded his approval. He pulled a business card from his pocket and handed it to Brooke. "I have a friend who installs alarms. He's the best. Tell him I referred you. He'll give you a good deal."

"Thank you." Brooke slid the card into her pocket.

"I'll have the night shift drive by during the night. Don't hesitate to call if you see anything suspicious. Anything at all. If a branch rubs your window the wrong way, I want you to call us." The chief turned to Luke. "If you hear a noise outside, do not check it out by yourself. Call us. You do not want to leave her vulnerable while you play hero." A harsh light in the chief's eyes made the statement seem personal.

Luke swallowed. "Don't worry. I'm no hero."

---

Brooke set her empty mug on the table. Thumps and thuds emanated from the open basement door. Ethan carried a large, unwieldy bag through the doorway and out of the house.

The mannequin.

She shivered and rubbed her crossed arms. Luke went to the stove and turned on the burner under the teakettle.

Ethan went back into the basement and made several more trips to his car with boxes of evidence. Finally, he closed the door. "I'm finished down there. You should board up the window."

"I will. Thanks." Luke showed him out and disappeared into the basement. Trying not to jump at each hammer strike, Brooke made fresh tea, but the hot liquid did little to banish the chill in her belly.

The hammering stopped. Luke came back upstairs and slipped into a chair. "I covered it, but I'm not feeling too secure here. How about we check into a hotel for the night?"

"Can't." Brooke dropped a hand to the dog plastered to her side. "There's no way to sneak a dog this big into a hotel."

"And I guess it's too late to start calling dog sitters."

"I'm not leaving her here alone." Brooke hugged Sunshine close. Joe or whoever left the mannequin in her basement could have hurt her dog. The only threat Sunshine posed was tripping over her. In fact, Brooke wasn't even comfortable leaving the dog home while she went to work tomorrow, and she would much prefer sleeping in a hotel than with a loaded shotgun under her bed. "I guess I could leave her with Abby for a few days. We trade dogs for vacations."

Brooke reached for her cell and made the arrangements. Upstairs, she stuffed pajamas, a change of clothes, and a few other essentials into a small bag. When she came back down, Luke was packing up the dog's food. "Where are we going?"

"Just trust me."

She already did. "I guess I have to take a day off tomorrow."

"You've had a hell of a week." Luke slid his laptop into his bag and loaded the trunk.

In the car, she called the school secretary's number and left a message. Fifteen minutes later, they pulled up in front of Abby's narrow house. Brooke led the dog from the back seat. She leaned in to wipe a puddle of drool from the soft leather. Oops. Dog fur covered the seat and carpet. She made a mental note to vacuum Luke's vehicle.

Luke carried the bag of dog food to the front door. Abby's porch was decorated with pumpkins and cornstalks. Orange light twinkled from the hedges under the front window.

A throaty *woof* and the sound of heavy paws sent Luke back a step.

"It's OK. That's just Zeus," Brooke said.

Sunshine wagged her tail. In a flannel robe that covered her from neck to feet, Abby opened the door. The dog at her side was the size of a compact car. The house was a shotgun, built one room behind the other. Brooke led Sunshine into the living room. Behind it were the dining room and a small kitchen.

"Holy shit." Luke edged past Abby's mastiff and set the bag of dog food on the dining room table. "How big is he?"

"About two hundred pounds." Abby said. "But he won't hurt her. He loves other dogs, and he's very mellow."

Brooke unhooked Sunshine's leash, and the dogs went on a sniffing and wagging spree.

"Good thing," Luke said.

"Are you sure you don't want to stay here?" Abby put a hand on Brooke's arm. "Zeus is a much better watchdog than Sunshine."

"Thanks for the offer, but I think a hotel is the safest option. No one will know I'm there." Brooke could not put her friend at risk.

"OK." Abby hugged her. "Don't worry about the dog. She'll be fine."

"If she's still favoring that leg in the morning, you can give her one of these." Brooke handed her friend Sunshine's arthritis medicine. "Thanks."

Back in the car, Brooke looked over the back seat. "I'll vacuum your interior tomorrow."

"Don't worry about it." Luke shrugged. "It's just a little hair."

"Actually it's a lot of hair."

Luke laughed. "Still doesn't matter."

"Where are we going?" Brooke settled back. "Did you decide on a hotel?"

"I couldn't find anything local with enough security." Luke turned out of Abby's development and onto the main road. "It's a long drive, but I'd rather go where I know you'll be safe tonight—my place in Manhattan."

"You want to drive all the way to New York City?"

"I live in a very secure building, and I have a separate alarm system in my apartment. I really need a good night's sleep and so do you." Luke headed toward the interstate. "I don't want to worry about Joe or anyone else for the rest of tonight."

Brooke shook her head. "The mannequin in the basement doesn't feel like Joe. Too much forethought. He's angry and impulsive. He put roadkill in my mailbox and threw a rock though my window in plain sight. This was different. Whoever set the scene had to find a mannequin, research Karen's murder, and figure out when we'd be out. When did he do all that if he was in jail the night before?"

"All good points, but Joe was mad. Maybe he already looked into Karen's murder."

"And had a mannequin lying around?"

"You never know. Somebody had one handy and that's creepy enough." Luke scratched his chin. His beard stubble rasped against his fingers. "Is there anyone else who could want to hurt you like this? What about that history teacher?"

"Tony?" Brooke pulled back. "You've got to be kidding."

"He has it bad for you." Luke reasoned. "And he was very unhappy when he visited the other day."

"Tony has attached himself to other teachers. He's never stalked them."

"So? Did he ever show up on any of the other teachers' doorsteps?"

"I don't think so."

"Maybe he's more obsessed with you. His mental state could be deteriorating."

Brooke turned to the passenger window and watched the dark night roll past. Luke was right. She'd call Mike and tell him about Tony in the morning. She'd totally missed the cues that Tony was getting attached to her. What else had she missed?

She went through a mental list of everyone she knew and came up empty. Was there anyone else she'd misread? Someone who wanted to hurt her?

# CHAPTER TWENTY-SEVEN

"Brooke, we're almost there."

She jumped. Luke's hand dropped from her shoulder to her arm. "I'm sorry. I hated to wake you."

She blinked and looked out the windshield. Heavy rain poured onto the glass. The wipers struggled to keep up. Traffic streamed by even though it was past midnight. Brightly lit high-rises lined the street, their images blurred by the downpour. Manhattan.

Luke turned into an underground parking garage and stopped next to a manned booth. A yellow mechanical arm blocked the entrance. With a wave to the guard, Luke pushed a button on the sun visor, and the barrier lifted. They drove underneath, turned down two aisles, and parked in a numbered slot.

Brooke stretched and got out of the dripping car. Luke grabbed their bags from the trunk. They walked through two rows of cars. She shivered as their footsteps rang on the concrete in the damp and empty space. An elevator went up one floor and opened to an expansive marbled lobby. The setup was much like Ian's place in Philly, but there were two security guards on duty, one at a desk, the other standing unobtrusively near the elevators. A sign on the wall that read FITNESS CLUB OPEN 5 A.M. TO 11 P.M. pointed to another hallway. From an archway across the lobby, muted voices and the metallic sounds of utensils hitting plates echoed from a restaurant.

The desk guard looked up at Luke. "Good evening, Mr. Holloway."

"Good evening, Max." Luke swiped a keycard through a reader on the desk. It blinked green. He led Brooke toward the elevator.

"Mr. Holloway." The second guard had already pushed the elevator button. He held the door while Luke and Brooke boarded.

"Thank you, Phil." Luke pushed number three.

The doors closed. The ride was three seconds long. Their steps were silent on the carpet in the hall. He pulled his key from his pocket and opened the door. Brooke walked into a modern, sleek apartment. A short hall led into a spacious living room of gleaming hardwood, mahogany furniture, and deep red accents. Floor-to-ceiling windows looked out over the city street. Lights sparkled through the raindrops cascading down the glass. Everything was low-slung and long. The black granite and stainless-steel kitchen opened onto the living space.

"Wow." She ran a hand across a sideboard polished to a high gloss. Her dog and kids would trash this place in three seconds flat. Heck, *she* was afraid to touch anything. She checked to see if she'd left fingerprints on the wood. All clear.

Luke crossed the room to another short hall. He nodded toward a doorway. "I'll put your things in the bedroom. You can have the bed. I'll take the couch."

Brooke followed him into the bedroom. Space was tight, but more floor-to-ceiling windows made the room seem bigger. A king-size platform bed faced the view.

"You don't have to give up your bed for me."

"It's not a problem."

But Brooke didn't want to be alone. She wanted him. She wanted human contact, skin and heat and enough physical sensation to block out the ugly images in her head.

She glanced around the beautiful but stark bedroom. His apartment was luxurious but it wasn't warm or welcoming. Even the bed, with its perfectly smooth crimson duvet, didn't look inviting.

His apartment made it clear. They were very different people with polar opposite tastes and life goals. A relationship between them would never work. But she still wanted him.

"The bath is through here." Luke flipped a wall switch.

She glanced into the adjoining bath, full of black granite and glass. Everything gleamed. A huge multi-jet shower dominated the space. Not a smudge or speck of dust to be seen.

Luke would be returning to this life in just a few more days. She couldn't have him forever, but maybe she could have him for one night. She was damned tired of sleeping alone. She followed him back into the kitchen.

With tense movements, he opened an under-the-counter wine cooler and selected a bottle of white.

"Would you like a glass?" He uncorked it.

"I'd love one, thanks." Brooke leaned over and read the label: PINOT GRIGIO.

He poured out two glasses. Perching on the edge of a tall stool at the counter, she sipped. The wine floated, light and crisp, over her tongue and into her fluttering belly.

"How about a snack?" Luke put together a plate of cheese and crackers.

Neither crackers nor cheese settled her. She gave up and concentrated on the wine.

"Done already?" Luke gave her glass a questioning glance.

"It's very good." It flowed into her blood and settled warm over her nerves.

Luke tasted his wine. "It's a nice vintage." He ate some crackers and gestured toward the plate. "Aren't you hungry?"

"Not really." Not for crackers anyway.

Luke's apartment felt like a whole new world. One in which she didn't have to think about Karen or Maddie or bricks through windows or horrible pranks.

Just for once, she wanted to purge her mind and let her body take over.

She turned around to face his chest and slid her arms up and around his neck. "You don't have to sleep on the couch." She rose up on her toes and planted her lips against his. Her hands drifted down to unfasten the top two buttons of his shirt.

He tasted like wine and cheese. His body went ridged, and she desperately hoped she hadn't made a huge mistake. When his tongue swept into her mouth, Brooke opened to welcome it with relief. She let her hands roam across the hard planes of his chest.

"You don't have to do this, Brooke." Luke murmured against her mouth, and she hesitated. Was she doing this wrong? Was he not turned on?

Brooke slid her hand down further to cup the bulge in his jeans, and he gasped. He was definitely turned on. She unbuttoned his shirt the rest of the way. *Holy cow.* There was his stomach, all lean and ripped in a classic washboard she'd never seen outside of a magazine ad. But this was no picture. He was solid and real and within reach.

"Brooke, I don't want to take advantage of you." Luke stopped her, holding her arms firmly. His breath came in hard pants, his face was flushed, and his erection strained rather obviously against the front of his pants.

Brooke stifled a laugh at the ridiculousness of his statement. She'd kissed him. She'd unbuttoned his shirt. She'd tried to unbutton his jeans. He hadn't touched her with anything but his lips, except to keep her hands from removing any more of his clothing. Yet he was concerned about taking advantage of her.

"You've got to be kidding me."

"No. Really. It's not that I don't find you attractive. Believe me. I want you too, but you're in a vulnerable state right now. I want to be sure this is really what you want. I'm not relationship material."

Brooke just stared for a minute. She didn't know what to say. *Actions speak louder than words.*

"Luke, what I want is for you to stop talking. Now." Her hands itched to stroke his bare skin. Dark hair swirled across his chest and down into the waistband of his jeans. Brooke's eyes followed the trail. She broke the trance and pressed her body up against his. With her hands still restrained, she began to kiss her way across his chest, which turned out to be exactly the right move.

The hold on her arms relaxed as his hands slid down her upper arms in a gentle caress. Brooke swirled her tongue around his nipple, and he groaned.

"Brooke." The single word he breathed onto the top of her head did not sound anything like "please stop." It sounded much more like a "keep going, baby" kind of statement.

Brooke slipped her arms free from his grasp and flattened her hands against his bare chest. Desire swelled in her chest in a consuming wave. An ache pulsed in her belly as her mouth found his skin again. She wanted more of him. All of him. She licked her way down his chest.

He looked male, smelled male, tasted male. Her mouth moved lower, and his body jerked as her tongue rimmed his navel. His hands moved to her shoulders, but rested there, trembling lightly, almost limp.

Brooke glanced up. His eyes were riveted on her face, the lids half-closed. Sweat dampened his chest. He looked powerless, as if he was under some spell that she had cast.

Power flooded Brooke's body, and her blood began to hum through her veins. She'd never felt in charge, as if she'd entranced a man with her sexuality. Sex with Ian had always been pleasant but predictable. Ian didn't like to lose control. Ever. At the time, she hadn't minded, but then she hadn't known what she was missing. The feeling was liberating, intoxicating, freeing her from the helplessness she'd experienced all week. Luke had barely touched her, and she was more turned on than she'd ever been in her life.

Her clothing rasped against her skin, and she ached to be free of it, to feel Luke's skin sliding over hers.

Brooke stood up and grasped the hem of her sweatshirt, prepared to draw it over her head. Then she stopped. If she could see him this well, and she was enjoying the sight, then he would be able to see her just as clearly. Running kept her in decent shape, but her flat stomach was marred by silvery stretch marks that the bright kitchen lights would highlight. She'd experienced a sexual revival in the past few days, but her confidence hadn't recovered *that* much. Dimmer lighting was definitely a necessity. Candlelight would be perfect.

"What's wrong?" Luke's voice was edged with concern. "If you're having doubts, you don't have to go through with this. We can stop anytime you want."

"No. Believe me. I want to go through with this. You have no idea how much I want to go through with this." She hesitated.

She did not need to point out any more of her insecurities. "Let's go in the bedroom where it's more comfortable." She took his hand and led him from the kitchen.

In the bedroom, she pulled him close again, letting her hands trail across those amazing abs. City lights filtered through the rain-splattered glass, but the room was more shadow than light. She spread her fingers across his flat, hard belly. Good Lord, those Abercrombie & Fitch models had nothing on him.

Luke pulled away. "Hold on." He moved a switch on the wall. Blinds lowered over the windows with a soft whirring sound. He reached for the bedside lamp.

She put a hand on his arm. "How about lighting those candles instead?"

"I want to see you." His voice was thick and hoarse and turned her on even more. But still.

"Ah, but that's the thing. I'm not so sure I want to be seen." Her eyes dropped to the floor. "My body's not exactly perfect anymore."

"Brooke." Luke reached for the light and switched it on. "No one's body is perfect. I want to see everything." He stood there for a few long seconds, silently weighing some unspoken factors.

Brooke held her breath. Was he changing his mind?

Finally, he took a step backward and spoke. "I'll tell you what. I'll show you mine if you show me yours. Then we'll see if *you* still want to sleep with *me*." The stoic expression on his face told her he feared her rejection, and her heart swelled at the courage his offer had required. He shrugged out of his own shirt and turned around.

Brooke barely contained the breath that wanted to *whoosh* right out of her lungs at the sight of the angry scars that covered his back like badly matched patchwork. Despite the months that had passed since he incurred his injuries, some of the scars looked fresh and raw.

"Does it hurt?" The question came out in a whisper.

"Not much. The skin has no feeling in some spots, and is unusually sensitive in others. Sometimes it itches. It's stiff." He turned back around to face her. "Still interested?"

Had he really thought she wouldn't be? If anything, his display of trust turned her on even more.

She nodded and raised an eyebrow. "Oh, yeah."

The smile spread over his face slowly, and then turned into a humorous leer. He wiggled an eyebrow back at her. "Your turn."

Brooke grasped her sweatshirt and drew it up over her head. Luke's eyes brightened as he stared at her breasts, held into a lovely and enticing position by a worth-every-nickel push-up bra. Her nipples tingled and tightened as if he'd touched them. She hooked her thumbs in the waistband of her jeans and slowly drew them down over her hips and legs. In just her string bikini, she stood in front of him, just out of reach.

"Take them off." His demand was more breath than voice.

Brooke reached behind her and unhooked the bra. The straps slid down her arms as it fell to the floor. She bent to wiggle out of her panties and looked up at Luke. The hunger on his face as he surveyed her naked body wiped out all her doubts. Her blood began to hum again.

Standing before him as he stared at her, Brooke found the fact that she was nude and he was still mostly dressed erotic. He hadn't moved, but the vein in the side of his neck bulged rhythmically with each beat of his heart.

Brooke stepped toward him and pressed her bare breasts up against his chest, rubbing her nipples against the coarse hair. He raised his hands tentatively to her shoulders and separated their bodies a few inches. Brooke watched, fascinated by the slight tremble in his fingers as he slowly stroked downward over her breast with one hand. He cradled her in his palm. She closed her eyes and leaned into his touch.

"I want to savor every bit of you. There's no rush." He whispered as his lips brushed her temple.

Actually, there was, and his statement only fueled the fire within her. Brooke was going to blow a fuse if she didn't get him inside her soon. But Luke seemed content to just touch her breast, staring at his own hand as if he was completely fascinated with the weight and softness of her in his fingers. Brooke, however, had lots of other body parts that begged, yelled, clamored to be stroked. An ache that only Luke could satisfy.

He needed to feel the urgency that coursed through Brooke's veins in a thick and hot rush.

She raised her eyes to his again and pressed a palm against his erection through his pants. His breath caught and quickened as her fingers worked the button of his jeans. She drew the zipper down carefully and freed him into her palm. Well, more than her palm. He was huge and heavy as she cradled him in her hand. Satin over steel.

His thumb moved to brush her nipple, and Brooke felt the tingle all the way deep into her belly. Urgency replaced her need to feel powerful. She drew his jeans down to his knees and pushed him backward toward the bed, his erection as impressive as a Manhattan high-rise. As she tossed his pants aside, his hand closed over hers. The veins in his forearm corded with tension. So much for him not being as aroused as her.

"Nightstand." His words were guttural and strained.

Brooke reached into the drawer and drew out a box of condoms.

She handed him one and tossed the rest onto the nightstand. Vaguely she thought she should be nervous, but her belly only tightened with anticipation.

The foil was slippery in Luke's sweaty fingers.

"Maybe I'd better get that." She took it from him and tore open the package, wondering if she'd remember how to put one of these on. It had been many years since she'd needed to use a condom. Luckily, it turned out to be much like riding a bike, and the basic design hadn't changed in two decades.

Brooke climbed on top of him and straddled his hips.

His hand slid across her belly and down between her legs, gently exploring and testing. He needn't have worried. She was more than ready. She was so far beyond ready; she was going to finish all by herself if he didn't get a move on.

And damn, wouldn't that be a shame?

One finger slid inside of her, and he tensed. As she moved to lower herself onto him, his hands gripped her hips, stopping her descent.

"What's wrong?" Brooke panted, trying to keep the edge of irritation out of her voice. So close and yet so far away.

"I don't want to hurt you." His face tinged red, both from exertion and a faint trace of embarrassment. "I'm a . . . a big guy, and you're so . . . ah . . . small."

Brooke could not contain the short burst of laughter that shot from her lips. She quickly covered her mouth to stifle any further giggles. If there was one steadfast rule about men and sex, it was that a woman shouldn't laugh when they talk about their man parts. It tended to spoil the mood.

Luke raised one brow.

"I'm sorry. I'm not laughing at you. Really." She took a deep breath and calmed herself. She did not want to talk. She wanted his huge erection inside her right now, rubbing her where she ached, but he was so darned considerate. "Trust me. I'm going to appreciate everything you've got for me." With that last statement she took him into her body in one long stroke.

*Holy . . .*

He filled her completely. She held still, letting her body adjust to his presence.

Whoever said that size didn't matter was *so* full of shit.

Brooke rose and eased down on him. Luke's body snapped tight and arched up off the bed. Sweat beaded his forehead and chest. His hands reached up to cup her breasts. Callused thumbs stroked her nipples.

With palms flattened on his stomach, she moved again, savoring the feel of the slow stroke inside her body.

He pulled her down to his chest and breathed in her ear, "Brooke."

Luke's hands grasped her hips. Fingers circled around to squeeze her ass. His chest heaved as she slid up and down on his chest. "Easy. Don't want it to end this soon."

But Brooke couldn't control the movement of her hips. They pulsed faster until Luke wrapped both arms around her and, with a quick roll, flipped her onto her back.

He slowed his movements, but Brooke was already too far gone to stop.

"No. Faster. Please." *Almost there.*

He grunted and rose over her. Supporting his weight with his arms, he drove into her. Brooke clutched at his shoulders as the climax built. The pressure increased until she could barely breathe.

Sweat mingled. Luke's hips thrust faster. Her body slid on the sheets. Brooke reached for the headboard and held on.

Brooke closed her eyes as bright, multi-colored lights flashed and pulsed behind her eyelids. Tension coiled deep in her belly. Her body jerked and she closed tight around him as pleasure burst through her core, flooding her veins with heat.

Luke's back arched, and his body stiffened for a long moment. Then he groaned, shuddered, and collapsed on top of her. "Thank God."

He drew his elbows under his arms and supported his weight. Then neither of them moved as they both sucked air into their deprived lungs.

Finally, Brooke opened her eyes. She planted her hand in the center of his chest. His heart hammered against her palm. Luke smiled and leaned down to kiss her on the lips. "Thank you."

"I think that's my line." Brooke grinned back at him. His face was more relaxed than she'd ever seen him. Her hand stroked down his rib cage. He could use a little weight, but the man was fit.

"That was amazing, but I'd envisioned something a little . . . slower."

"Sorry. Couldn't wait any longer." Brooke twirled her fingertip in the hair on his chest. "We could always do it again."

"Practice does make perfect."

# CHAPTER TWENTY-EIGHT

The shadow of the three-story brick building fell over his car. In the darkness, rain sluiced off the windshield. He stared through the rivulets at the apartments in front of him. What would be seen by some as an inconvenience tonight was a blessing to him. The downpour would obscure visibility and keep people inside.

The apartment complex, comprised of three buildings surrounding a courtyard full of crabgrass, was large enough that residents surely did not know all their neighbors. Scraggly shrubs flanked the entrances. The parking lot made up the fourth side of the square. Each building had its own secure entry. Guests needed to be buzzed inside. But he knew all he had to do was wait.

Selena, the waitress in 12B, started her shift at 10:00 p.m. He checked the luminous dial of his Timex. She should be coming out any minute.

A young woman appeared in the glassed-in lobby. Right on time. He flipped up the hood of his jacket, reached for his door handle, and got out of his car. Rain pelted nylon as he sprinted for the building. His boots splashed in shallow puddles. He reached the door just as she was exiting.

"Here you are." As polite and sweet as usual, the pretty brunette held the door open with one white waitress shoe while popping up an umbrella.

"Thanks." He kept his face turned down and his shoulders hunched over as he stepped inside and shook the water from his jacket, dog-fashion. Huddled under her umbrella, the waitress jogged to her car. Lovely. He'd spent some time watching her before he'd selected Maddie as his prize this year. Perhaps that hadn't been the best decision.

One he could rectify at some point. Not now, though. He already had his hands full tonight.

He waited until Selena drove off, then lingered a few more minutes. The rest was a bit tricky, but if he could pull it off . . .

Well, Brooke was going to get quite a shock.

He wished he could have seen her reaction when she found the mannequin. All this preparation was like tenderizing her, letting her marinate in her own terror until she was ready to be his main course.

All was dark and quiet. He shoved a large rock between the door and the jamb, holding it open. Then he returned to his car.

Sheets of rain poured down on him as he pulled the tarp-wrapped bundle out of the trunk. He staggered. The woman was much heavier than the mannequin he'd stashed in Brooke's basement, but she was more pliant. He shifted his grip, and pain shot through his wrist. Normally, he'd be able to lift her deadweight without issue, but the earlier adventure at Brooke's house had taken its toll. Too bad he hadn't had time to kill the stupid dog that tripped him.

Rain dripped from the visor of his hood as he stumbled across twenty feet of concrete to the entrance. He toed the door open and scanned the stairwell. No one above or below. Using the handrail for balance, he took her down one flight.

He turned and nudged the basement door open with the back of his shoulder. In the dim light of an emergency-exit sign, two pairs of washers and dryers were lined up on one side. The storage units on the right were cheap, chain-link jobs, more dog kennels than proper storage lockers. Tenants secured their bikes, skis, and other outdoor gear with combination locks. The cloying scent of fabric softener mixed with the smell of mildew.

He carried her toward the far corner, just beyond the laundry area, and stretched her out on the floor. Holding the loose end of the plastic with one boot, he gave the body a shove with his other. She rolled over twice, the tarp falling away, her arms slapping onto the cement with a fleshy sound. The neatly folded sheet he'd stashed inside the tarp with her fell loose. He dragged her by the armpits to the corner and propped her up. Then he shook out the sheet, covered her body, and folded the edge over her head. Her face, once so pretty, was too battered to interest him any longer, but he hardened at the memory of how it got that way. His fists alternately pummeling her face and encircling her throat while he pumped between her flailing legs. The whimpers rasping from her bloody lips had sounded just like the mewling of a dying kitten.

The whole time he'd pictured Brooke's face and body in place of his victim.

What would it be like to render such a strong woman helpless? To invade her body in every way he could envision. He had quite an imagination and plenty of experience to call on.

His hand drifted to his crotch. He stopped himself. He needed to practice self-control before his time with Brooke came. Their night together couldn't be a repeat of tonight's premature finish. No. He had big plans for Brooke.

He adjusted the sheet over the bloody face. Now for the finishing touches. He threaded the earring through the hole in her ear. He struggled to hook the tiny backing with his latex-gloved fingers. He jammed it onto the post. There. From his pocket, he drew a necklace. Sterling silver glimmered in the emergency-exit light. He fastened the chain around her neck and adjusted the pendant to the center of her naked chest, right over the name he'd carved in her skin.

Perfect.

# CHAPTER TWENTY-NINE

*Luke stumbled down a smoke-filled stairwell. Pain blasted through his back. With every step, the unwieldy load of guilt he carried grew heavier. He staggered under its weight. His lungs screamed. His head reeled. The toe of a wing-tip caught on a tread. He tripped, grabbing the metal handrail to steady himself.*

*Pausing for two deep breaths of foul air, Luke swayed.*

*Can't stop now.*

*He gathered his panic and harnessed it to propel him forward again. A concrete landing. A one-eighty. Another flight of steps. He turned again, his aching thighs rubbering out on him. Another group of people rushed past. An elbow brushed his ribs, the small jostle enough to throw his stride off again.*

*An older man coughed. He wiped soot from his face with the sleeve of a silk shirt and squinted at Luke through the haze. "Can I help you?" he asked in Spanish.*

*But Luke couldn't let him. Couldn't let go of the railing. If he stopped to think, he'd never get moving again. He shook his head and continued downward, spiraling into nothing.*

Luke jerked awake, his body covered with a film of sweat. His breath came in pants and his heart hammered against his rib cage. His eyes darted around the strange room. The nightmare had been as vivid as usual, in full color and surround sound, and it was a few minutes before he oriented himself in his bedroom.

In bed. With a very naked Brooke. Her hand rested on his chest. The top of her breast swelled over the edge of the comforter.

Thank God he hadn't fallen out of bed, and what a shame he needed to move.

But the adrenaline that rushed through his veins like class-five rapids demanded a physical outlet. Sleep would be impossible for the remainder of the night. As would lying still and trying to pretend it hadn't happened. Folding back the warm down blanket, he eased his body away from Brooke and toward the edge of the bed.

"Luke?"

He glanced over at Brooke's tousled head as she sat up behind him. The concern in her eyes sent a flood of humiliation through him. "Everything's fine. Go back to sleep."

"Everything is not fine. You look like you just ran the fifteen-hundred meter." The slight edge of anger in her voice took Luke by surprise. "And I will certainly not go back to sleep."

He paused, reluctant to share any of the gory details about his horrific experience. Brooke had enough of her own terrible memories to carry. Part of him wanted to unload some of his guilt and pain, but Brooke didn't need more violent images in her head. Besides, talking about it didn't really help. It just made him think about it more, and his epic failure was the last thing he wanted to reflect on.

Plus, he liked keeping her separate from his nightmares. She made him laugh, made him forget sometimes, just for a little while, what had happened over there. Well, maybe forget was too strong a word. He'd never forget. But when she was nearby, those memories weren't always front and center in his mind.

Right now, Brooke waited, her eyes turned up expectantly toward him.

“Sometimes I have nightmares. I’m sorry that I woke you.” He explained. He crossed the room and rummaged for a pair of sweatpants.

“Where are you going?”

“I can’t go back to sleep. I usually go for a run.” He pulled the pants over his hips and went back to the dresser for socks.

“It’s the middle of the night.” Brooke shifted to dangle her legs off the edge of the bed, holding the covers up over her breasts against the chill in the room.

“I know.”

Brooke turned her head toward the window. “It’s also cold and pouring rain outside.”

“That’s OK.” He shivered and reached for a shirt. “I’m sorry, Brooke. A couple of miles ought to do it. I won’t be long.”

Luke pulled away, drawing back into that lonely, painful place like a wounded animal seeking its den. Last night he’d talked with her, laughed with her, made love to her, but as soon as his memories resurfaced, he slammed himself shut. He didn’t want to close himself off from the world; he couldn’t help it.

“Stop apologizing. And stop getting dressed. You can’t go running in the freezing rain. You’ll get pneumonia or hypothermia or something.” Her matter-of-fact tone left no room for argument. She rose, letting the quilt fall away from her body, and strode, naked, to stand in front of him. She was beautiful and wholesome, the exact opposite of all the visions swirling inside his head. “Besides, you promised you wouldn’t leave me alone.”

More guilt. He clenched his hands in his shirt to conceal the shaking. Not possible. No doubt Brooke noticed but was kind enough to pretend she didn’t. Denied his routine energy outlet, he was lost. His heart raced through his chest, as if looking for a place to hide.

"What you need is a hot shower. Come on." She grabbed a condom off the nightstand, took him by the hand, and pulled him into the bathroom with her. He followed with no resistance.

He eyed the condom she set on the shower ledge. "Brooke, I don't know if this is a good idea."

"Sh. Just relax. That's just in case. I know you're probably not in the mood." After leaning in to turn on the spray, Brooke turned and tugged his sweatpants down his legs.

She pulled him under the warm water with her. Her hands slid up and around his ribs. Moving up his back, her fingers passed over a burn scar. Luke flinched.

"I'm sorry. I didn't mean to hurt you. Is the water too hot?"

Unsettled and speechless, he simply shook his head, trying to concentrate on Brooke instead of his still-weak knees.

The warm water sluiced over their bodies, and a few moments was all it took for Luke's lagging brain to figure out that it had a wet, naked woman at its disposal. His hand drifted toward her breast, then stopped.

"You can touch me if you want." Her voice was husky with desire.

"I'm too sweaty." His voice strained in his throat as he reached for the soap.

"Hey, one of the rules for showering with another person is you're not allowed to wash yourself. It takes all the fun out of the experience." She took the soap from him and lathered his chest and arms, massaging the muscles firmly as she moved across his skin. As Brooke's hands slid over his torso, his empty ones sought her body automatically, running on pure primal instinct.

Something shifted inside him, from helpless confusion to arousal. His hands stopped trembling and squeezed her flesh with purpose. They kneaded her breasts and slid down to her hips. For a brief second he slid one hand between her legs, stroking, testing. Then, his control shattered. He dropped to his knees and pressed his mouth against her center. His mouth suckled and his tongue lapped with a desperate need to replace every sense—every memory—with Brooke. The scent and taste of her flooded his nose and mouth. Her soft moans filled his ears. His hands held her smooth skin. He looked up. Her head was tilted back, her eyes closed. Her body bowed back against the tiles as he devoured her, drove her. Her back arched and her hips jerked uncontrollably against his relentless mouth.

Luke lurched to his feet. His slippery fingers fumbled with the condom. Finally, he curled his hands around the backs of her thighs and lifted her up, pinning her to the cool tile, burying himself deeply with one desperate thrust.

Need made him huge and hard. Fresh, deeper pleasure speared through Luke from his toes to the base of his spine. He'd never wanted a woman with this intensity, needed her for his very survival.

"Shit. Brooke." Still for a moment, he panted in her ear. "I don't want to hurt you."

His heart galloped toward the finish line, and fresh sweat broke out across his back as he fought for command of his body. His control slipped through his grasp like water.

"You're not. Please, Luke. Harder." Brooke gasped, holding on to his shoulders as his pace quickened, arching her back and wrapping her legs around him to take him deeper into her body. "God, yes. That's it. Just like that."

He responded to her encouragement with the force of the tide, driving harder and deeper with each thrust. Her back slapped against the wet tile. She clung to his shoulders and rode out the storm. Her body tightened around him, the pressure bringing him to the precipice. The tension deep in his spine coiled tighter until he couldn't hold it back any longer. It burst forth with lightning speed. His muscles gathered and heaved. He shuddered and jerked, surging against her and shuddering again before quieting.

His depleted body pressed against her, his forehead resting on the smooth skin of her shoulder. Air bellowed in and out of his lungs. Drained, Luke shivered violently. The water pounding on his back had grown ice cold.

She pushed lightly against his chest and he released her, letting her slide slowly to the floor. His thighs Jell-Oed as he reached behind him and turned off the spray. No wonder. After what had just happened between them it was a miracle his legs would hold him upright.

He'd never experienced anything like that ever before in his life.

Luke shivered again. He brushed a hand across Brooke's wet shoulder. Goose bumps had broken out all over her arms. Leaning out of the door, he grabbed two thick towels, wrapped one around her body and rubbed her from head to foot. When they were both dry enough, she took the lead once again, leading him back into the bedroom and pulling him down to the bed. She tossed the heavy comforter up over their chilled, damp bodies.

Luke wrapped his long arms around her and held her against his chest. He tipped her chin toward his face, momentarily speechless. That had been the most amazing sexual experience of his life. Nothing in his history could even come close. It felt as if he'd never truly made love to a woman before tonight.

Sex with Brooke was a miracle. She was a miracle.

Luke concentrated on the woman in his arms. He inhaled deeply, drawing the scent of her sex into his nostrils. He could still taste her on his lips, feel her soft skin pressed against him. She filled his senses with pleasure and blotted out the pain.

He would never have enough of her.

“Brooke. I . . .” He didn’t know how to express the gratitude that swelled in his chest and clogged his throat.

“Sh.” She pressed her finger against his lips. “I’m going to consider what just happened as one major benefit to dating a younger man.”

“Thank you.” Luke lightly kissed her temple and pressed his forehead to hers. She had no idea what she had just done for him, what he felt for her.

“I wouldn’t thank me just yet. Now that I know what you can do, I’m going to want a lot more of that.” She smiled up at him.

He grinned back at her. “Sure as hell beats a ten-mile run in the freezing rain.”

“I should hope so,” she answered with mock indignation and smiled up at him.

He tucked her against his chest, her body soft and warm against his, her scent in his nostrils. And for the first time since he returned home, he fell back to sleep.

# CHAPTER THIRTY

The basket of laundry dug into her hip. Selena Vasquez trudged down the three flights of stairs to the basement of her apartment building. Her slippered feet scuffed on the dingy blue carpet, worn to a muddy gray down the center of the treads. In the vague light of the stairwell sconces, she rounded the last turn, the metal handrail wobbling under her grasp. At 5:45 a.m., the sky was still dark. Her aching head and feet yearned for sleep, but she didn't have a clean uniform for tonight's shift. She just couldn't bring herself to put one on that already stank of grease. It didn't matter that the fresh outfit would absorb the oily odors within minutes of starting her shift at the diner. She just couldn't do it.

Nor could she rest well with chores undone. She blamed her mother, who had ruled the family house with a combination of hard work and Catholic guilt. Selena would wash the scent of French fries from her hair and finish her English paper while her clothes washed. Then she'd sleep until her night class at the community college and yet another shift.

Two more years.

She bumped the door open with a hip and flipped the wall switch. The bare bulb flickered and went out. Awesome. Just what this creepy room needed—more creep. She propped the door open. Light from the hall trickled in. The pocket full of quarters jingled as she crossed the concrete and dumped her clothes into the empty machine. She added detergent and closed the lid. Six coins were inserted in their slots. She slid the metal tray in with a *click*. Water rushed into the tub and the machine churned.

Dust tickled her nose. She sneezed and sniffed. Another odor reached through the dust, something simultaneously sweet and raw. She set her basket on top of the dryer and scanned the space. Dirty and dark, it was not a room she cared to dwell in any longer than necessary, but something was wrong. The hairs on the back of her neck lifted. A primitive alarm cramped her belly. Was someone hiding in here? She squinted into the shadows. Her gaze fell on a form in the corner.

A sheet draped over something.

She shuffled two steps forward. Her eyes adjusted to the dim light. Her gaze fell on a lock of dark hair poking out from under the gray fabric. Her belly clenched tighter. Her eyes refused to believe what her instincts were telling her. Her slippers scuffed the concrete until she stopped a foot from the base of the bundle. She reached forward and tugged on the bottom hem of the sheet. It slid down to reveal the bloody face of a dead woman.

Selena stumbled backward and screamed.

---

Gray light washed over the stark bedroom. Brooke moved her legs under the covers. The crisp sheets slid, smooth and decadent, against her naked skin. Luke's apartment was stark, but she couldn't deny enjoying the luxurious linens and fixtures, like an indulgent vacation in a five-star hotel. She felt safe here too. Isolated from the fear that had taken over her usually routine life, but also separated from the responsibilities of single motherhood and her teaching career.

When was the last time she'd slept naked? She couldn't remember, which was just plain sad. Nudity was something a mom of teenagers just couldn't indulge in outside of the shower. But here, with Luke, she wasn't just someone's mom. She was a desirable woman.

She turned her head. Next to her, Luke slept on, the covers pooled around his waist, his bare torso on display. Her hands itched to stroke the sinewy muscles of his chest and shoulders, but he needed the rest after last night's panic attack—and all that had come after.

He hadn't shared the source of his pain, but he'd no doubt dreamed about the explosion. The incident had left deep scars on his back—and in his soul. Strangely enough, his vulnerability had drawn her closer to him, like she wasn't the only one with a violent past she couldn't shake. In sharing his pain, she was less alone.

She snuggled back down into the duvet and pillows. One heavy arm was thrown across her waist, and the possessive feel of it pleased her more than it should. This was temporary. She shouldn't get used to it. But a warm bed and a sexy man were an intoxicating combination she hadn't experienced in many, many years. She deserved some time to enjoy it, but the fact that this moment was fleeting dimmed her pleasure.

Luke had grown on her more than she should have allowed. The joy booming in her chest after last night's lovemaking blindsided her. One night together and she was this attached? How would it feel when he left for another continent?

*Buzz.*

She tracked the sound to the nightstand, where her cell phone rested next to the clock. She hadn't slept until nine in years. Of course, she hadn't exactly slept through the night. Satisfaction and heat pulsed through her veins at the memories. Her heart might be timid, but her body was definitely not. Maybe he could be persuaded to take another shower together this morning. She closed her eyes, determined to ignore the phone. It vibrated again, and the irrationally worried mother inside of her reached for it on instinct.

The number read TOWNSHIP OF WESTBURY. Her heart jolted as she pressed the green ANSWER button. "Hello?"

Luke stirred. Bedding rustled as he turned toward her.

"Brooke?" A male voice asked.

"Yes." Brooke's voice quivered with nerves. She cleared her throat.

The caller exhaled hard. "This is Mike O'Connell. Are you all right?"

"I'm fine, why?"

Next to her, Luke rose to his elbow and watched her with groggy but worried eyes. She lifted the phone an inch from her ear so he could hear.

"We called your house, but no one answered," Mike said.

"I took your advice and left town for the night." Why would the police be calling her house? Fear pulled Brooke to a sitting position. She tugged the duvet up over her breasts and hugged her knees. "What happened?"

"That was smart. I need you to come down to the station and answer some questions." The chief evaded. "Where are you?"

"New York City."

"It's important, Brooke." Mike's tone was dead level. "Can you come in later this morning?"

Brooke's empty stomach clenched. "Why don't you tell me what happened?"

Mike hesitated. He breathed the words out in a sigh. "A woman was killed last night."

"Maddie?"

"No. Maddie is fine."

"Who?" Brooke felt Luke's hand on her arm, steadying, calming. She took it in hers and held on.

"We don't know yet." Mike said in a soft voice. "We were hoping you might help us figure that out."

"Why do you think I might know her?" Panic rose in Brooke's chest. Luke squeezed her hand tighter. He scooted over to wrap his other arm around her shoulders. Brooke leaned into him as she waited for an answer she knew was going to be horrible.

"Because she was laid out like your roommate." The chief paused. "And your name was carved into her skin."

---

Brooke shielded her eyes against the late morning sun as she got out of the car in the Westbury police station parking lot next to a Coopersfield PD cruiser. The breeze that swept dead leaves across the asphalt was bitterly damp and cancelled out any warmth the sunshine could have provided. She burrowed deeper in Luke's borrowed sweater.

Luke opened the door and steered her through the entrance. In the lobby, Brooke wiped her shaking hands on her jeans. The rest of her body was twitchy too, each round of trembles started in her bones and radiated through the rest of her before fading like the final tremors of an earthquake. Her knees were loose as yarn. She hugged her arms and concentrated on the warmth of Luke's hand at the small of her back. It was the only part of her anatomy not freezing cold, and those six square inches of support might be all that was between Brooke and the floor.

Ethan spotted them and waved them past the counter.

"This way." He led them to a small conference room. Chief O'Connell and another man in his late forties sat on the backside of an oval table. Officer Kent occupied the chair on the right. Open files and papers were strewn across the pale gray laminate.

As they entered, O'Connell closed a file of photos. He stood, his face straining with the effort, and shook their hands. "Thanks for coming."

Ethan followed them inside and closed the door.

"You know Officer Kent from Coopersfield." The chief introduced them. "This is retired Philadelphia homicide detective Jack O'Malley. Due to his experience with violent crime, I've asked him to consult on this case."

The former cop was tall and thin, with some gray mixed into a head of short, dark hair. A cane hung on the back of his chair. "Call me Jack." He stood to shake their hands.

"Please sit." The chief waved toward the empty chairs opposite him. "Thanks for driving back."

"After the break-in last night, I wanted to get Brooke away from here." Luke pulled out an office chair for her.

"I can appreciate that." The chief frowned. "Unfortunately, it gets worse."

Brooke sank into the cushioned seat. Luke sat and edged his chair closer. Under the table, his hand found hers and gripped it tight. She gathered strength from her reserves—and from him. After last night, she knew he had faced enough horror to understand. "What happened?"

The chief began. "A woman was found in the basement laundry room of an apartment building early this morning. She was positioned similarly to the mannequin in your basement."

Brooke held on to Luke's hand. "Do you know who she is?"

The chief's fist balled up and thudded once on top of his file. "We're waiting on confirmation."

"I don't understand." Terrible-information overload was frying Brooke's brain. "Why wouldn't you . . .?" The dots connected themselves. Her empty stomach rolled over, and her head did a quick swim. She hadn't even been able to get a cup of coffee down this morning.

"Her face was too damaged for a visual identification," the chief confirmed. "But there is a local woman who's been missing since late Wednesday night."

"Who?"

"I'm sorry. I can't say anything until we have confirmation. The family deserves to know first." The chief lifted the corner of his file. He slid a picture out. "Do you recognize this?"

Brooke pulled the picture toward her by one finger as if it were tainted by violence. Her lungs collapsed. "That's Maddie's earring, the match to the one her assailant left on her hospital tray. You're sure Maddie is all right?" *Please, please, please God.*

Luke wiggled his hand from her grip and wrapped his arm around her shoulders. Did he know she needed help staying upright?

"Maddie is fine," the chief said. "I spoke to the officer at her house this morning."

Relief sent another wave of dizziness spinning through Brooke's head. She inhaled deeply, then remembered that a girl was still dead. It just wasn't Maddie. Brooke wanted to ask why she was here, but her throat locked up, dry and tight as if packed with chalk dust.

Luke's hand rubbed her shoulder. He reached across his lap with his free hand and interlocked their fingers. "What do you want from Brooke?"

Jack looked up from his notes. Though Luke asked the question, Jack addressed Brooke. “We’re hoping you can give us information. Are you sure you’re up for all this?”

Brooke nodded. “Yes.” Her voice was a breathy rasp.

“Ethan,” the chief said. “Get Ms. Davenport some water.”

“Yes, sir.” The young officer exited.

Mike gestured to the seated cops. “Kent, why don’t you start with an update on Maddie Thorpe’s assault?”

“Right.” Kent opened his file. “We recovered DNA samples from under Maddie Thorpe’s nails. Those samples are being run through the national DNA database, CODIS. So far, we haven’t gotten any hits. Three weeks ago, a woman was raped in Hillside. DNA was recovered in that case as well. Since both of the victims were joggers attacked in the woods, we’re comparing the DNA in both assaults. The blood type is the same, but it’s O positive. Roughly forty to fifty percent of the population is O positive, so that doesn’t tell us much. You saw the composite sketch?” He raised his brow at Brooke and Luke.

“Yes,” Luke answered. “Chief O’Connell showed it to us.”

“We have no other leads. No one saw or heard anything. Hillside PD is still working their case, but they haven’t come up with anything new.” Kent turned his attention to Jack. “We don’t really know if the two cases are related. What do you think?”

“It’s hard to say. There are similarities in the cases, but enough differences to give me pause.” Jack glanced down at the paper. “We are, however, proceeding on the assumption that the killer from last night is the same man who attacked Maddie and left the mannequin in Brooke’s basement. He left Maddie’s earring with the corpse to make sure we connected the cases. The substance on the mannequin’s face was human blood. It matches the blood type of our murder victim, B positive. It’s not the most common blood type, roughly nine percent of the Caucasian population. It will take a few weeks for the DNA reports to confirm, but with the earring, I'm betting it's the same guy."

Jack flipped to the next yellow-lined page and set a pair of reading glasses on his face. "Both Maddie and this victim were beaten. He used his fists, which tells me he likes to get personal. He wore gloves, so he's also careful. With Maddie, the blows could have served the more general purpose of subduing her. But victim number two was beaten far beyond what would have been necessary for compliance. It was rage."

Brooke flashed to the sight of the killer straddling Maddie in the woods. The sound of his fists striking her face. With a sharp inhalation, she ripped her attention from the past.

Jack followed his notes with the tip of his pen. "Victim number two wasn't killed at the laundry. He brought her there afterward. She had multiple ligature wounds. She had other, er, injuries that suggest he kept her somewhere for a while. He needed time and privacy to do what he did. I also suspect he drugged her, but we'll have to wait for the toxicology reports for confirmation."

She knew Jack was trying to be kind in not revealing the gory details, but his vagueness wasn't helping. Brooke's imagination filled in the gaps.

Jack looked up. "My guess is that's what he would've done with Maddie if you hadn't interrupted him. He would have taken her somewhere else and he would have killed her."

Ethan returned with several bottles of water. He handed one to Brooke. Fresh from a refrigerator, it chilled her already cold fingers. She twisted off the cap and took a small sip. Her stomach protested the onslaught of icy liquid. She set the bottle on the table. "Why is he doing this?"

Jack put his hand flat on top of the closed file. He leaned over the table toward Brooke. “On the surface, he’s punishing you. You’ve devoted a portion of your life to protecting young women. He knows that hurting young women is the best way to get to you. Not only did he copy Karen’s murder, but he carved your name into the victim’s skin. That’s personal.”

“You said *on the surface.* Why?” Kent asked with a tilt of his head.

“Because that’s just his excuse.” Jack tapped a finger on his file. “I believe he’s really hurting and killing women because he likes it.”

“Do you profile?” Kent asked.

“Hard to profile on one case.” Jack’s mouth thinned. “The FBI has specialists who might be able to do a better job, but I will say he’s not on the young end of the spectrum nor is this his first kill. There’s too much planning involved. Plus, he switched gears easily to incorporate Brooke’s past. That tells me he has some experience. Serial killers tend to be males between the ages of twenty and forty. While we do see teen killers, few are over the age of fifty. They tend to kill within their own race, so he’s likely white.”

“Can’t you give us anything else?” Kent tapped on his paper with his pen. “Any suggestions of where to start looking?”

“You could try positions of authority. A store security guard or some other job that would give him a sense of power.” Jack scratched his chin. “Remember we don’t have any proof we’re dealing with a serial killer, just my gut.”

“Your gut is usually pretty accurate,” Mike said.

Brooke wrapped her arms around her middle. She’d thought she’d faced the worst horror of her life when she found Karen’s body. But this was open-ended. What would he do next?

Mike grabbed a water bottle. “I called the prison. David Flanagan is still in prison. He has regular visits from his family and lawyer. We’re checking out the family to see if anything looks amiss.” He clenched a frustrated fist on the table. “I’ve been in contact with the state police and the FBI, but so far we haven’t turned up any open cases that fit these parameters.”

Kent’s phone beeped. He checked the display. “I have to get this.”

“I think we’re about done anyway.” Mike held out a hand. “Thanks for coming.”

“Anytime. Let me know if anything breaks. I’ll do the same.” Kent let himself out of the conference room.

Brooke’s throat constricted, but swallowing water was not a possibility.

A girl had been murdered and left to taunt Brooke. Jack suspected a serial killer, but they had very few leads. The murderer knew Brooke well, and he could be anybody.

# CHAPTER THIRTY-ONE

What if the police didn't catch the killer before Monday? Luke paced the small room, torn between wanting Brooke to stay out of the police investigation and helping the police find the killer. If Brooke went into hiding, would the killer forget about her?

No. He wouldn't.

Brooke cleared her throat. "Luke and I had some ideas about this guy stalking Maddie via her various social media sites. Maddie is very active online. She gave out a lot of personal information all over the Internet. When you confirm the second victim's identity, we could try and cross the two girls' online activities and see if there are any intersections."

"That's a possibility." Mike swept both beefy hands over his head. "The state police are equipped to do that sort of analysis. We don't have the expertise in-house."

"I could do it." Luke pivoted toward the table. "My background is in network security. My first task with every new client is to hack their system and find its vulnerabilities."

"I'll take all the help I can get. As soon as we have a confirmed identity, I'll let you know." Mike flipped his legal pad to a fresh page. "In the meantime, Brooke, I want you to think hard about all the men you know, even casually. Is there anyone new in your life?"

Brooke's face was blank. Dwarfed by Luke's sweater, the

sleeves hung over the tips of her fingers. For the first time since Luke had known her, she looked lost. "I can't think of anyone who could do this. Wait. What about Joe?"

"No one knows where Joe is." The chief clicked his pen. "But we're looking hard for him."

Luke went back to his chair and took her hand. Her fingers were colder than the water bottles fresh out of the fridge. Shit. There must be something they could do. "Isn't there a list of sex offenders in the area?"

"Yes, and we're working our way through the list." Jack patted a stack of folders at his elbow. "In fact, I wanted Brooke to look through these photos and see if she recognizes anyone." He slid the top file across the table to Brooke. She paled, which was saying something because she came into the room the color of bleached cement. "They're just mug shots."

She lifted the corner of the folder by the very edge as if the photos could jump out at her.

The stack of pictures was thicker than Luke expected. "How many are in the pile?"

"Fifty-seven offenders with histories of violence against adult women." The chief frowned. "We can expand the territory and the parameters later, but this gives us a start."

Brooke turned pages and studied images. She made two piles. In fifteen minutes, she'd finished the first pass. She patted the facedown pile. "None of these men look at all familiar. I'm not so sure about these three." She spread them on the table like playing cards. "It's possible I've seen them, but I can't remember when or where or in what context."

"Take all the time you need." Jack stood and stretched. "In fact, I could use a sandwich."

The chief looked at his watch. "We'll order lunch in. Any requests?" He gave Brooke a critical sweep.

She shook her head. "I'm not hungry."

"I have to check on a few things." He heaved to his feet and crutched-it toward the door. He caught Luke's eye.

"I'll be right back." Luke released Brooke slowly. When he was sure she wasn't going to keel over, he followed the police chief into the hall.

The chief nodded toward his secretary. "Nancy has a take-out menu. Order something for yourself and anything you think Brooke might eat." He headed for an office in the back of the station. "I'll be back."

Nancy handed him a white tri-fold menu for a local sandwich shop. Luke ordered a ham sandwich, a bowl of chicken soup, bread, and crackers.

"Good choices," Nancy approved. "She's taking this hard?"

Luke glanced back at the open conference room door. Jack had emerged from the room and was stretching his back.

On the other side of the counter, the station door opened. A young woman rushed in, tears streaming down her face. Luke recognized her from somewhere. How did he know her?

She shoved messy brown hair away from her face and leaned on the counter with both hands. "My roommate said an officer came to our apartment looking for me."

"Your name?" Nancy's face went from helpful and concerned to dead serious.

"Gabrielle. Gabrielle Quaker."

Nancy picked up her phone. Glancing over her shoulder at the chief's office, she hit one number.

"I'll take you back to see Chief O'Connell." With the air of a funeral procession, Nancy escorted her through the station. She opened the chief's door. The girl hesitated. Her body language was that of a person who knew what was coming was the worst news. Mike was walking around his desk to meet her. He shut the door.

Luke suddenly placed the girl. *No.* He glanced back at Brooke. Pain welled around his heart. This was going to break her. He started toward the conference room.

A muffled wail came from the chief's closed door.

Brooke appeared in the conference room doorway. She glanced around the station, spotted Luke, and started toward him.

The chief's door opened. He came out of his office and waved for Nancy. She hurried across the floor to confer. One hand splayed on the strand of pearls at her throat.

Luke heard Brooke's sharp intake of breath. She was staring at the open office door. The dark-haired girl huddled in a chair in front of a desk. She lifted her tear-streaked face.

"No." Brooke's knees buckled.

Luke launched himself across the ten feet that separated them, but she caught herself on the edge of a desk. She leaned, breathing heavily.

Luke grabbed a chair and shoved it under her. He eased her into it and rubbed her shoulders. "Deep breath."

Jack handed him a paper bag. Luke put the opening over Brooke's mouth and nose. "Just try to breathe normally."

Air wheezed in and out of her lungs. A few minutes later, she exhaled hard and pushed the bag away. She propped her elbows on her knees and bent forward until her forehead rested in her palms.

"The dead girl, it's Natalie, isn't it?" she asked without lifting her head.

Jack didn't have to answer. Brooke's body trembled.

The killer had murdered one of Brooke's self-defense students.

# CHAPTER THIRTY-TWO

He switched on the news and watched the breaking story. Behind a somber newswoman, law enforcement personnel swarmed around Selena's apartment building. Yellow tape fluttered in the breeze.

*Yes!* He loved watching his work on live TV.

His new plan was risky, but he hadn't had this much fun in years. Breaking out of the rut he'd been stuck in was well worth putting aside his one-kill-per-year rule.

Now to put step three into play. He started his computer, then peeled and ate a tangerine while he waited for the machine to boot up. The orange taste lingered on his tongue, the combination of tangy and sweet reminding him of Natalie. Bright and beautiful on the outside, and just enough zest on the inside to keep her interesting. For a while, anyway. How convenient that Natalie had posted online about attending Brooke's class. He so enjoyed putting the personal touch on his gift.

Until excitement had taken over.

He went to the kitchen for a second tangerine, but the bowl was empty. He must have eaten more than he thought. His hunger had been increasing lately, and not just for food. He wanted his double feature.

His home screen popped up on the computer. Time to get to work. There'd be time to satisfy his *appetites* later. Right now, he had an abduction to plan. There was no way he was going to get

Brooke away from her new beau. She would have to come to him, and for that to happen, he would need some bait. There was only one perfect lure to reel Brooke in.

He opened his social media application and scrolled through updates.

There she was. How interesting. Someone had a new boyfriend.

With a crack of his knuckles, he went to work hacking the young man's account. This was going to be the best night ever.

# CHAPTER THIRTY-THREE

Natalie was dead, and it was Brooke's fault.

Numbness spread through Brooke's body, the shock of her student's death flowing through her veins like a morphine drip. Luke picked her up and carried her into the conference room. He lowered her into a chair. Sitting across from her, he took both her hands in his and held them without speaking.

She lifted her head. The room tilted. "Two women are dead because of me."

His brow creased. "Wait. Two?"

"Natalie and Karen."

"Karen was your roommate."

"Yes."

"She was killed by her ex-boyfriend." Luke rubbed her hands. "How can that be your fault?"

Her gaze locked on the files spread across the conference room table. The words poured out, the secret she'd kept since that awful night breaking free. "I found her. Karen went down to do laundry a little before midnight. She was a night owl and the machines were always empty at that hour. I've always been a morning person. I used to get up early before work and run four or five miles. By midnight, I could barely keep my eyes open. I fell asleep on the couch after she left. By the time I woke up, it was 3:00 a.m. I knew right away that something was wrong.

Karen always shook me and sent me to bed when I dozed off in front of the TV."

She paused for a wavering breath but couldn't look at Luke. "Her bedroom was empty. No Karen. No laundry. I went downstairs. At first I thought the basement was empty . . ." The vision intruded, every detail clear as a high-resolution photo. She stopped to steady herself. "I went in and looked around. Karen's clothes were scattered on the floor, her laundry basket upside down, her sheets piled in the corner. Karen was under the sheets. The police said she'd been dead for three to four hours."

Brooke's voice failed.

Luke squeezed her fingers. "Look at me."

But she couldn't. She tightened her grip on his hands, holding onto to him as she blurted out the rest. "The basement always smelled like mold. We used to prop the window open. I was the one who forgot to close it earlier that day when I went down to do my wash. If I had remembered to close the window, Karen would still be alive."

"Or he would've simply broken the window. I'd say you shouldn't blame yourself for what happened, but I know that's not possible." Luke exhaled. "I still blame myself for Sherry's death. I know it's not rational, but I feel like there must have been something I could have done to save her."

Luke lifted her chin with his forefinger. His eyes reflected the despair compressed inside her own rib cage, the pressure constricting around her, tightening until she could barely breathe. "I won't tell you to let go of the guilt because I have no idea how to do that. I guess we just have to learn to live with it."

She thought of Natalie's family. How could they learn to live without their daughter? Brooke's suffering was nothing compared to what they were enduring. Her eyes filled with tears. A few escaped to roll down her cheek and drop from her jaw. Sadness clogged her throat. A lone sob burst through.

Luke pulled her forward and wrapped his arms around her. Her head fell onto his chest, and tears spilled onto his shirt. She recovered her breath with a full-body shudder. He tucked her under his chin. One warm hand rubbed a slow circle in the center of her back. Brooke had no idea how much time passed as she drew strength from Luke's quiet presence.

A knock sounded on the door. It opened. Chief O'Connell came into the room, his crutches banging on the metal doorframe. He produced a pack of crackers and a can of ginger ale from his pocket and set them on the table. "Luke, can I talk to you for a few minutes?"

Brooke lifted her head. She wiped her face with a hand. "You don't need to leave the room."

Mike gave her a quick appraisal. "We have the account information and permission from Maddie and from Natalie's parents to access their online accounts."

"How sure are you that it's Natalie?" Her voice cracked.

The answer was in the chief's pale blue eyes. "Dental records confirmed her identity a few minutes ago."

Another wave of grief crashed over Brooke. Poor Natalie. "She was targeted because she attended my class."

Chief O'Connell shifted on his crutches. "We don't know that."

Brooke stared him down.

"But it's a strong possibility." The chief's face tightened. "I have to interview her family and friends. He handed Luke a piece of paper. "Here are the girls' accounts, log-in information, passwords, etcetera. See what you can do with it. I've sent it to the state police too, but it's not their only case."

"I'll get on it right away." Luke pocketed the list.

"Let me know if you come up with anything." O'Connell turned to Brooke. "Is there anything you can tell me about Maddie or Natalie that might tie them together?"

"I didn't even know Maddie before this week." Brooke rubbed her forehead. "Natalie and her sister attended my last women's self-defense course, which obviously didn't help much." What else could she have taught Natalie to keep her safe? How had she failed?

"Brooke." The chief leveled a serious gaze at her. "Natalie's Mini Cooper was found on the side of the road on her route home from work. Her bumper was mangled. Both rear tires were flat. He didn't just run her off the road. He rammed her car with his. There weren't any houses or businesses in sight. Nowhere for her to run for help. The driver's side window was smashed. She probably locked the door to try and keep him out. She tried to contact the police on her cell, but the signal out there was weak. The call didn't go through. There were injuries to her hands and forearms that suggest she fought." His voice trailed off. "But he was bigger and stronger."

Brooke's lungs expanded in a painful, shaking breath.

"This was not the work of an amateur. He knew what he was doing. The fact that Natalie couldn't fight him off is not your fault."

"But if it weren't for me, she wouldn't have been his target." And thinking about targets, Brooke pulled out her phone. "Excuse me for a minute. I want to check on the kids, and I have to let Ian know what's going on."

She knew her kids were safe at Ian's high-security apartment building, but a mother's worries weren't always about being rational. Fear for her kids was pure instinct.

---

Drizzle hit Brooke's face as they walked from the police station to the car. "Where are we going?"

"I booked us into a hotel about twenty minutes from here."

"I want to go home."

"I know, but this is safer." Luke steered her with a hand on the small of her back.

"For who?" Brooke protested. "I'd rather have him find me than take out his anger on another innocent young woman."

"Brooke, I'm not going to let this guy have you no matter what." Luke waited until she met his gaze. "And do you really think he would stop if he got you?"

"No." Brooke settled into the passenger seat. "I'm out of clothes. If we're going to be hiding for an indeterminate length of time, I'd like to pick up my computer. And I left my phone charger on my nightstand, and my phone is almost dead. It's broad daylight. All this guy's activity has been at night. How about we go back to my house for a few hours now and check into a hotel later?"

He considered her compromise for a few seconds. "All right." He drove back to her house and parked out front. "Wait here with the doors locked. If you see anyone but me, drive away and call the police."

Brooke stared at the house while Luke went inside. He didn't return for ten long minutes.

"OK. Coast is clear." He carried their bags into the kitchen. "I'll heat up some soup."

"I'm not hungry." She dumped her purse on the table.

"You should eat anyway." He set up his laptop on the table. He plugged in and booted up, then poured some soup into a saucepan. He turned on the burner under it.

Unable to sit, Brooke paced the kitchen. Good thing her knee had improved. She couldn't contemplate being still with this much turmoil churning through her. Natalie's face kept popping into her head, Brooke's imagination battering it beyond recognition.

Standing at the stove, stirring soup, Luke frowned over his shoulder. "I'm going to work on identifying parallels in social media activity between the two women. With multiple sites and profiles, just downloading all the information will likely take a while. Why don't you access Natalie's accounts, read through them, and see if anything jumps out at you?"

She grabbed her laptop from her office and opened it next to Luke's computer. He placed a bowl of chicken soup on the table at her other elbow, then brought her crackers. The scent wafted to her nose. She picked up a spoon. It hovered over the bowl as guilt rolled through her. How could she be hungry when a young woman was dead because of her? How could she eat when Natalie's family was making funeral arrangements?

Luke sat down with his own late lunch. "You need to eat, Brooke. Making yourself sick serves no purpose. Helping the police find the killer is the best use of all that guilt and anger right now."

Could he read her mind? She switched her computer on and ate a few spoonfuls while the laptop warmed up. Her stomach protested, then settled as the warm broth soothed her. Brooke managed to eat half the bowl while she checked her e-mail. Same old, same old from school. Pushing the bowl away, she braced herself and started surfing through Natalie's social media profiles.

Natalie was active online, but she didn't announce her minute-to-minute activities as Maddie had done. Brooke scrolled. Natalie subscribed to updates from Forever Fitness and the Coopersfield High School alumni page. Brooke moved to the photos section and stared at the pictures of the beautiful smiling girl whose ruined body was lying in a stainless-steel morgue drawer. Brooke's stomach cramped. She breathed through her nose and fought the rise of nausea. Her emotions were not helping. Natalie's killer had to be stopped, and Brooke needed to lock down her guilt if she was going to contribute.

Brooke scrolled through two years of pictures and stopped on a shot of Natalie's high school soccer team. She opened a second window, signed on to Maddie's account, and clicked the PHOTOS tab. Maddie's field hockey team pictures popped up in the first few screens. Something clicked in Brooke's brain. She went back to Natalie's team picture. The photos were similar, which made sense because all the athletic team yearbook pictures looked alike. She arranged the windows to view the images side by side. Tiny words ran vertically up the left edge of both photos. Photographer's credit? She enlarged the pictures until she could read the letters.

"Luke."

"Did you find something?" He shifted his position.

"Maybe." She angled the computer so he could see the screen. "Look at these pictures."

Luke leaned in. "We know both girls were high school athletes. Why would having their team pictures on their profiles be unusual?"

Brooke pointed to the name on both images.

Owen Zimmerman Photography.

"Coincidence?" Luke scratched his chin. "How many schools use the same photographer?"

"I don't know." Brooke sighed. "We've used Owen for years. He gives us a great package. You're right. It could be the same for all the local schools."

"It's worth passing that on to Chief O'Connell."

Brooke picked up her cell and dialed. She was instructed to dial 911 only if the call was an emergency. The line switched to voice mail. She left a message for the chief to call her back.

"The only two things that jump out between the girls' accounts are Forever Fitness and the team pictures." Brooke couldn't let go of either. "Let's take a ride to Owen's studio. It's right in town."

"Brooke, we are assisting the police, not acting in their place."

But the police were working on their own theories, and Brooke's connections were spiderweb thin. "Whoever he is, he could be planning another murder right now."

"And visiting Owen will accomplish what?"

"I just want to get a look inside his studio."

"Why? I doubt a killer would leave evidence out in the open."

"Then it won't hurt to stop by. I'll just say I want information on getting some family portraits done. Nothing suspicious about that. Besides, you said it yourself. The link between Owen and the girls is tenuous. Maybe I can find out where he was last night and eliminate him from our list." Brooke jumped up, the thought of doing something active to help energizing her. She headed for the hall at a brisk pace. "Grab some workout clothes. I'm in the mood to try out some exercise equipment on the way back."

"Damn it, Brooke!" Luke yelled from the kitchen. "We cannot go looking for a killer. What if you tip him off?"

"We'll be very casual. I can't just sit here. He could be hurting another woman right now." Ignoring his expletive, she darted up the stairs. She found a pair of yoga pants in decent condition at the bottom of a drawer and tugged them on. What did she hope to find at Owen's studio or Forever Fitness? Did she think she'd recognize Natalie's killer?

Her research told her that killers often blended in with society. That's how they got away with their crimes. Still, she had to try. What if she didn't and another woman died tonight?

Natalie had been murdered because of her involvement with Brooke. She couldn't let another one of her girls suffer the same fate. The killer was fixated on Brooke. Who knew what else he was planning. She had to do everything possible to find him before he acted out another sick plan.

---

Luke glanced at Brooke in the passenger seat of his car. "You called Ian earlier. How did he take the news?"

"Not well. He wants to keep the kids until this is all over."

Great. More incentive for Brooke to pursue the killer.

"Why did I let you talk me into this?" Luke parked in front of a small brick house on Second Street. A discrete sign on the mailbox read OWEN ZIMMERMAN PHOTOGRAPHY in tasteful print.

"Because the association is weak and you don't think we're accomplishing anything." Brooke got out of the car. "Basically, you're humoring me."

"So, why are we here?" And why did the idea of paying the local photographer a visit give Luke the willies?

Brooke led the way. "You said your program would take about an hour to run. We might as well do something useful while we're waiting."

He followed her up the walk. Hell, in those tight yoga pants, he'd follow her anywhere. A matching yard sign and arrow directed them to the side door, marked STUDIO.

Luke knocked. He angled his body slightly ahead of Brooke's, just in case.

The door opened. The man who opened it was about forty. Shaved head. Shorter than Luke but stockier. Probably strong enough to carry a dead body.

Surprise puckered Owen's brows. "Brooke?"

"Hi, Owen." Brooke smiled and introduced Luke. "I'm sorry, I should have called first. Did we catch you at a bad time? I wanted to ask you a few questions about getting some family portraits done. For my mother. For Christmas. Is it too late to order for the holidays?"

"No, it's OK." Owen stepped back. "Come in."

The left side of the studio was bare, dark wood floors, white walls. Lights on wheels and props were pushed into the far corner. Roll-down screens, like giant roller-window shades, hung from the back wall. In the front of the room, a couch, two chairs, and a coffee table were set up in conversation mode. Photo albums were spread on the table.

"What did you have in mind?" Owen asked.

"I'm not sure. Something plain but not cliché, if you know what I mean." Brooke rolled a vague hand in the air. "I thought maybe you'd have some ideas."

"Let me grab the proofs from a few recent sessions." Owen walked to the coffee table. He rooted through a few stacks of small photo albums and selected two. He gestured to the sofa. "Have a seat and take a look at these. See if anything catches your eye."

Brooke dropped onto the couch. Owen took the chair diagonal to her. Luke stayed on his feet. Sitting and looking at pictures wasn't going to get them anywhere.

"Do you have a restroom?" Luke asked.

Owen pointed. "Through that doorway. First room on the left."

"Thanks." Luke followed Owen's directions.

"Oh, I like this." Brooke's voice faded as Luke closed the door behind him.

Just as he'd hoped, a small office was opposite the bathroom. Luke ducked inside. If Brooke wanted answers about Owen Zimmerman, Luke was going to get them for her. Then he was going to get her somewhere safe for the night.

A computer hibernated on the desk. Images faded and appeared in a screen saver slideshow. He tapped the space bar and kept his ear on the muffled conversation in the other room. A quick perusal of the desk drawers didn't yield anything interesting. The credenza was equally uneventful. The computer blinked to life. Luke took a quick peek at the hard drive files. Most of the files were full of images, as to be expected from a photographer, organized in folders by client name. A few layers down he pulled up an obscurely labeled folder: SPECIAL JOB.

The thumbnails were shocking enough Luke didn't click to open any of them. He pulled out his keychain. A flash drive the size of a stick of gum dangled. Luke inserted it in the USB slot and copied the entire folder. Then he closed the files window and slipped out to the restroom to flush the toilet and run the sink for a few seconds.

In the studio, Owen had shifted to the couch next to Brooke, far too close considering Luke's new opinion of the photographer.

Brooke smiled. "What do you think of this?"

It was an outdoor shot of a family in jeans and sweaters gathered around a German shepherd.

"Nice and natural." Luke put on his game face and sat on Brooke's other side.

She showed him a half-dozen pictures. "Which one do you think the kids will like?"

"The one with the dog, no question." Luke would have said anything to get Brooke away from Owen. The flash drive was burning a hole in his pocket.

"I like that one too." Brooke closed the book.

Owen opened an agenda book. "Do you want to set up a time to do the shoot?"

Brooke pursed her lips. "I'll call you next week to make an appointment. I have to see which days the kids are with their father."

"No problem." Owen closed his book and set it on the table.

Brooke stood. "Thanks, Owen. My parents are going to love this picture."

"Thanks for coming by." Owen showed them to the door. "Talk to you next week."

They walked to the car and got in. Luke started the engine.

Brooke hooked her seatbelt. "Maybe I was wrong about Owen."

"You weren't." Luke pulled away from the curb. "While you were looking at pictures, I took a quick tour through Owen's computer."

Brooke's head snapped up. "I'm impressed."

Luke clenched his fingers on the steering wheel. “Don’t be. What I did was illegal and dangerous. In fact, I can’t believe I did it. You’re obsession is contagious.”

“What did you find? Let me see it.”

“No way.” Luke turned toward Main Street and switched on his headlights. Above the quaint town, clouds were rolling in, bringing early twilight with them. “I’m handing the copies of the files over to Chief O’Connell. Although I obtained them illegally, so I’m not sure what he’ll do with them.”

“With what?”

“Pictures. Seriously, once you see them, you can’t unsee them. I’d really like to unsee those pictures. I’m not going to show you.”

“Will you just tell me what the hell you found?”

“Some very disturbing BDSM porn.”

Brooke shrugged. “People are into that these days.”

“Are you?”

Brooke blushed. “No, but to each his or her own.”

“This wasn’t a little bondage or submission session for bored suburban housewives to get off.” He felt like he needed to bleach his eyeballs. “This was violent.”

And bloody.

# CHAPTER THIRTY-FOUR

*Scrape.*

Maddie bristled as the branch outside rubbed against her window. The hairs on her neck lifted.

*Just the wind. Just the wind. Just the wind.*

But repeating the facts didn't subdue her rampant paranoia. Her brain knew she was safe here with her parents, but her heart jolted at every noise, no matter how routine. Would her terror ever fade? Would she ever get back to normal? Tomorrow she had an appointment with a psychiatrist. Her dad was taking her, but she was already dreading leaving the house.

She'd survived her attack, only *she* was the one imprisoned. *He* was still out there, free to do whatever he wanted. Her parents had tried to shield her, but Maddie had seen the news about the murdered girl. That could have been her. That would have been her if it hadn't been for Brooke.

Her gaze shot to the window, now black with nightfall, but all she could see was her own reflection. Anyone outside, however, could see her.

Maddie's phone buzzed.

She picked it up and smiled. She opened the message from Tyler.

MISS YOU.

Her grin spread when the pain in her face was barely an ache. She texted Tyler back.

U2.

He'd stopped to see her yesterday and brought her flowers. He'd also offered to drive her to school and work when she was ready to go back. Until her attacker was caught, Tyler didn't want her going anywhere alone.

He cared about her, even after she'd broken up with him. Despite the chill of knowing her assailant was still on the loose, warmth glimmered inside Maddie. She wasn't ready to go back to work or anywhere else just yet—she was barely able to tolerate an hour or two in her room alone, but someday . . .

Another message from Tyler came through. He was stopping to see her when he got off work.

*Scrape.*

The high pitch of the sound sent an ache through her teeth. She dropped her phone on the bed and eased to her feet, slowly and carefully. The room spun but settled in a few seconds. The carpet was soft under her bare feet as she walked to the window. She stayed to the edge of the room so she wasn't visible to anyone outside. The property was backed by woods—the same woods in which she'd been attacked. He could be out there. Watching. Waiting.

Maddie yanked the curtains closed. The sudden movement sent a shaft of pain through the sore muscles of her shoulders. Her head and face had taken the worst of his beating, but the rest of her body hadn't escaped injury. She went to the top of the stairs. Her hand gripped the banister in case a dizzy spell intruded.

At the bottom of the steps, her feet protested the cold wood floor of the landing. Maddie shivered as she turned toward the family room at the rear of the house. "Dad?"

Her father was in the doorway before she'd traversed the fifteen feet of hallway. His rifle dangled in the crook of his elbow. In his late fifties, balding with a belly that showed his addiction to both Pringles and his recliner, her father wasn't a threatening physical specimen. But he bagged his buck every season. Maddie had no doubt he'd love nothing better than mounting her attacker's head on the wall.

His expression softened. "What do you need, sweetheart?"

"Could you trim that big branch on the tree out back tomorrow? It's rubbing on my window and . . ."

"I'll do it right now."

Maddie glanced at the window. Anxiety rolled through her in a greasy wave. "Tomorrow's fine."

But her dad was already moving. "It'll take three seconds." He handed the rifle off to her mother. "It's loaded."

Mom accepted the heavy weapon with an awkward shift of her slight frame, and Dad headed for the back door.

A fresh burst of fear sprinted through Maddie's belly. "You don't have to do this tonight. It's raining."

"Sweetheart." He flipped a wall switch next to the door. A small circle of light spilled onto the deck. "I'll be right back. It's barely spitting."

He opened the door and went outside. His boots clunked across the wood. He descended the steps and exited the yellow sphere cast by the bug bulb. He turned toward the shed at the rear of the property where the yard tools were kept. Then the night swallowed him.

"Close the door, honey," her mother said.

Maddie squinted into the darkness. A few seconds passed. Sweat ran down her back and soaked her hoodie. Her heartbeat accelerated, pulsing fear through her veins with each quickening pump.

Something rustled.

She darted out the door.

"Maddie, get back inside," her mother called, but Maddie couldn't stop. She couldn't let anything happen to her dad.

---

He crouched beneath a tree. Under the hood of his jacket, a cold wind blew across his exposed face. Drizzle peppered his cheeks, but he barely felt the chill. The excitement churning in his belly was more than enough to keep him warm.

In the tree's shadow, he watched the rear of the building. He loved the dark, reveled in the possibilities it created, the metaphorical doors it opened for him.

Certain acts couldn't be contemplated in the light of day.

Tonight was the culmination of all his experience in hunting prey. In planning. In paying attention to the smallest details.

The door was opening. A figure was coming outside. Was it her?

No. The form was too large. A man walked briskly by, dead leaves scurrying from his path. He burrowed deeper into the shadows, held still, and waited for the man to pass. A moment later he relaxed. There. Her slight, hesitant form slipped out the door and into the night.

A fresh thrill coursed through his veins. This was it. The beginning of tonight's challenge. He moved into position.

Crossing her arms and rubbing her biceps against the dropping temperature, she walked by, her steps tentative, her eyes searching the darkness. She stopped. Her eyes widened when she saw him. Her face froze in terror.

He grabbed her wrist and yanked her into the shadow. Before she could make a sound, his fist slammed into her temple. She crumpled, and he scooped her limp body into his arms.

Last time he'd made plenty of mistakes. He's been lazy and over confident.

He hurried toward his vehicle. He juggled her lax body and searched for his keys. Pain blasted through his injured wrist as he shifted her weight. A press of his thumb unlocked the doors. With a quick glance around to make sure no one was watching, he maneuvered her onto the back seat. He pulled a small plastic case from the pocket behind the driver's seat. Inside, the syringe was filled and ready. He couldn't put her in the trunk; that was reserved. Nor could he risk anyone seeing her flailing around, bound in his car.

Yes, ketamine was cheating, but he'd only measured a small dose, just enough to keep her quiet until showtime. She'd wake up in time for the festivities. Who wanted to fuck an unconscious woman? Might as well switch to necrophilia, and what was the fun in that? No, he liked them alive and kicking.

He arranged her on her side. If anyone looked in the car, she would appear to be sleeping. When he was closer to his destination, zip ties and a blindfold awaited.

Now, on to step two.

# CHAPTER THIRTY-FIVE

Brooke read Chris's response to her text. He was playing video games. Haley was in her room. Though she knew the kids were fine at Ian's, her son's message gave her a sigh of relief.

"Do you still want to go to the gym?" Luke asked.

She considered his question. From his tone, he'd prefer to skip it. But what if the killer wasn't Owen? "I do."

"I don't like it." He switched on the wipers as a few tiny droplets of rain hit the windshield. "I wanted to have you somewhere safe by dark. The hotel isn't as secure as my place, but it's our best option for tonight."

Thick cloud cover had hastened the arrival of nightfall.

"What if Owen is just a pervert, not a murderer?"

"You didn't see those pictures." Disgust rang through Luke's voice. "I really want to get those files to Mike."

"He'll call back. Considering you stole the images, I don't want to leave them with anyone else."

"Even so, I don't know what you hope to accomplish at Forever Fitness."

"Both girls were members."

"Could be a coincidence. The girls lived in the same town. They likely crossed paths in more than one way." Luke stopped at a stop sign, then turned onto Main Street. "Plus, the police already know about the connection between the girls and the gym."

"I'd still like to check it out. That guy at the desk was certainly strong enough." And the super-fit Zack had given Brooke the creeps.

He huffed. "OK. On one condition."

"What?"

"Afterward, you eat a real meal, and we go to the hotel for the night."

Brooke's stomach cramped at the idea of food, but she needed to go to Forever Fitness. It was the only other link they'd found between the two girls. What if they didn't stop and it turned out that the killer was connected with the gym? She couldn't live with any more guilt than was already piled on her shoulders. "Deal."

"Why don't you call the police chief again?"

Brooke dialed O'Connell's cell number. A mechanical voice answered and instructed her to press one if her call was an emergency. Brooke pressed number two for voice mail. She left another message. He was probably still tied up with Natalie's family. Sadness and the urge to help find the young woman's killer bloomed fresh in Brooke's belly.

A few minutes later, they pulled into the strip mall that housed Forever Fitness. Luke parked in the puddle of a streetlight and grabbed a gym bag from his trunk. They went inside. The air was humid and smelled of sweat. "I have to change. Please stay in the public areas while I duck into the locker room."

"Sure."

Inside, they handed their temporary IDs to the pretty blond girl manning the desk.

"Is Zack working tonight?" Brooke smiled.

"No, he's off." The blond entered their membership numbers into the computer. "Did you want to leave him a message?"

"No, thanks." Brooke scanned the room. She'd really wanted to have a casual conversation with Zack. A few young men grunted in the free weight section. Two girls jogged on treadmills, eyes on the TVs hanging on the opposite wall, earbuds plugged into the machines. She didn't recognize anyone. What to do? Standing and staring at the other members wasn't the best way to blend in. She sat down at a chest-press machine. How much weight could she press? She inserted the pin under the forty-pound mark. That's what the bags of dog food weighed that she carried from the car to the house.

"I thought you called in sick today?"

Her head spun around toward the voice.

Greg was standing next to her. His T-shirt was soaked through, and sweat dripped from his face. He dried his forehead with a towel. "Playing hooky?"

"I took a personal day," Brooke corrected, her tolerance for Greg's lack of social grace lower than usual.

"Hey, I could care less." Greg held up his hands in a defensive gesture. "You never take off."

"I didn't see you when I came in." Brooke scanned the gym.

"I was in the cross-training class." He jerked a thumb toward the exercise studio. A group of fit-looking men and women were filing out. In fact, Greg was fitter than Brooke had realized. No bulky muscles, but his body was lean and hard-looking. He had the kind of body that could heft dead women and still slip through a narrow basement window. *Oh, stop.* This was Greg. She'd known him for years. "It's a tough workout. How's your knee?"

"Better, but I'm sticking with upper body today."

Greg nodded. "Smart. So is lifting weights, especially as you get older."

Brooke bit back the sarcastic retort that wanted to spring free. Instead, she made a noncommittal sound of agreement.

"Well, I have to go shower. Have a great weekend." He sauntered toward the locker room.

With a nod of acknowledgment, Luke passed the teacher on his way out. He walked over to Brooke and leaned close. "See anything suspicious?"

"Not yet."

Luke headed for the free weights, where the grunting men gathered.

Brooke turned her attention back to her machine. She gave the handles a push. She could barely budge the lever. Maybe she did need to join the gym. She backed the weight down and tried again. *Ugh.* Weight lifting sucked. A dozen half-hearted presses later, she moved on. The biceps machine didn't feel any better. She stood. The room tilted.

Maybe working out with more stress than food in her system wasn't the best idea. She faked it through another machine with the minimum weight.

She signaled to Luke, who was leg pressing an impressive stack of weights. A couple of minutes later, they were walking toward the car.

"Well, that was a bust." Brooke wiped a raindrop from her cheek. "We were probably the most suspicious people in the gym."

"True." Luke tossed his gym bag in the back seat of the car. "What about that dinner?"

Brooke spotted the Jade Dragon at the other end of the shopping center. "I could probably eat some wonton soup."

"Works for me. It'll be quick too." Luke surveyed the parking lot. "I didn't want to go back to your house in the dark."

"Your computer should be done working its magic by the time we get home. We'll eat and run." Despite Brooke's attempt at courage, the darkness raised the hairs on her nape. She moved closer to Luke. Every shadow represented a potential ambush.

---

A sense of isolation closed in on Luke. He turned at Brooke's mailbox. The headlights swept over her front lawn. He parked in the driveway and looked up at the dark house.

Damn it.

They hadn't left any lights on. He'd planned to have Brooke away from here and in a more secure location before nightfall. He'd even booked the room using his corporate credit card to eliminate any link to Brooke. In a decent hotel, there was no longer any such thing as a cash room under a fake name. Photo ID was required for just about any travel arrangements these days. Even though he made a career in the industry, sometimes he longed for the days before 9/11 had raised the world's security flags.

"Wait here while I check things out." Luke leaned across the seat and withdrew a flashlight from the glove box. "Lock the doors and—"

"I know." Brooke cut him off.

He glanced at her. Would she actually drive away and call the police if she thought he was in danger? Probably not. She was a hero. He got out of the car, closed the door, and waited for the locks to click before heading to the house.

The front door swung inward. Darkness swallowed the foyer. Stepping inside, Luke led with the beam of his flashlight, holding it away from his body so he didn't present a target to anyone who could be hiding in the dark.

Leaving the front door open, he swept the beam around the living room and down the hall. Nothing. The house felt empty without a dog to trip over. Reaching behind him, he flipped three wall switches by the door. Lights illuminated the foyer, the porch, and the lamp post next to the front walk. A glance out the doorway reassured him that Brooke was fine, and no one was lurking on the lawn. He searched the first floor, then every nook and cranny of the basement before heading upstairs to check under beds, in closets, and behind shower curtains. Every light in the house blazed when he went outside to escort Brooke into the house.

She carried the take-out bag to the kitchen. "Did you check your program?"

Luke locked the door. "Not yet." He checked his laptop. The screen was black. He tapped the touchpad and woke up the hibernating machine. "Finished. Let's see what we have."

Brooke brought two bowls of soup to the table. Luke ate while he scanned through the files. Both girls had been very, very busy. "I'm going to sort the results."

He took his time, letting Brooke finish her dinner before they got back into the case. The list of common links between Maddie's and Natalie's profiles grew steadily. Brooke pushed her bowl away still half-full, but it was better than nothing.

"They had more in common than I'd anticipated." Luke scrolled through the list.

Brooke took her bowl to the sink. She returned to lean over his shoulder. "The list is two pages long."

"Apparently, they're both very popular."

"How do we narrow it down?" Brooke's voice rose with the tint of desperation.

"*We* don't." Luke saved the results in a separate file. "The police will investigate. Have you heard back from Mike?"

Brooke pulled out her cell phone. "Shoot. The battery is dead. I'll go get my charger. It's in my overnight bag."

She went down the hall.

"Repack it while you're up there," Luke called after her. His own bag was still in his trunk from the night before. "I want to get out of here soon."

Brooke returned a few minutes later. A charging cord dangled from her hand. She dropped her bag by the doorway. "I have an idea."

*Uh-oh.* Brooke's ideas meant trouble.

"I'm going to call Maddie and go through this list with her." Brooke plugged in her phone. "She can at least tell us how she is connected to these people and organizations. Let me see the list."

Luke turned his computer around. "Brooke, I think you should leave this to the police."

"It's just a phone call." She waved his concern away.

"That's how it starts." Luke pushed his bowl away, anxiety unsettling his stomach. "We're going to drop off these files and the pictures I *stole* from Owen Zimmerman at the police station. Then we are holing up somewhere safe for the night."

"Of course." Brooke nodded. "This won't take more than a few minutes. If Maddie can eliminate anything from this list, it'll save the police time. We have to stop Natalie's killer before he hurts another girl."

*We,* not *the police.* "Brooke, you have to stop doing this."

"Doing what?" Brooke's face paled. "She's not answering."

"Maybe her phone is dead too."

"No." She shoved a hand into her hair, her eyes white rimmed, her lips compressed in a flat, bloodless line. "I might let my battery run out once in a while, but Haley would never let that happen. That phone is practically fused to her hand. As much as Maddie posts online, I'm sure she's the same way."

Brooke paced a frantic circle as she redialed. "Damn it. Where is she?"

"Brooke, let it go. Please." Luke stared at Brooke as she dialed her phone. His anxiety over protecting her had gone way beyond a promise to a friend or even the fear of failing Brooke the way he'd failed Sherry. Fear for Brooke and for what he would do without her spun through him. His breaths accelerated. His pulse climbed. Clammy sweat broke out on his forehead.

"I couldn't take it if something happened to Maddie."

"Well, I couldn't take it if something happened to you."

Their stares locked. Neither yielded.

Brooke's expression tightened. "I can't put myself before her."

And that would make him a coward if he asked her to give up. Distance. He needed some privacy to get his shit together.

"Excuse me for a minute." He ducked into the bathroom and splashed cold water on his face.

"Mike left me a voice mail," she called from the kitchen.

Concern churned into panic in Luke's chest. Guilt had taken over her mind. She was never going to back off. She was going to pursue this killer until she found him or vice versa. Neither option was acceptable. How the hell could he keep her safe if she refused to take care? She was a car without brakes going over the top of a hill. Once she gathered momentum, there was no stopping her. She was going to steamroll right into a brick wall.

Luke couldn't stand to watch her crash.

---

Brooke listened to the chief's voice mail. He was back in his office. She dialed the number.

Mike answered on the first ring. "Did Luke find something?"

"He's still sorting through the data," Brooke said. "But two major connections jumped right out at me. Forever Fitness and Owen Zimmerman."

"We know both girls belonged to the gym, but who is Owen Zimmerman?"

"He's a local photographer." She explained about seeing the athletic team photos, all taken by Owen, on the Internet. "I know it's a thin connection, but when we went to see him—"

"You did what?" The chief's voice went flat.

"We went to get some information about having portraits done," Brooke backtracked.

Mike didn't say anything, but anger radiated over the line.

She blazed ahead. "Anyway, while we were there, Luke found some violent pornography on Owen's computer. He copied it for you."

"Brooke—"

"I know it's not legally obtained, but at least you know to start looking at him as a suspect."

Mike mumbled, "Christ, Brooke. What are you trying to do to me?"

Brooke considered his question to be rhetorical. "Now, we have those pictures for you, plus Luke will have the downloaded and sorted data for you. Where should we drop them off?"

"I'll be in my office." Mike sounded tired.

"And another thing." Brooke twirled the charging cord around her finger. "Maddie's not answering her cell phone."

"There's a car parked in front of her house. I'll contact my officer and make sure everything is all right."

"Thank you."

"Brooke, I know this is hard for you, but you need to stay out of this investigation."

"Of course."

"Promise you won't go looking for any more suspects?"

"All right." Brooke exhaled. "I was only trying to help." Mike didn't understand. She *had* to help.

"I realize that, but this is a dangerous situation. I don't want you walking into a killer."

Brooke ended the call. Her phone buzzed in her hand. She read the screen. UNKNOWN CALLER. A flurry of alarm floated into her throat as she put the cell to her ear. "Hello?"

"Hello, Brooke." The voice was a gravelly whisper. "Are you looking for someone?"

*Oh, no.*

With a frantic sweep of her gaze, Brooke scanned the room for Luke, but he hadn't returned.

"I'm watching you. Don't move. Don't speak. Just listen. If you don't obey my instructions exactly, I will shoot her right now."

*Maddie.*

A click sounded over the connection. Brooke flinched. A weapon being cocked? She couldn't tell.

"Turn around and walk out your back door."

Brooke hesitated. Maddie's life—and her own—hinged on her decision.

"I said walk out your back door. I'm in control now. Don't forget it. You have three seconds, or I'm going to kill her. Don't hang up. Don't signal your boyfriend. Keep the phone to your ear."

With no alternatives, Brooke did as she was told. She unplugged the charger and prayed that in the last ten minutes her battery had charged enough for whatever he had in mind. She stepped outside. Darkness shrouded the yard. Her workout clothes were no match for the dropping temperature, and cold drizzle bathed her skin.

"Run toward the garage."

She broke into a jog. The wet grass soaked the hems of her yoga pants. Pain zinged through her still-healing knee. She focused on it, used it to keep the fear from paralyzing her brain. If she didn't keep her cool, Maddie was dead. The old building loomed ahead. A figure stood at the corner. Medium height and build. Dressed in a bulky black jacket and pants. A ski mask covered his head and concealed his features.

As she approached, he backed away. "Around back," he whispered.

She slowed to a walk and obeyed, following his retreating shadow. A plain four-door sedan hunkered behind the garage, out of sight of the house. The front bumper was dented. This was the car he'd used to ram Natalie's vehicle. The trunk and one rear door were open. The dome light illuminated the figure of a girl wedged on the floor in front of the backseat. She was bound, her head covered with what appeared to be a pillowcase.

He stood near the open vehicle door, a handgun pointed at the girl's limp form. "End the call and drop the phone."

Brooke punched END. Her cell hit the dripping weeds with a wet thud.

He tossed something at her. It landed in the grass at her feet with a metallic jingle. The car's interior light gleamed on silver. Handcuffs. "Put those on."

She bent down and picked them up.

Possibilities raced through her mind. She had no weapon. He wasn't close enough to strike, and he was pointing a gun into the car. What choice did she have?

She snapped the bracelets over her wrists.

"Get in the trunk."

She paused. Sweat dripped between her shoulder blades. He slid his phone into his pocket, then leaned over, yanked the pillowcase from the girl's head, and pressed the muzzle to her temple.

Brooke's heart stopped.

# CHAPTER THIRTY-SIX

*Haley.*

The sight of her daughter's face swept away Brooke's balance. She stumbled forward.

He held up a hand in a stop gesture. "Get in the trunk or she's dead. Right here. Right now."

He'd already proven his willingness to kill. Reason told her to run for help, but her body propelled itself forward on autopilot, her maternal instinct preventing her from leaving her child, even as she was well aware that her mere presence did nothing to diminish the danger.

Brooke walked toward the vehicle, her heart slamming against her ribs. Fear dried her throat as she climbed over the bumper. Easing into the trunk's interior, the smell of rubber and gasoline gagged her. She shifted onto her back and lifted her feet. If he came close enough . . .

He didn't. "And no funny business. I will leave you by the side of the road, drive somewhere else, and take all my frustrations out on your little girl. On the other hand, maybe if you cooperate, I'll only kill you tonight."

The trunk slammed, and she was enveloped in darkness. The weight of her decision and the confining space smothered her. Her breaths came faster, until small dots of light appeared in the black void.

The primary rule in women's self-defense? Do everything you can to prevent being taken to a secondary location. Once a killer had you in a private, secluded place, your chances of survival rivaled lightning strikes and shark attacks. If it were only her life at risk, she'd have run and taken the chance he'd have missed her in the dark. Hitting a moving target with a handgun was a lot harder than it looked on TV. Even if he shot her, Luke would have heard. Help could have been summoned.

But none of her training prepared her for a gun pointed at her child by a man more than willing to commit torture and murder.

Despair and guilt wrapped around her heart and clenched hard.

What had she done? She should have run for help. Gone for assistance. There was no way he was letting either one of them go.

But she couldn't leave her daughter, even if her training told her that was the most logical move. She'd frozen and obeyed. Panic raced through her veins, spreading icy certainty to her limbs. She'd done the exact opposite of everything she taught her girls, and she'd condemned her daughter to death.

---

Luke dried his face and stared at his reflection in the mirror.

*Man up.*

He'd promised to protect Brooke until he returned to work. Tonight, he'd finish sorting the data for the police and take her to a hotel. In the meantime, he was backing off on the personal relationship they'd developed. He'd book two connecting rooms. No more making love with Brooke, though his chest already ached with the loss. The connection they shared was unlike any other in his experience. But in that link he sensed not only the power to heal him, but the ability to break him just as easily. So, he would keep his promise to Wade, but he wouldn't risk his recovery. Brooke couldn't change. She was caught in a hopeless spiral of guilt he understood too well. She endangered herself recklessly, and he couldn't suffer another loss.

He went back into the kitchen and checked his computer. The program was finished. "Brooke?" he called.

No answer.

He checked the den and her office. Empty. He took the stairs two at a time. "Brooke?" All four bedrooms were empty. The bathrooms too. An eerie silence settled over the house as alarm triggered inside him.

Luke checked the basement and then ran through the first floor one more time. In the foyer, he shoved a hand over his head. Brooke was not in the house. Where the hell was she? Her car and his both sat in the driveway. The front door was locked. Luke opened the door and went out onto the porch. "Brooke?"

A frigid gust of wind sent dead leaves scrambling across the walk.

Luke went back inside. He raced down the hall. The back door was unlocked. He grabbed a flashlight and went outside. One lap around the house yielded no sign of her. Dread pumped through his body. "Brooke?"

The garage?

It was the only place left on the property to check. Luke ran across the grass, a surreal horror cloaking him, like a nightmare he couldn't wake from. Why would she come out here?

No reason. Something had happened, and he'd missed it because he'd been freaking out in the bathroom.

The garage was empty. He dialed the police chief. Mike answered on the first ring.

"Did you talk to Brooke?" Luke closed the garage door.

"She called me about fifteen minutes ago to tell me about the fitness center and the photographer. I didn't approve of either action, and I told her she had to stop interfering in the case."

"Shit." Luke circled the building, sweeping his beam across the grass in rhythmic arcs.

"What's wrong?" Mike clipped off the words.

Luke spun in a frantic circle. His light bounced around the countryside, ineffectual beyond a distance of twenty feet. "She's gone."

"What do you mean, she's gone?"

"I went into the bathroom. When I came out ten minutes later, she was fucking gone. The back door is unlocked. That's the only clue."

"We'll be right there."

Luke ended the call. In the beam of his light, a glimmer in the grass caught his attention. He walked toward it. Anxiety shifted into terror as he recognized Brooke's cell phone. He scanned the grass as far as his light would reach. Ten yards ahead, tire tracks led toward the road, fresh in the damp earth from tonight's drizzle.

Simultaneously sweating and freezing, he wiped his forehead with his sleeve. The police were on the way, but it was too late. Brooke had been taken.

Luke had failed.

# CHAPTER THIRTY-SEVEN

Agony and confusion pounded through Haley's temples. She tried to raise her head, but it felt floaty, almost as if it wasn't attached to her neck. What happened? She opened her eyes to see only darkness. She tilted her head to listen. An engine hummed. Fabric slid on the skin of her face. What was over her head? She reached up to remove the covering, but her hands were tied together. The hood was secured somehow too. She couldn't pull it off.

*No.*

She pulled at the binds, but her skin gave instead. Thin and inflexible, they dug into her wrists. Pain shot up her arms. She inhaled the stale air that surrounded her face. Her feet were free, but her muscles refused to obey her commands to move. Her legs flopped when she wanted them to bend.

Had he drugged her? She had no other explanation. She pressed her fists against her mouth to hold back her scream.

She wriggled her torso. There wasn't much room to maneuver. She was wedged in a tight space. She tried to roll over, but her head smacked into an object. A wave of nausea rolled through her. She flexed her tingling fingers and encountered flat, coarse carpet.

A car.

Was she in the trunk? No. She moved her hands as far as her possible and encountered the smoothness of leather. She must be on the floor in the back, stuffed between the seats.

A cough startled her. The driver? Haley froze. Though she couldn't see, she sensed a person close to her. The sound of his breathing confirmed his presence. The floor shifted as the car made a turn. The chips she'd eaten earlier roiled in her belly, flooding her chest and throat with a sour, acidic burn. And her body still floated . . .

What had happened?

She'd been in her room, flipping through an old issue of *Cosmo*, her eyes barely skimming over the flashy ads and thinking about how unfair her parents were acting.

And then . . .

*Someone knocked at her bedroom door.*

*"Haley?" Dad called through the door.*

*"What?" Her tone was rude, and she didn't care. Mom could cover for him all she wanted, but Haley knew it was her dad's idea to drag her down here and ruin her life.*

*The door opened, and her dad stuck his head inside. "I have to run to the office. I won't be long. Stay inside, OK?"*

*Holding nothing back, Haley scowled up at him. "Fine."*

*She dropped her attention back to her biology book. His sad stare was hot on her face. She knew her rebuff hurt his feelings. She only saw him two weekends a month since the divorce. But whose fault was that? He was the one who'd left them and moved too far away to see them more often. Anger nudged the guilt aside.*

*None of this was her fault.*

*Did either of her parents know what this weekend meant to her? Had they cared that she was missing the most important night of her life?*

*No. They hadn't. Her mom was being ridiculous and overprotective as usual. All she ever talked about was safety. Haley had had it with the lectures.*

*"Want me to bring you anything special for dinner?" Dad asked.*

*"I'm not hungry." Which was actually a dumb thing to say because she was. But letting him do something nice for her would make him feel better. She didn't want him to feel better. She wanted to share her misery.*

*He closed the door.*

*Haley gave up on her studying. She shoved her books aside and flopped onto the fluffy comforter. Her dad had fixed this room up for her in her favorite color: purple. But she wasn't here enough for it to feel like "her" room. Her suitcase was opened on the dresser. She'd live out of it until she was allowed to go home on Monday. Dad wanted her to leave some things here, but Haley lugged everything back to Westbury twice a month. If she made herself at home in his apartment, he'd think what he did was OK. It wasn't.*

*She glanced at the clock by the bed. All of her friends were getting ready to go to the Halloween dance. She thought of the beautiful costume at home in her closet and her first pair of heels that she wouldn't be wearing tonight. And of Brandon, who'd asked her out on her first official date.*

*Would Brandon go without her tonight? Would he find another girl to dance with? Misery filled her until she choked on it. Her eyes overflowed. Tears rolled down her cheeks. She sniffed and wiped her cheeks with her hand. This was going to be the worst weekend ever.*

*Her phone buzzed. She checked the display. An instant message from Brandon. Flutters swam in her belly. She automatically glanced toward the door, and then remembered her dad had left. That's what he did best.*

*Brandon: MEET ME DOWNSTAIRS.*

*Haley: UR HERE?*

*Brandon: YES.*

*The flurries graduated to blizzard. He drove all the way down here to see her.*

*Haley: WHAT ABT THE DANCE?*

*Brandon: SKIPPED IT. WANTED TO C U.*

*Delicious warmth flooded her, washing away the sadness. Brandon would rather see her than go to the biggest dance of the year except for prom.*

*Brandon: COME DOWN.*

*Her thumbs hesitated. Dad said not to go outside. She picked at her fingernail. She wouldn't go outside. She'd go to the lobby, let Brandon into the building, and bring him upstairs. They could hang out here. Dad couldn't object to that.*

*Haley: K. WHERE R U?*

*Brandon: 20TH ST. WHERE'S THE DOOR?*

*Haley thought. The Twentieth Street entrance was actually in a narrow alley. The main lobby of the building opened onto Rittenhouse Square. She didn't want to go into the main lobby. That's the way her dad would come in. Better for him not to know she was downstairs at all.*

*Haley: IN THE ALLEY NEXT TO THE LUGGAGE STORE. MEET U AT THE DOOR.*

*Brandon: K.*

*The first floor of Dad's building was mostly stores. But you had to walk outside to get to them. There was a Starbucks and a small restaurant too. The luggage store was on the end, near the back exit to Twentieth.*

*Haley grabbed her phone and purse. She tiptoed down the hall. Her brother was playing a video game in the living room. Digitized gunfire and explosions boomed in the small space. Chris didn't notice as she slipped past him and out the apartment door. Down the hall, she smacked the elevator call button with a quick prayer that her dad wouldn't be back for a while. In the mirrored wall of the elevator, she smoothed her hair and wiped a smudge of mascara from beneath her eye.*

Ugh. *Why hadn't she stopped in the bathroom to check her makeup?*

*The elevator binged and opened at the lobby floor. Haley hung a quick left, breezed past the security guard, and strode for the Twentieth Street exit. She squinted through the glass door, but she didn't see him.*

*"Excuse me."*

*She startled. A gray-haired man about her dad's age stood behind her. He smiled and nodded toward the door. Haley stepped away from the door so he could exit. "Sorry."*

*Cool air rushed in as he left. The door closed with the soft sucking sound of the rubber weather seal. Cupping her hand over her eyes against the brighter light inside, she squinted at the dark street. Where was Brandon? She opened the door a few inches and called his name through the crack.*

*Nothing.*

*She pushed the door wider and stepped through the opening. Guilt and her father's words nagged at her. She'd only be outside for a minute. On the sidewalk, she shivered. It had been warm when she was out this afternoon. Now that the sun had disappeared, the air had turned cold.*

*She hugged her arms. "Brandon?"*

*The street was dark, the glow from streetlights obscured by trees and buildings and signs. She took a few more steps. "Brandon?" If he didn't come out in two more seconds . . .*

*A figure in a hoodie stepped out from under a tree.*

*She beamed at him. "There you are."*

*Her face froze. It wasn't Brandon. A chill sprinted through her veins. He sprang toward her. Hoping to startle him, as she turned away she lifted her phone and pressed the camera button, but the flash had no effect. Her boots dug into the pavement. She lunged for the building. Too late. Pain burst through her head. Her phone clattered across the pavement, and the world went black.*

Haley's stomach heaved at the memory.

*What had she done?*

She breathed through her nose and willed her gut to settle. Vomit would not improve the air under her mask.

*Stupid, stupid, stupid.*

It hadn't been Brandon messaging her. It had been the man who was waiting for her in the dark, and she'd walked right to him.

Tears burned her eyes. Visions of her parents and the mean things she'd said to them over the past few days played out in her head, an endless loop of selfishness. Would her angry, hateful words be their last memory of her?

Fresh sickness swept over her. She was going to die.

She tried to remember her mom's lectures. Keep calm. Think. Never give up. What would Mom do? Just because Haley was smaller and weaker didn't mean she was completely helpless. But drugged and bound, she felt pretty defenseless.

The car stopped, and Haley held her breath.

# CHAPTER THIRTY-EIGHT

Luke tamped down his spinning thoughts and focused on the computer screen. The best way for him to find Brooke was to figure out who had taken her. The only clues to her disappearance were her cell phone, the tire tracks by the garage, and the Internet trail of two teenagers. Mike was scrolling through Brooke's phone, and two police officers were outside casting the tire tracks. That left the Internet for Luke.

Mike gestured with Brooke's phone. "The call that Brooke received at 9:03 p.m. came from an unregistered cell phone."

Luke ripped his attention from his laptop. "Unregistered meaning a disposable cell?"

"Yes."

"So, you can't trace the call." Which was not a surprise.

"Right." Mike set the phone down. "Do you have anything?"

"I've gone through dozens of profiles connected to both Natalie and Maddie. But this one raises the most suspicion. Jeremy Brent, age nineteen, graduated from Coopersfield High School last year." Luke switched to his Internet browser, where he'd loaded the profile. "His account has all the earmarks of a fake profile. There's only one photo of him, and zero mention of any family members. None of his online friends seem to know him. There are too many "Thanks for the friendship. Do I know you?" comments on his page. He doesn't post updates, except for the initial activity when he set up his page. He almost exclusively interacts with young women."

"Any evidence of cyber-stalking?"

"No," Luke admitted. "This is more cyber-lurking."

Mike frowned. "Maddie didn't receive any harassing e-mails or online requests for personal information. If this guy is following her through social media, he got her address somewhere else."

Luke shrugged. "Frankly, both Maddie and Natalie gave out so much personal information, he wouldn't have to dig very deep. They both publically listed their places of employment. Hell, Maddie "checked in" at dozens of locations all over town. Anyone could have found her. All a predator would need to do is read her posts. Until she was attacked, I could tell you exactly where she was at almost any given time."

"Nothing illegal about reading public posts."

"No." Luke rubbed his forehead. "But I hacked into the Coopersfield High School alumni site."

Mike's mouth flattened to razor blade thin. "Officially, I didn't hear that, but go on."

"I can't find any record of him ever attending the school. I found a number of Jeremy Brents via Google, but none are in this area. You might not want to *officially* hear the rest of this either." Luke pointed at the screen. "The next site I hacked was one of his social media sites to obtain the IP, or Internet protocol, address his computer was using when he interacted with these girls."

The chief pinched the bridge of his crooked nose. "But that won't give us his actual physical address."

"That's right. The IP address is the numerical code that identifies a particular computer on the Internet. IP addresses are assigned by the Internet Service Provider. For most people, that's their cable or phone company."

Mike slapped the table. The phone jumped. "Shit. Getting his physical address from them will take a court order."

Luke went back to his keyboard. "You can wait for a court order. I'm going right to the source."

"You can hack into it?" Mike leaned closer, his interest and gaze narrowing.

"Actually, that's what I do for a living. I'm an ethical hacker. The first thing I do with every new client is hack their system and find out where they're vulnerable. Then I figure out how to protect their system and sell them our company's services. With fraud and identity theft so prevalent, client data security is a vital part of any business."

"Illegally obtained evidence won't be admissible in court."

"Admissibility won't mean much if we don't find her fast. She'll be dead." Luke's gut clenched as images of Sherry flashed through his mind. He couldn't fail Brooke the way he'd failed his assistant. "By the time you get a court order, it'll be too late for Brooke."

Brooke's phone buzzed. Mike looked at the display then at Luke. "Do you know who Ian is?"

"Her ex-husband." Luke's stomach steamrolled at the thought of telling Chris and Haley—and Wade—that Brooke was missing.

Mike answered the call and identified himself. His grim expression went grimmer. He took the phone into the dining room. Luke turned back to his computer. Mike came back into the room. His body leaned heavily into his crutches as if the news he'd received had taken a toll.

Luke's fingers froze. "What is it?"

The chief's jaw sawed. "Brooke's daughter disappeared."

"She's two hours away from here. We took her to Ian's to keep her safe."

"The Philadelphia police haven't confirmed any foul play yet. Brooke's ex ran to his office. He left the kids in his apartment. When he came back, Haley was gone. His son was playing video games. Chris thought Haley was still in her room. Building security saw her walking through the lobby a few hours ago. She was headed toward a rear exit." Mike started toward the door. "Philadelphia police have issued an alert for Haley, and we have every cop in the county looking for Brooke. Why don't you come back to the station? Jack is fielding calls there now."

"I can't stop in the middle of this." Luke pinned his attention back on his computer.

Mike gave him a pointed look. "Let me know as soon as you have the address."

"I'll call it in as an anonymous tip."

---

The stale air stank of carpet, rubber, and fear. Curled on her side, Brooke shivered. A piece of plastic sheeting crinkled beneath her. No doubt to prevent trace evidence from being transferred to the vehicle. Brooke combed through her hair for a few long strands. She tucked them in the rear of the trunk, beneath the sheeting.

A midsize sedan equaled a midsize trunk. She had a few inches of space around her body to maneuver. In the dark, she searched for an emergency trunk-release lever. The car looked fairly new, so it should have a glow-in-the-dark release of some sort. She didn't see anything. But then, if a man made a habit out of putting women into his trunk, he'd likely removed the mechanism to open it from the inside.

Where was the compartment that contained the tire changing tools? Wiggling until her back was wedged into the rear of the trunk, she pushed the plastic back and felt for the carpet edges. Her hand slid underneath and found the compartment lid. Her fingers pried it up. She stuck a hand inside and felt the hard rubber of the spare tire, but the well around it was empty. No tire iron. No jack.

Disappointment washed through her, and hope slid from her grasp like a handful of rain.

Jack was right. This guy was a pro. He'd planned this down to the smallest detail.

If she lived in a city, she could have pushed or kicked out the plastic taillight covering. She could have stuck her hand out and signaled to a passing motorist for help. But most of Westbury was rural. There was a good chance there wouldn't be a car in sight to help her. And she couldn't take the chance that her daughter would die because of her trick.

All of her training was based on self-preservation, but Brooke's one and only concern was her daughter. How could she protect Haley if they were separated? Was her daughter still in the car? Was she still alive? Brooke shut down that line of thought. She couldn't function if she even considered that possibility.

The car lurched to a stop.

In the darkness, she tensed, waiting. Were they at a stop sign? Over the sound of her own labored breathing, she heard a muffled rumble and a metallic squeal. Garage door? The car rolled forward. Metal groaned and slammed. A car door opened. The vehicle rocked gently as the driver got out. Another door opened.

Haley.

He was getting her out of the back seat. Tears slid down Brooke's cheeks. Helplessness and horror gripped her insides and squeezed. She held her breath and strained her ears for more sounds. What was he doing?

The car rocked. There was a scuffle and a slap. "You bitch!"

Brooke's chest compressed as if the vehicle was parked on it. Then everything went quiet, except for her heartbeat thudding in her ears and the labored sound of her next painful inhale. She repositioned herself so her feet were between her and him. If he leaned over, a solid kick to the face or head could knock him out.

Brooke pulled her right knee to her chest. Shoes scraped on concrete, and the trunk sprung open.

---

Luke stared at the screen. Every drop of blood in his body turned to ice water. He grabbed the phone and dialed Mike. As soon as the chief answered, Luke gave him the name and Westbury address of the account holder.

Mike was silent for two long seconds. "Shit."

"Yeah, shit." Luke gave the police chief extra points for not wasting time with a round of I-don't-believe-its.

Luke plugged the address into his GPS. Christ, it was only four miles from Brooke's house. The bastard could've walked over any time.

"Luke." Mike's voice went stern. "Don't go out there. He'll be armed."

*So will I.* And Luke was closer. "Since I got all this information illegally, an anonymous tip will be coming in as soon as we hang up."

Commotion sounded over the connection.

"Wait," Mike yelled. "I just got word that Haley's phone was found. She managed to snap a blurry picture of her kidnapper as he grabbed her. Cars are on the way to his residence now."

Luke ended the call and collected Brooke's shotgun from the den. Still loaded. Upstairs, he went into her closet, opened her gun safe, and filled his pockets with shells. His jeans were dark enough, but he tugged a black hooded sweatshirt over his light-colored T. In the car, he set the shotgun on the passenger seat.

Luke was no hero. If the police got there first, great. But if not, Luke wasn't waiting. He'd already failed to keep Brooke safe from this monster. He'd save her or die trying. Otherwise, he doubted he could live with himself. Even ten seconds could mean the difference between life and death.

# CHAPTER THIRTY-NINE

Luke killed the lights as the GPS told him he was approaching the address. The last house he'd passed had been nearly two miles back. A yellow glow appeared ahead. He pulled his car onto the shoulder and stared at the ordinary house fifty yards away. Two stories, two-car attached garage. What, no picket fence?

He double-checked the address. This was it.

Luke turned off the interior dome light before slipping out of the car. The shotgun was a welcome weight in his hands as he started across the grass.

---

Brooke blinked in the harsh light of the garage's bare bulb.

He was standing well back, away from any chance of her catching him with a kick. An unconscious Haley was draped over his right shoulder. His arm wrapped around her legs to hold her in place. His sleeve was pushed up, revealing a bruised and swollen wrist.

Her vision cleared, and shock shut down her brain.

"Out." Through a blood-smeared face, Officer Kent's mouth spread in an evil, "*Heeere's Johnny*" smile.

*Kent?* How could it be?

"You look surprised."

Brooke spit out a single word. "Why?"

"Why?" Kent sneered. "That's a stupid question."

Brooke sat up, pins and needles shooting through her limbs. "Why my daughter?"

"Because she's yours. She needs to learn some manners." He wiped blood from his face with the back of his hand, and then raised his handgun awkwardly over his shoulder with his left hand. He pressed the muzzle into Haley's lower back. "And so do you."

Brooke climbed out of the trunk. Her stiff, freezing legs protested. She put a hand on the vehicle to steady her balance.

"Turn around and walk." Kent nodded toward an interior door.

On trembling legs, Brooke stumbled across the cement slab and went into the house. The decor was shockingly normal.

"Keep moving."

A tidy kitchen opened to a living room outfitted with comfortable furniture and a flat-screen TV.

"The basement door is just ahead."

Brooke had a feeling the cellar wouldn't be so ordinary. She opened the door. Wooden stairs descended into darkness. A killer's dungeon. A strange detachment spread through her. This was it. Time was running out.

"Light switch is on the right."

She flipped it and illuminated the end of the staircase. Nothing was visible but concrete.

"Downstairs. Now."

Her sneakers made little sound on the wood treads. He stayed several steps above her, well out of reach of a back kick. She stepped down. A wall divided the room. In the center was a door. This half of the space contained a washer, dryer, some shelving, and a weight bench. Perfectly normal basement equipment.

"Step to the side. Over by the laundry basket."

Brooke moved five steps to the right. He opened the door with a key and turned on the lights. She needed him to put Haley down and lower the gun, just for a few seconds. Kent had injured his right wrist. She was pretty sure that was his dominant hand. His coordination seemed off. The injury just might give her a chance.

He backed away. "You first."

She walked through the opening.

He dumped Haley on a worktable. Equal parts fear and fury pulsed through Brooke's head. She could barely think. Haley was unconscious. Brooke squinted. Haley's chest rose and fell much too slowly. Terror spread through her belly in a heavy wave. "What did you give her?"

"Just a little Special K to make her more cooperative," he said. "She must weigh less than I estimated."

Special K, also known as ketamine, was a veterinary anesthetic and date rape drug. An overdose could cause respiratory depression or central nervous system damage.

The worktable was fitted with chains and other restraints. The skin of Haley's forehead was red and smeared with blood. But Brooke could see no break in the skin. She glanced back at Kent.

He wiped his bloody nose on his sleeve. Rage glittered in his eyes, the blue going cold and dead as a shark's. Haley had broken his nose with a head butt.

Haley's hands were bound in front of her body. One handed, he lifted her arms over her head. They flopped, limp and pale as dead fish, onto the table. He secured her binds to the table with a pair of handcuffs, his movements slowed by the use of his non-dominant hand. "There, now she isn't going anywhere."

He turned his focus to Brooke.

She was only going to get one shot at him. One debilitating blow or she and Haley were both dead. He walked closer.

Brooke clasped her bound hands together in front of her face, as if she were begging. "Please. Please don't hurt my daughter. I'll do whatever you say."

"Of course you will." He smiled. Perverse pleasure lit his eyes. "Let's see how you follow orders. Then I'll consider letting Haley go."

Brooke's mind spun. *Stall him, distract him any way possible.* "Why are you doing this?"

He sighed, the kind of sound one made when reminiscing a particularly fond memory. "If you hadn't come tearing through the woods to save Maddie, you and I wouldn't have reconnected. But, given your inclination, I suppose it was Karma."

"What do you mean, reconnected?"

"We met once before. Don't you remember?"

"No." Brooke searched her memories, desperate for a clue to her connection to this killer, information she might use against him.

"It was 1996. I was a rookie. I saw this red Trans Am roaring down Route 27, with a gorgeous girl at the wheel." His mouth twisted in a smirk, obviously waiting for her to make the connection.

*Oh my God.*

"Karen." She breathed out her friend's name.

"You remember." His eyes shone with excitement. "I pulled her over. She had long dark hair down to her ass and legs up to her chin. She was wearing this slutty little miniskirt that she hiked up to give me a better look. There was a girl in the passenger seat, but I barely noticed her. That was you, wasn't it?"

The memory washed over Brooke like an ocean wave. The balmy autumn night pouring through the open windows. The radio blaring. Karen belting out "Isn't It Ironic" at the top of her lungs with Alanis Morissette. Lights flashing in the mirror.

Karen had flirted with the cop and gotten off with a warning. She used to do it all the time. Brooke, in the passenger seat, hadn't even gotten a good look at the officer. Simultaneously embarrassed and enthralled by Karen's behavior, Brooke had tried to be invisible. Karen had been the lively, outgoing one.

"That was weeks before Karen's death."

"I couldn't get her out of my head, so I watched her. I didn't plan to kill her at first, but she'd been so confident, so convinced she was in control over me. She learned otherwise." His head tilted. "She was beautiful, though. I admit to being entranced. The only way to break the spell was to take away her power. She wasn't so pretty when I was finished with her. She was my first." He raised his chin in wistful pride.

"You couldn't have killed Karen. The police found evidence—"

Kent grinned. "I did a damned good job setting that dumb jerk up, especially since the frame was a last-minute idea. I smeared a little blood on his passenger seat, some more on the faucets in his condo. The fact that he didn't have an alibi was sheer luck." His smile widened. "Prison is going to be a rude awakening for that boring history teacher you jilted."

"No one will believe Tony killed me."

"Why not? He's a little old, but otherwise fits the profile: single white male, intelligent, a loner. He's home tonight, all alone, with no one to verify his alibi." Kent's eyes gleamed. "At first I was going to pin it on your new man, but the history teacher is a better fit. He has a better motive. Juries love to find angry ex-boyfriends guilty."

Brooke couldn't speak. She'd helped send David Flanagan to prison. The jury had only deliberated for an hour before giving their verdict.

"Natalie was a decent likeness to Karen, don't you think?" Was he looking for praise? Kent was sick and perverted, but there was nothing insane about him. He knew exactly what he was doing. "I've learned a lot over the years. Karen's death was over too soon. I couldn't risk being discovered. But I brought the rest, including Natalie, here." With the gun, he gestured to the table where Haley sprawled limp and helpless. "She screamed so loud the cinder block bled. It was beautiful."

Kent took off the bulky jacket. He reached across his body with his left hand, holstered his gun at his hip, and pulled a knife from a sheath on his belt. "If you didn't always have to be in control, you and your daughter wouldn't have to die tonight."

Kent's smile leaked pure evil.

He reached to the low ceiling. A pulley was affixed to the rafter. A hook, the kind a slaughterhouse might use to hang a side of beef, dangled from it. He rolled it toward her. "Put your arms over your head."

She raised her hands high with no hesitation and let her fear show through her eyes for a few seconds before casting them down in a show of submission. If he was overconfident, maybe, just maybe, he'd slip up. His arrogance was her only hope.

Her heart pounded hard enough to break a rib.

"Loop the cuffs over the hook." Oh, God. He wanted to hang her like a piece of meat. With Brooke incapacitated, Haley had no chance.

Brooke stretched. Her hands were level with the hook, but the short chain between the metal bracelets dipped two inches below. She was already on her toes. No matter how much he threatened her, there was nothing she could do. If he wanted her suspended from that hook, he was going to have to do it himself.

Kent watched her. Irritation flickered as he recognized his miscalculation, the single kink in his otherwise smooth chain of events. He'd planned everything down to the smallest detail, but he hadn't accounted for her shorter stature. He shifted the knife in his grip, his expression calculating, the blue of his eyes as cold as a layer of frost on autumn grass. Was he deciding how risky it would be to approach her?

Brooke held still, arms raised, poised as if obediently awaiting his next command. He stepped closer. She offset her hands and clasped them together like an opera singer. Then she slammed them down club fashion on his already-smashed nose. Fresh blood spurted. His head shot back. He dropped to his knees and glared up at her, evil and rage contorting his features as the monster within him took control.

One hand grabbed her ankle, the other thrust toward Brooke. Light glinted on metal.

The knife!

Instinct moved her body. Her scream punctured the dusty air as the blade sliced through her flesh.

---

The garage doors were solid, the sole window covered. Shotgun at the ready, Luke crept along the side of the house. Drizzle dripped from his face and slid into the neck of his hoodie. He rounded the corner and jogged to the back of the house. Curtains obscured the windows across the back as well, but light glowed behind them. In a crouch, he traversed the wet grass to the back door. Putting his ear to the metal, he listened for sounds of movement.

Nothing.

He put his hand to the knob and turned. Locked. A muffled female scream came from inside the house. A fresh burst of adrenaline coursed through Luke. The door was steel. The only way to open it would be to shoot his way in. Repeated blasts from a twenty gauge weren't the best way to conduct a surprise attack.

He ran to the nearest window and smashed the butt of the shotgun through the glass. The noise was louder than he liked, but he saw no other quick way to gain entrance to the house.

And the devil only knew what Kent was doing to Brooke and Haley right now.

A vision of Sherry's pleading eyes invaded his mind. Luke blinked it away. Screaming meant someone was still alive. If he was going to save them, he had no time for past guilt. Present guilt was more than enough.

He reached in, unlocked the window, and raised the sash. Climbing over the sill, he fell through the opening and landed on his hip in an empty living room, the heavy gun still clenched in his grip.

Luke held still, listening. Sounds of movement leaked through an interior door. He scrambled to his feet and hefted the shotgun. Leading with the barrel, he eased the door open and started down a flight of lighted stairs, his running shoes quiet on the treads.

Near the bottom of the stairs, he leaned forward and peered into the cellar. His gaze fixed on a door beyond, a flimsy interior job. It was barely a barrier. He tried the knob. Locked. Scuffling sounds came from the other room.

Luke stepped back and kicked the door open. He burst through and ducked sideways in case Kent had a weapon ready.

Brooke was ten feet away. She was handcuffed and bleeding. Kent was on his knees in front of her. They were too close together for Luke to shoot the bastard. Kent clenched a knife in one hand. Blood dripped from its blade and from Brooke's forearm. Kent's attention shifted to Luke. Brooke pulled her cuffed and clasped hands toward her chest and drove them, knuckles first, into Kent's windpipe. His eyes bulged. Gasping, he dropped the knife and grabbed for his throat. Short wheezes panted in and out of his lungs. He fell backward. His ass hit the concrete.

"You bitch," Kent choked out, red-faced, and swiped for the knife on the floor.

Brooke kicked him in the head. "Fuck you."

Footsteps pounded on wood. Ethan and Lieutenant Winters rushed in. They had Kent disarmed, rolled onto his face, and cuffed in seconds. One of the cops unlocked Brooke's handcuffs.

Luke yanked Brooke to his chest, but she pushed him away. "Haley."

His head snapped up. Behind Brooke, Haley lay on a workbench, unconscious and bound, her slight teen form utterly still, her face white as bleached bone.

"Please get her out of here." Brooke took the shotgun from Luke's grasp.

Ethan was beside him with a handcuff key. He released Haley from the table, then cut the plastic ties that bound her wrists. Luke took off his jacket and wrapped it around the girl. He gathered her in his arms.

"Brooke, don't do it," the lieutenant said.

Luke turned. Brooke was aiming the shotgun at Kent's head. Her eyes were leveled at him with a stare as frigid as the killer's had been. Her hands were steady, even the bloody one, and she radiated rage, raw and primal and deadly as a grizzly sow defending her cub.

"He took my daughter. He hurt her. He was going to torture and kill my baby." Brooke's voice was disturbingly flat. The shotgun didn't waver. "He doesn't deserve one more breath."

With one knee still ground firmly in Kent's lower back, the lieutenant shook his head. "I know, but you can't, Brooke."

Pressed to the concrete, Kent's face was red. Air rasped in and out of his lungs, his lips bluing as they watched. Luke thought the killer might not make it anyway. Brooke's strike to his windpipe had been on target. With some luck, his throat would swell enough to strangle him.

"Brooke," Luke said gently. "We need to get Haley out of here."

Brooke's shoulders fell. She handed the gun to Ethan and leaned on Luke as he carried her daughter out of the basement. As they emerged into the cleansing rain, Luke couldn't help but wonder. *If the police hadn't arrived, would she have pulled the trigger?*

# CHAPTER FORTY

"I am not leaving her for one second." Standing in the corner of the ER cubicle, Brooke pressed a towel to the bloody gash on her forearm.

The nurse tried again. "Ms. Davenport, your arm needs to be stitched. I have the next room all ready. You'll be ten feet away."

"I am not leaving." Brooke stated through clenched teeth for the tenth time.

Dr. Wilson, the ER doctor checking Haley's pupils, looked up at her. Kind blue eyes met hers. "I'll stitch her right here in a minute."

The nurse shrugged and walked out.

"Her vital signs are good. I don't see any visible injuries other than the bump on the head. I'd like to schedule her for an X-ray and an MRI." He checked Haley's pulse again, turned to the computer mounted on the wall, and typed. "Ketamine is a powerful drug, but the effects are short-lived. She should be coming around soon. One of the side effects is amnesia. She might not remember any of tonight."

Which would not be a bad thing.

The nurse wheeled a metal tray into the room.

Dr. Wilson washed his hands at the tiny sink. He yanked two latex gloves from a box on the wall. "Have a seat."

Brooke dropped into the plastic chair. She'd remained standing this whole time because she wasn't entirely sure she'd be able to get up again once she was down. Now that Haley had been checked out, she supposed it didn't matter all that much.

"Local anesthetic." Dr. Wilson picked up a syringe and injected her forearm in three places. She flinched. Considering all she'd been through that night, the injection hurt more than she expected, as if her pain threshold had maxed out. He irrigated the wound. Tears filled her eyes at the sting.

"We'll give that a minute to work." He tapped on her arm. "Can you feel that?"

Brooke shook her head.

"Don't watch," he said. "Look at your daughter. She's going to be all right."

Brooke turned her head away from the deep gash to watch Haley's monitors blink and beep with regular assurance. Her mind was simultaneously numb and reeling, and the *blip, blip* of Haley's heart monitor was mesmerizing.

The energy drained from her body like water from a tub. A tear slipped down her cheek.

"All done." Dr. Wilson snipped a thread. Brooke glanced at the neat row of stitches on her arm. He covered the stitches with rolled gauze. "I'm keeping Haley overnight. We'll move her to a room shortly. Are you all right?"

Brooke's lips could barely form the word. "Yes."

"You're not injured anywhere else?"

"No." Brooke glanced back at Haley. *Blip. Blip.*

"In the meantime, then, we'll get you a more comfortable chair." Dr. Wilson rose, wheeling the tray away with a foot. "And I'm going to have a psychiatrist check in on you both tomorrow. You can't ignore psychological trauma any more than physical injuries. Both need treatment to heal properly."

After he left, Brooke leaned her head back against the wall.

The events of the night were too much to comprehend. How would Haley cope with the trauma? How would Brooke?

Kent had killed Karen. How could that be when Karen's ex-boyfriend had been in prison for sixteen years for the crime?

Brooke's mind shut down. It was all too much. She slid her chair closer to the bed and grasped her daughter's hand. She could have lost everything tonight. She was making changes in her life. She was going to get the counseling she should have had all those years ago. It was time to let Karen, and the grief that smothered Brooke's life, go.

A shadow appeared in the hall. Luke peered in. "Is she OK?"

"She will be."

Relief and exhaustion dragged at his face, while gratitude swamped her heart. He had come for them. Risked his life and faced a killer to rescue her and Haley. If she hadn't loved him before, last night was the clincher. She couldn't resist a man who kicked down doors to save her child.

Wait. *She loved him?* She stared up at his too lean face, and his intense green gaze focused on her.

Her heart thumped in answer. She couldn't regret an ounce of her love for him.

He glanced down the hall. "Ian is here."

Ian. A small surge of anger lent her strength. It was going to be a while before she forgave him.

"The police want to talk with you. Are you up to it?" Luke asked. "It you're not, I'll tell them to come back tomorrow."

"I can talk to them." But Brooke dreaded getting to her feet. Luke put his hand out, and she took it, letting him help her stand.

"Brooke?" Ian stood at the entrance, his hair and clothing rumpled, his eyes desperate, his usual composure erased. His gaze settled on Haley.

"The doctor said she should be all right." Brooke took pity on him. No one could have predicted that the killer would follow Haley to Philadelphia.

Ian's body deflated. "Thank God."

"I'm sorry," Brooke said in a low voice. "This is my fault."

"Your fault?" Ian's brow wrinkled. "Why would you think that?"

She lowered her chin. If she'd had a tear left in her soul, she would have wept. "If I wasn't obsessed with Karen's murder, I would never have gotten involved in this."

"My God, Brooke. You can't blame yourself for saving a young woman's life." Ian scrubbed his face with both hands. "I'm the one to blame here. I put Haley in danger. You saved her. I was only going to be gone a short time, but I shouldn't have left them alone at all. I specifically took Haley and Chris to keep them safe. I shouldn't have put work first. Not for one second." His face tightened, deepening the lines around his eyes and mouth. "The police found her cell phone in the street. She thought she was messaging with that boy she likes. She went downstairs to let him into the building. She even told him she couldn't come out."

Poor Haley. Her impulsive decision would haunt her, but Brooke would make sure she got the help she needed, so her daughter wouldn't pay for her mistake for the rest of her life.

"I don't know her as well as I should." Ian would need to deal with his guilt in his own way. "I could have lost her."

"Will you sit with her?" Brooke asked. "I have to give a statement to the police."

His face brightened. "Of course." He tentatively reached for Haley's hand.

Luke was waiting for her outside the cubicle. He wrapped an arm around her. With equally heavy heart and body, she leaned on him. He was there for the moment, and she appreciated his support, but she was going to have to let him go too. In a few days, he'd be off to Argentina, and she would be alone again.

---

Two days later, Luke took Brooke to the police station. This was the first time she'd left Haley's side. But her daughter was being looked after by Abby and her monstrous dog. Plus, a security expert, some friend of the police chief, was currently installing a security system in Brooke's house. Brooke had referred him to Maddie's parents too. Physically, Maddie was recovering nicely, but Brooke knew the harder battle would be to overcome her emotional trauma.

Unfortunately, Kent had survived.

Mike and Jack were in the conference room. Files and photos were spread across the table.

"We have a lot to tell you." Mike gestured toward two chairs.

Brooke sank into a chair. "Thanks."

"In the storage bins in Kent's basement we found scrapbooks of more than a dozen murdered women. He detailed how he stalked them. Kept track of their daily schedules, their friends, jobs, and hobbies. He then identified someone in the woman's life who would be set up to take the blame for the killing, usually a boyfriend or ex-boyfriend. Kent took particular pleasure in planting the evidence." Mike looked up. "He had a brand-new file on Brooke."

Brooke swallowed her queasiness. "He told me he killed Karen. Is this true?"

"Yes." Mike opened a file. "Karen Edwards was his first killing. He planned her murder in the weeks after he pulled her over for speeding. Setting up the ex-boyfriend was an afterthought. But he enjoyed following the trial so much that framing someone else for his murders became part of his ritual. And being a cop gave him the knowledge to do it right. His frame-ups were successful in all but two of his killings."

"This is why no one suspected a serial killer was active," Jack added. "He didn't leave a trail of unsolved murders. Most of the cases were closed. Interestingly, Maddie was the first woman he attacked this close to home. His crimes started farther away and spiraled inward. Maybe he got overconfident?"

A knock sounded. The chief's secretary opened the door. "There's an Ellie Springer to see you. She says it's about her brother, Timmy."

Mike got up and crutched his way into the lobby. He returned a few minutes later with a woman in her fifties. Straight-backed with determination, she clutched a purse with both hands against her belly. Years of labor and exhaustion showed in her lined face and red-knuckled hands. The graying hair scraped back from her face in a severe bun didn't help. Her pink hotel maid uniform was just as worn.

At Mike's direction, Ellie lowered her stooped body into a chair.

"Ms. Springer is Tim Kent's older sister." Mike introduced them.

Ellie gave Brooke a grim stare. "I'm sorry for what my brother did."

No, *how is he?* No claims of innocence. Guess they weren't close.

Ellie pulled a pack of cigarettes from the front pocket of her uniform. She tapped one out and held it between her fingers.

Ignoring the NO SMOKING sign on the wall, Jack slid an empty diet soda can in front of her. "Go ahead."

No one protested as she lit up, then sucked down smoke like it was air to a drowning victim. "Is he in prison?"

"He's still in the hospital." Mike said. "You're not surprised by any of this?"

She blew out a stream of smoke. "The only thing that surprises me is that it didn't happen sooner."

"Why?"

"Timmy was an accident. I was in high school when he came along. Our parents were tired and busy. They hadn't wanted another child. He was pretty much left to himself. They were killed in a house fire when Timmy was six. By that time, I was in my twenties. I was working and going to school at night. All the sudden I had Timmy to look after. I quit school and took a second job. A rented trailer was the best I could afford. I did my best with him for six long years, until the social worker came and took him away. She said I was abusive. I think the little shit called social services himself."

Mike stopped her. "I don't understand."

"My baby brother was a sick, sick little boy. I tried everything to set him straight, but he was wired wrong. Something was missing, maybe a soul. I don't know."

"What did he do?" Mike asked.

She leveled a gaze across the table. "He killed things. Bugs, frogs, animals, whatever he could catch. I remember the first time clear as day. It was nighttime. I was making dinner, macaroni and cheese, because that was his favorite and that's all we had left until payday anyway. In the beginning I thought he was holding his sadness about our parents' deaths inside. It was only later that I realized he didn't show any grief because he didn't have any feelings. That boy was colder than February snow."

She took a drag on her cigarette. "I found him in the bathroom. He'd caught a mouse. The poor thing was all over the floor, all over his shoes, all over the hammer he'd used to beat it to death. Blood and bits of fur were stuck to the metal." She shivered and took another long pull on her cigarette. The color had leached from her face. "Timmy looked up at me. He had this huge smile on his face. It was the first time I'd seen any emotion in him since he came to live with me. The first activity he'd enjoyed was hammering an animal to death."

Luke's stomach turned.

"It got worse from there. I watched him as much as I could, but if I wanted to feed him, I couldn't miss a shift. I tried everything. I lectured him. I took him to church. I gave him time-outs and grounded him. Got to the point I tried beating on him if I caught him torturing some poor creature. You wouldn't believe what he could do to a frog. Nothing worked. Punishing him had no effect. Screaming didn't faze him. He didn't care if I hit him. He just got mad that I made him stop what he was doing. He started fighting me on that. I'd have to lock him in the closet to get the mess cleaned up."

"Why did they take him away?" Mike asked.

"He must have told his teacher I'd hit him." The cigarette was down to the filter. She gave it a final pull. "Frankly, I was relieved when they took him away. He was getting bigger, and I was the only one who knew what he was inside. I'd been sleeping with one eye open and a locked door for a long time. If they hadn't taken him, maybe he would have killed me eventually. Sometimes, I wonder if the fire that killed our parents was really an accident."

"Your brother was transferred to City Hospital. He'll stay there until he can be transferred to the prison. You're his next of kin. You can see him if you'd like to."

Ellie lit another cigarette. "I haven't seen Timmy in twenty-five years. And twenty-five more would suit me just fine. I've never been a religious woman, but I didn't need a Bible to know that boy was the closest thing to the devil on this earth. He was born pure evil."

# CHAPTER FORTY-ONE

"This is your home, Lucas. I want you to visit whenever you want. You don't need to call or ask." Gran followed him to the car, hugging her thin frame against the chill.

"I promise to come more often." Luke hung his suit jacket on a hanger he kept in the back of his BMW.

She waved as he pulled out of the drive. In his rearview mirror, she grew smaller and smaller as he drove away, shrinking until he couldn't see her anymore. Luke ignored the empty space in his gut and focused on the road. She was getting older. There wasn't anything he could do to halt time. Her cold was fading, but he was still going to worry. What if she'd gotten worse instead of better? Who would take care of her?

Country roads turned into interstates. He veered onto the ramp that linked the Pennsylvania and New Jersey Turnpikes. His heart, and his sweat glands, kicked up a notch. By the time he entered the Lincoln Tunnel, his hands were clammy and his stomach was curling up like a nervous child.

But he had something to resolve before he went back to his job and moved on with his life.

The morning sun shone on his head, the day's first note of warmth after the cold night. He locked his car, parallel parked at the curb between two American sedans. Under the watchful eye of two young mothers, three preschool-age girls jumped rope on the sidewalk. The sing-song chanting of an alphabet rhyme followed Luke up the steep flight of steps of the three-story brownstone, converted from one huge home into three large apartments. He pressed the buzzer labeled number three.

"Hello?" a man's voice answered.

"It's Luke Holloway."

"Come in. Come in." The exterior door buzzed. Luke opened the door and stepped onto the black-and-white tiles of the lobby. His muscles were sluggish and reluctant as he climbed to the third-floor landing. A couple in their mid-fifties waited just inside the threshold to an apartment. Mr. and Mrs. Leonetti.

Sherry's parents.

They'd passed their dark eyes and olive skin on to their daughter. Mrs. Leonetti was plump, her short hair dyed a uniform dark brown. Sherry's dad was bowling-ball bald.

"Please, come inside." Mr. Leonetti stepped back and waved Luke inside.

He walked into a high-ceilinged room. As was typical of converted townhomes, there was more height than space. Light streamed in through two narrow windows overlooking the street. Worn furniture, framed pictures, and oddly shaped knickknacks, the kind of things grade-schoolers made with clay, crowded the space. The effect was more comfort than clutter. A mass card from Sherry's funeral lay on the hall chest.

Sherrylyn Mary Leonetti.

Guilt crawled its way up Luke's chest into his throat.

"I'm sorry I didn't answer your calls or return your messages." He lowered his head. They'd lost their daughter, and he hadn't even offered his condolences. Hadn't been able to face their grief for a woman he couldn't save.

He didn't offer an excuse because he had none. Sherry's parents had reached out to him a dozen times since the explosion. He'd avoided them like a coward.

He'd lived, Sherry had died, and there hadn't been a thing he could have done to change that. Luke opened his mouth to explain, but he choked on the words.

"We understand." Mrs. Leonetti reached forward and grasped Luke's hands with strong fingers. Her warm eyes glistened. They were deep brown and swimming with sadness, a bottomless pool of sorrow. But other emotions lingered there too. Kindness, faith, strength.

Mrs. Leonetti steered him toward a leather sofa. One of them pressed a cool glass into his hand. Water. Luke drank, swallowing some of his guilt. It settled in his empty stomach, cold and achy. He stared ahead, at a sideboard filled with pictures of Sherry and her sisters. Close in age, all three were curvy and petite, with long dark hair and laughing eyes. Mr. and Mrs. Leonetti sat on either side of him, flanking him with their solid presence.

"We came to see you in the hospital. You weren't awake." Mr. Leonetti put a hand on Luke's shoulder. "We wanted to thank you."

Luke didn't register the last words right away. They sunk in slowly, the way rainwater seeps into parched earth. He lifted his head. They wanted to thank him? For what? Watching their daughter die?

"You carried our Sherry out of that building." Tears streamed down Mrs. Leonetti's wrinkled face. Mascara trailed onto her cheeks. She grabbed Luke's hand and clenched it tight. "You brought her back to us."

Luke studied the worn Persian carpet. Intricate patterns of beige flowers and vines bordered a navy center. "I didn't save her."

"No one could have saved her." Mr. Leonetti's fingers dug into Luke's muscle. "But you tried and risked your own life to do it. For that we will always be grateful."

"Three floors burned up completely." One of Mrs. Leonetti's tears dropped onto his hand. "Without you, she wouldn't have come home at all."

An hour later, Luke stood in front of his office building. He stared up at the towering glass structure. The Leonettis had settled his nerves, but fresh panic rattled his skeleton and turned his stomach as he reached for a door.

The truth hit him like an ax.

He didn't want to go inside.

He didn't want to go to Buenos Aires.

He hated his apartment in New York. He hated the whole fucking city. His panic attacks hadn't been brought on by high-rises or elevators. He'd freaked out because he didn't want to return to constant travel and never-ending stress.

The explosion had changed him. Before Manila, Luke was the most dedicated, type A person in the company, except for his boss. But now everything had changed. His priorities had shifted under his feet like tectonic plates. He had one foot on each side, and his ass was hanging out over the crack. Which way should he jump?

---

Brooke left the cafeteria. On her way out, she spied Haley at a table with her friends. Haley had no memory of being abducted. Brooke wasn't sure if this was good or bad. They were taking it one day at a time. Brooke opened the bag of chips she'd bought as an excuse to walk down here.

Joe Verdi's daughter sat at a table by the door. The police had found her father. He'd checked himself into a rehab center. Joe had been too humiliated to tell even his own father where he was. There was hope for the family, Brooke supposed. While Joe could never take back his actions, at least he realized he had a problem.

"Hey, Brooke."

She stopped and turned. Owen Zimmerman was hurrying toward her. Brooke pulled back. Owen might not be the killer, but Luke had said his tastes were of the nasty variety.

"Aren't you done with the yearbook photos?"

Owen nodded. "Pretty much. Just had a few makeups to do this morning."

Brooke wondered if she should talk to the principal about getting a new photographer. How could she justify it? *My boyfriend illegally obtained some photographs . . .*

He shoved his hands in his front pockets. "I know you've had a rough weekend, but if you still want those photos for a Christmas present, don't wait too long to make an appointment."

"Yeah, about that." She inched backward.

"What's wrong?"

"Look, Owen. I'm just going to say it." She lowered her voice to a whisper. "I know about those violent pictures on your computer."

Owen's forehead wrinkled. "What pictures?"

"Does BDSM ring a bell?"

"Oh." Owen's eyes widened. "*Oh. Those* pictures. How . . .?"

Brooke didn't answer.

The light bulb went off in Owen's eyes. "You didn't think those were real, did you?"

"What do you mean?"

He laughed. “I was hired to do a photo shoot for a very adult Halloween fright night: 50 Shades of Zombies. The BDSM theme is really popular these days. People can’t get enough of it.”

Mental. Head. Smack.

“Seriously, you thought that was real?” Owen asked. “That was some weird shit.”

“I’m sorry, Owen. For snooping and for jumping to conclusions.”

“It’s OK.” But Owen was still laughing when he walked away.

She returned to her classroom. Pretty blond Sara was waiting by the door. Brooke had promised her student extra help with her algebra today.

“I’m sorry. Am I late?” Brooke checked her watch and unlocked the door.

“No. I’m early.” Sara swept her long blond hair over her shoulder. “My mom wanted to know if you got the cookies she baked you.”

Brooke dropped the chips on her desk. “The macaroons were from you?”

Sara pulled a student desk close to Brooke’s. “Yeah. My mom wanted to thank you for helping me so much. She dropped them off at the office, but one of the other teachers said he’d bring them to you.”

Brooke dropped into her chair. “Please thank your mother for me.”

Sara pulled out her notebook. “I’m really confused.”

Hours later Brooke parked in her driveway. She glanced at Haley in the passenger seat. She’d said her first day back at school had been “fine,” but exhausted circles rimmed her eyes.

They went into the house. A *beep* drew Brooke to the hall closet. She stepped over the dog, opened the door, and turned off the new alarm. Worth every penny. Without it, she doubted she or Haley would be able to close their eyes at night.

The kitchen was a mess again. All of Luke's efforts destroyed in the few days he'd been gone. She pressed a hand to the center of her chest, where the emptiness had settled. He'd promised to visit when he returned to the States but that would be six to eight weeks from now. Then he'd be off to another exotic location.

She went into her office. The sight of her extensive files and notes reminded her of Kent's detailed records with a surge of nausea. She grabbed a box from the shelf and started emptying drawers. An hour later, her desk was cleared of everything relating to violence. One by one, she carried the boxes into the attic.

The sound of a car door brought her back to the hall. She looked out the sidelight. A silver BMW sat in her driveway. Luke got out of the car and walked to her front porch.

She opened the door. Hope lifted her heart as he stepped into the house.

"I thought you were going back to work."

Luke leaned down to kiss her. "I did go back to work."

Disappointment brought her back down.

"I quit." He grinned.

"What?"

"I quit."

"Seriously?"

Luke took her hand. "I'm an unemployed thirty-four-year-old man who's going to move in with his grandmother. I have some money put away, and I'd like to start my own business, maybe do some consulting eventually, but honestly, right now, my only plans are to paint Gran's house. But if you don't mind a man with no real life plan or prospects in mind, I'd like to take you on a date."

"A date?" Brooke stammered.

Luke nodded. Behind the pain in his green eyes, light glimmered. "Yes. A real date. We've faced a killer and almost died together, but we've never gone out to dinner or a movie. Do you like movies?"

"I love movies." Brooke's heart was stuck in disbelief gear.

"Are you teaching your self-defense class tonight?"

"No. I'm taking some time away from all that."

"Really?" Luke said. "You don't have to. If it's important to you, I'll even help you. Your girls can beat me up every week if it makes you happy."

"Here's the thing. It wasn't making me happy." Brooke took a deep breath. "I was reliving Karen's death as a punishment."

Luke took her in his arms and held her close. "You can't blame yourself for not being able to predict the future any more than I could."

"I know." She sniffed. "That's why I have to take a break. I need to let some of the hurt go. I need to let Karen go."

"We're a mess."

She leaned back. He hadn't shaved, and the shadow on his jaw made her yearn to feel the rasp. "Maybe that's the point. No one else ever really understood. You get it."

"Oh, I know all about survivor's guilt, no question."

"I went to a psychiatrist this week." She pressed her forehead into his chest. "I wasn't about to let Haley suffer like I did. So I thought maybe I deserved the same."

Luke kissed her temple. "You found your roommate's body and never had any therapy?"

"I went when Ian made me, but I didn't get anywhere." Brooke shook her head. "I didn't want to get better."

"But now you do."

"Yeah." She really did.

"I assume you don't want to leave Haley alone yet." He turned and wrapped an arm around her shoulders. "How about we rent a movie on the TV tonight? We'll do that real date whenever you're ready."

"As long as it's a comedy, I'm in." Brooke leaned against his shoulder. "I've had enough suspense and sorrow for a lifetime."

Luke steered her toward the den. "What's going to happen to the guy who went to prison for Karen's murder?"

"He's being released, along with twelve other innocent men who were imprisoned for Kent's crimes." Brooke pulled back. "I want to see him, to apologize for helping to put him behind bars. Would you go with me?"

"Brooke, I'll go with you anywhere." Luke hugged her close. "Any news on Kent?"

"No, but I'm hoping for a guilty-plea-to-avoid-the-death-penalty deal. I really don't want to have to testify against him. I will if I have to, but I'd rather not."

"I know." Luke leaned back. "But I'll be here if you do."

"Won't you miss the city?"

"No. And even if I did, it's only a short drive away." He brushed a stray piece of hair from her cheek. "I've lived in dozens of places, and I have very few people in my life to show for it. I want roots, Brooke."

"I'm about as rooted as a person gets." She smiled.

"I want to wake up in the same bed every day." He leaned close and whispered in her ear. "Preferably with you. Naked."

Picturing him naked, Brooke sighed. "You know that's not going to happen that often for a few years. The kids need—"

He wiped a tear from under her eye with his thumb. “Stop worrying. I’ll take whatever you can give me. One day at a time, OK?”

“OK.” She kissed him back.

Sunshine butted her head against their legs. A pungent scent wafted up.

“Oh, my.” Brooke reached a hand to her nose. “The movie will have to wait.”

“I’ll get the dog if you get the towels.” Luke laughed. “I’m glad I won’t have to do it by myself this time.”

“No.” Brooke rose up on her toes and planted a kiss on his mouth. “We’re in this together.”

THE END

# ACKNOWLEDGMENTS

Thanks to Dan Boucher for reviewing the brain-numbing geeky details. Any omissions or errors are my fault. Also, thanks to Kendra Elliot, my friend and fellow Montlake author. It's amazing how much support a person can provide from three thousand miles away.

Publishing a book is a group effort. I'm lucky to have the support of an entire team of incredible people. As always, a gigantic thanks to my agent, Jill Marsal, for making my dream a reality. My managing editor, Kelli Martin, and the entire staff at Montlake Romance (especially author herder/technical goddess Jessica Poore) also deserve credit for doing their best to take care of the process and let an author focus on writing. Finally, thanks to developmental editor Shannon Godwin for her help in making this book come together.

Don’t miss Melinda Leigh’s next
spine-tingling romantic thriller

# SHE CAN HIDE

# CHAPTER ONE

A *whoosh* and soft impact jolted Abby's body. She slid forward. The seat belt caught her and snapped her back. Pain ripped through her temple. What happened? Her vision blurred, and she rubbed her eyes to clear it.

The steering wheel and dashboard came into focus. She was sitting in the front seat of her Subaru sedan. Icy pellets bounced off her windshield. When had it started to sleet? Blinking hard, she stared through the glass. Water splashed over the hood. *Oh my God.*

She swiveled her head to get her bearings. A thin sheet of ice edged the opposite bank twenty feet ahead. Water bubbled over rocks down the center of the flow. Behind the car, fifteen feet of water stretched to an inclined embankment. Her car was door-deep in a river.

The Subaru bobbed for a couple of seconds. The front end tilted down, and water swished over the floor mat. This had to be a nightmare. But her personal horror didn't usually involve water. Abby's bad dreams were all dark all the time. But a minute ago she'd been in the parking lot of the high school where she taught math. How did she get here?

Water swirled around her feet and seeped through her running shoes. Cold. No, beyond cold. Liquid ice. Shocking pain washed over her ankle and jolted her from her dreamlike state.

This was real.

Terror swept through her confusion and jerked her from numb disbelief into panic. Fear, bitter and acidic, bubbled into her throat. Her lungs pumped like pistons, forcing air in and out at dizzying speed. Tiny dots flashed in her vision. Out the window, water rushed past the car, the surface level with the hood and rising.

The interior closed in on her, claustrophobia overwhelming her senses.

The water was going to rise. She was going to be trapped, and then she was going to drown. She was going to die.

A chunk of ice scraped across the windshield. The noise jolted her.

She had to get out of the car. She fumbled for the seat belt release, the frigid temperature and horror destroying her dexterity. Frantic fingers yanked at the nylon. Her thumb found and depressed the button, and the strap loosened and recoiled with a snap. Abby reached for the door handle and pulled, but she couldn't budge it. Water pressure held the door closed. Until the pressure was equalized . . .

No! She couldn't sit here and wait for water to fill the car. She'd drown. She had to get out now. Water inched up the glass. The sense of confinement suffocated her. Her heart catapulted blood through her veins.

The window.

She pressed the lever. Nothing happened.

*Oh, no. It had to open!*

Did electric windows work underwater? The car shifted again, the hood dropping thirty degrees. Sliding forward, Abby braced her upper body on the steering wheel.

Water advanced beyond her calves to her thighs. Her winter running tights were designed to facilitate moisture transfer, not keep water out. The cold bit into her skin like teeth. Pain and numbness spread up her legs and reached for her body with a greedy splash.

Tears leaked down her cheeks and terror sprinted through her heart as she pressed the window button harder. The glass lowered. Yes! Her flash of relief was cut off by the flow of water. It poured through the opening and washed over her torso in an icy fall. She had an exit, but now the car was flooding even faster.

With a groan, the car tipped as the weight of the engine pulled the vehicle deeper into the eddying river. Abby fell forward as the car went vertical. She lost her grips on the wheel. Her world tilted. Her forehead slammed into the dashboard. Blood spattered, but she felt nothing.

The water rose, swallowing her pelvis and chest in the span of two panting breaths. She twisted her body sideways to fit through the opening, but the force of the water pouring through the window pushed her back into the vehicle.

Frigid liquid enveloped her neck and face. The shock seized her muscles. Her breathing sped up in a reflex to the agonizing cold. She pressed her face to the ceiling to suck in a last lungful of air. But the car dropped again, turning as it sank. Her body tumbled like clothes in a washing machine.

Where was the window?

Disoriented by the car's shift, she searched with frantic desperation. Icy water stabbed her eyeballs. In the murky underwater scene, she saw it.

*There!*

Her arms tangled in her heavy wool coat. She shrugged out of it and pushed her shoulders through the opening. Once her hips cleared the window, the current pulled her free. The surface was a bright layer just above the car roof. Lungs burning, she stroked upward, toward the light, away from the darkness below. Her head burst free of the water and she gasped. Oxygen flooded her brain. With the infusion of air into her body, her limbs went from cold to numb to dead weight in an instant.

She could barely move to keep her head above the surface. Dirty water sloughed down her throat, choking her. She looked for the bank, but the water carried her farther from the vehicle, toward the center of the rapids that bubbled white down the center of the waterway. With one final desperate lunge, she grabbed the bumper of her Subaru protruding from the surface. She'd never make it to shore. She'd escaped the car only to drown anyway.

Acceptance washed over her, as numbing as the temperature, then sadness. Her poor high school students would grieve. Her only friend and fellow teacher, Brooke, and the young neighbor Abby tutored would be devastated. Zeus, too, for as long as his dog memory would allow. That was it. She hadn't let many people get close. Her mother was dead, and she hadn't seen her father in three years, since the last time she'd come close to dying, when he'd made his lack of interest clear.

Loneliness rivaled fear in her heart as the current tugged harder. For the second time, she was facing death alone. But if she could do it over again, would she change?

Could she change?

It didn't matter. She wasn't going to get another chance. Her frozen fingers faltered, then slipped. The wet metal slid out of her grip. Icy water closed over her head.

# ABOUT THE AUTHOR

John Tannock Photography 2012

Melinda Leigh abandoned her career in banking to raise her kids and never looked back. She started writing as a hobby and became addicted to creating characters and stories. Since then, she has won numerous writing awards for her paranormal romance and romantic-suspense fiction. Her debut novel, *She Can Run*, was a number one bestseller in Kindle Romantic Suspense, a 2011 Best Book Finalist (The Romance Reviews), and a nominee for the 2012 International Thriller Award for Best First Book. When she isn't writing, Melinda is an avid martial artist: she holds a second-degree black belt in Kenpo karate and teaches women's self-defense. She lives in a messy house with her husband, two teenagers, a couple of dogs, and two rescue cats.